Reader praise for Elaine Cunningham's *The Dream Spheres*

"*The Dream Spheres* is a true triumph."

☉

"A . . . gripping book with an intricate plot with some delightful twists and revelations."

☉

"I absolutely devoured t̶ . . . ̶ningham does not disappoint with t̶ . . .

"The plot is . . . and will grab the reader's attentio̶ . . .

Novels by
Elaine Cunningham

Songs and Swords

Starlight and Shadows

Evermeet: Island of Elves

The Magehound

Counselors and Kings • Book I

Elaine Cunningham

Dedication

To my brother, Myron, who takes time to read these books.
Don't think I don't appreciate it,
even if you do steal Mom's copies.

THE MAGEHOUND

Cover art by John Foster
First Printing: April 2000
Library of Congress Catalog Card Number: 99-66047

9 8 7 6 5 4 3 2

ISBN: 0-7869-1561-7
T21561-620

U.S., CANADA,
ASIA, PACIFIC, & LATIN AMERICA
Wizards of the Coast, Inc.
P.O. Box 707
Renton, WA 98057-0707
+1-800-324-6496

EUROPEAN HEADQUARTERS
Wizards of the Coast, Belgium
P.B. 2031
2600 Berchem
Belgium
+32-70-23-32-77

Visit our web site at **www.wizards.com**

halruaa

Bandit
Wastes

Mhair
Jungles

The high Aluar

The
Nath

Temple
of
Azuth

River halar

River Aluar

Swamp of
Akhlaur

halarahh

Lake
halruaa

Khaerbaal

halagard

Bay
of
Taertal

house
Jordain

Zalazuu

Kilmaruu
Swamp

N

W   E

S

Great
Sea

PROLOGUE

The wizard's shoulders burned with fatigue as he forced himself to lift the machete one more time. He hacked at the flowering vines, but the tangled mass was so thick that it seemed to shrug off his blows. A burst of shrill, mocking laughter erupted from the green canopy overhead, a maniacal sound that held a rising note of hysteria. Several of the men with him froze, their dark eyes glazed with trepidation.

"Nothing but a bird," the wizard snapped, desperately hoping that he guessed correctly. "Are you masters of magic or timorous milkmaids? Has Akhlaur's treasure lost its allure? Perhaps you'd prefer to pass your remaining days as a magic-dead wench crouched beneath a cow's udder? I assure you," he added darkly, "that could be arranged. Now, get back to work." He punctuated his command with another angry whack.

He focused on his anger and goaded his men into doing the same. Anger kept them moving. Fear was something they ignored as best they could, for in the Swamp of Akhlaur, even a moment's hesitation could be deadly.

An enormous, luminous green flower snapped at the wizard, missing his ear but dusting him with pollen that glowed softly and smelled like mangoes and musk. He sneezed violently and repeatedly, until he feared that the next explosion would surely expel his liver through his nostrils. When at last the spasms passed, he lashed out with his machete and sliced the blossom from the vine. He knew better than to kick the massive flower, but he dearly wished to.

The wizard had come to loathe the swamp and everything in it, but for these flowers he reserved a special enmity. Monstrous in size and appetite, the swamp blossoms snapped randomly and unexpectedly. Their cup-shaped blossoms were ringed with thorns that curved like a viper's fangs and held poison as deadly as venom. What they caught, they kept. A spray of iridescent blue tail feathers protruded from one tightly clamped blossom. On the ground nearby, low-growing vines entwined the nearly skeletal form of a wild boar. Tendrils of green spiraled around exposed ribs. A flower bud nodded over the juncture of a dagger-sized tusk and massive skull, like a child admiring the work of its deadly parents.

The wizard redoubled his assault on the vines. His hair clung to his forehead in wet strings, and his fingers itched with the desire to cast a spell that would wither the dangerous green barrier into dry and crumbling twigs.

But he dared not. He had brought a company of wizards into the Swamp of Akhlaur, armed with enough spells and potions and enchanted weapons to take them from one new moon to the next—or so he had thought. Already their store of magic ran dangerously low.

How was it possible that in just three days they were forced to replace magic with muscle? What other equally vital errors might he have made? What secrets did the swamp hold that might prove beyond their dwindling powers?

Doubts plagued the wizard as he and his men hacked their way through the thick foliage. Three days in the Swamp of Akhlaur had thinned his patience, his confidence, and his ranks. Twenty men had followed him into the swamp; only thirteen had managed to stay alive. That was no small accomplishment, not when every day brought unexpected dangers and merely breathing was a great effort. His chest throbbed with a dull, heavy ache from battling air as thick and hot as soup.

The wizard had thought himself well accustomed to heat, for Halruaa was a southern land where seasons were defined by patterns of the rains, the winds, and the stars. But never, never had he known such heat! The swamp was a cauldron, a fetid, foul thing that simmered and bubbled and spat.

Water was everywhere. It dripped from the leaves, it enshrouded the shallow waters with mist, it sloshed about the men's ankles. At present they skirted a strangely brooding river. The surface of the water rose in slow, green bubbles that spewed stench and steam into air too moisture-laden to receive either. Odors lingered in the stagnant air, as land-bound as shadows, commingling but still distinct enough to identify: swamp gas, decay, venom flowers, sweat, fear.

Fear. The wizard could taste the sharp, metallic bitterness of it in his throat and wondered why. He, Zilgorn of Halruaa, was no coward. Wizardry was a demanding and difficult path, and no wizard without a strong will and a stronger stomach could become a necromancer. Zilgorn courted death, he bought and sold death, he shaped it to his will. It seemed reasonable to him that he should succeed in the deadly swamp where so many other wizards had failed.

He glanced at the ancient, sweat-stained map he clenched in one hand. His first master, Chalzaster, had spoken of his ancestors' lost village as a place on a hill overlooking a fair meadow, with the swamp beyond. The meadow and village were long gone, swallowed by the eerily growing swamplands, but a hill was a landmark worth seeking. It was all Zilgorn had—that, and the legends that whispered of magic-rich treasure, and the knowledge that many had died trying to claim the legacy hidden in the swamp.

"How much longer?" demanded one of his apprentices. The young man squinted up into the thick green canopy. "We've been working since dawn, and it must be nearly highsun. Yet how far have we gone? A hundred paces? Two hundred?"

"Would you rather swim the river?" snapped Zilgorn.

His retort drew no response but sullen stares. The apprentice shrugged and lifted his machete high overhead. He swung hard, and his blade grated against hidden stone.

Several of the men exchanged hopeful glances. "Akhlaur's tower?" one of them breathed.

The wizard chuckled without mirth. "Hardly! If this quest was so easy, why has no one yet succeeded?"

His followers looked doubtful. This, easy? In three days, they had spent more time in battle than in exploration. Two men had been lost in sinkholes, and another had been crushed and swallowed by a giant snake. Four battle-scarred figures shuffled along behind them with the obedient, mindless gait of the animated dead. The presence of these zombies, their former companions, unnerved some of the younger members of the party, but Zilgorn knew better than to leave the dead lying around untended.

"Not Akhlaur's tower," he said in a milder tone, "but worth exploring all the same. Strip the vines from the stone."

They fell to work, grunting and sweating as they attacked the foliage, ripping at it with knives and their bare hands. Suddenly one of the wizards fell back with a startled oath.

Zilgorn hurried over for a better look. The skeleton of a tall man stood erect, arms held out dramatically high as if to cast a final spell. Vines twined through the dead man's empty chest, and his skeletal back was propped against a tall, rune-carved stone. Lying amid the moldering tatters of his robes was a tarnished medallion. Zilgorn could barely make out the engraving: a rising flame in a circle of nine stars, the symbol of Mystra, goddess of magic. He turned the medallion over and studied the sigil, a magical design unique to a particular wizard, that was engraved upon the back. It was a mark he knew well.

"Chalzaster," he murmured, lifting his gaze to the empty eyes of his first master. "So this is what became of him."

A heavy silence fell over the group. The name Chalzaster was familiar to them, for they had seen it on many a spell scroll. An archmage of the illusionist school, he was most famous for creating defensive spells against attacks by sea. Many would-be invaders had been kept at bay by his illusions of pirate ships, sea monsters, and waterspouts. His name had become proverbial: "Chalzaster's shadow" was a catchphrase for anything fearful but insubstantial.

"The swamp killed the archmage Chalzaster," one of the men muttered. His tone and his eyes were hopeless, defeated.

"Yes," Zilgorn agreed evenly. "This is an unexpected bounty. You, Hazzle. Collect the finger bones."

The young wizard set to work without hesitation. He was well on his way to learning the necromancer's art, and so he understood that the bones of an archmage were most likely components of some rare and powerful spell. After a few moments, Hazzle spilled the grim treasure into his master's hands.

Zilgorn carefully slipped the bones into a bag tied to his belt. "Look around. Who knows what Chalzaster might have found before he died."

They worked until the shadows turned dusky and deep, until the distant snarls of night-hunting creatures heralded a rising moon. At last they freed Chalzaster's bones from the vines. The great wizard had died guarding the portal to a large, crumbling stone building that had long ago been swallowed by the swamp.

Zilgorn thrust the skeleton aside and peered into the darkness. "Bring a light. Quickly!"

It occurred to him, too late, to specify that he wanted a mundane torch, an oil-soaked reed set aflame by sparks from flint and steel. Out of habit, one of the wizards conjured a floating sphere of soft blue light. The glowing sphere bobbed gently, then glided into the room.

Zilgorn's reprimand died unspoken as azure light fell upon the room's grim occupants. Chalzaster had not died alone.

The bones of at least a dozen large humans and the more delicate remains of three half-elves lay sprawled on the floor, the skeletons strangely intact. Bony fingers still curled around valuable weapons: swords, pikes, and daggers. These people had died quickly, and they had been left to lie where they fell.

The wizard glanced around the room in search of some explanation. The walls, though ancient and crumbling, were decorated with remnants of carvings depicting legends told of the goddess Mystra. Zilgorn could barely make out a shattered marble altar amid the heap of stones against the far wall. From one tilting pillar dangled a hanging censer designed for the burning of incense, but which now held an abandoned bird's nest. Clearly this had once been a Mystran temple, and most likely the ancient site from which Chalzaster's forebears had come. Apparently the archmage had returned to his ancestral village. But why had he died here?

Zilgorn stooped to tug a sword from a crumbling fist. He studied the markings on the blade. They were magical, of that he was certain, but he felt no pulse of life within the steel. A very fine tiger's eye, a golden gem nearly the size of a pullet's egg, had been set into the ornate hilt. But the stone was dull and milky, as if the sword had been blinded.

"Not blinded," Zilgorn murmured with sudden understanding. "Drained."

"Master, look at this!"

Hazzle's voice blended excitement and awe. The necromancer dropped the magic-dead sword and strode across the room. His apprentice pointed toward a crystalline statue, a transparent, life-sized image of an elf warrior frozen in a battle-ready crouch, muscles tensed for a sudden charge.

The statue was female, exquisite in the beauty of its subject and the artistry of its crafter. Zilgorn had never seen its equal. Yet certain things about the statue troubled him. The elf woman's lovely features were frozen in a rictus of pain, and her crystalline hair hung strangely lank.

Absently he brushed at his own damp black locks. A horrible suspicion took root in his mind and began to blossom.

"The warriors fell with their weapons," he mused. "Chalzaster, an archmage, died on his feet. But what of this elf woman?"

"Elf woman?" Hazzle was clearly disconcerted by this notion. "This is but a statue, a treasure from some long-lost time."

"Is it?" said Zilgorn with dangerous calm. He fisted his hand and drove it toward the crystal warrior. As he suspected, his hand plunged deep into the translucent image. What he did not expect was the bitter chill that assaulted him, not merely the cold of death, but the utter absence of warmth that spoke of a void, a frigid absolute emptiness. Zilgorn jerked his hand free and showed his student the blue-white skin.

Hazzle sucked air in a quick, startled hiss, and several of the men made signs of warding—a superstitious, peasant-brained response to the unknown, something that would have irritated Zilgorn had he not been consumed with more important matters.

The wizard shook his hand until a measure of warmth and feeling returned. He tore a corner from the parchment map and walked back to the bones of his former master. Taking Chalzaster's medallion in one hand, he pressed the parchment against the sigil. During his apprenticeship, he had been magically empowered to affix Chalzaster's sigil to the spell scrolls he copied, thus marking them as authentic copies of the archmage's work. This power was his to command until the day he died, so by this reasoning the sigil should burn a glowing red shadow of itself onto the parchment.

But it did not. Whatever magic the medallion had once held was long gone.

Zilgorn rocked back on his heels and considered this. Chalzaster had no patience for anything mundane or magic-dead, so every person with him had surely been a wizard, or possibly a cleric. All had died quickly, according to the power they held: most of them in the act of attacking, the great Chalzaster in mid-spell. But the elf woman, a creature whose essence and body and soul were fashioned of magic as surely as a rainbow was made of light, had been drained so quickly that she had left nothing but a transparent, profoundly empty image. Zilgorn had never heard of such a thing, but he knew death well—well enough to see his own death foretold by the bones of Chalzaster, and his pretensions of magical power mocked by the elf's frozen ghost.

The necromancer stiffened. "Away from here! Flee this place at once!"

The panic in his voice lent wings to the other men's feet. They charged from the ruined temple and stumbled frantically down the narrow path.

They pulled up short at the water's edge, eyeing the dark, simmering surface as they struggled to calm their frenzied breathing and quiet their pounding hearts.

Quiet.

It occurred to Zilgorn suddenly that the swamp had become eerily silent. At twilight, the swamp usually seethed with life, but no crocodiles roared from the shallows, no birds shrieked or twittered in the canopy, no monkeys scolded. Even the insects had stopped humming. The swamp itself seemed to be huddled down, wary and watchful.

Then a terrible thrumming roar ripped through the air, at once both as deep as thunder and as shrill as a falcon's cry. Zilgorn, dazed and defeated though he was, thought he heard a dissonant chorus of lost voices reverberating through the inhuman roar. One of those voices he knew well.

The necromancer squared his shoulders and prepared to join Chalzaster in whatever afterlife their efforts had earned them. He summoned a lightning sphere, the most powerful spell left to him, suspecting that magic would act as a lure and make his end quicker. That wasn't cowardice, he assured himself. Didn't Chalzaster die on his feet, ready to hurl one last spell?

But the magical weapon quickly dissipated, fizzling in Zilgorn's hands like a campfire in a monsoon. He hardly noticed, for his eyes were fixed on the creature that rose slowly, silently from the dark water.

The creature's face was enormous, hideous beyond words, the sort of visage that surely haunted the nightmares of demons. The face was framed by huge elf ears that were not only pointed, but also barbed. Its massive skull was covered not by hair, but by a tangle of writhing, snapping eels. Black as obsidian were its eyes, and they showed no intelligence that Zilgorn could understand; they were as soulless and single-minded as a shark's. As the creature waded toward shore, it revealed a muscled body shaped roughly like that of a man, but utterly devoid of beauty. Each sinew was corded like a drawn bow, and its gut was sharply concave beneath the massive chest. Four arms, each ending in grasping talons, reached toward Zilgorn.

"A—a laraken," he breathed, though in truth the monster was larger and mightier than any measure Zilgorn knew of such creatures. The approach of death lent its own clarity, and Zilgorn recognized the monster as a kindred spirit: a creature of power and hunger. He remembered all that he had done over the years and understood that this was the death he had earned. Nothing in all of Halruaa could have frightened him more than that knowledge.

Zilgorn had seen death in all its forms, and he had dealt death in manners that stretched the bounds of normal possibility. He had summoned and commanded creatures so fearful that a glimpse of them would stop most men's hearts and turn a warrior's bowels to water. But the necromancer could do nothing to stop the screams that tore from his throat.

Tore from his throat! Zilgorn's head snapped back, forced by an unseen power as he felt his voice, the instrument of his magic, wrenching loose. The pain seared through him and was gone, leaving him empty and mute. Instinctively he lunged forward, as if to seize back his voice, and he watched in horror as his outstretched hands withered to skin-shrouded bones.

He wanted to flee, but his limbs would no longer obey his will. Power and life flowed out of him like blood from a mortal wound. The laraken, which had reached the riverbank and loomed over them at twice the height of a man, slowly began to gain flesh. Its sunken belly swelled as it drained the magical essence of the wizard Zilgorn and the dying men behind him.

The proud necromancer's last thought was one of relief, for without a voice, he could not die screaming, and there was no one to witness his final defeat.

He was wrong on both counts.

In a tower room that overlooked Halruaa's western mountains, a place far from the Swamp of Akhlaur, an elf woman bent over a low, round scrying bowl. The death of Zilgorn played out before her in all its detail, and her sharp ears caught the new note in the laraken's roar: the necromancer's trained voice, raised in a final keening shriek of pain and terror.

When the magical vision ended, the elf woman leaned back and brushed a glossy green curl from her face. She glanced at the wemic, a lion-like centaur, who crouched in watchful silence by her side.

Neither elves nor wemics were common in Halruaa, and together they were as oddly matched as any two companions in all the land. Kiva, the elf woman, was of wild elf blood, and her coloring was common among forest folk in the southern lands. Her abundant hair was deep green in hue and her skin a rich coppery shade. Her face was beautiful but disturbing, for there was no gentleness in its sharp lines, and her eyes were as golden and enigmatic as a cat's. She was resplendent in a gown of yellow silk and over-dress of gold-embroidered green. Emeralds flashed on her fingers and at her throat. The wemic, in sharp contract, was clad only in his own tawny hide. He was a massive creature, with the lower body of a lion and the brawny, golden-skinned torso of a man. A thick mane of black hair fell to his shoulders, and his eyes, like the elf woman's, were a feline shade of amber. His only ornaments were the ruby earring fastened in one leonine ear and the massive broadsword slung over his shoulder.

"Zilgorn was the best of the lot," Kiva mused in a singu-larly clear, bell-like voice. "I thought he'd make a better showing for himself."

The wemic frowned, misunderstanding. "You thought he would succeed? That he could free the laraken from the swamp?"

Kiva's laughter rang out like crystal chimes. "Never a chance of it! That is our task, dear Mbatu. But with each wizard we entice into the swamps, we learn a bit more."

Her companion nodded, and his golden eyes flamed at the prospect of battle. "We go into Akhlaur soon?"

The elf's face clouded. "Not yet. Zilgorn proved . . .dis-appointing. A necromancer's magic offers no better protec-tion from the laraken than that of any other wizard. We must find another way."

"So this last expedition was money and effort wasted," Mbatu concluded, gesturing to the scrying bowl.

Kiva's smile held an edge that could have cut diamonds. "Not a waste," she said softly. "Never that. I would pay any price to bring death to Halruaa's wizards, and count it a bargain."

CHAPTER ONE

If asked, many of Halruaa's people would swear that the world ended in a circle of snow and sky. This proverb referred to the Walls of Halruaa, the nearly impassable mountain ranges that encircled their land like a gigantic horseshoe. Such words were spoken with great pride, and only partly in jest.

It was harder for Halruaans to dismiss the seas beyond their southern border and the ships and merchants that came and went with the tides, but trade was regarded as an exchange of goods and not of culture. Halruaans purchased luxuries such as silk from the far-eastern lands and musical instruments crafted in the distant city of Silverymoon. They sold their potent golden wine and the trade bars of electrum taken from the dwarf-mined tunnels that honeycombed the foothills. But the best of Halruaa they kept fiercely to themselves. Theirs was a magic-rich land, a kingdom ruled by wizards, and a living legend whose reality far exceeded the tavern tales brought home by awestruck merchants.

To be sure, most of these merchants had little true understanding of Halruaa's wonders, and the wizards of Halruaa went to considerable pains to keep them unenlightened. Foreigners were confined to the port cities and carefully monitored both by magic and militia. Many well-traveled visitors considered Halruaa to have the least accessible culture and most suspicious people they had ever encountered. If that was so, it was not without reason. Halruaa's history was that of an oft-besieged castle, for many of her neighbors saw the land as a treasure trove of unique spells and incomparable magical artifacts.

Dangers from within—dangers spawned by magical failures or wildly ambitious successes—were just as deadly as the threat offered by pirates or dragons or the drow-spawned Crinti raiders that prowled the wastes beyond the northeastern mountains. The ruling wizards understood that only hard choices and constant vigilance kept Halruaa from going the way of lost Netheril, and Myth Drannor, and a hundred other legendary lands that lived only in bards' tales.

That was not to say that life in Halruaa was grim. Far from it! The clime was soft and balmy, the soil yielded a succession of abundant crops in every season, the wilderness provided adventure for those who desired it, and the cities offered luxury for those who did not. And magic was everywhere.

Nowhere was that so true as in Halarahh, the capital city and home of the wizard-king Zalathorm. The skies were full of curving towers resembling graceful dancers frozen against the clouds, structures too fantastic to stand without magic. Exotic beasts known nowhere else roamed the public gardens and graced the homes of wizards and wealthy merchants. Shopkeepers casually displayed rare spell ingredients, as well as magical items that could shame a dragon's hoard and reduce most northern wizards to tears of despairing envy. Many of the common folk could boast of a magical item or two, practical things that aided in daily chores or provided a bit of simple luxury or whimsy. Even those who had neither the talent to wield magic nor the means to purchase it could join with the elite to enjoy the city's frequent spectacles.

They gathered this night at the shores of Lake Halruaa to celebrate the spring regatta. As the rains and storm winds of the winter season abated, the skyships once again took flight. It was a sight that never failed to coax sighs from jaded archmages and swell the hearts of the common folk with awe and pride.

No magical secret was more jealously guarded than that of Halruaa's flying ships. At first glance, a ship in dry dock or tied at port appeared to be nothing more than a mundane sailing vessel, broad-beamed and carrying three masts. The skyships were not particularly maneuverable, and they could not lift high enough into the air to clear the mountains. Skyships required constant magical renewal, and they were too slow and clumsy for aerial combat. None of this mattered at all, and reminding a Halruaan of these details would be as pointless as criticizing the artistic merit of a family coat of arms. The skyships were a legacy from their ancestors, the wizards of ancient Netheril, and as such they were a potent symbol of what it meant to be Halruaan.

The launching of the skyships came at the end of Lady Day, a spring festival honoring the goddess Mystra. Everyone donned festive red garments, lending the crowd at lakeside the appearance of a vast field of scarlet flowers. As the sun set, the music of street musicians faded away and the cheerful clamor of voices dimmed to an expectant hum. Every eye turned toward the waters of Lake Halruaa.

Slowly, slowly the great ships began to rise from the lake. Starlight seemed to gather in their white sails, gaining brilliance as the sky darkened and the skyships rose. There were ten of them, moving into perfect formation: nine ships forming a circle of starlight around a central ship, the great vessel owned and occasionally flown by King Zalathorm himself.

Suddenly Zalathorm's ship appeared to burst into crimson flame. The starlight captured by the attending ships began to blink on and off in a pattern that made it appear that the circle of ships was moving faster and faster until giant stars seemed to spin around the dancing flame—Mystra's symbol, and therefore that of Halruaa.

The crowd responded with huzzahs, stamping their feet in quickening rhythm, dancing and holding their arms out toward the light. The display ended in a brilliant burst, and a cloud of sparkling motes descended upon the cheering people. These tiny lights would cling to their red garments until the sun returned, forming patterns that, according to tradition, spoke of Mystra's favor.

Laughing and chattering, the people hurried away to enjoy the evening's festivities, most of which revolved around having their fortunes told. Some went to the temples to joyous rites to the goddess of magic, while others sought counsel from diviners who read such signs through incantations. The common folk held parties for neighborhood wise women, who pieced together credible stories using bits of folk magic and a lifetime of experience with the people who sought their advice. Wherever they went, most people came away satisfied. Ill tidings on Lady Day were as rare as snow in the swamplands.

In the sky over the lake, the now-dark skyships prepared to return to port. Procopio Septus, the Lord Mayor of Halarahh and captain of the skyship fleet, nodded to his helmsman. Before the man could relay the orders to the crew, the scrying globe beside the helm began to pulse with light.

Procopio skimmed his fingertips over the smooth crystal. A face took shape on the surface of the globe, a round, cheerful, and distressingly familiar face. The wizard stifled a sigh as he regarded his friend and nemesis, Basel Indoulur.

"We *conjured up* a good show, eh what?"

"And a fine Lady Day to you, Basel," Procopio told his fellow wizard, ignoring the sly humor in the man's words. Basel Indoulur was a wizard of the conjuration school, which was not as highly regarded as divination, Procopio's discipline. But Basel never lost an opportunity to tease the diviner with the opinion that conjuring accomplished things, while divination merely nosed about in whatever other wizards were doing or were likely to do.

Nor was their school of magic the only difference between them. Procopio was a small man with a prodigious beak of a nose and strong, blunt hands. He wore his thick white hair clipped close to his head. His appearance was always meticulous, and his garments, though honoring Lady Day with the traditional red silk, were quietly fashionable. Basel Indoulur was a fat, jovial soul who was frank and vigorous in his enjoyment of Halruaa's finer things. He was brightly clad in a tunic of crimson silk with beaded trim and voluminous sleeves. As was his custom, his black hair had been dressed with fragrant oils and worked into scores of tiny braids. When he laughed, which was often, the beads at the tip of each braid set up an echoing twitter. Procopio did not measure Basel by his appearance but by his ambition. The conjurer had reached a high level of magical skill and was the Chief Elder of his home city of Halagard. It did not escape Procopio's attention that Basel lost few opportunities to attend events in King Zalathorm's court. Much good may it do him. King Zalathorm was a diviner, as were most ruling wizards. It was widely accepted that only a diviner had hope of ascending the wizard-king's throne.

"Lady Day was a great success. All went well, as I *anticipated*," Procopio added, getting in a subtle dig of his own.

"Deft riposte!" Basel threw back his head and laughed delightedly.

The compliment dampened the diviner's self-satisfaction, but not for long. Procopio had other ways of making his opinions and his powers known.

"A fine night," he said mildly. "A shame to take the sky-ships down so early."

The image of Basel pursed his lips, probably to avoid grinning like an urchin. "And there's a sprightly wind," he agreed. "Seems to me a good ship, well captained, could race a dragon on a night like this."

Procopio permitted himself a smile. "You read my

intentions. Figuratively speaking, of course. Shall we wager, say, a thousand skie?"

It was a princely sum, for the electrum coins were as dear as gold, but Basel did not blink. "Past the western banks of the River Halar," he suggested. "First man to the green obelisk takes it."

Procopio nodded, accepting the daring wager. The night winds were capricious, and the ships could not venture far out over the turbulent lake. Moreover, the junction of river with lake was a common site of wind tunnels. Here the river water, cooled by melting snows from the mountains, met the steamy air that seeped northward from the swamp. It was a volatile mix at the best of times and especially risky in the spring.

"Captain?" the helmsman said hesitantly.

The wizard waited until Basel's image faded from the globe, then gave a sly wink. "Hard astern, on my mark."

The helmsman picked up the horn and shouted orders to the crew, then repeated Procopio's count. He turned the wheel hard, and the starship began to trace a slow, wide arc in the sky. Her sails fluttered, then snapped tight as they filled with wind.

"There be twisters tonight, m'lord?" the helmsman asked with studious calm. "You looked ahead to see, so to speak?"

Procopio turned to regard the man. "Would I have accepted Lord Basel's wager if I had not? There will be a bit of weather as we pass the city's storm break, however. Basel's apprentices plan to cast spells of wind summoning. Could be nasty to someone whose ship or crew are ill prepared." He paused for a small, cool smile. "Pity about poor Basil's aft mast."

As if in response to the diviner's words, the third mast of the *Avariel*, Basel Indoulur's skyship, began to groan in the gathering wind. The conjurer turned and regarded it with mild puzzlement. The wood was flexible, taken from the date palms that lined the stormy Bay of Taertal. Spells of binding kept the masts firm, and Farrah Noor, one of his most competent apprentices, had been charged with renewing the enchantment.

The wizard shrugged and turned back to the grinning trio of apprentices that awaited his command. "Ready to cast the wind charm?"

They nodded and began to chant in unison, their hands moving through the graceful gestures that summoned and shaped the magic. Basel left them to the task and turned his face into the wind, enjoying the bracing rush.

Suddenly a powerful gust caught the ship and sent it listing dangerously to one side. The spellcasting wizards stumbled to the deck and slid, smashing into the side of the ship in a tangle of limbs. Wood began to creak alarmingly and the sails flapped thunderously. Basel braced his feet wide and seized the control rod himself, chanting as he struggled with magic and skill to right the *Avariel*.

The ship fought him like a panicked mare, and the aft mast began to creak and splinter. Resignedly Basel knew what must be done. Reaching out with a spell of unbinding, he magically severed the ropes that fastened the sails to the masts. The heavy canvas whipped away, and at last the ship came upright. They were safe, but hopelessly becalmed.

Basel watched as his apprentices rose to their feet and brushed at their crimson finery. All three of them looked rumpled and rattled, but the expression of puzzlement on Farrah's pretty face confirmed Basel's growing suspicions. He gestured the young woman to his side.

"Let me see the gestures to the wind spell," he said mildly. "Leave out the chant, if you please."

The apprentice went through half the spell before she flushed and faltered. "I seem to have forgotten the third quatrain," she admitted. "Only this morning I knew it perfectly. On my life, Lord Basel, I do not know how this thing could have happened!"

Actually, Basel had a fairly good idea. "And the enchantment of the mast? You spoke the spell of binding this morning, as you were bade?"

An expression of complete befuddlement crossed Farrah's face. "You gave me this task? My lord, I have no memory of this."

The conjurer nodded. Loss of memory was a common side effect of magical inquiry. Most likely Procopio had had his servants follow Basel's apprentices during the day's festival and had cast spells of divination upon the first one they'd found. Unfortunately for the *Avariel*, it had been Farrah.

Basel swallowed his anger, lest his stricken apprentice think it was directed at her. "Did you bring your flying carpet, Farrah? Fine! Calm yourself and take a bit of wine, then ask the ship's steward to pack a thousand skie in a sack. Follow Lord Procopio to the green obelisk and pay him his winnings."

"But my lord, the law says you need not pay a crooked wager," protested Mason, a commoner with uncommon talent and a habit of speaking plainly. "I practiced the spell with Farrah this morn. Nay, more than practiced: She all but taught it to me. As Mystra lives, Farrah did not forget the wind charm."

"Of course she didn't," Basel replied evenly. "I know what you imply, but have you any idea how difficult it would be to prove your suspicions?"

The young man folded his arms and glowered. "Not so hard. After a goose is stolen, you look for the man who's eating eggs."

"No doubt that's a useful proverb in many circumstance," the wizard said. "But you cannot charge Procopio Septus with divination. That would be like accusing birds of flight. Perhaps he bent the edges of tradition, but he broke no laws. Complaining would make us appear ridiculous. No, worse than ridiculous, for who was it who attempted to win a race by conjuring a wind charm?"

"So we do nothing?" the youth said incredulously.

Basel's smile was as bland as a cherub's, but his eyes turned flat and hard. "If that is all you see, perhaps you should spend less time eyeing Farrah and more time observing your fellow wizards. Halruaa is more than spells and skyships. Did you think that you came to me to learn nothing but magic?

"Watch," he concluded in an uncharacteristically grim tone. "Procopio Septus has larger ambitions than winning a race, and if he succeeds, we've more to lose than a skyship."

❂

An ancient elf stood on the deck of Starsnake, watching as the events foretold by his patron played out. "A small ship approaches," he said mildly, pointing to the craft leaving the damaged *Avariel*. "It would seem that Basel Indoulur is a man who honors his wagers."

If Procopio Septus heard the rebuke in the elf's voice, he gave no indication. "That is not a ship but a flying carpet. Your eyes begin to fail you, Zephyr. How reassuring for both of us that your counsel has not."

The elf did not miss the implied threat. "You are pleased with the new jordain I selected? Rualli is doing well?"

Procopio smiled thinly. "Not so well that I intend to replace you, if that's what you're asking. But let's speak of your recruitment efforts."

For a moment Zephyr's heart thudded painfully, then he realized that his patron could not possibly know of Kiva and Zephyr's secret efforts on her behalf.

"There are several promising students at the Jordaini College," Zephyr said mildly. "Tell me more about what you desire in your new counselors, so that I might make a closer match. For that matter, I could serve you better if I understood why you wished to hire so many. Most wizards content themselves with the counsel of a single jordain."

Procopio nodded toward the approaching carpet and the

small woman seated on it. "He who lives by the sword dies by it. The same could be said of magic. You have seen the problems that occur when a wizard surrounds himself with mages of lesser skill. It creates vulnerability. That I cannot have."

The elf understood this, for he himself was a jordain, a superbly trained counselor chosen not only for his keen mind, but also for his utter lack of magical ability. The jordaini were highly resistant to magic and bounded by a multitude of rules that kept them separate from the normal flow of Halruaan life. They underwent rigorous training and took sacred vows: service to the land, their wizard patron, and truth. Death was the penalty for using magic or speaking untruth. Harsh, to be sure, but it was one of many things that kept the jordaini honest. Infractions were rare. Zephyr did not know of a single living jordain who flouted these rules—save for himself.

"It is a comfort to speak plainly," Procopio said. "No one can take my secrets from your mind. A man in my position can afford to surround himself with any comfort he desires."

"That is at best a partial truth, my lord," the elf said sternly. "You hire jordaini who are outstanding in the art of warfare. Why? You are lord mayor of this city and captain of its skyship fleet, but King Zalathorm directs the military."

The wizard turned to face Zephyr. "As will he who rules after Zalathorm."

For a moment they stood in silence. "So there it is," the elf said softly.

"There it is," Procopio agreed. "I would be king. Tell me how. You have lived long and seen kingdoms rise and fall."

"Indeed," Zephyr murmured. He marveled that the wizard did not hear the bitterness in his voice.

"I am greatly skilled in the art of divination," Procopio went on, too absorbed in his own dreams to consider any nightmares his jordain might have lived. "But many wizards can captain a skyship as well as I, and military science is not my discipline. I need men who know it as well as I know my own business, and," he added with a sly smile, "that of Basel Indoulur."

Zephyr nodded thoughtfully, putting aside his own whirling thoughts to concentrate on his patron's situation. "Then you will need a master of horse to replace Iago. Regretfully, the outpost militia stationed in the Nath region found no trace of him. We assume he was carried off by raiders. There have been recent sightings of Crinti shadow amazons in the foothills," he said, referring to the race of gray-skinned, gray-haired horsewomen who ruled the land of Dambrath and haunted the wild eastern borders of Halruaa.

The wizard grunted. "Then we've seen the last of that jordain. Did we lose all the horses he purchased?"

"Only one, my lord. It would seem that Iago took a promising stallion out for a run and was not seen again."

"Pity. What of his replacement?"

"Several promising candidates, my lord. In this year's class, I would recommend Andris, whose grasp of military strategy is quite astonishing. Matteo is skilled with weapons and rides extremely well. Both are promising leaders. Either would do admirably."

Procopio considered this. "But do I really want another green jordain? What of those who are already in service to a wizard lord? Why not hire a seasoned counselor out from under his current patron? It's done all the time."

"True, but the practice holds risks," the elf cautioned. "You are not the only wizard to employ more than one jordain, but if you concentrate too blatantly on gathering a military council, it will not be long before your rivals perceive the pattern. The young men I mentioned have other skills that will distract the eye from your main purpose for them."

"Wise advice," the wizard mused. "Very well, then, see to it. Pick whichever one you think best."

The elf bowed. "I will send messengers to the Jordaini College as soon as we reach the villa. It is prudent to bid early for the services of the most talented students."

In truth, Zephyr started the process long before the sky-ship reached land. He took his leave from his patron and shut himself in his tiny cabin below decks. Once the door was barred, he moved a loose plank from the floor and took from its hiding place a small milky sphere. He blew gently on it. The swirling clouds parted to reveal the face of a beautiful forest elf.

"Lady Kiva," he said softly.

Her jade-colored brows furrowed. "Speak up. What's wrong? Are you alone?"

"Would any jordain use a magical device if he were not? It could mean my life if someone found me speaking with you." The ancient elf smiled sadly. "And I have not endured these many years to leave our lifework undone."

Kiva inclined her head in a single nod, a gesture of agreement and solidarity. "What do you have for me?"

"I have recommended two jordaini to Procopio. Either will suit him. I have to make a few more inquiries before I know which one will best suit your purposes."

"Why don't I take both?" Kiva suggested. "Certainly I could use them."

"Too risky," the old elf cautioned. "One of the group you can take, and the rest will be glad that your eye fell upon someone else. But there will be talk if two of the most promising students disappear. Your religious order might start an inquiry."

"The Church of Azuth?" she said with scorn. But she saw his point. She shrugged and moved on. "You will contact me when you know which of these jordaini will best serve."

"Of course. How is Iago working out?"

"He is resistant, even for a jordain," the elf woman admitted. "Can you get me another?"

"It seems unlikely that Procopio will believe that two of his jordaini counselors were abducted by the Crinti," Zephyr said dryly. "Have you no hope of working with Iago?"

"Very little. He remains unconvinced that my claims he

was recruited by a great wizard for the service of the land and truth. That is the problem with the jordaini—they are so damnably hard to turn! Magic does not work on them. They cannot be bribed or threatened. They have brilliant minds as humans measure such things, but no passions. What I need," she mused, "is a jordain with a weakness. Find me one."

"You would do better to say, 'Find me another,' " Zephyr commented.

Kiva's eyes turned almost gentle. "A desire for vengeance is no weakness, my old friend," she told him. "We are getting closer to our goal, I promise you. We will make things right."

"You have found the secret?" Zephyr asked eagerly. "You know how the laraken might be destroyed?"

For a moment the elf woman did not answer. "I know how to make things right," she repeated. Her face abruptly vanished from the globe.

Zephyr quickly returned the scrying globe to its hiding place and began to prepare the letters to the Jordaini College. Not until the skyship touched down at the docks did he think about the laraken. He wondered if his life's quest and Kiva's were truly one and the same.

CHAPTER TWO

The battle wizard smirked and made a circular open-handed gesture. A miniature sun appeared in the air above his upturned palm. It promptly exploded, sending an arrow of brilliant liquid fire racing toward Matteo.

The young man shifted his stance wider to absorb the impact and lifted his matched daggers into a gleaming X. The bolt of magic hurled itself against the crux of gleaming silver, then skittered along the daggers, dissipating in scattered motes that sparkled off the razor-sharp edges of the blades.

Matteo followed the classic parry with the recommended attack. With one smooth, practiced movement he flipped one dagger into the air, caught it by the tip, and hurled it toward his opponent.

The older man's eyes widened as the blade whirled toward him, but he stood his ground and began to gesture frantically. Matteo kicked into a run, not waiting to see the outcome of either attack or counter spell. He heard the metallic click of steel upon stone and shielded his eyes against the quick flare of sparks, but still he came on.

At the last moment, he dropped to the ground and spun, sweeping one leg out wide and hard at the wizard's ankles. Matteo grimaced as his shin met seemingly solid stone, but he sucked up the pain and quickly got his throbbing leg back under him. He leaped toward the fallen wizard and seized one of the man's stone-hard ankles. With his remaining dagger, he slashed at the sole of the wizard's foot. The silver blade sliced through the leather and drew a yelp of surprise from the downed man.

The stoneskin spell was a common defense, but like most spells it was not invulnerable. Its creator had over-looked a common manifestation of the natural magical world: like repels like. The natural stone beneath the wizard's feet rebuffed the flattery of the stoneskin spell's imitation, leaving the soles of the caster's feet vulnerable. Learning the weaknesses of each spell, parrying and coun-tering close-in magical attacks—these were some of the most important fighting strategies a jordain learned in his training. Matteo couldn't help feeling a surge of satisfaction as he rose to his feet and held out a hand to his fallen master.

But the wizard sat cross-legged on the packed earth of the training field, holding his insulted foot and regarding his sliced shoe dolefully.

"Was that last bit truly necessary, lad? You can make your point without actually using it."

"Always wield the sword of truth, for it is the keenest weapon," Matteo quoted blithely.

"And the leg of stone is the hardest one," said a wry voice behind him.

With a grin, Matteo whirled to face his closest friend. Andris was a fifth-level jordain, a student in the same form as Matteo. They were both due to graduate at summer's end. Classmates and friends since infancy, they competed in all things like fond and contentious brothers.

No observer would take the two men as natural brothers, however, for they were as unlike physically as two men could be. Andris was tall and lean and exceedingly fair for a

Halruaan. His narrow eyes were a greenish hazel, and his long, braided hair a dark auburn. No amount of sun could turn his skin the rich golden brown common to the dozen or so other jordaini who practiced on the training field, shirtless and sweating and gleaming like chiseled bronze in the hot sun.

Matteo was more like the other men in appearance. He stood perhaps a finger's width below the six-foot mark, and he possessed the olive skin and dark chestnut hair common to Halruaans of good blood. His eyes were nearly black, his features strong, and his fine, narrow nose was curved like a scimitar's blade. Despite the more than a handspan's difference in their height, the two young men balanced each other in mass. For this reason, they were frequent sparring partners on the teeter boards and cloudcarts, two devices that taught the jordaini to fight under magically imposed circumstances. Wizards were known to drag themselves and their opponents into the sky for aerial combat, thinking to thus gain the advantage. The jordaini might be utterly devoid of magical ability, but they did not cede a single pace of battleground to wizardly tactics.

Matteo folded his arms and sent a cocky grin at his friend. "A stone leg is a hard weapon, that much is true. But you notice that good master Vishna has found himself a comfortable seat and a sudden need for new shoes."

"I've also noticed that your shin is turning an unbecoming shade of purple," Andris returned dryly. "There's a better way."

Instantly Matteo lost interest in their repartee. "Show me."

The tall jordain sent an inquiring look at Vishna. The master nodded and rose to his feet. Andris ran at the wizard, dropping to the ground as Matteo had done and executing the leg sweep in much the same fashion. But when Andris dropped into the crouch, he did not face Vishna as the attack pattern prescribed, but instead presented his right side. When his leg struck the wizard, he hit with the hardened muscle of his calf rather than the poorly padded bone of his shin.

Matteo could see the sense of it. There would be less pain, and the modified attack virtually eliminated the risk of broken bones, a not uncommon hazard of this particular sequence. At this very moment, there were two second-form students in the infirmary, wearing plasters and glumly enduring the ministrations of Mystra's clergy. They would be back on the field in days, but in the meantime, they would have to suffer many sly comments from their fellows.

"There is a problem," Matteo observed. "The initial attack is vastly improved, that I readily concede. But once the wizard is down, you are out of position for the knife thrust."

"Not so," Andris countered. "I'll show you."

"Not with my help, you won't," protested Vishna as he struggled to his feet. "Stoneskin or flesh, my bones are sufficiently rattled from clanging about on the ground. I'm for the baths."

"May you walk in truth's light," both students said in unison, speaking the formal leave-taking between jordaini. The wizard flapped a hand in their direction in a less than formal gesture of acknowledgment as he walked gingerly away.

"I'll be your wizard," Matteo offered, speaking with the recklessness that only a jordain could understand.

Andris made a small involuntary sign of warding. "Mind your tongue, fool!" he said with quiet urgency. "You've more brass than brains."

"A metaphor," protested Matteo. "It was only a metaphor. An occasional borrowing from bardic style enhances a jordain's discourse."

"That may be, but metaphors can be risky things. There are many among us who consider truth a grim and literal matter, and some that might take you amiss if they overheard such claims."

Matteo sighed. "Just do the attack."

His friend nodded and burst toward him in a running charge. Before Matteo could brace himself, he felt the ground slam into him and saw stars dance in the morning sky. He blinked away the sparkles of light and watched as Andris continued his spin. But the red-haired jordain seized Matteo's ankle, using the hold to come to an abrupt stop. He pulled hard, reversing his direction and swinging his free hand toward Matteo's foot.

Andris slammed his fist into the ball of his opponent's foot. In real battle, he would hold a knife. There were points of power and pain on the sole of the foot, and a jordain knew them well. Even without the weapon, the precisely placed attack sent icy lightning coursing up Matteo's leg. He gritted his teeth to hold back a howl of pain.

"That works," he conceded in a gritty whisper.

Andris rose to his feet and extended a hand. Matteo grasped his friend's wrist and hauled himself up. His leg was numb nearly to the waist, and he hobbled around in small, pained circles as he awaited the return of blood to the offended member.

"Reminds me of the time I failed to dodge the aura of Vishna's cone of ice," Matteo said ruefully. He looked at his friend with great admiration. "You have improved the attack."

The tall jordain shrugged. "This tactic would not work for everyone. Speed is needed, and it does not hurt that I am built more like a snake than a bull. A man with more muscle couldn't halt his momentum quickly enough."

"Not without ripping off the wizard's leg at the hip," Matteo said dryly. He snapped his fingers and grinned. "There's an interesting variation. Why couldn't Themo execute your attack, then use the wizard's stone leg as a bludgeon?"

They both smirked at the image this painted of their classmate. Themo was taller even than Andris, and as thick-bodied and strong as the huge, hairy Northmen who occasionally came to the port cities for trade or adventure. At heart, Themo was less a scholar than a warrior, and he'd gotten in trouble more than once for sneaking away to the taverns to provoke battles.

"He could have used just such a weapon at the Falling Star," Andris agreed, his eyes twinkling at the memory.

But Matteo turned sober. "Indeed. Had you not been there to devise a battle tactic, the fool might have died that night, and his friends with him."

The jordain gave another diffident shrug. "I cannot match you in feats of memory or debate," he said frankly. "Strategy is the thing that interests me."

"Obsesses you," his friend corrected him heartily. "Have you made much headway with the Kilmaruu Paradox?"

It was meant as a rhetorical question. Matteo chose his words to express Andris's fascination with even the most difficult and obscure military puzzles. He was therefore surprised and intrigued by the light that leaped into his friend's hazel eyes.

A studiously casual expression settled over Andris's face. "It is a classic dilemma," he said. "The Halruaan navy has been occupied with it for many years. Not only does this question absorb the best minds stationed at the naval base at Zalasuu, but also the two thousand troops who hold the fort beyond."

"Not to mention the dozen or so adventurers and wizards who disappear into the swamp each year," Matteo added. "As the proverb goes, the Swamp of Kilmaruu keeps the numbers of fools in Zalasuu low."

"Ah, but therein lies the paradox," his friend said slyly. "It is written that the mages and adventures who disappear into the swamp only seem to whet the appetite of the undead who haunt it, drawing them out into the surrounding countryside. Massive attacks into the swamp have proven disastrous to the city and its outlying villages. Yet if the military does nothing, the undead will slip into the Bay of Azuth and bedevil the ships. Disaster lies at the end of either course, action or restraint."

Matteo nodded. History, particularly military history, had been part of their studies for years. But at the moment, he was more interested in the subtle implication in his friend's words than in this old puzzle.

"The paradox has always been understood as the futility of either action or restraint. Your words imply a different interpretation."

The tall jordain clasped his hands behind his back, absently watching a winged lizard crawl across the sky as he chose his next words. "Suppose that someone devised a formula for attack. Suppose he researched it extensively, worked out the strategy from every conceivable variation fate could present. Suppose that someone proposed this solution to his masters as his fifth-form thesis. Do you suppose that such a man might get an appointment as counselor to a battle wizard? Perhaps," he added wistfully, "such a man might flout tradition and gain not just a counselor's role, but his own command."

Matteo's jaw dropped. For a long moment he struggled to take in this revelation. "Is it true? You have solved the Kilmaruu Paradox?"

"I think so," Andris said modestly.

"You think so?" Matteo echoed reprovingly. This matter could determine the entire course of his friend's life. It was too important for light words and imprecise speech. "A jordain thinks first, and only then speaks."

It was a familiar proverb, one that had guided their training for over twenty years. The words had the desired effect. The young man's chin lifted confidently.

"Yes. Yes, I have devised a battle strategy that will clear the swamp of undead."

Matteo let out a whoop and threw his arms around his friend, spinning him around and off the ground. They fell into a tangled heap and began to wrestle like puppies at play.

After quite some time, they tired of this sport and broke apart, sprawling out on the ground and panting with contented exhaustion. Andris sent a wistful look at his friend. "You really think that this will earn me a position with a patron of note?"

Matteo linked his hands behind his head and smiled. "I wouldn't be surprised if Grozalum himself demanded your hire," he said, naming the powerful illusionist who ruled the port city of Khaerbaal, Halruaa's most important naval base.

"Jordaini at alert," demanded a deep, sonorous voice from the gatehouse. "First honors. Wizards in the house."

The two young men scrambled to their feet and hurried into position at the edge of the training field. Their fellow students gathered there, standing at respectful attention, feet at precise shoulder width, hands clasped behind their backs, and eyes level as they awaited the arrival of the visiting dignitary.

Life in Halruaa was orderly, governed by laws and customs that were detailed and precise. Protocol was an important part of any higher education, for each stratum of society was afforded certain privileges and honors. Wizards enjoyed the highest position, hence first honors. The posture assumed by the jordaini showed the respect that propriety demanded, but it also bespoke their own high status. Second in class only to the wizards, they were a highly trained elite. After all, they represented truth, a power quite different from magic but just as powerful in its sphere. Law and custom decreed that only a jordain could meet a wizard's eyes at all times. Those of lesser rank lowered their gaze respectfully before addressing a strange magic-wielder.

Matteo's eyes widened as the wizardly entourage swept into the compound. Quickly he schooled his face into a more seemly composure, but he couldn't help but stare at the unusual visitors.

A score of well-armed men marched into the field, following each other in two lines that framed two extraordinary creatures. The larger of these was a wemic, a centaur-like creature that appeared to be half man, half lion. The beast's body was massive, nearly the size of a small horse, and his golden-skinned torso was as thick and muscular as Themo's. Matteo made a note to compose a satire for his classmate on this theme at first opportunity.

The wemic's face would be considered handsome in a man, though his nose was larger and broader than human features were wont to be, and the pupils in his golden eyes were vertical, like a cat's. A thick mane of glossy black hair fell to his shoulders, and an earring set with a large red stone glittered in one rounded, leonine ear.

But it was the other being upon whom Matteo's eyes lingered longest. Elves were a rarity in Halruaa. A few elf folk, most of them half-blooded, were drawn to Halruaa by their love of magic. Some of them even advanced to the Council of Elders and were counted among the four hundred most regarded wizards of the land. But Matteo had never heard of an elf reaching the rank of inquisitor.

She was beautiful, in an exotic, alien fashion that tightened Matteo's throat with awe and evoked in him a strange and foreign longing. Her skin was a coppery hue, and the thick hair braided and coiled about her shapely head was a green deeper and more lustrous than fine jade. Her eyes were as golden as those of the wemic at her side and nearly as feline. Though her head rose no higher than Matteo's shoulder, he did not for a moment make the mistake of thinking her fragile. There was a fine coiled strength in her slender form, like the liquid steel of a cat's muscles. She wore the bright clear yellow that proclaimed her an inquisitor in the service of Azuth, the god of wizards, whose worship was slowly gaining credence among Halruaans, and the only god other than Mystra, Lady of Magic, whose worship was permitted in the land.

The elf woman's gaze swept down the line of young men. "I have heard good things of this year's form," she said in a peculiarly high, bell-like voice. "Although the time of your final testing is not yet come, I have been asked by several potential patrons to evaluate your battle skills.

"This is Mbatu," she said, gesturing toward the wemic. "He will test you in combat, according to a rank I will assign. I am Kiva, inquisitrix of Azuth." She smiled faintly. "Since we all know the common word by which such as I are named, let us speak it plainly. I am a magehound, and I prefer this title to the formal one. You have my permission to so address me."

She walked along the line, her head tipped back as she met the gaze of each jordain. Themo was third in line. He glanced down at the elf, but his gaze quickly returned to the fine sword the wemic wore over his shoulder. The expression on his face was that of a particularly hungry halfling regarding a pitcher of ale and a plateful of honey-cakes.

"You are first," she said. A flicker of anticipation danced through the big man's eyes. This seemed to please the elf. She reached up and patted his cheek as she might that of a child, then she continued down the line, passing by several men. She stopped when she stood before Matteo.

She regarded him for a long moment. "Second," she announced. The honor pleased Matteo, but he merely nodded his thanks. A student jordain might meet a strange wizard's eyes, but he did not speak unless prompted by invitation or dire need.

Kiva paused again before Andris. Her strange, beautiful face furrowed in puzzlement. After a long moment, she stretched out her hand. The captain of her guard hastened forward and placed in her palm a golden rod set with green stones and capped by a large green crystal.

The magehound reached up and touched the rod to Andris's forehead. Immediately the crystal began to vibrate, singing out a high, ghostly note. Kiva nodded, as if she had expected this. She took a step back and turned to the masters of the school, a distinguished ensemble of jordaini, scholars, warriors, and wizards. As was the custom, they'd come out to greet their important visitor. They were a diverse lot, ranging from deceptively frail Vishna to the burly, hook-nosed woman who in her youth had commanded the navy in the nearby port city of Khaerbaal. At the moment, however, all the masters regarded the magehound with identical disbelieving stares.

"Ordinarily I would call for Inquisition upon this jordain, but no further tests are required. The answer is abundantly clear."

"This cannot be! Andris is a fine student," protested Vishna. The old wizard stepped out of ranks, fairly quivering with distress. "He has been tested at the prescribed intervals, as are all the jordaini in this house. Never has he shown signs of latent magical talent."

"If he is so fine a student as that," Kiva returned coolly, "perhaps you did not look for these dangerous signs as closely as you might otherwise have done."

The accusation was potent and inarguable, but Vishna was not yet quelled. "If Andris is to be accused, he has the right of Inquisition. Let it be done."

"It is the law," agreed Dimidis in his thin, querulous voice. The aged jordain spoke seldom, but when he did his words held the weight of verdict—small wonder, considering that Dimidis served as judge of the Disputation Table, the court that settled differences between jordaini and meted out occasional punishment for rule infractions.

"That is quite enough, both of you," decreed Ferris Grail, the wizard who served as headmaster of the school. "The magehound has passed judgment upon a false jordain. That is her duty, and that is also law." The headmaster spoke quietly, but his deep voice tolled out over the stricken jordaini like a death knell, as indeed it was.

Vishna bowed his head in defeat and fell back into line.

Now that the opposition was silenced, Kiva turned back to Andris. A strange light burned in her golden eyes. "I accuse you, Andris, of possessing magic power and hiding this knowledge from your masters."

Her gaze swept the line of young men, taking note of the disbelief and horror dawning on their faces. "I see that I do not need to tell you the penalty for this offense."

CHAPTER THREE

The streets of Khaerbaal were quiet, for the sun
burned high overhead and every Halruaan who
could sought the comfort of darkened rooms and,
if they were fortunate, magically cooled breezes.

Tzigone was unaccustomed to such comforts,
so she didn't miss them. If anything, she enjoyed
the hour or two of relative solitude. A few street
people huddled in the shade offered by alleys and
arbors, and visitors from other lands mopped at
their streaming faces as realized their error and
sought a cool tavern. Few spared a glance at the
small, thin figure clad in a loose brown tunic and
leggings that ended several inches above her bare
feet. With her tousled, short brown hair and
slightly smudged face, she looked more like a
street urchin than a young woman. If an observer
cared to look more closely, he might notice that
beauty was hers if she wished to claim it. Her face
angled sharply from high cheekbones to a small
pointed chin, and her eyes were big and brown,
lively with intelligence and unusually expressive.

At the moment, those eyes were deeply shad-
owed, for she'd lost another night's sleep to that
thrice-bedamned wemic.

Tzigone shifted the sack off her shoulder and
looked around for a likely recipient for its contents.
She didn't keep anything for long. Possessions,

things, had a way of betraying those who held them too close. The last thing she'd treasured had been a silver brush, and keeping it had gotten her captured and nearly killed.

Her gaze fell on an old woman huddled in the shade of an almond tree, wearing thick cast-off garments that might have been comfortable during the coolest winter days. Tzigone pulled a long, red silk kirtle from the bag.

"A fine day to you, grandmother," she said cheerfully, using the friendly greeting common to peasant folk. "Lady's Day has come and gone."

"Mystra be praised," muttered the crone, not bothering to look up. "Crowded, it were. And noisy, too."

Tzigone dropped the simple gown into the woman's lap. The fine fabric glided down as softly as a shadow. "Have you any use for this, grandmother? I can't wear it now that Lady Day has passed. There are too many travelers in this town with odd notions about a lone woman in a red dress." When the crone shot her a quizzical look, Tzigone placed her hands on her hips and took a couple of steps in a dead-on imitation of a doxie's strut.

"Them were the days," the old woman said with dry, unexpected humor. She fingered the silk with knotted hands. "This won't be bringing 'em back, but ain't it fine as frog's hair! I'll take it off'n your hands, girlie. And," she added shrewdly, "I'll not tell any who might ask where it come from."

Tzigone nodded and started to move off, but the woman seized the hem of her tunic, her face suddenly animated. "What of the stars, girl? Did the stars of Mystra what lighted up this gown foretell good fortune or ill? Mind you, I'll not be wearing an evil omen."

Tzigone painted a reassuring smile on her face. "Don't worry, grandmother. My fortune was the same as always."

This seemed to content the crone, for she hauled herself to her feet and hurried off, clutching her treasure.

For once Tzigone had spoken no more than the unadorned truth. Magic slid off her like water off a swan.

The tiny magical lights that rained from the sky at the close of the Lady's Day festival had refused to touch her. She closed her eyes and sighed as she remembered how people had fallen back from her, their own red clothes glittering with Mystra's stars and their faces holding the somber, shuttered expression usually reserved for funerals. And why not? No stars, no future. "You're dead," their eyes had said. "You just don't know it yet."

"Don't rush me," Tzigone muttered.

What bothered her more than the crowd's reaction was her own small lapse. She'd quietly borrowed a red gown from a local garment shop so that she could move unnoticed through the crowd, forgetting what would happen at the festival's end, not thinking how her starless gown might draw the attention of the wemic who of late had been stalking her.

And that was the problem. She had survived this long because she forgot nothing. That was the law that ruled her days. Never did a slight go unavenged. No kindness, no matter how casual or even unintentional, went unrewarded. But for her, sleep had always been the true time of remembrance. Sometimes, when she was deep in dreams, she could almost remember her real name and her mother's face.

Sleep beckoned her, and she found her way through the narrow back streets to one of her favorite hidden spots. She sank into slumber as soon as she settled down.

Despite her exhaustion, she fell at once into dreaming. The dream was a familiar one, poignant with the sights and sensations of childhood. It was twilight, and the breeze had the rich, silken feel that came when night lured the winds inland from Lake Halruaa, making the humid summer air flow and swirl like a mage queen's skirts. The breeze was especially pleasant on the rooftops overlooking the port city of Khaerbaal. On the tiled roof of a portside inn, the girl and her mother chased floating balls of light that dipped and danced against the purple sky.

Many Halruaan children her age could conjure lights, but hers were special: gem-colored and almost sentient, they eluded pursuit like canny fireflies.

"That one!" she shrieked happily, pointing toward a brilliant orange globe—a miniature harvest moon.

Obligingly her mother hiked up her skirts and ran after it. The child laughed and clapped her hands as the globe cleverly evaded capture, but her eyes lingered longer on the woman than on the dancing light.

Mother was her world. To the child's eyes, the small, dark woman was the greatest beauty and the wisest wizard in all of Halruaa. Her mother's laughter was music and fairy song, and as she ran, her long brown hair streamed behind her like a silken shadow.

No other children had ever joined their game, but the girl did not really miss them. In the city below, children were being led through chanted prayers to Mystra and then tucked beneath insect netting for a night's sleep. Seldom did the wizard's daughter envy them or wish to join them.

She had never lacked for companionship, for all creatures came to her mother's call. Just this morning she had romped with a winged kitten, and she'd eaten her mid-day meal in the company of two sun-sleepy lizards with scales that shone like commingled emeralds and topaz. Her favorite companion was Sprite, a lad no bigger than her small, pudgy hand. He always appeared so promptly that she suspected he followed them from place to place in hope of hearing her mother's summoning song. She understood this impulse completely, for there was no sound dearer to her or more lovely.

Even so, she hadn't asked for Sprite in many days, for reasons she did not like to examine too closely.

Fiercely she thrust the thought aside and ran toward a small crimson globe. She stopped short just as the globe dodged, then crouched and pounced at it as she'd seen the flitter-kitten do just that morning. She caught the ball in the air and bore it down to the ground with her. She landed hard, and the globe exploded beneath her with a satisfying pop. She scrambled to her feet, a triumphant smile on her face and a splattering of luminous red on her tunic.

Her mother applauded enthusiastically and then made a small, graceful gesture with one hand. The red stain lifted from the girl's tunic and spun out into the night, forming a long, glowing thread.

The child grinned expectantly as she waited for the next part of their game. The thread would twist and loop until it etched a marvelous picture against the darkening sky. Sometimes her mother sketched exotic beasts, or a miniature skyship, and once she fashioned a stairway to the stars that the girl could actually climb—and did, until her mother took fright and called her back. But most often the threads drew out maps that traced paths through the back streets and over the rooftops of whatever city or village they currently explored.

Tonight, however, the thread formed none of these things. It wandered about aimlessly, hopelessly tangling itself. Finally it dissipated altogether into a smattering of faint and rapidly dimming pink motes.

Puzzled, she looked to her mother. "I'm tired, child," the woman said softly. "We'll make pictures another night."

The girl accepted this with a nod and dashed off after a pair of emerald lights. Since there would be no pictures tonight, she made a new game of her own. Earlier that day she had tied a short, stout stick to her belt. This made a fine sword. In her imagination, the globes became a swarm of multicolored stirges—giant, thirsty, mosquito-like creatures that hummed macabre little tunes as they drained sleeping men dry. She sang a stirge song now in a childish soprano, making up nonsense verse as she went along. Each imaginary monster ended its days in a splash of colored light. It was a fine game and helped her put from mind the small failing of her mother's magic. On nights like this, she could forget a good deal.

She could almost forget that they lived on the run.

Her mother tried hard to make a game of it, and the little girl played along, as children tend to do. She understood far more than her mother suspected, but there were still many things that puzzled her. For some time now, questions had been building up inside her like the swell of magical power during a summoning. She was certain that she would explode like one of her globes if she didn't speak out. Soon. Tonight!

But she waited until all the dancing lights were spent. They left the roof and took shelter for the night in the crowded upper room of a dockside inn. The child always felt safest in such places. Nocturnal "adventures" seemed to occur more frequently when they took solitary refuge. She felt reassured by the sonorous snores coming from the trio of ale merchants who shared a bed by the shuttered window, and took comfort in the sword that lay, bright and ready, beside the earnest young man her mother had described as a questing paladin.

She waited while her mother emptied the common washbasin into the back street and refilled it with fresh water from the pitcher. She sat stoically while her mother wet a square of linen and scrubbed off some of the dirt that the child seemed to attract, much as spellcasting drew cats. She waited until her mother took out their greatest treasure, a small brush with a silver handle engraved with climbing roses, and began to ease it through her daughter's tousled dark hair.

Usually she loved this nightly ritual; often she wished she could purr throughout the brushing like a petted cat. Tonight, though, she would have answers or she would burst.

"Who is following us?" she demanded.

The brush paused in mid-stroke. "Great Lady Mystra!" her mother exclaimed in a low, choked voice. "You know?"

She gave an impatient little shrug, not sure how to answer this. "Who?" she repeated.

Her mother was silent for a long moment. "Many are the tools, but the hand that wields them is that of my husband."

The little girl picked up an oddly discordant note in the music of her mother's voice. It occurred to her, for no reason that she could yet understand, that Mother did not name their shadowy pursuer as her child's father. Perhaps this was because in Halruaa the two were ever the same. Children were born within marriage. Marriages were arranged by the local matchmaker, who was always a minor mage of the divination school. She had yet to live out her fifth summer, but she knew that much. Even so, the same puzzling instinct that sensed her mother's hesitation prompted her to leave the obvious question unasked.

She settled for another. "Is your husband a great wizard?"

"He is a wizard."

"Like you?"

The brush resumed its rhythmic stroking, but the effect was no longer soothing. The girl absorbed with each stroke her mother's emotions: tension, grief, longing, fear. The temptation to pull away was dizzying, but she fiercely pushed aside the impulse. She wanted answers. Perhaps this pain was part of the knowing.

"Once he was my apprentice," her mother said at last. "There is a proverb that warns masters to beware ambition in their students. Words of nonsense can be repeated as often as sage wisdom, but this one held true."

The little girl shrugged off the lesson, her mind on the recent miscast spells, the wandering magic. "You are the master still," she said stoutly, as if she could deny what was becoming clearer with every day.

Her mother's smile was sad and knowing. "How long has it been since you asked me to summon Sprite? It is a difficult casting. Surely you know that."

The girl's eyes dropped and her lower lip jutted. "He teases me. That's all."

"Really. That has never bothered you before."

"I've tired of it," she said, implacably stubborn. "And I'm tired of talking about that silly Sprite. Sing another song, one that will summon something fierce and strong. A starsnake!"

"They do not fly at night, child."

She folded her arms. "Then the name is stupid."

Her mother laughed a little. "Perhaps you are right. What fierce creature do you desire? A night-flying roc? A jungle cat, perhaps?"

There was a playful tone in her mother's voice. The girl understood that she was being humored, and she liked it not at all. "A behir," she said darkly, picturing a many-legged creature with the sinuous body of a snake, a fearsome crocodilian head, and a wide mouth full of wicked, translucent teeth. "It can follow us and lie in wait behind us. When your husband comes by, it will spring out and bite off his—"

"Foot," her mother supplied quickly, suspecting, quite rightly, that the little girl had placed her ambitions for the behir somewhat higher.

"Foot," agreed the child quickly, for she had lost interest in her imagined revenge. Her mother's eyes had gone wary, and her hand went to the small amulet that nestled in the hollow of her throat.

Carefully her mother eased her hand away from her amulet. "Your hair is so smooth and shiny! You look too fine for sleep. What if we run across the rooftops until we find a tavern still open? We could have cakes and sugared wine, and if there is a bard in the house, I will sing. And, yes, I will summon a fierce creature for you. A behir, a dragon—anything you like."

She wasn't fooled by the brittle gaiety of her mother's tones, or by the bribe of a rooftop romp. Though neither of them had even spoken the words aloud, the child understood that the hidden ways were safer than the streets. Quickly she tightened the laces on her soft leather shoes. It would not do to trip and fall into the grasp of her mother's husband.

"I'm ready," she announced.

Her mother eased open a shutter and lifted her onto the ledge beyond. The child leaned her small body against the wall and began to edge around the building, as confident and surefooted as a lemur.

Something caught her eye several streets to the east. A tendril of magic, so powerful that her eyes perceived it as a glowing green light, twisted through the streets toward them.

Lightning jolted through her, nearly knocking her from the ledge.

Tzigone frowned, puzzled. This had not happened to the child she had been, nor had it ever been part of her dream. A second jolt struck, and suddenly the ledge was gone and she was falling.

Tzigone awoke suddenly, gasping and flailing about for something to hold. A startled, almost panicked moment passed before she remembered where she was.

She'd picked the most secure resting place in Khaerbaal. She had followed the flight of a winged starsnake to this tree, an enormous bilboa that shaded and dominated the public garden. She'd climbed until she'd found this perch, and then bedded down on the broad limb. The snake was sleeping still, its gossamer wings folded and the blue and white scales of its long, coiled body glittering like moonstone.

Tzigone pushed herself up into a sitting position and shoved a hand through her short, sweat-soaked hair. The rope that lashed her to the tree had pulled tight around her waist, giving testimony to a restless sleep. She'd probably touched the snake while she was thrashing about.

Had she been almost anyone else, she would now be swinging from her rope, smoking like an overcooked haunch of rothe—not that she had much knowledge of these savory, shaggy beasts, overcooked or otherwise. Starsnakes she knew better.

The slumber of these winged reptiles was guarded by powerful magical defenses. A wandering sage had once informed her that creatures changed over the centuries in response to their surroundings and to thwart their enemies. In Halruaa, wizards were the most dangerous beings, potential enemies of anything that slithered, flew, or walked about on two or more legs. Few people learned to defend themselves against wizards, but the starsnake was more ingenious than most. No wizard had been able to negate their sleep shield, though from time to time there was tavern talk of darkly humorous tales of wizards who had tried and failed. No one in full possession of his senses would approach, much less touch, the sleeping creatures. That made this limb one of the safest spots in all Halruaa, provided that Tzigone left well before the creature awakened. This arrangement suited her just fine. She and starsnakes were frequent bedfellows.

The snake's wings rustled slightly as if touched by a night breeze. Tzigone brought her legs under her and crouched like a wary cat, one hand on the hilt of her knife and one hand tugging at her rope to make sure that she was firmly tethered. Sometimes the reptiles were roused by the release of their own killing magic, especially if they were hungry. The blast of magic usually provided them with a hot meal.

Tzigone couldn't tell if the snake slept or woke, for its blue eyes were always open. Suddenly the head reared back, a gesture that made the snake look absurdly like a person who had just glimpsed a surprising sight. The vertical pupils in the snake's strange, sky-colored eyes narrowed to dark slits, and for a long moment the starsnake regarded Tzigone sullenly.

"You touched us. Why do you live?" it inquired in a dry whisper.

Tzigone shrugged. "It's gotten to be a habit."

"An annoying one," the snake countered. "One that we can help you break."

The attack was a sudden blur of wings and fangs and ropes of moonstone. Tzigone dived off the branch, away from the lunging creature. As she fell, she slashed out with her knife. The blade tore through one of the beautiful wings, nearly severing it. Not taking any chances, Tzigone seized the wounded wing and gave it a hard tug. The short fall was enough to pull the creature from its branch. As she jolted to a stop, Tzigone released the wing. The starsnake's sibilant wail echoed through the tree as it spiraled down toward the garden below.

Tzigone swung gently back and forth as she listened for the distant thud. She tucked away her knife and seized the rope with both hands. She pulled herself up, then brought her legs arching up over her head until she could hook them over the branch. Strong and limber, she easily swung up into sitting position. Quickly she untied the rope, coiled it, and tied it to her belt. A glance at the moon told the time. Selune was half full, and thus visible during the day, looking out over the city like a single heavy-lidded eye. In half an hour's time, it would disappear behind the spires of the School of Augury. Tzigone's perch was high above the rooftops, and she figured it would take her about that long to scramble down the tree. As she climbed, she placed a whispered bet against the lady moon.

Her descent was faster than Selune's. She cast an impish grin at the wizard's school and then settled down to dress her kill.

The snakeskin was valuable and would keep her in coin for many days. Although the meat was bitter and unpalatable, she took a chunk anyway. The starsnake had fully intended to eat her; Tzigone thought it only fair to return the favor.

An hour later, she emerged from the back entrance to a small apothecary's house. The man possessed only a minor talent for potions and transformations, and his patrons were generally lackluster common folk: merchants, farmers, sell-swords, miners, and the like. Tzigone sold him strange things from time to time, spell components that he would take gladly and without question.

She walked along the back ways she'd learned as a child, utterly silent but for the pleasant chink of the shining Halruaan skie in her bag. The snakeskin had bought her a dozen portraits of King Zalathorm, duly minted on electrum coin.

"Tzigone, you're a bastard in every sense of the word and no mistake about it, but at least you're a rich one," she said softly.

She nodded, liking the sound of that. The clinking of coin made a pleasant counterpoint to the music of her chosen name. She liked the exotic sound of the word, the quick tap of the tongue for the T that led into the crisp accented syllable, and finally a quick slide out on two small sounds. "T-SIG-o-nee," she repeated softly, and nodded again.

The word meant "gypsy" in some obscure northern tongue. She'd liked it when she heard it several months ago and had claimed it as her own. Her latest name described what she was, if not precisely who she was.

For now—for a while longer, at least—that would have to be enough.

CHAPTER FOUR

Silence hung over the jordaini training field, heavy as swamp mist. The ingenious water clock in the nearby library tower tolled the hour, but no one bothered to count its chimes and no one hurried off to his next lesson. No one spoke. No one moved.

"No!"

The word burst from Themo like the cry of a wounded panther. The big jordain pushed his way through the line to stand between the magehound and his condemned friend.

"Surely there has been some mistake," he entreated. "There must have been! Andris is the best of us all. I will appeal this dispute to the Jordaini Council, as is my right."

"Dispute?" Kiva looked more amused than affronted. "In such matters, the word of a magehound is final. There is no appeal and no room for disputation. But since you speak with a passion unusual and refreshing for the jordaini, I am willing to listen."

She turned away from Themo to survey the suddenly hopeful faces of Andris's friends. "Have any of you seen this man use magic? You may speak freely."

A loud chorus of disclaimers rippled down the line, most of them framed by the formal phrases a jordain used to emphasize that his words were not satire or parable, but literal truth.

Kiva looked faintly bored but determined to see her duty through. "Perhaps he has some unusual abilities or accomplishes things that might be difficult to explain without magic?"

"He is skilled in battle strategy, my lady," Vishna said. "Unusually so. But that is no more than the application of a disciplined mind to the cultivation of natural gifts."

"Another proverb," Kiva observed dryly. "Must you jordaini always speak in forms and formulas? It is unspeakably dreary."

"Truth is seldom as interesting as lies," Matteo muttered.

The magehound wheeled toward him, her face incredulous. Immediately Matteo realized his mistake. If the elf woman thought he was accusing her of falsehood, his life was forfeit.

But after a moment Kiva smiled and nodded. "I agree. Unlike truth, lies must make sense. They demand an internal logic and attention to detail that truth, in its innocent arrogance, does not always achieve. Do you understand me, jordain?"

Matteo answered as he always did: honestly. "Not quite, lady."

Her jade-colored brows flew up. "Ah. We have a rare beast here—a man who will admit that he does not know something rather than speak a false word. You are a credit to your kind, jordain."

The lilt in her voice held true praise, but Matteo saw mockery glittering in her eyes. Puzzled, he answered as best he could. "I thank you for your *words*, lady," he said, adding subtle emphasis that acknowledged the hidden blade in her compliment.

The magehound looked intrigued. "You speak well, for a man whose wits are hemmed in with proverbs and platitudes. Perhaps you would like to tell me about your fellow jordain. What is it about him that makes the crystal sing?"

"I do not know of this crystal and its properties, lady, so I cannot answer your question."

"Actually, that's quite a good answer," she said approvingly. "You do not know the crystal. Well enough. But you do know the man and his character?"

Matteo hesitated, then inclined his head in a single curt nod.

"And do you know him well?" she prodded.

He glanced at Andris, whose face was more familiar to him than his own. "As well as one brother might know another," he said softly.

"You have never once perceived anything unusual about him, no act beyond the scope of any other magic-dead counselor?"

The morning's discussion about the Kilmaruu Paradox came unbidden into Matteo's mind. Quickly he willed the thought away, but some flicker of it must have entered his eyes.

Kiva's lips curved in a smile of feline satisfaction. "There is something, after all. Speak of it."

Matteo sent an anguished look at his friend. "You are pledged to speak truth," Andris said softly. "I would not have you do otherwise, whatever comes of it."

"Andris is indeed skilled in battle strategy," Matteo began reluctantly. "He has applied himself to this study more assiduously than any of us. He possesses an original mind and sees beyond the details of history to what might have been and what might yet be. Like a master weaver, he takes the threads and makes of them new cloth."

"Very poetic," Kiva said coldly. "Your disclaimer is noted. Get to the meat of the matter."

"This morning Andris revealed to me that he has solved the Kilmaruu Paradox."

A soft ripple of astonishment passed through the ranks of the jordaini. The magehound's hired soldiers looked shocked, and even the masters exchanged incredulous glances. Matteo noted that all of the masters seemed surprised by this news. Why so, when Andris indicated that he'd confided in at least one of them?

But Matteo could not consider the matter now. The magehound swayed closer to him, her lovely face dark with menace.

"Do you know how many wizards have made it their life-work to unravel that puzzle?" she said in a low, furious voice. "How many have died in the swamps? None but a wizard or an utter fool would dare attempt such a thing! Tell me, jordain, is your friend a fool?"

Matteo saw the trap at once. For the first time in his life, he regretted the vows that bound him to speak truth. "He is not," he said faintly.

"Then it would appear that he is a wizard." Kiva turned to the wemic. "Andris is a false jordain and a danger to his kind. Deal with it."

The creature crouched, tamping down his hind legs. Before Matteo could draw breath, the great catman leaped. The coarse fur of the leonine body scorched across Matteo's arm as the wemic flashed past. Matteo squeezed his eyes closed, willing back the unfamiliar moisture that gathered there.

But darkness could not block the sound, the terrible thud of impact as Andris hit the ground under the weight of the great wemic, the quick brittle crunch of bone. Matteo recognized the sound of a neck breaking, and he spoke a silent farewell to his friend. He watched in despairing silence as the wemic picked up the limp form of Andris with his manlike arms and slung the jordain over his massive shoulder.

Kiva turned to the masters, who stood as silent and stunned as their students. "There will be no further testing today. Judging from these long faces, it would be effort wasted. I will return when your students are at their best."

The magehound spun on her heel and walked out, followed by the wemic with his grim burden, and finally by her guard.

When the sound of their horses' hoofbeats had died away, the headmaster turned sad eyes upon his students. The wizard swallowed hard several times before he spoke. "The tides will be highest near midnight, and many ships will sail from the docks of Khaerbaal tonight. There will be much merriment in the town, and the taverns will vie with each other to draw in the sailors. Ale and wine will not reach prices so low for many moons to come. Since thrift is a jordainish virtue, I urge you all to partake," he said with forced lightness.

No one spoke or moved. With a deep sigh, the wizard abandoned his attempt. "Horses and coin will be available to all who wish them," he said in a softer and infinitely sadder tone. "Go, with Mystra's blessing and mine. Purchase a few hours of forgetfulness."

Several of the students slipped away, but none so quickly as Themo. Matteo noted the glitter of tears in the big man's eyes and the grim set of his square jaw. The combination did not bode well.

Vishna seemed to be thinking along the same lines. The old battle wizard came over to the place where Matteo stood alone, still reeling from the result of his unwilling betrayal. "Go with Themo, lad. Keep him safe."

Matteo's lips thinned in an ironic smile. "And how will I accomplish that? With the sharp sword of truth?"

The bitterness and anguish in his voice made Vishna wince in sympathy. The wizard sighed and placed a hand on the young man's shoulders. "Yours was not the hand that slew Andris. That thought is untruth, and arrogance beside."

"Arrogance? How so?" demanded Matteo in despairing tones. "How could I possibly boast of my part in the death of my friend?"

"You need not take pleasure in a thing to display pride.

Taking responsibility where none exists is arrogance. A child thinks that all things revolve around him and that his will and his words bring forth wishes upon the first star. You are no child. See that you remember that."

The wizard's tone was bracingly sharp. Matteo nodded, seeing both the purpose and the truth of the words. "Thank you, master," he said, speaking automatically the words he had been trained to use at the end of every lesson.

Vishna sighed. "The lesson is over. Go."

Matteo went, but reluctantly. The prospect of an evening in the boisterous port town held little appeal under the best of circumstances. But he quickly bathed and dressed in the traditional garb, a loose sleeveless tunic fashioned from white linen worn over matching leggings. Around his neck he hung the token of his class, a round silver medallion enameled with the jordaini emblem: the left half of the field green, the right yellow, and the two separated by a jagged bolt of cobalt blue lightning. He belted on the strap that held his daggers, then pulled back his dark hair and fastened it with a thin leather thong. These things—the clothing, the weapons, the medallion, and the few small things that aided in the care of his person—were the sum of his possessions. A jordain was allowed nothing but his knowledge, his reputation, and his friends.

Today Matteo had learned how tenuous was his claim to that last and most precious of possessions. He moved like a man asleep, stunned by the loss of Andris and by the realization of how fragile was his own position.

All his life Matteo had walked with pride, as befitted a man of his talents and station. Handpicked at birth—before birth, for that matter—he had been raised in the collective luxury of House Jordain and given the best training that this most civilized land could offer. He had worked hard, and he fully expected to be well rewarded. The jordaini were restrained by law from owning property and amassing wealth, but they lived exceedingly well and could advance in status. A truly talented counselor was in high demand among Halruaa's wizard lords and ladies, and such a man could expect to choose his own path and take whatever employment suited his ambitions.

But at this moment Matteo saw how incredibly hollow was this promise of a glowing future. All that it took was a word from a magehound, and the best of the jordaini was cast aside with no more hesitation or regret than Vishna might spare his ruined shoe.

There was little time to ponder the matter. Matteo had lost one friend today and was determined not to lose another. Themo was probably well on his way, and Matteo dared not leave the grieving man to his own devices for long.

The ride to Khaerbaal, the nearest city, took two to three hours, for the House Jordain was an isolated place. Set in the midst of a peninsula that jutted out into the Bay of Taertal, it was a vast complex of buildings and fields and training courses. The students spent some time each year in carefully supervised travel, for this was deemed an important part of their studies, but anything that Matteo had ever needed could be found in the complex. All the learning, arts, and sciences of this most civilized of lands was at his disposal. This created a sense of security and privilege that had defined Matteo's life. His studies were all focused on creating a counselor versed in many fields of knowledge, an entity in himself, loyal to the wizards he served but forbidden to develop personal ties with any magic-wielder.

Perhaps, he mused, this life had ill prepared him to deal with friendship, much less the loss of a friend. He was not even certain how to grieve. Though his mind and body were finely honed as a blade singer's sword, his own heart was a mystery to him.

He hurried to the stable and was relieved to find his favorite steed as yet unclaimed. No horse in House Jordain's extensive stables better suited his dark mood. A fine black stallion, the beast was at least a hand taller than any other horse Matteo had seen. His sire was reputed to have come from distant Amn, a land famous for its steeds. Although the stallion was the finest horse in the stable, Matteo was not surprised to find him still in his stall. Some blasphemous groom had dubbed the horse "Cyric," and the name had stuck. The stallion was as volatile and possibly as crazed as the evil god whose name he bore.

Matteo ordered a reluctant groom to prepare the horse, and then he sent another servant after a package of travel food. Khaerbaal was at least two hours' ride away, and if he left now he would miss the afternoon meal. He did not want the food and strongly suspected that his stomach would rebel, but he had been too well schooled in such matters to neglect his care. Jordaini were chosen for the unusual strength of their minds and bodies, as well as their nearly total resistance to magic. Harsh penalties ensured that the young men followed the rules that honed all their gifts. Though taverns were not strictly forbidden, an unsupervised trip to temptation-laden Khaerbaal was a rare event.

As soon as the marble gate of the jordaini complex was behind them, Matteo let Cyric have his head. The stallion seemed happy to run, setting an insane breakneck pace that suited Matteo's mood to perfection. He smelled the tang of the Bay of Taertal while the sun was edging toward its zenith, and he entered the north gate of Khaerbaal just as the temple bells were ringing the highsun warning. Native Halruaans knew to take refuge from the direct sun, but Khaerbaal was a busy port filled with strangers, many of whom were unaccustomed to the southern sun. Most quickly got the idea, and the crowds were thinning quickly as Matteo rode through the streets toward the dockside taverns.

Finding Themo was an easy task. Matteo merely fell in behind the group of local militia who trotted purposefully toward the Falling Star Tavern.

The din of battle reached him before the tavern itself came into sight: the thud of fists upon flesh, the splinter and crash of doomed furniture, and the shouted oaths that were more pungent than the dockside fishery nearby.

Matteo swung down from Cyric's back and tied the horse to a wooden post. He had no illusions that this precaution might actually contain the stallion. If Cyric tired of waiting, he would shatter the hitching rail and then attempt to do likewise to the skull of anyone foolish enough to stop him. The horse cocked his ears at the sounds of nearby battle and bade his rider farewell with an envious little whinny. Matteo dryly considered the possibility of teaching battle tactics to the stallion. Cyric would be a foe more formidable than many of the wizards Matteo had faced in his training.

The melee was in full foment when Matteo pushed through the door. He ducked as a familiar massive fist flashed toward his face, then reached up and caught Themo's wrist with both hands. As he rose, he twisted the arm, bringing it up behind the big jordain's back as he shoved him facedown on the nearest table.

He leaned in close to Themo's ear. "I'm going to let you up, then lightly hit you on the back of the neck. Go down as if you're stunned and stay down until the fighting is done, or I swear by Mystra's Truth that I'll drop you in earnest. Agreed?"

Themo's response was a small, barely perceptible nod. Matteo released his arm. As Themo rose, Matteo hit him hard, and the man dropped and sprawled as instructed. But he sent Matteo a blurred, reproachful look. Matteo wasn't sure whether his friend was upset about the more-than-necessary force of the blow or the fact that his sport had been spoiled. Either way, Themo's glare was giving away the game. Matteo nudged his friend's ribs with an ungentle foot, and Themo grudgingly closed his eyes.

Only then did Matteo notice the small magical storm raging in the tavern. A thick, smoky cloud filled the taproom. Sparks of light shot through it in bright random patterns. Matteo recognized the enchantment as a brightness spell from Obold's Spellbook, a rare book he had been required to learn last winter. The sparks were actually small bolts of lightning, which struck at random and drew yelps of surprise from the startled combatants. Themo, of course, possessed complete resistance to such puny missiles, and his impressive bulk had shielded a goodly number of the fighters. Once the big jordain was down, more of the bolts began to find their marks. Some of the brawlers staggered out of the cloud to escape the quelling magic.

It was an effective spell, and if Matteo let it rage on, it would settle the brawl before much more time passed. But any damage done to the tavern and its patrons would be blamed on Themo and would tarnish the reputation of House Jordain. Matteo's duty was to end the fight as quickly as possible.

He took a small gray stone from his bag and tossed it into the thickest part of the glowing cloud. There was no magic in the stone, but it was a lodestone mined from a particularly strong vein. Wizards used them to attract lighting, which often served to affix a spell into an enchanted item. There was a sharp sizzle as the lodestone drew the sparks. Then the cloud, deprived of much of its energy, began to dissipate.

The brawl settled down to a simmer of muttered insults and halfhearted shoves. Matteo wove through the mess toward the house wizard, a small dark man whom he had met before on his one trip to Khaerbaal. He stooped and picked up the lodestone, pocketing it and hoping that the wizard did not recall the last time Themo had visited this tavern.

But the little man glowered at Matteo as if the melee had been entirely his fault. Though Matteo kept his gaze level, he inclined his head in a slight bow. The wizard seemed somewhat mollified by this unnecessary courtesy.

"Your friend is trouble," he said scornfully but with less vitriol than Matteo had right to expect.

"He is young and greatly troubled," Matteo said mildly. He was tempted to contradict the wizard outright, but it seemed wiser to restate the older man's words and nudge them toward truth. "But he is jordaini, and therefore his deeds are mine. Perhaps these coins will purchase your master's forbearance."

The wizard opened the small bag Matteo handed him. Headmaster Ferris Grail, probably anticipating something like this, had instructed the jordaini's steward to dispense coins with a lavish hand.

The wizard's lips moved as he counted the sum within. "This will cover the damage," he agreed.

"And Themo's expenses? I assume he had a bit to drink," Matteo said dryly. His words held a rebuke, for by law it was forbidden to serve anything stronger than wine to a jordain. The effort made to keep the jordaini free of magic's influence would be wasted if their wits were confused by drink or pipe weed.

The wizard was too busy recounting the coins to notice Matteo's mild accusation. Since the amount in the bag far exceeded what Themo could drink or break in the course of a fortnight of grief, the wizard looked only too happy to call matters settled. He even clapped his arm around the young jordain's shoulders.

"Drink with me," he said expansively. "There's no bard in the house this day, but an entertainer or two stayed on when their troupe passed through. You might find such sport amusing."

Matteo doubted that sincerely, but he could find no polite reason to refuse the wizard's offer. He allowed himself to be guided to a table, and he sipped at a glass of pale yellow wine that the wizard poured from a silver decanter. The wizard launched into a tale of other battles he had quelled. Matteo listened politely but with scant interest as he watched the barmaids swiftly set the tavern to rights.

A few of the patrons stumbled out, perhaps to seek healers or to face scolding spouses, but most simply resumed their seats and paid little heed to swelling jaws or blackened eyes. Matteo didn't suppose that most of the tavern's patrons considered such things novelties, much less inconveniences.

He watched the mixed crowd with interest. Many of the patrons wore the blue-green uniform of Halruaa's navy, and an equal number sported the colors of various local militia. Sailors were plentiful, notable for garb as colorful as it was salt-encrusted. Matteo suspected that not a few of them were pirates, but forbearance was the rule at dockside taverns. Here there was no such thing as an innocent question. Asking a man's business was an insult that could result in a challenge to a duel. Most taverns in Khaerbaal had an alley behind kept remarkably free of debris for just such a purpose.

Many sorts of people came to the Falling Star. Matteo noted a pair of merchants, a blacksmith still wearing the apron of her office, and a dour trio of dwarf miners who hunkered down over their mugs, squat and silent as toadstools. There were a few foreigners as well. A tall, fair-haired man on the far side of the room was certainly a barbarian from some far northern land. The woman with him was a cleric. Matteo couldn't make out her deity's symbol from this distance, but he could see the faint red glow of the tattoo that marked it upon her forehead. Priests of all strange gods were so marked in Halruaa as a condition of entry. They were admitted to the port cities under certain strictures. They could not venture inland or attempt to proselytize. Either offense would activate the magic of the temporary tattoo, causing the mark to burn through the cleric's skull and into his or her brain. Matteo had seen this happen during his last visit to Khaerbaal in this very tavern. The grim process had taken a long time, and it had sent every one of the tavern's hardened patrons reeling into the alleys with green faces. It was that, even more than Andris's battle strategy, that had enabled Themo to walk away from the brawl with no more lasting harm than a broken jaw and a reprimand from Dimidis.

The house wizard's eyes suddenly brightened. He nodded to a table near the back of the room. "Now we shall have a disputation worth hearing!"

Matteo frowned, puzzled by the implication. Jordaini often held public debates or monologues, but always at the behest of their patrons and never in so rude a place. His puzzlement turned to slack-jawed astonishment when a small, thin lad climbed onto the table and touched a finger to his heart in the traditional salute to truth. Obviously the lad was not well acquainted with jordaini custom. He employed his middle finger rather than the prescribed digit.

The patrons stamped and hooted and banged their mugs on the dented tables. The would-be jordain acknowledged this acclaim with the traditional bow, bending at the waist, eyes never looking down, executing the graceful gesture perfectly yet somehow imbuing it with mockery. His face and movements projected an air that was both smugly self-important and wildly, blatantly effete. Several of the sailors chuckled, and a huge black-bearded man shouted a coarse insult.

The boy took this in stride, sending the burly sailor a wink that deftly turned the man's insult to unintentional invitation. The man turned scarlet as his mates guffawed and pounded the table with delight.

"Consider the starsnake," the boy said in a rich alto. "This is a puzzle that would confound Queen Beatrix herself."

This comment drew another round of chuckles. Matteo scratched his jaw as he considered the puzzle before him—and not the puzzle of the starsnake. The boy was a street urchin, yet he spoke with powerful, finely modulated tones that took years of study and practice to achieve. More disturbing still, the voice itself was eerily familiar. Female jordaini were rare, and this lad reproduced as faithfully as an echo the tones of the most famous jordaini woman: Cassia, counselor to King Zalathorm himself.

That accounted for the patrons' sly laughter. It was widely rumored some of the luster was off the shining love between the wizard-king and Beatrix, his latest queen. The jordain Cassia no doubt started some of these rumors. She took great pride in her post, and some said that her pride was too great and her ambitions too high.

What the truth of that was, Matteo couldn't say, but he had heard that the female jordain contrived to be at the king's side whenever possible. When this was not possible, Cassia often amused herself by declaiming scathing, subtle satires on such matters as absorbed the queen's interest. She had spoken at House Jordain, and Matteo would forget his own name before he would the music of her voice. And here it was again, pouring forth from this unlikely vessel!

The boy's commentary continued, deftly skewering both the foibles of the court and the pretensions of the jordaini. The house wizard nodded and smiled, but his face began to darken like a coming lake storm when the target shifted to wizards and their oddities.

"I like this not at all," he grumbled.

Matteo considered mentioning that the discourse was becoming amusing at last, but he decided that the remark lacked the discretion his rank demanded. "The lad has talent," he commenting, thinking this a suitably neutral remark.

For some reason, his words greatly amused the wizard. He threw back his head and laughed heartily and unpleasantly. There was a nasty gleam of satisfaction in his eyes as he regarded his guest. "So it's true, I suppose, what they say of you jordaini?"

Matteo longed to strike the malicious smile from the wizard's lips. "You have me at a disadvantage, sir," he said formally. "I am not aware of the particular gossip to which you refer."

The laughter disappeared from the wizard's face like an extinguished candle. Gossip was considered vulgar, and Matteo's polite words were a thinly veiled insult.

Before the man could speak, a low growl vibrated through the room like thunder. Silence fell over the tavern. Matteo turned to the door and let out a curse that earned him a respectful stare from a sailor at the next table.

The wemic Mbatu crouched in the open door, his tail

lashing and his baleful glare fixed upon the lad. Quick as a startled fish, the boy was off the table and darting toward the back door. Mbatu sprang, crossing the taproom with huge, bounding leaps.

At that moment something snapped within Matteo. Without thought of propriety or consequence, he leaped up from his chair and upended the table just as the wemic launched himself into another mighty leap.

Matteo's timing was perfect. The wemic crashed head-first into the thick, weathered boards and dropped like an arrow-shot bird. For good measure, Matteo hefted a chair and brought it down hard on the dazed wemic's head. The chair shattered and the creature went limp.

But Matteo's troubles were just beginning. His impulsive act had also upended his host. The wizard rose slowly to his feet, brushing at his robes. His eyes bulged as he stared at the massive, slumbering wemic.

"You attacked a magehound's personal guardian," he said incredulously, then repeated the words with obvious enjoyment. He was muttering them still as he hurried away, no doubt to report this grave infraction of jordaini law to the nearest authority. Matteo hoped that such a person was not currently in the tavern, or sentence might be passed and carried out this very night.

In moments the wizard hurried back, alone, looking more than a little disgruntled. The local militia had come and gone, dragging away many of the brawlers with them. No doubt the wizard had been unable to find an official representative of Khaerbaal's law and had returned to handle the matter himself.

A hunk of bread bounced off Matteo's head. He glanced in the direction from which it had come, annoyed at the petty distraction. The young entertainer peered around the frame of the back door, gesturing frantically.

"Psst! This way, and hurry!"

When Matteo hesitated, the boy rolled his eyes impatiently. "Your friend's out here. He needs you."

Matteo glanced to the place on the floor where he had left Themo "sleeping." Sure enough, the big jordain had slipped away, no doubt to pick a fight elsewhere. With a sigh, he quickly made his way to the back of the room and out into the street beyond.

He followed the lad to the end of the long dueling alley and then stopped. The corridor was empty but for him and the boy, as was the street beyond.

"Where's Themo?" he demanded.

"How should I know?" the urchin retorted. "Unless it's true what they say about jordaini, we'd better start running."

This was the second time someone had made that remark, and Matteo liked it even less on second hearing. He didn't have the leisure to inquire, however, for at that moment the wizard burst from the tavern, his face indignant and his open palm flaming with light.

"Damn," the boy muttered and dug one hand into the bag that hung at his belt.

Matteo drew his daggers and prepared to deflect the magical attack. As he expected, the sun arrow spell took deadly form and spun toward him. He formed the classic defense with a smooth, practiced movement.

But the boy was quicker still. His small hand flashed out, holding a shining bit of glass. Before Matteo could thrust the lad aside, the bolt struck the proffered target. It hit the small mirror squarely and bounced back at a declining angle toward the wizard.

There was a moment of stunned silence. The wizard let out a small, high-pitched whimper and began to topple slowly to one side, clutching with both hands at the smoking robes covering his groin.

Matteo sent an incredulous stare at the lad. The urchin shrugged and lifted the mirror to his own face, preening a bit and combing his cap of short brown hair with surprisingly delicate fingers.

"You told a deliberate lie," Matteo marveled.

It was the urchin's turn to be surprised. "I did a lot of things. That's the one that caught your fancy?"

Matteo glanced at the man writhing on the cobblestone and remembered the boy's deft and dangerous performance in the tavern. There was something to the lad's logic. But his next words, when he spoke, surprised him.

"What do they say about the jordaini?" he demanded.

The lad's laughter was rich and merry. "Many things, no doubt! I spoke of your ability to fight wizards. Why do you ask?"

"That wizard said much the same when I remarked that you had talent."

A knowing glint kindled in the urchin's eyes. "Repeat your exact words."

Matteo blinked, puzzled by the request but not confounded. He could repeat entire conversations verbatim. This was an important part of his training. "I merely said of your performance, 'The lad has talent.' Nothing more."

"Oh. Well, that explains it."

He folded his arms. "Not to me, it doesn't."

With a grin, the "lad" shrugged off a loose brown overtunic to reveal a shirt of thin linen and the slender but unmistakably female form beneath.

"They say that jordaini have little experience with women." She winked and thrust out a hand. "I'm Tzigone, and I'm here to change all that."

Dazed into rote compliance with protocol, Matteo took the offered hand. He balked, however, at accepting what the handclasp seemed to offer. "You are gravely mistaken. There is no place for a woman in my life."

"Make one," she said adamantly. "You just saved my skin. That creates a debt, and whether you like it or not, I'll be around until that debt is paid."

"I assure you, that is most unnecessary."

She glanced back toward the tavern and then took his arm. "Wrong again. Looks like I'll be paying the first installment sooner than expected."

Matteo followed the line of her gaze. The wemic reeled out into the alley and began to pad unsteadily toward them in a weaving but deliberate path. With each step, the creature seemed to gather strength and purpose.

Tzigone stamped her foot impatiently and tugged at his arm. "Are you going to stand there and shout 'Here, kitty!' until that thing pounces? Come on, before this gets worse!"

He remembered the dark, avid glee on the magehound's face as she condemned Andris to death. Yes, things could definitely get worse.

With a sigh, he turned and followed his new companion out into the street.

CHAPTER FIVE

Matteo soon learned that following Tzigone was no easy task. The lad—no, he corrected himself, not lad but maiden—could run like a lizard and climb nearly as well.

They were running full out down Sultan Street, batting away the filmy silk banners that served as shop signs, when Tzigone suddenly disappeared. In two more steps, Matteo saw where she had gone: a narrow alley, shaded by tall buildings on either side and almost obscured by the thick flowering vines that twined up the walls. He skidded to a stop and darted in after her.

Too late. As he rounded the corner, he heard the wemic's voice lifted in a sound that was half snarl, half guttural chuckle, and utterly triumphant.

Tzigone heard it, too. She cast a baleful look over her shoulder at Matteo and began to climb the vine-covered walls. "At least try to hurry," she muttered.

Matteo tested a handful of the fragrant vines and found that they would hold his weight. The rough stones on the wall beneath provided footholds. It was not unlike some of his training exercises, and he managed to almost keep pace with Tzigone.

The roof was smooth and broad. Tzigone rolled

to her feet and started off at a trot. She pointed toward the public garden in the midst of the city. "Going roof to roof, we can reach the bilboa tree from here. Once we're in the tree, Mbatu will never find us."

Matteo was momentarily startled to hear her speak the wemic's name. "You have had dealings with this wemic?"

She tossed a glance back at him. "How many lion-men have you seen in this part of the world? Stories are told, and I have ears to listen."

"Ah. Rumors."

"They've kept me alive so far," she retorted. She turned and planted her fists on her narrow hips. "Why are you just standing there? Are you coming or not?"

"Not." He folded his arms and leveled a steady gaze upon the incredulous Tzigone. "Do not think me ungrateful for your help, but I have had enough of flight. Go your way and leave me to mine."

"Which is?"

"I will confront the wemic in battle," he said simply.

The girl hissed with exasperation. "Did you see the wemic's baldric? The sword slung over his shoulder?" she said grimly.

Matteo sent her a puzzled look. He could recall both precisely: the baldric was a broad leather strap, tanned a light tawny hue, slanted across the wemic's great chest and joined to the belt that encircled his humanoid torso. The baldric held a scabbard that slanted over the wemic's back, fastened tightly at the top and secured at the bottom by a short strap so that the scabbard could tilt outward when the wemic drew his sword—a necessary adjustment, given the length of the blade. Otherwise the creature would have to reach behind his head to draw the sword, exposing the pit of his arm to his enemy's blades. No seasoned warrior would make himself vulnerable in this way. A quick stab or a thrown dagger could pierce the lungs and drown the wemic in his own blood. With the addition of the bottom strap, the wemic could simply reach over his shoulder and seize the hilt, thus drawing his weapon in half the time and with a fraction of the risk. All this Matteo had taken in with a glance.

"Yes, of course I noted baldric and sword. Why?"

"Why?" she demanded incredulously. "The sword's hilt rose above Mbatu's shoulder, and the blade crossed the breadth of his back. The wemic's reach is already longer than yours without that weapon. I don't care how good you think you are. You won't last long against him if all you've got is those daggers."

Her words smarted, but he couldn't deny her logic. "That may be, but I have no sword."

"I do. Follow me."

She took off, running down the length of the building and then leaping out over a narrow divide to a roof garden on a neighboring villa.

Matteo followed her to the edge of the wall. He glanced down and immediately wished he hadn't. He backed up a few paces, set his jaw and took the jump. He landed squarely in a patch of herbs. Mint filled the air with fragrant protest as he took off after Tzigone.

When she reached the edge of the roof garden, she uncoiled the rope at her belt and quickly tied on a small three-pronged hook. "Stand back," she warned, then she briefly twirled and let fly.

The rope spun out toward the outermost branches of the great bilboa tree. It struck the limb, wrapped around twice, and caught firmly. Tzigone tested the rope and then nodded. "Help me pull it in."

Matteo seized the rope and tugged until the limb was within reach. They both got a handhold and then, on Tzigone's count, dropped off the edge of the roof.

The limb dipped so low that Matteo would have sworn that it would break under their combined weight. As they began the upward swing, he glanced down. The wemic was directly beneath them, twisting his tawny body in midair in an attempt to get his feet beneath him. Obviously he had leaped up in an attempt to seize one or both of them. Matteo was chilled by the realization of how close the wemic had come to succeeding.

For several moments the limb bobbed up and down, each dip considerably more shallow than the last. When Tzigone decreed it was safe to move on, they began to pull themselves hand over hand toward the trunk. After a hundred feet or so, the limb grew broad enough to walk upon. Tzigone easily pulled herself up and extended a hand to help Matteo.

They edged along until they reached the massive trunk. As Matteo studied the odd arrangement of branches, he realized that the limbs grew in layers, like floors in a tall building. The next tier formed a roof about ten feet over their heads. The limbs were thickly entwined, and the leaves formed an apparently impenetrable barrier. Tzigone was right about one thing: Mbatu would not find them easily.

Matteo glanced down. The wemic paced beneath the tree, frustration and fury etched upon his golden face.

"A tree seems an unlikely refuge from any sort of cat," he remarked.

Tzigone sniffed. "Wemics are fast when they're on all fours, but they're no good at climbing. Too many limbs, too big from the waist up. The balance is all off."

He considered this and decided that she was probably right. What he did not entirely credit, however, was her claim to ownership of a sword. There were strict rules on what type of weapon each class could carry, and although he was hard pressed to define the girl's precise status, he doubted that she was either nobility, military, or militia.

Also dubious was her choice of hiding place for such a weapon. She had spoken a deliberate lie to get him out of the tavern. Quite likely she had done so again to lure him away from battle and into the safety of the massive tree.

"You hid a sword in a tree?" he said skeptically.

She dug her hands into the bark and began to climb.

"Many things are hidden in this tree. If you follow me closely and keep your eyes open, you'll survive most of them."

The trunk was thicker around than many a wizard's tower, and the bark formed raised patterns of ridges and whorls. Matteo found that climbing the sheer wall was not as difficult as he'd anticipated. After several moments they hauled themselves up onto a large limb.

Matteo stood and looked about him in wonder. The limbs were broad, the upper sides almost flat. They intertwined, forming a network of passages and nearly level platforms. Several paces away, several boards spanned the gap between two limbs. A bit of torn sailcloth formed a remarkably snug tent. Though sunset was still hours away, two pairs of booted feet protruded from it.

"They work at night," Tzigone said matter-of-factly as she began to climb again.

They passed several more small dwellings on the next tier, some established on the tree's branches and some carved into the larger limbs and in hollows in the trunk. Matteo marveled at the sheer variety of plant and animal life that took refuge in the bilboa tree. Tiny spiders, transparent as glass and invisible but for a faint rosy gleam within their bodies, spun delicate webs of red silk—webs that were unique to Halruaa, and much prized by wizards as spell components. Brilliantly colored birds roosted on the branches, some of which Matteo had never encountered in book or legend. A winged cat groomed itself, and insects bustled about with the importance of message boys.

Matteo wondered how many creatures found a home here. Here and there a limb had been torn away by storms, leaving small, snug rooms large enough to accommodate a small family of tree-dwelling creatures. Matteo would not be surprised if Tzigone herself found refuge in such places from time to time. She seemed as at ease among the limbs of the vast tree as she did in the city below. Indeed, the tree was like a small community within the city, teeming with life beyond the expected birds and insects. Matteo made a note to look into the possibilities presented by the arboreal cities. This could be useful knowledge.

"Careful coming around this bend. Don't touch the big web," Tzigone cautioned.

As Matteo maneuvered around a massive limb, he saw what she meant. A deep, narrow hollow was covered with a spider web that still glistened with dew. Some of the drops glittered silver and red and blue, reflecting the treasure hidden inside. Matteo noted the wistful look that Tzigone sent the trove, but she wisely did not attempt to despoil it. The spider that stood guard was as big as Matteo's palm. He recognized the breed as one developed by some wayward wizard who had been exiled long ago when his creations escaped into the wild. This creature was larger and more fearsome than common spiders. Its thick body was not furry but covered with incredibly strong, tiny scales. Despite its armor, the spider was exceedingly quick, and its bite was deadly poison.

"I begin to see why you would entrust a sword to this place," Matteo commented. "Have we much farther to go?"

Tzigone shrugged and kept climbing. Her lack of response deepened Matteo's suspicions, but he followed her as she ran across a broad limb to the far side of the tree. She counted off the side branches and then nodded in satisfaction.

"This is where we get off. Watch, then do as I do."

She leaped off the limb and seized the narrow branch. The strong, flexible wood bent under her weight, slowing just as her feet touched the wall that bordered the north side of the city garden. When she released the branch it snapped back up into place. She motioned impatiently for Matteo to follow.

He considered the situation and at once perceived a problem. With his greater weight, he would either hit the wall with great force or miss it entirely. Quickly he estimated the difference in mass between his tightly muscled body and

Tzigone's slender, wiry frame, then he ciphered the angle and tensile strength of branches on either side of her chosen limb.

Fortunately the branches were close enough for him to grasp both. He dropped between them, and his hands closed lightly around them.

The branches slid through his hands as he fell. He ignored the scrape of the bark against his palms, then gripped tightly when he reached the chosen spot. His calculations proved right on the mark. He dropped precisely as he intended and landed lightly beside the openmouthed girl.

She looked at him with new respect. "Huzzah!"

"It's a good thing that one of us considered the weight difference," Matteo commented.

She dismissed this with a light shrug. "It's been a while since I had to concern myself with someone else. Amazing how fast you get out of practice."

"Is there truly a sword?" Matteo demanded.

"Truly," she said, imitating his tone to perfection. His exasperated sigh amused her, and she chuckled as she walked along the wall of the public garden.

They climbed down onto Reef Street. Matteo couldn't help but stare as they walked down its length. Though this part of the city was well inland, the scent of the sea was strong. Aqueducts brought seawater in from the bay, and with the seawater came the creatures that constructed the houses and shops.

All the buildings on this street were fashioned from coral, and they ranged in color from pale sandy pink to a deep dusky rose. Sea motifs were much in evidence, from the wavelike patterns in the iron fences to the flowering topiaries carved in the shape of fish and merfolk. The gate of one particularly imposing shop was framed by a pair of stone sahuagin, hideous fish-men who stood guard with braced tridents and shark-toothed snarls. Matteo had heard that sailors considered this sort of decoration to be in terrible taste. Elves were more likely to mar the serenity of their temples with statues of drow raiders than seamen were to seek reminders of sahuagin.

Despite the occasional lapse in taste, such buildings were popular among the wealthy commoners. Growing a coral building took many years and an enormous amount of expensive magic. A new building was in the birthing process, and Matteo took great interest in observing first-hand how it was done.

A stout timber frame formed the skeleton, but the building grew from the top down. The city's artificers provided pumps—small marvels constructed of metal and magic—that lifted seawater through pipes to the roof, where it cascaded down into the cistern moat below. Tiny coral animals, summoned by magic, had risen with the water and over time had built a reef that reached almost halfway to the ground. Several artisans were at work framing in the lower windows and door with timber. A wizard hovered in the air, gesturing broadly and tossing fistfuls of odd substances into the portals that had already been framed. The debris vanished as it passed in, leaving some sort of magical ward in the windows that kept coral from filling them in. The magic they cast was as translucent as fine glass and far stronger.

It was a marvelous process, but Matteo also found it inexplicably sad. Generations upon generations of tiny creatures were induced to venture out of the wide sea into this narrow, artificial inlet, then tricked into building their reefs out into the inhospitable air.

Matteo wondered briefly if there were among these structures the tiny bodies of coral seers who perceived the deadly pattern, who strove to convince the others to give up the ways of untold generations. Clearly they did not succeed, but perhaps they, too, were part of the pattern.

"This way," Tzigone said, pointing toward a small shop shaded by a sea-green awning. No one was currently in attendance, which in itself was not unusual. Many merchants took long meals and short naps in the midday heat, trusting in powerful magical wards to safeguard their goods.

Tzigone strode purposefully toward the shop and studied the weapons on display. She reached in and took a simple but finely crafted short sword, considerably longer than a dagger but not so long that a jordain unfamiliar with dueling weapons would find it unbalanced.

"You keep your sword in a swordsmith's shop?" Matteo said dubiously.

She glanced up and down the street and then pressed the weapon into his hand. "For a while, I kept it in a perfumery, but every time I turned around I knocked down crystal vials. It was damned inconvenient."

Matteo's eyes narrowed. "You are quick to play games with words. Is this weapon truly yours?"

"Could I pass the swordsmith's wards if it were not?" she said impatiently. "Take it and let's be gone."

Matteo set off toward the harbor and the place where he had secured his stallion. He set a brisk pace, eager to find his horse and his friend Themo and take both back to the comparative safety of House Jordain.

Safety.

The word echoed in the great hollow that was his heart. Andris had found no haven there.

Matteo was unprepared for the grief that struck him like a tidal surge. Never had he experienced anything like this flood of emotion. He felt overwhelmed, as if he was being torn away from his moorings.

Several moments passed before he realized that Tzigone was studying him with interest. He caught her eye and braced himself for her questions.

To his surprise, she merely nodded. There was little sympathy in the gesture, but much understanding. Whatever she saw in his eyes was something she knew well.

For some reason, Matteo found this simple acknowledgment more comforting than any of the jordaini's beautifully honed and reasoned phrases.

He searched his benumbed mind for something profound to say and came up empty. "I have to get my horse," he said lamely.

"Well, good for you," she said approvingly. "I was afraid you'd want to look for Mbatu or some such foolishness."

"The wemic will likely find me. If he loses our trail, it would be logical for him to return to the place where we met. I left Cyric tied to a rail near the tavern."

She hoisted one eyebrow and sent him a sidelong look. "Cyric?"

"Yes. The stallion is named after—"

"I know who Cyric is, although frankly I'm surprised that you do. What did the horse do to earn a name like that?"

"Well, he is somewhat volatile."

"I'll bet." Her lips twitched. "You know, I thought all jordaini would be boring, seeing how you aren't allowed to add any color to your facts. It's nice to know that understatement isn't against your creed."

Her dry comment surprised a chuckle from Matteo. They fell into a comfortable pace as Tzigone wove a path through the streets.

Their shadows stretched out before them as they rounded a corner into yet another narrow street. The city was beginning to stir as the sunsleep hours passed. Though the sun was less direct, the heat did not noticeably lessen. Matteo noted that the day was in fact unseasonably warm. Heat rose in visible waves from the paved roads, distorting the scene ahead. A four-man patrol passed, their faces damp and eyes made surly by heat.

Matteo noticed the Tzigone was suddenly very interested in a shop window that offered fishing lures, small hammers, spools of wire, and other small metal devices.

"You have reason to avoid the city guard?" he asked.

"They usually seem to think so," she replied cheerfully. "It seems only polite to oblige them."

The jordain was about to challenge that dubious logic when suddenly the shadows at the far side of the street blurred, commingled into an ominous haze by the oddly shaped bulk closing in rapidly.

Matteo thrust Tzigone aside and turned, sword in hand, instinctively placing himself between the girl and the wemic.

The lion-man reached over his massive shoulder. Steel hissed like a striking snake as Mbatu drew his massive blade. The wemic crouched and then leaped, bringing his sword around for a high, smashing attack.

Matteo lifted his borrowed sword to meet the brutal assault. The weapons met with a high metallic shriek. The jordain didn't attempt to absorb the mighty blow, but shifted his weight to his right foot and let the force of the attack carry the enjoined swords to the ground. Deftly he twisted aside and danced back, sliding his sword out from under the wemic's blade. He darted in again, thrusting low, a point far lower than he would choose for attacking a human.

The wemic parried and retreated, trying to work his sword back into position for a high attack. Matteo would have none of that. He pressed in, stabbing and thrusting again and again, forcing the wemic to keep the battle low.

Never had Matteo fought a wemic, but he discerned what the creature's best strategy would be. Once the blades were high, the wemic could bring his leonine forepaws into play. By Matteo's estimation, the claws on Mbatu's feet could disembowel a man in three quick strokes or tear out his throat in one.

Again and again the wemic tried to draw back, tried to disengage the blades long enough to maneuver into position for a killing stroke. Matteo pursued, always taking the offensive and looking for an opening of his own.

The battle went on and on. The heat of the sun was punishing, and his arms ached from the unfamiliar weight of the sword. As if in a daze, he heard Tzigone mutter something about the damned horse and not being able to find the militia the one time you actually wanted them. From the corner of his eye, he saw her hoist a bucket of rainwater and heave it in a shining arc toward him and the wemic.

A fleeting smile touched Matteo's lips as he shook water from his eyes. Oddly enough, he understood at once Tzigone's intent. The water cooled him off but did not distract or inconvenience him. On the other hand, Mbatu's glossy black mane hung wet and heavy about his face, and his ears turned back with familiar feline distaste.

The wemic turned a murderous golden stare upon Tzigone. "Bring her in alive," he muttered, as if to remind himself of an onerous duty.

An eager, familiar snort drew Matteo's eye to the far end of the street. Matteo's black stallion trotted purposefully toward the battle, his eyes gleaming weirdly. His reins hung loose, and splinters of wood were tangled in his mane. For the first time, Matteo understood what the stable hands meant when they swore that they never heard that snort but they expected to see it accompanied by a burst of sulfur-scented steam.

Matteo spun to place Cyric at his back. He sent a quick glance toward the watchful Tzigone, hoping beyond hope that she might discern his battle strategy. To his surprise, she nodded and edged down the street toward Mbatu. She pulled a long knife from her boot and went into a crouch.

When the clatter of the stallion's approach stopped, Matteo danced back a couple of steps. The wemic saw his opening at last and lifted his sword high. Matteo moved with him, raising his sword in anticipation of the parry. As he expected, the wemic reared up and unsheathed his claws.

Tzigone threw herself forward, knife leading, and plunged her blade into the wemic's flank. Mbatu let out a roar of pain and instinctively twisted toward the new threat. But he could not halt the momentum of his own blow, and his great sword descended in a killing arc. Matteo tossed aside his borrowed sword and rolled clear.

His timing proved to be nearly perfect. Cyric had also

reared up, and his hooves slashed out at the wemic. One hoof grazed Matteo's shoulder painfully, but the other found the wemic's skull with a sickening thud. The wemic's head snapped back and he dropped to the cobblestone. He lay still, a steady trickle of blood matting his long black hair.

For a moment the street was silent, but for the whuffling, almost mirthful sound of the stallion's breath.

Matteo rolled to his feet and came over to pat Cyric's black neck. Tzigone tugged her knife free with a quick jerk and circled around to crouch by the wemic's head. She lifted one eyelid, then the other, staring into each orb intently.

"He lives," she said shortly. "No need to look over your shoulder, though. He won't remember any of this."

"You sound very certain of that," Matteo said warily. The tone of her voice held an odd resonance, one very similar to that he discerned in wizards after a spellcasting. "Speak forthrightly. Did you work magic on the wemic?"

"Me? A wizard?" She let out a short, derisive sniff. Rocking back on her heels, she rose in a swift, fluid movement. "The wemic is having a bad day. He's been hit on the head twice already, and it's only just past highsun. If things continue apace, by sunset he'll be lucky to remember his own name. Very lucky."

She spoke the last words with a bitterness that surprised him. For a moment Matteo puzzled over how, and if, to address this. No inspiration came, so he dealt with that which he understood.

"I would not have defeated the wemic without your help," he said honestly. "The debt is paid."

He swung up onto Cyric's back. The horse stood still for him, amazingly docile.

No, Matteo noted, not docile. A better word was "satisfied." It was as if the stallion had always longed to do battle and, having had the opportunity, was content for the moment.

Matteo extended a hand to the young woman. "May I offer you a ride to wherever you're staying?"

Tzigone eyed the big horse uncertainly. "You go ahead. I'll catch up later."

The notion was so absurd that Matteo almost laughed. "I'm returning to House Jordain to complete my training. The jordaini serve truth. Forgive me for speaking bluntly, Tzigone, but there is no place for you there."

She didn't seem daunted by his lack of encouragement. "There's a debt between us. I can't forget that. I never forget anything."

"I told you, the debt is paid."

"Because you say so? Is this the market, that we need to dicker?" she said testily. "Blankets and melons and such have no set price, but there are some things that do."

Matteo recognized the ring in her voice and the steel in her eyes. She spoke of honor, though in terms that he didn't quite recognize or understand. He responded in kind.

"Then when we meet again, I shall look to you for help and friendship," he said. "You may claim the same of me, without adding to the sum of your honor debt."

For a moment she looked startled, and then a thoughtful expression crossed her face. "You say that I use words too lightly, and maybe I do, but it seems to me that you're quick to speak of friendship."

Never had Matteo received so puzzling a response to the polite phrases he'd offered. It occurred to him that she might think he was suggesting something less than proper. "I meant no offense."

"And I took none. All I'm saying is that you're quick to trust. Maybe that's not such a good thing."

Amused now, he regarded her with lifted brows. "Are you warning me to beware of you?"

She stood her ground, yielding nothing. "I'm reminding you that you thought I was a boy and assumed that all cats can climb. Not everything is as it seems, jordain."

There was truth in that, and though it smarted to

acknowledge it, he responded with a respectful nod. "Thank you for your words," he said, showing the respect he would give a master after a much-needed lesson. "Thank you also for the use of your sword."

She shrugged and walked gingerly around Cyric, eyeing the big horse with interest. Cyric turned his head to regard her, and his expression seemed equally wary.

Matteo noted this exchange and found it rather fitting. He took up the reins and found that one had been sliced by the wemic's sword. He dismounted to retrieve it and tie it back on. Cyric was nearly impossible to control under the best of circumstances, and he dared not attempt to guide the horse with only his knees.

Tzigone watched as the young man bent over the repair. Moving like a shadow, she retrieved the sword that Matteo had flung aside. For a moment she regarded it and debated what to do. She couldn't take it with her, that much was certain. Penalties for dressing or arming oneself above one's station were severe, and the last thing Tzigone needed was another brush with the law. Swords were valuable, and in Halruaa, spells of seeking made sure that valuable objects didn't stay "borrowed" for long.

But she hated to leave the weapon in the street. Who knew who might pick it up and what use they might make of it? And judging from the day he'd had so far, Matteo was likely to need just such a sword before much more time passed. Certainly he'd handled it better than she had expected. It would be well for both of them if he had use of the sword when next their paths crossed.

Tzigone didn't require much persuading. She took a length of leather thong from her bag and quickly tied the sword to the back of the stallion's saddle. Fortunately the horse's back was broad and the sword short enough to conceal. She tucked the saddle blanket over the hilt. Judging by the shrewd, approving look in Cyric's eyes, she figured that the horse would find some way to alert Matteo of the weapon's presence if need arose.

She worked quickly and backed away just as Matteo looked up from the newly repaired bridle. "Peace to you, Tzigone," he said as he swung himself up on the stallion's back.

"And to you," she responded demurely.

She watched as the young man rode off, well content with her decision. Peace was a fine word and certainly something worth aspiring to, but in her experience, it was rarer than riches. If peace proved elusive, at least she'd seen that Matteo was properly armed.

And properly warded, too. The wemic was beginning to stir and groan, but when he awoke he would remember nothing of the day's events.

Just to be sure, Tzigone crouched by the wemic and repeated the small spell that she had cast, one that she had learned in a lifetime of seeking remedies for her own forgetfulness.

Her fingers still itched and tingled after the casting was complete. This didn't surprise her. Wizards seemed to think that all magical energy should dissipate with a spell, but Tzigone found this ridiculous. Magic was all around; all that wizards did was pick up pieces of it and combine them to make something new. They were so puffed up about their "great power," as if they actually created the magic they used. As if anyone could!

But there did seem to be an unusual amount of magic about. There was also some interesting treasure. Tzigone's fingers reached, almost of their own volition, for the wemic's earring. The stone was too big to be a ruby, but even it if were a garnet or carnelian, it would fetch a good price at the back door of many a respected gem merchant. She didn't worry about speeding the wemic's rise to wakefulness. Her fingers were so skilled that she could take the gem from him when he was fully awake without alerting him to his loss.

But she stopped just short of touching the stone. Acting on instinct, she jerked back her hand and clenched her fingers into a fist. Insight quickly followed. The ruby had been a lure, as most likely the red gown had been a lure. It had been so prominently displayed, so easy to steal, and so temptingly cut to her size. The last bit convinced her that she was right. The gown had been fashioned of expensive watered silk, yet it was far too small to fit the lush, extravagant figures cultivated by ladies of wealth and fashion. She'd bet skie against sand that it had been made to order with her in mind. And embued with a spell of seeking. No wonder the wemic had come so close to catching her.

With a single quick movement, Tzigone rocked back on to her heels and then rose to her feet. Resisting the temptation to give the wemic a final kick, she melted into the lengthening shadows of late afternoon, intent upon finding a way to finish paying her debt to the young jordain.

CHAPTER SIX

In a rented tower room not far away, Kiva leaned intently over the scrying bowl as she watched the battle between her friend Mbatu and the young jordain who had caught her eye earlier that day.

Matteo intrigued her. She had taken Zephyr's reports and done some research of her own. By all accounts, he was among the most promising of the jordaini students, as sharp and strong as any among them. Yet until this morning, she had not considered him to be a likely recruit. He was a true believer, steeped from birth in jordaini lore and the glamour of the jordaini myth. Such as he were never easy to turn.

She would believe this still, had she not witnessed the intensity of his grief over his lost friend. Matteo might have devoted his life to truth, but Kiva suspected that in time he would find rules and facts to be too bloodless a mistress.

At present Matteo was as proper and prideful as any young man of his elite class. But if that were to change, he could become a useful tool. His words suggested a subtlety of mind that pleased Kiva. He was still too young and naïve for that subtlety to prove a threat, but it would make the process of conquest more interesting and rewarding.

A faint groan came from the curtained bed. Kiva absently flicked her fingers toward her latest recruit, increasing the flow of scented smoke from the censer beside his bed and thus deepening his slumber. It was not her favorite method of inducing sleep. She preferred to use the spell that had apparently, and mysteriously, been worked upon the wemic.

Kiva studied the picture in the scrying bowl carefully. After casting the illusion that had enabled her to take Andris from House Jordain, she had followed the group of grieving jordaini students to Khaerbaal. She had two purposes for this: First she hoped to glean more information about Matteo by watching his behavior away from the strict rules of the school and the watchful eyes of his masters. In addition to this, she wanted Mbatu to finish the work of the previous day. If luck was with them, he would at long last run Keturah's daughter to ground.

The wench had been seen in Khaerbaal a few days ago, and the Lady Day festivities had offered a means of smoking her out. But the girl had managed to elude Mbatu in the crowds, and Kiva had been forced to leave the city or risk losing Andris to bids from other wizards.

Tzigone was a complication, to be sure, but her presence in Khaerbaal was also an opportunity that Kiva could not let pass. Three moons had waxed and waned since she'd last heard so much as a word of the slippery wench. So the wemic had left Andris sleeping in Kiva's care, exchanged his earring for an identical one linked to Kiva's scrying bowl, and gone off in pursuit of Tzigone.

The ruby and bowl were powerful devices, ancient beyond reckoning and reputed to have been created by an Ilythiiri wizard before the sundering of the one land. Kiva had carefully researched the claims of the adventurer who had sold her the bowl, and when she was satisfied that the man spoke truth, she had bought the treasure and then killed him. These days the Ilythiiri were called by another name: drow. These dark elves evoked such fear and horror that Kiva knew no one, human or elf, who would willingly use an artifact they had created, not even if it proved to be the most powerful device of its kind that Kiva had encountered in two centuries devoted to the study of such treasures.

Yet despite its power, the scrying bowl yielded no sign of the wayward girl. Kiva battled anger and frustration as she watched through Mbatu's eyes without actually seeing his prey. Her frustration had turned to fascination when Matteo stepped between the wemic and the fugitive. A jordain was pledged to follow the law, yet Matteo had risked his future to place himself between an unknown girl and a magehound's personal guard. Kiva noted the mixture of chivalry and rage that prompted the jordain's uncharacteristic response, and her plans for Matteo took a sudden shift.

She watched as the young pair fled together, tracking Tzigone by Matteo's exasperated responses to the girl's unseen actions and unheard words. The girl's shield against magical inquiry was absolute, even stronger than that of a jordain. In fact, this was the first scrying device Kiva had ever found that could actually track a jordain, who were bred for their magic resistance.

The girl would have been one of the strongest jordaini in Halruaa's history had her breeding been true. Such a waste—all the careful testing and meticulous records that made the marriage match between two wizards, not to mention the magical potions fed to the female for years. Who could have guessed that Keturah would disrupt the breeding process and take matters into her own hands?

Frankly, Kiva was surprised at the woman's initiative. It was true that Keturah had always been a strong-minded wench, but the humans of Halruaa were seldom capable of such blatant rebellion. Their lives and minds were ordered and constrained by laws, rules, customs, and magic.

Always magic, Kiva reminded herself. She could endure much for that. She could shrug aside nearly twenty years of training in their schools, the sly questing hands of their males, the idiocy of their rules. What were such things to an elf who had seen the birth and death of three centuries? If it took her another three hundred years, she would use Halruaa's magic to seize what was hers to claim.

And Matteo would help her to accomplish her goal. Of that Kiva was certain. He had the skill to defeat a wemic battlemaster and the independence to befriend an apparent street urchin. Of course, that tolerance would no doubt evaporate like dew in highsun once he found out that the girl spilled magic as carelessly as a fumble-footed tavern wench slopped soup.

But that knowledge could be long in coming to Matteo. Kiva had come to know Tzigone well enough to suspect that the girl would hold her secrets close and well.

Kiva bent over her scrying bowl. Matteo was on horseback, heading for the north gates. Kiva studied his posture and his placement on the saddle and decided that he rode alone.

The magehound waved a hand over the bowl to dispel the image and rose from the table. She went over to the cot and bent over her captive, lifting the lids on his hazel-green eyes and looking deep within, ensuring that his sleep was both safe and deep.

She quickly chanted a spell, one that would take her to the quiet street where Mbatu lay sleeping. When she emerged from the magical transport, she took from her bag a small square of black silk, which she unfolded again and again until it was many times its original size. This she dropped over the wemic. The gossamer veil floated down, draped over Mbatu's great form, and then sank again until it lay flat against the cobblestone.

Kiva snatched up the scarf and held it high, spinning in a quick circle and then letting it fly. The thin silk whispered around her as it fell, and she felt the quick, sure pull of the magic that drew her back to her rented room. At the last moment, she seized the corner of the portal with practiced ease, bringing the priceless device with her.

She tossed the silken portal aside and strode to the locked box she had left on her bedside table. Mbatu would fold the silk later, once he recovered from Tzigone's casting as well as from the magical inquisition that was to come.

Kiva took from the box a small rod—not the ornate, bejeweled toy she had brandished to confound the jordaini and their masters, but the real instrument of her office. Slim and silvery, it was no metal to be wrested from soil and rock, but captured lightning, pure energy converted to solid form. She knew of nothing that conducted magic so well— not water, not amber, not even moonstone. If there was a trace of magic in a living creature, she would know. The rod could reveal other useful and important things, but Kiva seldom used it. Lightning was never easy to hold, and the process was as painful to the magehound as it was enlightening.

She completed the spell that released the wemic from Tzigone's casting. Mbatu stirred and stretched painfully. His amber eyes opened, then narrowed as they focused upon the wand in Kiva's hand.

"The scrying bowl did not work?" he asked in a sleep-scratchy growl.

"It worked, but I need to know more. I need to know everything."

The wemic regarded her for a long moment. He shifted into a sitting position, folding his forepaws under him and using his humanoid arms to brace himself for the coming ordeal. It apparently did not occur to him to ask if the magical inquisition was necessary. If Kiva thought the pain was worth bearing, he could do no less.

"I am ready," he said in a stronger voice.

The magehound knelt on the floor facing him and slowly extended the wand until the tip lightly touched Mbatu's forehead.

Instantly she was swept by a great silent wind, a psychic typhoon that buffeted at her mind, her identity, her soul. It was no small thing to enter the mind of another sentient being, even that of a friend. Many a magehound had died shrieking after the first attempt, for sanity could be swept away by the onslaught, and a heart might burst from the burden of two separate rhythms that refused to become one.

But Kiva was strong enough, and so was Mbatu. The moment of agony passed quickly, and she slipped into the familiar pathways of the wemic's mind and heart. For a moment she paused, awed as a visitor to a grand temple, to marvel anew at the utter loyalty she found there. It was a quality Kiva valued, but not one that she understood.

She took from her friend's mind the tavern scene, and she suppressed a smile at the snippets of Tzigone's irreverent commentary that Mbatu had picked up before his charge. Through the wemic's eyes, she saw everything Mbatu had seen, and she noticed details and subtleties that he had not discerned. She saw Matteo's face as he leaped up and upended the table, and she marked the seeds of rebellion in the young jordain's fierce black eyes. By the time the vision was complete, Kiva knew that her decision was sound.

Slowly, carefully, she eased apart the magical ties that bound her to Mbatu. The wemic studied her with eyes glazed by pain but untouched by reproach.

"You will have this one, too, I suppose? He fights well enough," he added wryly.

"Matteo will fight for me in time," she agreed. "However, at present I have another use for him. His path will cross with the girl's, most likely quite soon. We can use that. We can encourage that. When the time is right, we can take them both unawares."

Mbatu snorted. "The jordaini have little use for women. Let a few moons pass, and he will not care whether Keturah's daughter lives or dies."

"I can change that."

The wemic misunderstood the sudden gleam in Kiva's eyes. "Is that wise? Dalliance with a student jordain will be frowned upon, even for someone in your high place. Perhaps especially so. Magehounds and jordaini do not mix. Personal involvement might taint the clarity and purity of your judgment and ill serve the cause of Azuth," he quoted.

They shared a chuckle at this notion. Her involvement was deeply personal, and her judgments had little to do with the workings of Azuth.

Kiva sobered first and told the wemic her plan. "Once Matteo has been taken, you can handle the horse? You will see that it is returned to the jordaini college?"

"I will do it," Mbatu grumbled. "Dark-hearted bastard that he is."

"Good. The moon wanes, and the new moon is three days away. The purification ritual will be performed that night. We must keep Matteo away until after this is done so he will not know the difference."

"Do you truly think he will not notice whether the rite is performed or not? Humans are not such eunuchs as that!"

"The jordaini do not know what awaits them. What Matteo does not know, he cannot dread. Students are taken to the ritual alone and hooded. The wizard who performs the rite does not know who comes under his knife. After the deed is done, the jordaini are sworn to secrecy and taken to recover in isolation. It will be a small thing to find a commoner to send in Matteo's place, especially if the man is seen riding into the complex on Matteo's horse."

"The masters of House Jordain are not so easily fooled. They will never permit this!" the wemic protested.

A small smile touched the magehound's lips. "You would be surprised what the jordaini will permit. Truth, as it happens, is a remarkably mutable thing. Go now and tend your part."

They left the tower room together, Mbatu to seek in the countryside beyond the city walls a young man who would stand for Matteo in the rite of purification, one who bore a passing resemblance to the jordain. Kiva's task was simpler: to report what she suspected to the captain of the local militia. Tzigone never carried a sword, or for that matter much of anything else. The canny wench knew that enspelled objects could be traced, and she changed possessions frequently. But Kiva was willing to bet that the young thief would not cast away so fine a sword. It was undoubtedly still in Matteo's possession.

Kiva quickly found a detachment of local militia. The captain took the magehound's report and set out for the northwest gate after Matteo.

Well satisfied, Kiva rode to a small holding she kept outside the city and settled down to await Mbatu, confident that the wemic would arrive shortly with Matteo's stallion and, more importantly, his substitute.

CHAPTER SEVEN

A sense of unease followed Tzigone like a shadow as she made her way to the Behir's Nest. As the sun dipped toward the west, the streets began to come alive. She worked her way through the crowd, paying less attention to her surroundings than usual.

Such weakness was often fatal and always dangerous. Like fear, inattention seemed to draw predators as blood in the water summoned sharks. From the corner of her eye, Tzigone noted that a street urchin had fallen into step with her, just slightly behind her and out of the normal range of vision.

For a moment Tzigone's throat tightened. The furtive, hollow-eyed child was a reminder of her early years and a mirror of what she had been forced to become. But that didn't stop her from seizing the thin, seeking hand that reached for her bag.

Tzigone spun the boy around, flinging him against the back wall of a milliner's shop. She caught him by surprise, and tossing him about was easy to do. But not until she had him pinned against the wall did she realize that the boy was fully her height and probably nearly as strong. That realization didn't change her intention in the slightest.

She turned his grimy hand palm up and slapped into it a coin, one of the skie that the starsnake's skin had brought her.

"You need a few lessons," she hissed. "Gwillon over on Low Street is looking for an apprentice. Give him this and mention my name. . . ."

She had to think for a moment before the name of the child thief she'd once been came back to her. "Tell him that Sindra says you have promise."

The lad eyed the coin, then lifted an awed gaze to hers. That single skie might be more riches than he'd held in five moons, but the name was worth far more to him. Gwillon was a master pickpocket and a legend among the shadows of this city. The man was getting along in years, but his training might be enough to keep this lad alive. Justice in Halruaa was swift, and few thieves were caught twice. She'd given the boy a rare second chance, and he knew it.

The boy fisted his hand around his apprentice fee and darted off in the direction of Low Street. Tzigone nodded approvingly and went on through the back way to the shop where she was currently employed.

Chimes sang musically as she opened the door. Tzigone glanced up, marveling anew that something so beautiful could be made from the sort of scraps that a butcher might toss to stray dogs. Behir's bones. Who would know by looking at the ugly creatures that they housed such fey beauty?

Halruaans were never content to leave any creature as nature intended, and behirs were a special target of their breeding programs. Miniature behirs of various sizes were raised for purposes ranging from moat guardians to exotic pets, but like pigs and poets, they garnered most of their acclaim after their deaths. Their primary purpose was spell components.

It seemed that nearly every part of a behir was good for something. The long, slender horns that flowed back from their heads were ground into powder and added to ink used in writing out spell scrolls for various lightning spells. Their talons and hearts went to making inks that were used to create spells offering protection from poison. Even the mundane uses of their leavings were marvelous. Their bones were crystalline and were used for scrimshaw. Like musical ghosts, the behir bones sang at the doors and windows of Halruaan homes long after the flesh that had clothed them was distant memory. The teeth, however, gave rise to the most creative uses. They were translucent and multicolored, often imitating and rivaling the hue and sparkle of gemstone.

Tzigone crept silently to a large, oddly shaped wooden box that stood on a three-legged stand. It was a musical instrument, a special creation of Justin, the artificer who owned this shop. Inside the box were strings fashioned of behir's gut and electrum wire, and on the wide end of the box was a row of neat ivory keys. When one of the keys was pressed, a curved fang was lifted by a complex series of levers until it plucked at the string. The sound varied greatly, depending upon what instrument the musician called to mind. These instruments were much in demand in the city, and Justin was building another, his back to Tzigone and his attention wholly absorbed by his work.

She chose a sound and struck the key attached to the lowest, thickest string. The behir's fang flashed up, and the electrum cord vibrated. A deep, full-throated sound reverberated through the room—not a musical instrument, but a wemic's roar.

Justin leaped and spun in one quick, startled movement. His glare melted into a reluctant smile as he met Tzigone's grin.

"A good jest," he conceded. "But bear in mind, boy, that not everyone cares to be the brunt of your mischief. Keep it up and you'll come to grief soon or late."

Tzigone had learned early in life that letting people think

she was a boy was safer, if marginally so, than being seen as a young woman alone. "What can I do today?"

"Behirs need feeding. There's a clutch of new hatchlings to record, too. Three of them, and fine beasts all. Ethan's brood, out of Blue Bess."

She followed him out into the back, where a series of long narrow pools housed the creatures. Sure enough, three new behirs, each not much bigger than a cat, lounged on the sunning rocks. All of them were covered with soft scales of the light topaz blue that Justin favored, and all had only six legs. Each would develop another three or four pairs before adulthood. They had yet to grow horns, and but for their length and color, they looked very much like sky-colored crocodiles.

Justin watched Tzigone as she chopped fish and eels. She clicked her tongue, and the miniature monsters came to her like obedient hounds, swarming about the wall as she tossed them their food. The babies had to be nearly hand-fed, an exceedingly dangerous task for anyone whose fingers were less fleet than Tzigone's. The hatchlings' teeth, already gem-colored and sharp as needles, flashed and snapped as they ate.

The artificer nodded approvingly. "You've a sure, quick hand with the beasts. I could use an apprentice, especially when it comes to the slaughtering. Gathering and treating spell components can be tricky work. Have you been tested for magic?"

The question was rhetorical. Every child in Halruaa was first tested before the age of five, and often thereafter until his or her talents and destiny were decided. Tzigone had sidestepped the formal process and learned whatever skills suited her needs and caught her fancy.

"I've less magic than a stone," she lied in a rueful tone.

"Ah." Justine looked both disappointed and uncomfortable. It was not exactly a disgrace to lack magical talent in Halruaa, but except in the case of the jordaini, neither was it an honor. "Well, someone has to cook the soup," he said in a conciliatory tone, falling back on a familiar proverb.

Tzigone gritted her teeth and forced herself to smile and nod. She hated proverbs, and nothing annoyed her more than people who were so lazy or lacking in imagination that they allowed their words to travel only well-worn paths. Jordaini were often the worst. And here she was, indebted to a particularly arrogant member of the breed.

So far today she'd been stung by a starsnake, chased by a wemic, and indebted to a jordain. And to cap matters, here she was, up to her elbows in fish guts.

Tzigone shrugged. Chances were, tomorrow could be worse.

When all the behirs had been fed, she went into the back room to record the new births. Her heart quickened as she dragged the heavy tome down from the shelf, and it beat like a wild elf's battle drum as she paged through the complex birth records.

Genealogy was vitally important in Halruaa. Records were assiduously kept in books filled with intricate lines and patterns. Tzigone was determined to learn the meaning of those markings. It was for this purpose that she risked her fingers to Justin's behirs. Behir-tending was a job that few people would take, and he had gladly trained her in what little she needed to know to keep his records. The rest she would teach herself.

When the light from the single small window began to fail and her eyes swam with the effort of deciphering the tiny markings, Tzigone slipped out of the back room to her next lesson, one that was closely related to her study of behir heritage.

Each village, each city neighborhood, had a resident matchmaker. They were minor mages of the diviner school, and with the help of the birth records listed in the Diviner's Registry, they saw far enough into the future to decide who should marry whom.

Since matchmakers started with a woman and found an

appropriate male, Tzigone needed to change her appearance before she presented herself. Two colorful scarves, nearly dry when she'd tugged them off someone's line, would serve in her transformation. One tied around her waist would make a skirt, and the other she'd drape over her linen shirt. But first she stopped at a public fountain and scrubbed her face and arms clean. A bit of dirt lent her a more urchinlike appearance, but that wasn't suitable to her desired image as a winsome, marriageable girl.

Both the theft and the deceit lay easily on Tzigone's conscience. She had lived on the streets for as long as she could remember, and she had learned early to survive. But more basic than that was the gypsy code that such a life had inscribed upon her mind and spirit. She had no real sense of property, at least not as most Halruaans seemed to regard it. Ownership was not a sacred right but a temporary thing. A coin was quickly traded for something she desired more, such as a hot meal or a pair of boots, nicely broken in and not too badly patched. She was as quick to give as she was to take, and that was the way of many who lived as she did. The scarves she draped over her slender form today would probably form an awning tomorrow to keep the sun from a sleeping baby's face, or perhaps reawaken, if but for a moment, the vanity of some aged coquette. In Tzigone's eyes, it worked out well enough. Nothing made of wood or cloth or metal was important enough to warrant the fuss people made over it.

She'd just finished dressing when a spray of water arched toward her. Although she jumped back, the water drenched her borrowed finery so that the thin cloth clung to her legs.

She looked up into a familiar dark face enlivened by a long, waxed black mustache and a teasing leer. Gio was a traveling entertainer, and as near to family as any she could remember during her waking hours. Laughter crinkled the man's eyes, lingering there in pleasant lines and whorls. Though well into middle life, he was still a child who delighted in play and whose antics brought laughter and evoked childhood memories from those who had forgotten such things. There was a kind of magic in that, and Tzigone had enjoyed her years of travel with Gio and his partner.

She laughed and splashed him back. "Still in town, Gio? I thought you and Viente planned to move on to Sulazir."

He laid a hand over his heart, pantomiming great insult. "Planned? Since when does Troupe Gioviente plan? Are we merchants or greengrocers, to trudge through our days in so dreary a fashion?"

"I will not insult you by offering apology. For such words, I should slice out my tongue and throw it to the ravens!' she said, placing the back of her hand against her forehead and mimicking his extravagant delivery.

The entertainer saw nothing amiss in this gentle mockery. "Sulazir has lasted this long without Gioviente. The city will survive a few days more."

Tzigone rephrased her question in a manner more likely to elicit information. "What kept you in town?"

Gio cast his eyes skyward and shook a fist at some unseen power. "Carmelo is what, and I curse the day I took on that boy. Always getting fancy, he is, and getting us all dragged in for inquisition. We're clean, as you know, but one of us had to spend some time in the hold for creating disturbance. It was his turn."

Tzigone smirked. Gio didn't mind visiting his friends in the hold and doing a few tricks for the bored guards, but when it came to paying off a public debt, it was always someone else's turn. She'd spent time in various dank, barred rooms herself.

The diversions offered by the entertainers were not actually illegal, but someone was always challenging their claim that their tricks and illusions and feats of skill were simply that, unbolstered by aid of magic. Magic was common currency in Halruaa, and although Tzigone wouldn't exactly say that her countrymen had lost their sense of wonder, they seemed both impressed by and skeptical of anything that was accomplished without magic. Fraud had to be proved, and once an accusation was made, the entire troupe would be hauled away for inquisition by the local magehound. Tzigone, of course, had always appeared to be utterly magic dead, a fact that did nothing to increase her confidence in wizards.

Wizards had dogged her footsteps for years, laying traps and ambushes. Nothing they had produced against her so far had prevailed. She'd had a bad moment when she'd come close to nicking the wemic's earring, a deep sense that touching the gem would be a grave mistake. Fortunately she was as sensitive to magic as she was immune from its effects.

"So how is Carmelo?" she asked quickly, eager to think about more pleasant things.

"Tolerable, all things considered. Tomorrow is his last day in the hold, and it will pass quickly. They just threw a jordain in the cell across from him, and you know Carmelo. He'll tease every story and song out of the man before day's end."

Tzigone's ears pricked up. "A jordain? What did he look like?"

The gypsy shrugged and spat. "Much the same as any I've seen, though better-looking than most. Dark hair, white clothes, both of which looked a bit worse for wear. Looks as if he'd made the militia earn their wages before they brought him in."

"That I doubt," she said with certainty. Matteo had looked considerably scuffed up when they'd parted ways, and he probably was in much the same condition now. "If we're thinking about the same man, this one would walk to the hold and lock himself in if someone so much as suggested that he bent a law."

"If he's such a paladin as all that, why is he in the hold?" Gio asked, reasonably enough.

As to that, Tzigone had a fairly good idea. It seemed she would have a chance to erase the debt the same day it was incurred. She thought fast. "If I wanted to get into the hold, how would I do it?"

"Getting in is never a problem. It's the getting out that tasks me," the man pointed out. "What's this jordain to you, girl, that you'd waste your breath on such crazy words?"

"I owe him a debt," she said simply.

The gypsy nodded. Property was something that neither would ever understand, but they knew the worth of things that mattered. "Well, then, I've just the thing for you. You remember how to walk on stilts?"

She sniffed. "If you're out to insult me, just call me an ugly bastard and get it over with."

"Biggest weapon first," he said approvingly. "Not the usual strategy, but it should be. Might cut down on time wasted fighting."

"You were saying something about stilts?" she prompted.

Gio's eyes glittered with mischief. "Now, if you were the law and saw a pair of stilts lying inside the wall of the hold, what would you think? Someone's trying to breach, that's what. But a single pole? No one would think much of it."

"I don't think much of it myself," she retorted. She could vault a wall using Gio's pole, and said so.

"Ah, but not one like this," Gio said slyly. He shouldered off his pack and took from it a bundle of oddly shaped sticks. "They fit together into one long piece," he explained, demonstrating with several of them.

"What are those notches for?"

"Footholds. You can balance the pole and climb it at the same time. But mind you, stay well away from the walls. Lightning sheets cover the inside walls almost to the top. If you lose your balance and lean against the wall, you'll be sizzling like bacon."

"Stay away from the walls? So how do I get out?"

"Moss hangs from the cherrynut tree just outside the south wall. It is strong, and hard to see in the failing light. You'll be in the tree before any of those lazy guards notice what you're about."

Tzigone studied the placement of the notches and decided that the balance might work. To limber up, she bent backward until her palms rested on the ground, just behind her feet. Slowly she shifted her weight onto her hands and brought her legs up straight, then slowly lowered them down into another tight arc. She rose, standing in nearly the same spot as she'd been before the exercise.

Gio nodded approvingly and handed her a length of pole. She braced it and hopped up, placing her feet on the lowest notches. She swayed for a moment until she found her balance. Then she found that she could indeed climb. She went up about six feet and then let the pole tip, keeping her grip on it as she lightly dropped to the ground. Even if someone noticed her performing this stunt, she would be up and in the tree before they realized what she'd had in mind.

"This will help," she said with gratitude.

"It's not an easy trick, but you make it look as if it were," the gypsy said admiringly. "Like climbing a rope, or so it looks. If you were still with the show, you'd have us dragged in for magical inquiry sure as sunrise."

A thought crossed her mind and brought a wry scowl to her face. "Now that you mention it, the climbing will be the easy part," she grumbled.

Gio looked mildly offended, as if she'd insulted his latest toy. "You know a better trick, girl?"

"Convincing a jordain to break out of the hold."

The gypsy considered this and then placed a hand on her shoulder in silent commiseration. "One more word from an old friend?"

"Don't bother telling me he's not worth the trouble. I never met a jordain who was."

"I wouldn't think of trying to sway you, seeing that your mind's set on getting him out," Gio protested. "Just do me this favor: If you're caught, at least try to throw the pole out over the wall. I'd hate to lose it."

"Pride of ownership, Gio?" she teased him.

He looked puzzled. "Just pure common sense. There's not a man or woman inside the hold that would make good use of the thing. It'd be a shame to see it go for firewood."

CHAPTER EIGHT

The sun hung low over the mountains when Mbatu returned to the travel house he shared with Kiva. The wemic had a peasant man slung over his shoulders, much as a hunter might carry a deer. He shifted the man casually and tossed him at the magehound's feet. The captive groaned from the jolt of impact and then curved into a tight, pained ball.

Kiva didn't see any marks on the peasant, but she didn't expect to. Mbatu was too skilled and shrewd to mark his prey unless it pleased him to do so.

The elf woman regarded their captive thoughtfully. He was a young man, about the same height as Matteo. His muscles had been honed by hard labor and his skin browned by the sun. There the similarity between the two men ended. The farmer's face was twisted in pain but would not be considered particularly handsome in the best of circumstances. His hands were square and blunt-fingered, the nails ragged and grimed with soil. His hair was a similar shade of deep chestnut, but it was coarser than the jordain's and not quite as long and lustrous. Darkness, however, would blur these small details. Magic and simple mundane extortion would cover the rest.

"Will he be missed?" she demanded.

The wemic shrugged. "Not particularly. He is a day laborer on another man's fields. Such men come and go with the crops."

"Good. Let's finish it, then."

Kiva quickly cast a spell to ease the man's pain and make him biddable to her will. At her command, the farmer stripped off his rude garments and replaced them with white linen tunic and leggings, as befitted a jordain about to endure the ritual of purification.

Getting him onto Matteo's black stallion proved a greater challenge. The horse pitched and reared and snorted, refusing to let the peasant mount his back. Even Kiva's magic couldn't bend the stallion to her will.

At last the magehound admitted defeat and gave the peasant a lesser steed to ride. As for the stallion, Kiva found a way to entice him back to his stable. She rode her preferred gelding, but brought on a leading rope a mare in season. They set a brisk pace and found that the black male was more than willing to keep up.

They rode to the village on the outskirts of House Jordain, to the neat row of villas where the masters lived. Kiva had made good use of Zephyr's research, but she had additional sources of her own. One of the masters of the Jordaini College had good reason to hold his secrets quiet and close.

The man didn't look pleased to see her, but he gave her the prescribed courtesies. After they had exchanged the usual tiresome phrases of polite ritual, Kiva told the man what she had in mind.

The master's eyes flashed to the young substitute, who awaited them outside. He was still mounted on his borrowed steed, and his dull, enchanted eyes stared fixedly ahead.

"With all due respect, lady, I must protest. Put aside for the moment the matter of jordaini honor, or even the laws of this land," he pleaded. "Consider this young man, who will never sire a family. It is no small loss. The men and women who till the land depend upon their children's small hands.

The tasks that farm children perform are not busy work or play in imitation of adults, but a most important contribution to family. The farmer who lacks strong children is accounted a poor man, and with good reason!"

The magehound waved away these concerns with a quick, impatient flick of one hand. "House Jordain is ridiculously wealthy, for all your protestations of personal poverty. If you're so concerned for this peasant, recompense him. He will not have children. Well enough. A mule and a milkmaid should fill the breach."

"But what of his wife?" the man said softly. "If ever your arms ached to hold a child, you could not condemn even an unknown woman to this emptiness."

Rage set the elf's golden eyes aflame, then banked with a control so absolute that the lack of emotion was more terrifying than her sudden anger.

But the old man would not be deterred. "What of Matteo? You are a high servant of Azuth; you know the hidden mysteries of this land. He cannot be excused from this ritual. I need not remind you of what can happen when the jordaini breed."

In response, she handed him a small jeweled token. No bigger than the nail of her small finger, it was a tiny pellet studded with scales the colors of topaz and garnet and filled with magic. It was the token of the queen, and it carried both sentence and decree.

"I have my orders," Kiva said evenly, "and now you have yours."

For a long moment the man regarded the jeweled pill, and not because he wished to contemplate its beauty. Then he quickly swallowed it. He knew that from this moment, to speak of what was done this day would mean his death.

"Come along," he said harshly. "Let's get this travesty done and over with."

The magehound shook her head. "I must return to the city on business. You can handle this from here, I trust. Oh, and one thing more. I've brought with me a black stallion,

Matteo's chosen mount. Take the beast back with you to complete the subterfuge. You may board my mare at your stables for several moons and keep the foal that the stallion has most likely got on her while we spoke," she said generously. "The foal is likely to be quite valuable and will provide some recompense."

"Recompense for what?" the man snapped. "My honor? This poor man's virility? Or perhaps Matteo's life? Where is the boy? What has become of him?"

"That is the very business I must attend. You see, Matteo was detained in the city. Some unpleasantness surrounding the big jordain known as Themo, I believe. A tavern brawl with unfortunate consequences," she said, invoking a half-truth that the master was certain to accept.

The man sighed. "You can bring Matteo back to us? What of this so-called 'unpleasantness?' Is this a matter that you can handle?"

"Of course. Though it would be best that your student knows nothing of what passed between you and me."

"It is unlikely that he will know any of it! The jordaini are told of the purification rite, but most think that it is nothing but a time of solitary contemplation. Afterward they are sworn to silence. So far none has broken oath. And so far," he said pointedly, "none has birthed or fathered children that the entire land must fear. Think carefully upon what you do."

Kiva's lips twisted in a sneer. "Do not attempt to take the moral high ground. You couldn't find it with a map and a ranger to guide you! How dare you lecture me! You, who would rather see your own son castrated than see harm done to a peasant whose name you need never know."

The wizard paled. "The parentage of a jordain is a secret thing, never to be spoken of lightly."

"Then do as I say, and we need never speak of it at all," Kiva said implacably. "Matteo need never learn of what was done to assure his impressive talents and high status. I have seen how he took the death of his friend. How would he receive the truth about his mother? How would he regard the man who had a part in such a thing?"

For a long moment silence filled the room. "Go," the man said in a choked voice. "As always, everything will be done as you say."

❧

Matteo slumped against the cold stone wall and stared out the single window in the door of his cell as he tried to take it all in. Andris was dead. Mystra only knew what had become of Themo. And he, Matteo, was imprisoned on a charge of carrying a weapon that was not only proscribed but also stolen.

He sighed and surveyed his prison. The hold was a rarity in Halruaa, a land of swift justice and very few prisons. The port city of Khaerbaal was more rough-and-tumble than most, and though a few minor offenders were sentenced to a few days of confinement, for the most part the hold was a place to store criminals until the resident mage could attend to his or her case. Guilt was quickly determined through magical inquiry and the sentence carried out according to law.

Matteo had no fear of the outcome. His innocence would be determined by the prison magehound. Even so, the temporary disgrace carried a crushing weight.

A shadow passed by the small, barred window, silhouetted against the flickering light of torches thrust into metal brackets on the walls outside. Matteo gave an impassive glance toward what he thought was the guard, then leaped to his feet. The light was dim and uncertain, but Tzigone's face was forever burned into his memory and he would know her anyplace.

"You!" he declared in a tone that dripped with wrath as he pointed an accusing finger at the young woman.

Tzigone rolled her eyes. "And I thought Gio's performance was overwrought. Save the drama for the supper crowd. Right now let's think about getting you out of here."

If possible, the mention of rescue only served to increase Matteo's ire. "I am jordaini, bound by the laws of the land. You insult me by suggesting that I would attempt to escape justice."

"Justice?" she repeated incredulously. "Is that what you think happens around here? I know the magehound who works the hold. He's an ugly little monkey of a man who holds a grudge against anyone better favored than he. One look at that handsome face of yours and he'll be howling for an Inquisition. If I were you, I wouldn't bet my future on the outcome."

Matteo's first impulse was to protest this as blasphemous. A magehound's word was final and fair. This was the underlying premise of his culture, the assurance of the jordain's status and power.

Yet he himself had harbored such thoughts. How could he not? Andris was dead. Andris, who was his dearest friend and the best of them all. It was enough to make any man lose faith.

Faced with such a dark and unfathomable void, Matteo clung to what he knew. "I do not fear the magehound's judgment. Truth is a sword that cuts all bonds."

She threw up her hands. "The 'truth' is that you were caught with a weapon crafted by Zanfeld Yemandi, the city's premier swordsmith."

"You said the sword was yours!' he protested.

"Mine, his," she said impatiently. "I had need of it at the moment and Zanfeld did not. Who had the better claim to it?"

Matteo groaned and buried his head in his hands. Though Tzigone obviously intended to aid him, her words condemned him as surely as they informed him. When the magical inquiry was done, it would be discovered that he knew beyond doubt at the time of inquisition that the sword was stolen.

"I an undone," he muttered, slumping lower against the wall.

"Then get off the floor and do yourself back up," she said tartly. "I'll get you out of this. Trust me."

He sent her a quick incredulous glance. "Need I remind you that it was you who got me into this?"

She shrugged away his words with the same impatient unconcern that she might have in dismissing a comment about the political situation in distant Cormyr. The expression on her face clearly proclaimed, What has one thing to do with another?

Tzigone cast her eyes toward the ceiling. Then, with the air of someone who has better things to do than engage in meaningless chat, she dropped out of sight. Metallic whispers gave witness to picks and knives being employed on the lock.

Matteo walked over to the door. "I will not go with you," he said with calm finality. "If you open the door, I will pull you inside and shut it behind you."

Tzigone's face popped back into view, and she regarded him with an insouciant grin. "What woman could resist so poetic a ploy? Look at me! I'm swooning!"

"I didn't mean—"

She cut him off with a jab to the forehead with the blunt end of her pick. "How stupid do I look? I know what you meant. Now be quiet and let me work."

Again she disappeared. Matteo heard the distant tread of footsteps. "Someone's coming. Go now before you're forced to join me here."

This logic finally struck a chord. The woman rose and sent a quick look over her shoulder, then leaped for the iron bracket set high on the wall. She pulled herself up onto the torch's shelf and nimbly rose to her feet. From there she reached the lowest edge of the rafter and swung herself up onto it. Swiftly she walked across the broad beam. The only sign of her passing was a silvery sprinkle of dust and the appearance of a couple of indignant spiders, disturbed from their perches and swinging like pendulums from gossamer threads.

Matteo breathed a gusty sigh of relief. Though Tzigone's understanding of life was vastly different than his, he was moved by the fact that she would try to rescue him. All the same, he was glad that she was safely out of it.

He had just settled back down on the floor when the lock began to clatter in earnest. He surged to his feet as the door swung in, ready to unleash a blistering tirade at the persistent girl.

But the face in the doorway was not what he expected, not the impish charm of Tzigone's pointed chin and big, dark eyes, but the exotic, dangerous beauty of a wild elf female.

Kiva the Magehound raised a single jade-colored brow. "You are most eager to leave, Matteo. Strangely you don't seem pleased to see me."

Matteo had no answer for that. Instead he regarded the steady, golden stare of the wemic at Kiva's side. Judging from Mbatu's expression, Matteo guessed that the wemic remembered quite well what had passed between them earlier that day. Tzigone's assurances of forgetfulness were nothing more than another of her comfortable lies.

Kiva slipped a slender arm around the wemic's waist, a gesture that struck Matteo as warning rather than affection. She glanced over her shoulder at the hold's magistrate, who was all but wringing his hands in distress.

"Deepest apologies, lady, but you cannot simply take this prisoner and go."

"Oh? And why is that?"

"He must be examined by the hold's inquisitor. You know the rules."

Kiva's smile was chilling. "I also know Chartain. He was assigned this post because he could get no other. Do you put more faith in his judgment than mine? If I say that this jordain is no thief, let that content you."

The magistrate gave one last try. "You walk in Azuth's light, lady, and speak through the sure sight of magic. If you say this man is no thief, I will swear my own life against his innocence! But you cannot deny that he was carrying a sword, though it is against local custom for a jordain to do so."

"What need have they of such weapons when they are armed with the sword of truth?" she said sweetly, neither confirming nor disputing the accusation.

Once again Matteo heard the hint of irony in her voice, a music not unlike the faint, mocking echoes of the Unseelie folk, dark fairies who haunted the mountain passes around Halruaa and played seductive tunes known to lure men from the paths into the wilderness.

"He had the sword when the militia stopped him," the magistrate stated again.

"But did he know at the time that he was carrying it? Did you?" she said, turning abruptly to Matteo.

"I did not know about the sword. The magehound does not lie . . . about this," Matteo said, adding subtle emphasis of his own.

Her angry gaze snapped to his, and for a long time they locked fierce stares. Matteo remembered a cobra and trainer he'd seen frozen in just such a posture. Like the snake trainer, he suspected that a misstep would cause the deadly creature before him to strike.

But after a moment Kiva's lips curved in a delighted smile. She turned to the magistrate. "You heard him. We all know that the jordaini place truth above all. Let him go at once."

CHAPTER NINE

Matteo's troubles did not end when the door of the hold clanked shut behind him.

Kiva wished him well in her sweet, ironic voice and then disappeared. The wemic, after a final long, challenging stare, followed the magehound, leaving Matteo entirely to his own devices.

He started out to find Cyric and soon realized that this effort was both futile and costly. The stallion had shattered the hitching rail by the Falling Star Tavern to get loose, and the innkeeper demanded payment. Matteo had spent all of his allotted coin to ensure that Themo would not come to grief over the brawl in the tavern. It took all his persuasive powers to get the man to agree to accept a note, payable upon demand by the stewards of House Jordain.

Matters did not improve from there. Ordinarily many hostlers in Khaerbaal might have been willing to lend him a mount, certain of payment from the jordaini order, but none believed Matteo's claim to being a member of that house. His battles, his jaunt with Tzigone through the bilboa tree and the dirty back streets, and his confinement in the dirty cell had left his white linens dingy and stained beyond recognition. Worse, he had inexplicably lost the pendant that proclaimed him a jordain.

There was nothing to do but walk, so Matteo set out at a brisk pace. By sunset, he left the city gate behind. He walked as late into the night as he dared, then took a page from Tzigone's book and took refuge in a large, vine-shrouded mazganut tree.

Sleep did not come, for he was all too aware of the numerous night sounds around him. He recognized the snuffles and grunts of the wild boars who rooted for fallen nuts at the base of the tree, the not-too-distant shriek of a hunting panther, the hum and chitter of the tiny, often malevolent sprites who made their lairs in the uppermost branches.

Worse were the faint, unearthly echoes of the Unseelie music. Matteo had heard tales of the dark fairies that haunted the mountain passes and danced widdershins upon the ruins of ancient cities and long-forgotten graves, and he'd read that on occasion they ventured close to civilized lands. All these things he recognized from his studies, but the knowledge did little to prepare him for the chilling actuality of their song. After a time, he began to talk to himself, reciting tales and histories and royal genealogies—anything to drown out the faint, darkly compelling music.

It occurred to him more than once during that long night, and during the day's trudge that followed, that perhaps there was more wisdom in Tzigone's warnings that he had perceived at first consideration. He had spent his entire life within the confines of House Jordain. His studies had ranged the world and touched on all of its sciences, some lightly, some in considerable depth. Yet truly how well prepared was he for the world beyond the counselors' school?

The moon was a new crescent when Matteo arrived back at the school the next night, dusty and footsore. He knew at once that word of his disgrace had preceded him. The set, disapproving expression on the face of the gatehouse guard left no doubt.

"The ritual of purification took place last night. You're to go to the meditation huts at once."

Matteo groaned. After all that had happened the last few days, he had forgotten about this important rite. No jordain left the college without it. He brought to mind a list of his masters and settled on the one most likely to help him resolve this situation.

"Can you take a message to Vishna for me?"

"No messages," the guard said adamantly. "When they want you, they'll let you know."

Matteo nodded and went at once into his belated solitude. The meditation huts were scattered among the orchards on the far western side of the compound. Matteo's hut was furnished with a cot, table, and a large pitcher of water. Not having any other option, he settled down to think and to wait.

On the third day after his return, the servant who came each morning to leave a tray of food knocked on the door and handed Matteo a pile of fresh clothes. "Prepare quickly. You are bid to present yourself at the Disputation Table."

Although Matteo had been expecting this, the summons brought a lump of dread to his throat. He had been released from the hold and would not be tried for theft, but he had still committed a number of infractions of jordaini law and custom. And now he had missed the final ritual. It was likely that he would have to repeat the fifth form before leaving the school. Or, far worse, he might be dismissed altogether and stripped of rank and title.

He quickly dressed and made his way to the large high-domed building that housed the jordaini court. The entrance hall was round, and in the floor was set with mosaic tile the emblem of the jordaini: a circle that was half yellow and half green, the colors separated by a lighting bolt of blue. Matteo rubbed at the empty spot on his chest where his medallion usually hung, then took a long, steadying breath and strode through the hall toward the council chamber.

The Disputation Table was not only the name of the court, but a literal table, a huge structure comprising two very long tables connected at the far end by a smaller raised table. At this high place sat Dimidis, the judge who would render a verdict. The other masters and the jordaini students sat around the outer rims of the long tables. They all regarded him with somber faces.

Matteo had been in attendance during many sessions, for the court was a busy place and was often called upon to interpret a jordain's advice to his patron, as well as to deal with occasional disputes between jordaini and the less frequent infraction of rules.

But the vast, hollow room had never seemed so ominous as it did now. Matteo held his chin high as he walked down the long center aisle to stand before Dimidis, painfully aware with each step of the eyes upon him.

The aged judge was one of the few jordaini who took his status from his own position, rather than that of a patron. Dimidis was known for his stern and often inflexible judgments, as well as his tendency to form opinions and dislikes with distressing haste. Judging from the sour expression on the man's lined face, Matteo guessed that he had earned the judge's enmity.

Dimidis rattled a sheaf of parchment. "We've all read of this young man's misdeeds: tavern brawling, destroying property, attacking a magehound's guard. He attended a performance that mocked the jordaini and then aided the performer's escape. He has fought a duel with a weapon proscribed to his class—a stolen weapon, which was later found in his possession. When questioned in the hold, he defied the magistrate and refused to name the thief. This name would have been taken from him through Inquisition but for the intervention of the Inquisitrix Kiva."

The old man stopped and glared at the assembly. "These are the charges against Matteo of House Jordain. Who, if any, will speak for him?"

"I, Lord Dimidis."

Matteo was grateful but not particularly surprised to see his favorite master, Vishna, the battle wizard, rise to speak.

"Like many of the students, Matteo went to Khaerbaal with a heavy heart. You know that Andris, a close friend to Matteo, was slain that morning at the command of the magehound Kiva."

"Which was both her function and her right," Dimidis pointed out. "Continue."

"I sent Matteo to the city, knowing that some of the students would find outlets for their grief. If mischief came of it, I am in part to blame. Indeed, I expressly requested that Matteo watch over one of his fellows. This he did admirably. The other student returned to us on time, unscathed and held blameless for his actions. It was he who started the tavern brawl and Matteo who ended it."

"The deeds of one jordain reflect upon us all. That is why this court exists. Matteo did no more than his duty."

"That is my point," the wizard said earnestly. "This young jordain did his duty and did it well, despite his personal sorrow. If he was perhaps a bit impulsive in his subsequent actions, surely we can consider the circumstances."

The judge looked at the battle wizard as if he had been speaking Turmish, or Common, or some other barbarian tongue. "Is that all? Have you nothing relevant to add?"

For a moment the wizard stared incredulously. "Apparently not," Vishna said shortly and sat down with an abruptness that spoke more of anger than defeat.

To Matteo's surprise, Ferris Grail was the next to speak. He was also a wizard and the headmaster of House Jordain, but Matteo had had little direct contact with him. The headmaster was apparently better acquainted with Matteo. He spoke ringingly of Matteo's scholarship, intellect, and unblemished record.

"We have had eleven petitions for this jordain's services," the headmaster concluded. He placed a sheaf of parchment on the table before Dimidis. The judge picked it up and paged through it, his expression turning more dour by the moment.

"I would also speak," said Annalia Gray, the school's logic and rhetoric professor. The woman was the only female jordain in the complex and as gifted in disputation as any among them. Usually Matteo listened keenly to any words she had to say so that he could commit them to memory. Though his future depended upon her argument, he could not listen today. Instead, his eyes were drawn by the green and gold figure gliding down the aisle toward the judge's bench. He barely noticed when Annalia Gray concluded, even though she took her seat in a burst of applause.

Kiva, the Magehound, had come to speak for him.

This Matteo had never anticipated, nor was he entirely happy to have such an ally. He listened with growing unease as Kiva repeated what had already been told, leaving out some things that had not yet been reported: Matteo's battle with the wemic in the backstreets of Khaerbaal and the name of the girl he had defended. Tzigone was referred to only as "the thief" in reference to the sword, and "the entertainer" when Kiva spoke of Matteo's attack on Mbatu in the Falling Star Tavern. Indeed, to hear Kiva talk, it sounded as if there had been two distinct people.

Finally Matteo was called upon to speak for himself. He bowed first to Dimidis, then to the assembled court.

"All that you have heard against me is true. I thank Master Vishna for his words and for his compassion, but I must stand for my actions and not the circumstances that prompted them. I regret my infractions of jordaini law and will accept humbly whatever penalty this council assigns. I ask only that I might be permitted to ask the inquisitrix a question that has confounded me."

Dimidis looked pleased with Matteo's manner and his request. "You may speak."

Matteo turned a steady, challenging gaze upon the elf woman. "A dragon does not quit the skies to chase a rabbit into the thicket. Why then was the wemic Mbatu, a magehound's right hand and personal bodyguard, in pursuit of a young woman who has been described only as a tavern performer and common thief?"

Everyone in the room looked startled, then intrigued. "A good question," Dimidis said approvingly, looking at Matteo with the first sign of real interest. "Lady Kiva, we are most eager to hear your response. Most eager indeed. By your words, I had gathered that Matteo had fallen in with two scoundrels, not a single girl."

Fury flashed through the magehound's eyes, followed quickly by a flicker of indecision. Her cool mask was back in place so quickly that Matteo, had he not been studying her so intently, would have wondered if he'd imagined her initial response.

"There is nothing to explain," Kiva said in her cool, bell-like tones. "The girl is reputed to have a sharp and clever tongue, and the jordaini were not the only targets of her jests. She insulted Mbatu the day before. The wemic is quick to anger and quicker to attack. He tended his own business, not mine. For that, he has been duly rebuked. As to the misunderstanding about the girl's identity, please recall that I speak your language as a second tongue. I have not the precision of speech that a jordain employs. One scoundrel or two, the girl was the wemic's concern and not mine. I know nothing of her, and that is more than I care to know."

Dimidis looked faintly disappointed by this mundane explanation. "Then I suppose we're finished here. I have little choice but to dismiss the matter. Among the petitions for Matteo's services is one we could hardly ignore. Procopio Septus, Lord Mayor of Halarahh, finds himself in need of counsel."

Matteo's eyes widened at this most unexpected news. Procopio was a powerful diviner, the mayor of Halruaa's capital city and the captain of that city's skyship militia. This was a coveted position and one that far exceeded his aspirations for his first post.

For a moment pride surged, washing away some of the humiliation of the past few days. Then it occurred to him that this post would probably have gone to Andris, had he lived.

Even so, it was a far better fate than he had expected. Matteo dipped into a deep bow. "Humbly I accept this post, Lord Dimidis, if that is the council's desire."

"My wishes have little to do with this," Dimidis said in a sour tone. "Just see that you have no further cause to stand before the Disputation Table, and I will be content."

❂

Several days passed as Matteo traveled to Halarahh, the capital of the land and the home of Zalathorm, the wizard-king. It was not so very far a distance as the raven flies, provided that a raven could be persuaded to fly across the lower edge of the Swamp of Akhlaur and brave the winds that roiled over Lake Halruaa.

The best and safest way to travel was by ship. Matteo set sail from Khaerbaal, skirting the coastline of the Bay of Taertal and moving along the western shores of Lake Halruaa.

The days passed swiftly, despite his increasing anticipation. Matteo had not traveled to Halarahh since his twelfth year. His first glimpse of the city, as the ship rounded the storm break, proved more than equal to his memories.

Much of the city was organized around the docks. But Halarahh was not like Khaerbaal, where prim rows of wooden docks jutted out into the sea and led to businesslike warehouses, inns, and taverns. The royal city had docks, certainly, and ships came and went briskly. But beyond the harbor was a wonderfully broad and open area, paved with colored stone and shaded by trees and fanciful pavilions. This was the site of colorful festivals, seasonal fairs, and open-air markets.

"What fair is currently running?" Matteo asked one of his fellow passengers, a merchant from the eastern foothills.

The man's eyes lit up. "The Monster Fair. It'll be a sight, if you've time to take it in. Good bull aurochs, for farmers who've got the pasturage to feed fuzzy elephants. Don't hold much with them myself. Meat's too gamey. Much prefer a good haunch of rothe."

A faint stab of disappointment assailed Matteo at this mundane description. "It's a market for cattle, then?"

"And everything else. The fancy lizards that ladies keep as pets these days. Birds from the Mhair Jungles. Griffon kittens, dragon eggs. If you can eat it, cage it, put it on a leash, or chop it up for spell parts, like as not it'll be there. I hear tell they've even got a unicorn up for bid."

It was on the tip of Matteo's tongue to ask which of these fates awaited the unicorn, but he decided he would rather not know. He thanked the man and went off to collect his few possessions.

The ship moved smoothly into the dock, and Matteo was met at the plank by men wearing jordaini white and distinctly unpleasant expressions. They looked him over in a manner that made Matteo suddenly sympathetic for the creatures in the market square.

"You're Procopio's latest?" one of them demanded.

"I am Matteo, and I am here to enter the service of Procopio Septus," he agreed.

"Well, come along," the speaker said grudgingly.

The men spun and stalked off, leaving Matteo to follow or not.

He was surprised by the less than enthusiastic welcome, but he was too fascinated by his surroundings to take much offense. Halarahh was a wondrous city, the largest in the land, home to nearly eight thousand souls. Yet as Matteo's escort led him through the market square toward the villa of Procopio Septus, he didn't once get the feeling of being in a close or crowded place.

The villas they passed were sprawling and spacious. Even the homes of middling folk boasted comfortable grounds filled with gardens and flowers. Public parks and gardens greeted them at nearly every turn. Wide streets opened into large courtyards, many of which housed open-air markets, smaller versions of the vast dockside square.

The city was comfortably cool, a welcome respite from the punishing sun of Matteo's sea journey. Perched on the northern banks of Lake Halruaa, the city sat at the confluence of two of the land's greatest rivers: Halar and Aluar. Soft breezes wafted off the waters and were captured and magnified by many innovative magical devices.

Although Matteo could not work magic, he had spent most of his life in study of it. Never, however, had he seen so much of it concentrated in one place. Almost half the inhabitants of the city were spellcasters, and at least three hundred made their livelihood by working magic. Wizards' towers leaped toward the azure sky, giving the city an aspect of a forest fashioned of marble and crystal and stone. Magical lamps lined the streets and enlivened the homes and shops. As they passed the open doors of some of the grander shops, they were treated to a soft caress from the soft, scented breezes that magically cooled the merchants and their customers. Flat-bedded carts trundled by at regular intervals, laden with magically created ice blocks that cooled folks of lesser means.

But what most amazed Matteo were the skyships. Although Halruaa was famed for these marvelous cloud-going vessels, Matteo had never seen one close at hand. His last trip to Halarahh had taken place during the winter, when most skyships kept close to land. He had observed the spring regatta at the Lady Day festivals that took place in every city in the land, but he had always seen the skyship display from a distance. It was considered unseemly for a jordain to be sprinkled with fortune-telling magic.

So he was vastly pleased when the road his fellow jordaini traveled led toward the docks where the ships came to roost. Several of the graceful ships wheeled through the sky as they traced the edges of the lake like fine ladies on a summer evening's promenade. Each of the ships boasted three masts, plus a flying jib aft and two sails astern on swinging booms. The bodies of the ships were plated with armor from giant sea turtles, so from below they looked much the same. But much color and design had been lavished upon the sails.

"You're staring like a peasant," one of the jordaini observed coldly. "Have you never seen a skyship?"

"Never so close at hand. What stately grace," Matteo marveled. "They look rather like kites flown by giant, powerful children."

"A fine way to describe your new patron," observed a dry voice behind him.

Matteo turned. A short, thin man stood behind him, arms folded and head tilted to one side as he returned Matteo's gaze. The newcomer was a striking man, one who would draw eyes in a crowd despite his lack of stature. His nose was hooked like a hawk's, and his thick snowy hair had been cut exceedingly short so that it bristled about his head. His medallion proclaimed him a wizard of the divination school, and the ring on his hand was etched with the seal of the city: a triangle pointed downward with a star at the tip to represent the shape of the land on which Halarahh sat. Wavy lines etched over the whole completed the crest of the windswept city.

"Lord Procopio." Matteo swept into a formal bow.

The wizard waved aside this courtesy. "You took your time in coming, young man. The crew has been holding the skyship for your arrival."

This was an unexpected treat. Matteo's eyes lit up. Then his gaze darted to the other jordain for confirmation. They regarded him with narrowed eyes and scowls. Puzzled, Matteo turned back to his new patron. "You wish us to accompany you on the skyship?"

"Just you. Come aboard, unless you can fly on your own power," the wizard said tartly. He turned and strode toward one of the docked ships.

Matteo followed, studying the vessel with interest. The image of a long, sinuous snake had been painted in rainbow colors on the side of the ship and continued to coil its way up the foremost mainsail. The other sails depicted a starsnake's wings, and elaborate curved runes painted onto the hull confirmed that *Starsnake* was indeed the ship's name.

Lord Procopio led the way to the forecastle and twisted the gold and silver rod mounted there. The skyship rose gracefully into the sky, more rapidly than Matteo would have thought possible.

The wizard looked at him sharply. "You look surprised. Have you not learned the properties of such ships?"

"I have, my lord. Knowing is one thing; experiencing is quite another."

"True enough. How fast are we going?"

Matteo considered what he knew of the ships and calculated the effects of the winds off Lake Halruaa. "Seventeen knots," he said firmly, glancing toward the helmsman for confirmation.

The helmsman nodded. Procopio shrugged, unimpressed, and pointed out toward the center of the lake. "Take her out. Let's give our new counselor a bit of a challenge."

The man at the wheel looked none too happy, but he did as he was bade, leaning his weight into turning the heavy wheel.

This put Matteo in the uncomfortable position of needing to give advice before any was requested. He wondered that he would have to do so, for the dangerous winds of Lake Halruaa were proverbial. No ship sailed the interior of the lake, not on the surface and not in the air.

"Lord Procopio, if I am to fulfill my duty, I must advise you against going out over the lake," Matteo said respectfully.

Procopio's only response was to point toward another ship, skirting the shore and rapidly approaching them.

"That is the *Avariel*, owned by the conjurer Basel Indoulur. He is a reckless man, proud enough to consider himself my rival. If we engage him in challenge, he will not turn away."

Procopio turned to a blue scrying globe mounted on a pedestal and gestured over it. Clouds swam in the circular sky, then parted to reveal the face of his apparent rival. The man was portly, with pillowy cheeks and small, shrewd eyes. His black hair had been oiled and worked into many small braids that hung nearly to his shoulders. The wizards exchanged the expected pleasantries, then Procopio got down to business.

"Fine winds today, Lord Basel."

The image of the wizard nodded happily. "Aye. The *Avariel* is giving near to five and twenty knots. I wouldn't have thought the old girl could dance to so merry a tune."

"Small wonder. You sail deep into the lake winds."

"No deeper than you," Basel retorted. "If you've something on your mind, man, have out with it."

"A challenge. A contest of will and nerve."

Basel's eyes bulged, then he laughed. "A game of chicken, in other words. Come, Lord Procopio—a child's game?"

"Made interesting by a man's wager. Say, two thousand skie? And I'm no such fool to suggest a collision course. A contest of skill and speed. The first to reach thirty knots takes it."

The wizard's small eyes glinted. "I'm not so good a friend that I won't take your money," he agreed, and then his image winked out of sight.

Procopio turned to Matteo. "Imagine that this is your first campaign. You will advise the general, who has been ordered to follow your counsel. The outcome of this battle is entirely in your hands."

Matteo longed to retort that this was a silly wager, not a battle worth fighting. To achieve those speeds, the ships would have to venture far out over the waters, where the winds were strong and unpredictable.

But the wizard had created the situation, and it was Matteo's duty to make of it what he could. He scanned the clouds and the shoreline as he ciphered the weight of the *Starsnake*.

"What crew does the *Avariel* carry?"

Procopio nodded his approval of this query. "Same as *Starsnake*, to the man. Six and twenty. The skyships were built by the same shipmaster, and the rods of levitation were enchanted by the same wizard. The ships are sisters. This contest will not be determined by the vessel, but by the wisdom of the captains."

Matteo was tempted to point out that a wise man didn't take such large risks for sport or pride. Young as he was, he understood that not all truth should be spoken aloud. He turned to the helmsman, a thin, balding man nearly a head shorter than the wizard. "Your name, sir?"

The man blinked, obviously surprised by the question and the courtesy. "Spalding, m'lord, an' it please ye."

"You do me too much honor," he said with a smile. "Procopio Septus is the only lord here. My name is Matteo."

"As ye will, m'. . . Matteo."

"Thirty degrees toward starboard, Spalding."

Procopio scowled as the ship turned and slowed. "You're heading back toward shore. That's a coward's course, and certain defeat. Turn back into the lake winds, if you've the stomach for it!"

Being chided for a coward stung, but the jordain shook his head and studied the shoreline. "Hold steady, Spalding. On my mark, turn hard to starboard. Head directly to the shore by the shortest route and hold course. Trim the sails as needed to maintain speed."

The helmsman blanched, but he faithfully relayed the order to the crew who manned the ropes. Matteo waited until the moment was right, then bade the man turn. The ship swung in a slow, ponderous arc, losing speed as she went.

"Bold move!" Procopio taunted.

For a moment the sails fluttered slack. Then, as Matteo expected, they snapped taut and the ship leaped forward.

The wizard's brow furrowed with puzzlement. "This course seems destined to take us directly into the *Avariel's* path."

"That is my intent."

Procopio stared at him, slack-jawed with astonishment. He shut his mouth with an audible click and shook his head. "You've gone mad. I've seen it before. Some men just can't fly—the thin air addles their thinking. I'm taking over command, Spalding."

"No," Matteo said calmly. He noticed the speculative gleam in his new patron's eyes, and at this moment he understood that this was not pointless folly, but a test. If he meant to win Procopio's respect, he had to see this through. "You bade me win this battle for you, and that is precisely what I am doing."

"Victory is sweet, but I'd rather have my ship, whole and skyworthy!"

"Then stand by. To turn aside now would be dangerous." To add weight to his words and to signify the seriousness of his intent, Matteo stepped between the incredulous wizard and the helmsman. He held the little man's eyes with an unflinching gaze, one that held a different sort of challenge.

This was clearly not what Procopio had been expecting. The wizard's face turned purple with a mixture of anger and bruised pride. He could not compel Matteo by magic, and it was equally certain that he could not enforce his will by strength of arm. Procopio stepped back, his eyes black with anger, and began the gestures of a spell that would sidestep the jordain and impose his will on the helmsman.

Matteo recognized the spell and deftly countered it. He seized the wizard's right wrist and swept it up high, then hooked his thumb around the small finger of the left. This altered the gestures, turning the intended spell into a harmless illusion. Colored lights began to dance upon the sail, casting images of lithe women dancing in a circle, dressed in the feathers of the painted starsnake's wings.

Procopio dropped his hands to his sides and stared incredulously at the flickering image, all that remained of his interrupted spell.

"You take too much upon yourself, jordain. An enormous

risk, with a ship not your own! Do you know the worth of such a vessel?"

Matteo told him precisely what it was worth, give or take a handful of gold pieces. The flash of surprise in the wizard's eyes told Matteo that he had hit the mark. But more truth remained unspoken, and Matteo didn't shrink from it. "Great risks were taken, that is true, but not by me."

Procopio's eyes narrowed, but his expression remained unreadable. "How so?"

"I spoke against venturing over the lake. The winds are strong and unpredictable. Once you determined to follow this course of action, my task was to keep you alive. I turned at the proper time, not before. It was not cowardice but calculation. Will you let me finish the task you gave me without further interference? If not, speak now. Soon there will be no time for disputation."

"I swear it," Procopio grumbled. "The ship is yours to command."

Matteo nodded and turned his attention to the rapidly approaching skyship. He could see it now in more detail. Upon the sail had been painted elaborate runes and symbols, and the polished plates of the sea turtles that armored its hull had been gilded with electrum in similarly ornate patterns. But it was on the sails that Matteo concentrated. The winds were strong, and they filled the sails of both ships. If even one of the *Avariel's* sails rippled and went slack, he would know that Basel Indoulur had lost his nerve. But if the approaching ship held course, then Matteo would evade it and leave Procopio to deal with his bruised pride and lightened purse.

Yes, there it was, a soft fluttering of the foresail. The *Avariel* was taking evasive action. One uncertainty remained: Which way would Lord Basel turn?

"How will he evade us?" Matteo demanded. "Will he turn toward port or starboard? Which sails will he drop, and which will he tack?"

"He will not turn aside," Procopio asserted. He gave

Matteo a sour look. "Until today, I would have named Basel Indoulur the most stubborn and arrogant whore son in all Halruaa. Now he stands close behind you for that honor. He will not turn aside."

"Is this your opinion, or the word of a diviner?"

Matteo's words were a potent challenge. If Procopio were wrong, he would lose not only his ship, but his reputation as a wizard who could foresee what was to come.

The wizard locked stares with his young counselor, then hissed and turned aside. "I will do the divination."

"Quickly," Matteo urged.

The wizard swept a hand over the globe and stared intently at something Matteo could not see. In a moment he looked up, and a wry smile touched his lips. "I'll be a necromancer's apprentice! You were right: Basel will turn aside. He will drop jib and foresail, tack hard to starboard with the aft sails, and use the lake winds to turn him hard out to sea."

Even as he spoke, the sails on the approaching starship began to flutter and shift. Matteo marked the arc of the starship's turn and concentrated on the winds that whipped at his hair and cloak. Suddenly he felt a shift in the airflow, the outer edges of a small circular maelstrom, a storm in miniature.

Matteo touched the helmsman's arm. "Turn toward the *Avariel* ten degrees, on my mark. One—"

"This is folly!" sputtered Procopio. "The ships will surely collide."

"Two," Matteo said coolly.

The wizard braced himself against the rail for the coming impact and glared at his young counselor. "Consider yourself discharged, jordain."

"Now!"

The helmsman gave the wheel a violent twist, and the *Starsnake* nosed about into the turning path of the rapidly approaching skyship.

Just then the full impact of the expected wind seized them. The ship hurtled forward, leaping through the sky like a breaching dolphin. There was a soft hiss as the wooden rails of the two ships kissed gently in passing.

The sudden squall died as quickly as it came, and the Starsnake slowed to a more sedate pace. Procopio turned an incredulous gaze upon his young counselor.

"What was that?"

Matteo permitted himself a smile. "About three and thirty knots, I daresay."

"Four and thirty," the helmsman corrected in an awed tone.

The wizard waved this victory aside. "But the wind . . . how did you know it was going to pick up just then?"

Matteo pointed to a long, low building that lay below on the shores of that lake. "That is the city icehouse. See the large blocks being loaded onto those wagons?"

"What of it?"

"When water is magically changed to ice, much heat is given off. Some of that energy is channeled into magical power, but much of it is wasted. It rises swiftly, creating a strong updraft."

"Heat from ice," the wizard muttered. "Never would I have thought of it quite that way."

"The effect upon the winds does not stop there. The chill given off by such large quantities of ice creates a strong pull for the warmer air, which in turn creates a strong circular wind. That is what caught us and brought us forward in a sudden surge. Had we not turned precisely when we did, we would not have caught the full power of the wind and would have collided despite Lord Basel's evasion."

The wizard regarded him with interest, the near miss apparently forgotten. "Heat from ice. What battle applications might that have?"

Matteo thought this over. "The ice works with the winds to create a small storm. If the clouds from this storm are low, a starship could rise above and seed them. A sprinkling of fine sand would be enough to engender a strong hailstorm. With or without magical amplification, such a storm could provide a diversion, at the very least, and quite possibly a devastating attack."

"Ice below draws ice from above. Under certain circumstances, that might prove useful. Ah, we hear at last from the intrepid *Avariel*," Procopio said snidely as he turned to the softly humming globe.

Basel Indoulur's face appeared, ashen but smiling. "Well done, my friend! Half my crew are wishing for a clean pair of breeches and the feel of solid land beneath their feet. You've earned your two thousand skie. Or should I say, your new jordain has earned them for you," he added slyly.

A velvet bag appeared from the empty air and fell at Matteo's feet with a weighty chink.

"What say, lad?" continued Basel. "I could use an adviser with your nerve. Mine cluck and flap about like a passel of brooding hens."

Matteo noted the wary expression on Procopio's face. The wizard had discharged him; he was free to take any employment offered him. But Matteo sensed that yielding anything, much less the services of a valuable counselor, would mean a loss of face to the wizard.

"I am honored by your words, Lord Basel, but I have just recently entered the employ of your friend Procopio. I have no wish to leave."

It might not be the whole truth, but judging from the relief in the diviner's eyes, it was the right answer.

"Nor would I willingly let him go, Basel, and shame to you for trying to steal him out from under me!"

The conjurer shrugged. "Ah, well. A man must have his sport. We will meet soon, I trust."

Basel's image faded from the globe. "Too soon, most likely," the diviner grumbled.

When he turned back to Matteo, he was smiling. "That was well done all around. You displayed knowledge, judgment, confidence, and, not least important, loyalty. I am well pleased," he said in a patronizing tone.

Matteo inclined his head in a bow, less out of courtesy

than to hide the flash of anger that he couldn't fully suppress. He had hoped to prove himself, but through true service and not in foolish games.

"Thank you, Lord Procopio, but I had thought that you found me unsuitably arrogant."

The wizard tossed back his head and laughed. "That's no failing as long as it is justified. Arrogance is only intolerable in the inept."

"I shall keep that in mind," Matteo said dryly.

They spoke of other things, and the skyship came to port without further incident. Matteo suspected, however, that his time of testing had just begun.

His suspicions were confirmed when he was taken to the jordaini quarters. His two escorts were not the only counselors in Procopio's employ. Matteo was the youngest of eight. That night at dinner, six attended, and all of them seemed devoted to taking Matteo's measure and ensuring that he understood his lowly status among them. It was not a pleasant meal, and Matteo was not sorry to see it come to an end.

That night the oldest of the jordaini came to his chambers. To Matteo's surprise, the jordain was a full-blooded elf and very old indeed.

The counselor thrust out a slender hand, much wrinkled but still strong enough to offer a firm grasp. "I am Zephyr. If you have any questions, ask freely." The elf smiled briefly. "Then when you are finished, I will supply answers to those questions you were too tactful to ask."

This introduction brought a smile to Matteo's face. "Procopio finds himself in need of much advice, it would appear. Eight jordaini to one wizard?"

The elf shrugged. "It is a matter of status. Procopio Septus collects counselors as some men collect horses, and I might add, he regards us in much the same light. Surely the starship flight convinced you of that."

"You heard of it?" Matteo asked, somewhat chagrined.

"From one of Lord Basel's counselors," the elf confirmed.

"Your boldness surprised and pleased both wizards, but rest assured that Procopio stood ready to magically transport his ship to safety had you failed."

The enormity of such a casting stole Matteo's breath. "If he doesn't have need of me, why am I here?"

"You have a name as a good fighter with a head for strategy. Procopio wishes to strengthen his understanding of military tactics. You can expect him to stage other games to test your wits and nerves."

That made little sense to Matteo. "Procopio is mayor of the city, but it is the king who directs the defenses."

The elf stabbed a finger at him as if to award a point. "Precisely. And Procopio intends to be king after Zalathorm."

There was something almost treasonous in that notion. Zalathorm had been king all of Matteo's life, not to mention the lives of his unknown parents and grandparents. Life under another ruler was almost as unfathomable to him as the idea of moving to a strange land.

"You must become accustomed to this notion," Zephyr said dryly. "Our task is to aid Procopio in reaching this goal."

"Our task is to serve truth," Matteo pointed out.

The elf gave him a level stare. "And I'm telling you what our particular truth is. Measure all others against that, and you will do well here."

They chatted for a few moments more, then the elf jordain tired and excused himself to rest.

For a long time, Matteo lay abed and considered what the elf had said. He had long understood that Halruaa was a society controlled by many rules and customs. For the first time, he considered the complexity of political maneuvering beneath the mannered and orderly surface.

It was hard for him to find a place for himself amid this. A jordain's stated role was to see and speak truth, cloaked perhaps in satire or other rhetorical garb, but truth untainted by either magic or personal ambition. The honor and veracity of the jordain was proverbial. Things were true or they were not. It was that simple.

But what of Andris? Was it possible that truth was a changeable thing, that the inviolate judgment of the mage-hounds, perhaps even the Disputation Table, could be bought with subtle coin?

These were disturbing thoughts, and they followed him into his dreams when at last he fell asleep.

The following days proved no better than the first. Matteo learned that although the king had no heirs, Procopio was abundantly blessed with them. The jordaini in Procopio's service were entrusted with the education of these would-be princes and princesses—nine of them, by Matteo's best count.

His charge was Penelope, a girl of about eight, with long, fat black ringlets and a permanently petulant expression. Matteo got out a finely carved game of Castles and began to instruct her in the strategy.

The tiny buildings held her interest for a few moments, but her attention soon wandered. Matteo quickly surrounded her fledgling structure with his pieces.

"You are encircled, child. Next time keep a closer eye on the board and think with each move of what might come next."

Penelope's lip thrust out, and her small hand flashed forward. Pieces of carved sandalwood and ivory scattered across the marble floor.

"You cheated," she said heatedly.

Matteo blinked, not sure how to respond to such an absurd accusation. "Not so, lady. You simply lost the game."

She folded her arms and glared at him. "I don't lose. I've never lost any game, ever."

Matteo began to understand the situation. "Why don't you play in the courtyard gardens, and we will try again after midday meal."

The child shrugged ungraciously and left the room. Matteo made his way directly to his patron's study. He told the wizard in a few words about the child's response.

"Next time let her win," the wizard decreed.

"That is dishonest, and a disservice to the child, "Matteo

protested. "Strategy games are designed to develop the reason and intellect, but learning to win and to lose with grace is a skill as important as any other."

"A lesson she will learn in time," the wizard said. "Ease her into it."

"With all respect, I cannot teach in that manner."

Procopio shrugged. "Fine. Tell Dranklish to take over the girl's tutoring. You can deliver a diplomatic message for me. That is, if your scruples don't prevent you?"

He ignored the wizard's sarcasm. "I would be honored."

For several days to come, Matteo served largely as messenger, memorizing a sentence or a speech and repeating the messages, faithful to the word and nuance and inflection. He did not see Zephyr again except at an occasional meal, and his attempts at befriending the other jordaini were soundly rebuffed.

Matteo found none of the camaraderie and good-natured teasing he had known in the school. Here, satire was in deadly earnest and usually held several sharp, hidden layers of meaning.

After a few days of this, Matteo began to feel rather despondent. When he was not on duty, he spent his time learning the city or reading alone in his bedchamber.

He was engaged in study one evening when a soft rustle drew his eye to his open window. A surge of pleasure engulfed him at the sight of the small, pointed face peering over the ledge, and his smile mirrored the grin on the young woman's face.

"Tzigone!" he exclaimed. "How did you find me? For that matter, what possessed you to travel so far?"

She hauled herself over the sill and into the room. "I take my debts very seriously. Or had you forgotten? I thought jordaini were supposed to have memories like palaces with endless rooms."

Matteo had forgotten nothing, and his wariness returned as he recalled all that had passed between them. "I remember that you advised me not to trust too easily."

She nodded in understanding. "You'll be reminded of that often enough of in a place like this. I'd rather live in a behirs' nest than a wizard lord's villa. You've had a hard time of it, I suppose."

"It is a fine position," he said stiffly.

"Hmmph," she said, unconvinced. "Where wizards are concerned, the only 'position' you're likely to find yourself in is over a barrel with your breeches about your ankles."

Matteo stifled a chuckle. "I am not supposed to hold such dim opinions of wizards."

"Nice evasion," she complimented him. She sat on the windowsill, her bare feet dangling into the room. "This place is as good as any. I suppose that after your last few days at the jordaini complex, you would be happy to go almost anywhere else."

"I'm not sure I understand."

A flicker of pity crossed the girl's face. "I followed you back to the school, as I said I would. I witnessed that so-called rite of purification."

"I was late to come," he said shortly. "But in the time allotted me, I had much to contemplate."

"Contemplate?" she echoed incredulously. "Is that what you call what I saw?"

Matteo shrugged. "Granted, it probably was not much to watch. Observing the growth of crops would be as exciting as watching jordaini in solitary contemplation. Though I do not complain. I arrived late, but the two days I spent in thought were most enlightening."

Tzigone's eyes lit with understanding. "And as far as you know, that's the extent of this rite."

"The ritual of purification is a time of solitary contemplation," Matteo said, puzzled by her reaction. "Mine was shortened, but I made what use of it I could."

For some reason she found that comment amusing. "No offense, Matteo, but that's something I'd expect one of your less fortunate comrades to say."

"I don't understand," he repeated.

"Someday you might. When that day comes, be sure to tell me if you consider my debt paid. After talking to you, I think it might be."

With that cryptic comment, she disappeared into the night, leaving Matteo staring after her in puzzlement.

CHAPTER TEN

Kiva enjoyed a few quiet days in her retreat outside of Zalasuu, but she was just as happy to see this time draw to a close. She had spent a very long time preparing for the assault upon Akhlaur, and today she expected to make more progress than she had in a decade.

The villa was well outside the walls of the city. Small but luxurious, it was surrounded by deep forests and warded by virtually impenetrable magical wards.

That morning the magehound broke her fast with tea and fruit on the piazza, a tiled courtyard encircled by gardens. An elaborate iron trellis curved over the breakfast table, providing shade and lending support for the profusion of grapevines that entwined it. Bunches of grapes, some yellow and some a soft, sunrise pink, hung in fragrant clusters overhead. The morning rain had come before dawn with a sudden bursting of clouds, and moisture still hung thick in the air. The air, despite the heavy perfume of the garden and the braziers of scented smoke that kept away the insects, was fetid with the scent of the nearby swamp—the Kilmaruu Swamp, and the origin of the paradox that Andris had been brough there to solve.

Kiva heard the soft tap of approaching footsteps and watched as the tall jordain walked onto the piazza. For many days he had lain in deep slumber. Since magic had little effect upon the jordaini, Kiva had resorted to burning in his room incense made from powerful herbs and giving him sips of strong herbal infusions. Though she had been tapering off the dosage so that he might awaken, she had given him enough over the past several days to leave him disorientated and confused.

She studied the tall young man as he approached. His auburn hair was still damp from the baths, but he had not made use of the razor that had been left for him. This was telling. The jordaini custom was for men to be meticulously clean-shaven.

She gestured him to take the seat across from her. "You look well, Andris. Your long sleep seems to have agreed with you."

"I was given no opportunity to disagree," he pointed out.

"True enough." She put down her cup and folded her hands on the table. "I must apologize for the way you were brought here. You have been chosen for an important task, as counselor to a hidden lord."

"Counselor?" The young man eyed her warily. "I am no longer jordain. No man tainted by magic can hold that office."

"And do you have this 'taint,' Andris?"

"So you say. I myself have seen no sign of it."

Kiva rose and walked over to a small table. She took something from a carved wooden box and returned to him. "This is a test given to the children of Halruaa. Light is the first and simplest of magical energies. It moves more swiftly than heat or sound or substance. Read this scroll and imitate the gesture written upon it."

The bit of parchment was the simplest of spell scrolls, suitable for children who could not yet read. On it was sketched a small curved pattern.

"Hold your hand so, fingers all together so that the tips touch your thumb, and trace this pattern in the air before you. Begin at the red dot and move toward the blue."

Andris did as he was bade. A ball of faint greenish light appeared, bobbing listlessly over the breakfast table. He dropped his hand onto the table and regarded the enchantment with bleak eyes.

"You have produced light," Kiva pointed out. "You don't look pleased."

"Should I be? There are fish and fungi that can do as much."

Kiva chuckled. "Now that you mention it. But you can also do many other things, and do them well."

"Nothing that matters. Nothing for which I am trained. I am disgraced, dead in the eyes of my brothers."

"Your death was a necessary illusion. Your new patron required it," she said softly. She settled back in her chair. "But let us speak of more pleasant things. There is in your training much that interests me. Tell me of the Kilmaruu Paradox."

A spark of interest lit the man's hazel eyes. "You know the problem as well as I. The Kilmaruu Swamp is a hive of undead. Many wizards and adventuring parties have sought to clear the swamp, but they only seem to strengthen the creatures. Each incursion into the swamp brings a retaliatory strike on the villages and farmlands beyond. On the other hand, if nothing is done to contain the undead, they slip into the harbor and scuttle the ships."

"And how would you solve this problem?"

Andris leaned forward. "In Zalasuu, there is a proverb: 'The swamp helps keep the number of fools in town low.' That is truth, but invert the statement and another truth is revealed. Increase the number of fools in the town, and we could keep the number of undead in the swamp low. Do you know the etymology for the word 'jordain'?"

"All too well," she said dryly. "In Old Netherese, the language from which Halruaan descended, it was the word for 'fool.' At that time the word had a meaning more elevated than it now enjoys. A fool was a counselor to kings and wizards, a bard of sorts who entertained and advised through satirical songs. I suppose this charming little history has a point?"

"In time. Permit me to explain one step at a time," Andris said, his animation increasing with each word. "What element is common to all who enter the swamp to explore and conquer? What weapons do they employ?"

"Magic, of course."

"And magic feeds the undead. The creatures seem to require it. Why else would they venture into the harbors to attack ships? I have made a study of the cargo lost to these attacks. Without exception, the ships carried a goodly number of spellcasters and magical items."

Kiva nodded thoughtfully. "I had not thought to seek a pattern there, but your reasoning seems sound to me."

"For reasons I do not completely understand, the undead in the swamp need magic to survive. The adventuring wizards and warriors and clerics armed with their magical weapons and holy artifacts feed the undead, like so many tavern wenches delivering hot trenchers of stew."

Kiva suppressed a smile at the analogy and noted at the faint disdain in the young man's voice. In time, he would come to regret both. "And your solution?"

"There are many in this land who possess no magical talent whatsoever. The jordaini are chief among them, but there are others. Gather them together and go against the undead denizens of Kilmaruu without magic."

The words hung in the air like a challenge, like a curse or foul blasphemy. Both the elf and the man understood that this strategy flew in the face of every instinct and tradition of the land.

"And who would command this army of jordaini?"

"I would have done so gladly, were I still jordain." Andris glared at the fading magical light.

The magehound dispelled the globe with a flick of her coppery fingers and then picked up the scroll. She smoothed it and put it on the table before him.

"Cast the spell again, jordain."

Andris set his jaw and formed the gesture as before. This time no light came to his call. He lifted a puzzled stare to Kiva's face.

In response, she reached into the folds of her gown and retrieved the jeweled wand that had damned Andris. She touched it to the grape arbor that curved over the breakfast table. A high, ghostly note vibrated through the iron trellis.

Understanding, pained and incredulous and furious all at once, dawned in the jordain's eyes. Kiva nodded acknowledgment of his insight.

"Yes. The result would be much the same if I were to touch this wand to a stone, a toad, or a pile of goosedown. It finds magic in everything, whether there is any to find or not."

"My brothers think me dead," Andris said, speaking first of that which troubled him most.

"Would it comfort you to know that you will see and work with many of them again? That in doing so, you will be doing what you trained for? You and your jordaini brothers will attend powerful wizards, using both your talents and your resistance to magic for the good of the land."

Andris regarded her thoughtfully. "You make a powerful point. But why the deceit?"

"It was a necessary thing. Truth might be meat and drink to the jordaini, but most men order their lives by other impulses. There is great status in having jordaini servants, and the wizards clamor over you like hounds snarling over bones. A man of your talents was needed for this great task. Other opportunities would soon be offered to you. We could not entrust the outcome to fate."

"You could have told me of your plans outright. A jordain is free to choose among employments offered him."

Kiva smiled and laid her slender hand on his arm. "Forgive me, Andris, but I did not know your true measure. Status is all-important in this land. I have on good authority that both Procopio Septus of Halarahh and Lord Grozalum of Khaerbaal intended to petition for your service. The admiral of Halruaa's navy reports to Grozalum. If Procopio has his way, he will be king after Zalathorm. Most ambitious jordaini would be sorely tempted by offers from such patrons. I feared that you might find such an uncertain undertaking less attractive if you knew what glories were available for the taking."

Andris scratched at the unfamiliar stubble on his chin. "But I am jordain. I serve the truth and the land."

"And what of yourself, Andris?" she said softly. "What do you want for yourself?"

The question seemed to puzzle the young man. Kiva tried again. "How content are you with the life that lies before you? You will advise, wizards will command, and others will do. Is that what you want? Correct me if I have read you falsely, but I think you were born to command."

Andris was silent for a long moment. "It is not the tradition of this land."

"Nor is it tradition to mount a campaign without magic. Yet you have devised just such a campaign, and you long to command it. Is this not truth?"

There was mockery in her voice, but the young jordain's face remained thoughtful. "Who commissioned my services?"

"I cannot say. This land is ruled by wizards, but none have been able to contain the undead monsters of Kilmaruu. Let's just say that it would be . . . awkward if someone so highly placed were to seek a nonmagical solution to this problem."

Andris's face suffused with wonder as the alchemy of hope transformed her lie into his greatest hidden dreams. Every wizard, every fighter in the land aspired to serving the great Zalathorm. This, then, was what Kiva seemed to offer. His own command, at the king's bequest!

The young jordain rose and fell to one knee before her. "Since you speak for the wizard who commissioned my service, you are my patron. Tell me what you desire me to accomplish, and I will find a way to do so," he said earnestly.

The elf woman patted his arm. "You have made a fine start, Andris. Far better than you know."

☉

The next day Mbatu stood at the edge of the camp, watching as Kiva's recruits trained. Though he could find no fault in the warriors' efforts, neither did he take any pleasure in watching them.

Yesterday he had been the battlemaster; today all that remained for him to do was watch as the tall, red-haired man put the fighters through their paces.

To his amazement, the men were no longer Kiva's captives and mercenaries, but an army. The wemic didn't know what Kiva had told the young jordain, but something had set him aflame. His passion had spread like wildfire to every man in his command.

The men were armed with rattan swords, so they could get used to the unfamiliar weight and length of them before using steel. Andris chose five men and bade them to swarm him. They charged in, whistling their practice blades through the air.

Mbatu chuckled, expecting the tall man to be facedown in muck before he could lift his sword.

He should have remembered his own encounter with a jordain. Within moments, all five of the fighters had been sent reeling back to nurse their bruises.

"Iago," Andris called, pointing to a slim, dark blade of a man. "You play the role of the out-numbered fighter."

"An honor," the man said dryly. "It will be excellent practice for playing the role of the corpse."

Andris joined in the laughter this comment elicited, then his face turned serious. "Remember that we will not be fighting honorable duels. We need to work together if any of us are to survive. Imagine that Iago is surrounded by undead. I'll show you how to work the perimeter and finish off the attackers as he pushes them back. You three—you can be the first wave of undead."

The men lifted their swords and rushed in for the attack. Andris fell back, so that for a moment, Iago was standing alone. The smaller man parried the first thrusting attack.

Before the rattan swords could disengage, Andris stepped in and seized the attacker's hair. He drew his sword lightly across the man's throat and then spun toward the second attacker, fist clenched as if it were still gripping a handful of hair. He swung hard into the second man's gut, doubling him over.

"Freeze," he commanded.

The men stood as they were, though the man he'd just hit wobbled as he struggled to stand in his bent-over position.

"Let's say that I beheaded the first zombie and used the head to shield-smash the one coming up behind. What now? Iago?"

The slim jordain nodded toward his "headless" companion. "This creature cannot see. He will flail around for a time before falling. I need to move beyond reach of his blade."

"You can do better. Turn it toward the other monsters," Andris suggested. "Like so."

He whirled and used the flat of his sword to strike the man who was bent over and off-balance. The man stumbled into the "headless zombie," who obligingly turned and started swinging at this new attacker.

Iago skirted the pair and lunged at the third man, who parried and riposted high. Iago caught the blow with his sword and then planted a foot on the man's chest, pushing him away—and directly onto the point of Andris's waiting sword. At the last moment, Andris sidestepped so that the man splashed down into the water. He rose dripping but smiling in relief. Rattan swords did not draw blood, but all of the men were covered with livid bruises.

"You see?" Andris said. "Working together, small bands of men can fight large numbers. Let's try it again, this time with four attackers."

It was a precise sequence, a deadly dance with finely timed moves. Again and again Andris walked them through it, showing how to fight against four, against six, how to vary the defenses and attacks against humans, against wights and ghouls.

The wemic was both impressed and troubled by this display. He had always been Kiva's strong right hand. She had purchased him when he was a cub, a child too young to remember the ways of the pride. The elf woman was his only family. What she said, he did. His strength was prodigious, and he had never known fear. Few men or elves could best him at arms. What he knew, he did very well.

Mbatu was beginning to realize, however, how limited his knowledge was. Oh, he could fight. In honest melee, few could match him, much less overcome him. Yet in less than a moon's time he had been outmaneuvered by one jordain and replaced by another.

The wemic watched as the men sloshed through the shallow, fetid water and drove stakes into the muck. To these they fastened several straw figures. Andris moved the men into position, encircling the straw zombies like a pack of wolves and closing in. At his mark, each man tossed a handful of coarse, sandy substance into the water. The swamp began to roil and sizzle. Foul gas rose from it, writhing like sickly green ghosts. One of the fighters tossed a torch into the vapor. There was a sudden sharp sucking sound, and then the swamp was aflame.

The fire died almost as suddenly as it had erupted. The only trace of the straw men was the charred sticks that had supported them. The zombies and ghouls wouldn't leave even that much of a legacy.

Kiva came up behind him, her nose wrinkled in disgust over the scent. "How goes it?"

"The jordain knows his undead," the wemic admitted. "If the men fight as he tells them to do, they will win."

"I am glad to hear it. It will be good practice," she agreed.

Mbatu studied her, his leonine face troubled.

"Practice?"

"For Akhlaur," Kiva said calmly. "The men will learn to fight in a swamp, to deal with the undead."

"But what of the laraken?" demanded Mbatu. "What will prepare them for such a monster?"

"What could?" she retorted. "I daresay the fiend will be as much a surprise to them as it was to us. Fortunately, we are better prepared now."

"We?" the wemic repeated suspiciously. "But you will not be there."

"Actually, dear Mbatu, I rather think that I must."

A low, angry growl came from the wemic. "You cannot," he said fiercely. "The laraken feeds upon magical energy. How many wizards have you sent into the swamp? Few of those wizards survived. Those who did were utterly stripped of their magic and more empty of mind than if an enfeeblement spell had been cast upon them. What will happen to you if we go into that place?"

The magehound traced his set jaw with her coppery fingertips. "Don't fear for me, dear Mbatu. I have learned quite a few of the swamp's secrets. Have I never told you how the wizard Akhlaur was defeated? No? He was dragged into the elemental plane of water by the very creature he summoned to help create the laraken."

"Yes. So?"

"So a tiny gate remains. Water leaks through, and with it the powerful magic of the elemental plane. It is this leak, this magic, that sustains the laraken and keeps it dependent upon the swamp." She smiled slyly. "If I could close this gate, the laraken would be forced to seek sustenance elsewhere."

The wemic's tailed lashed with anger and frustration. "But how? We could take a hundred jordaini into the swamp, and the laraken would still be drawn to you!"

The magehound's face hardened. "Why do you think we have been chasing Keturah's daughter?" she demanded. "If she's truly her mother's daughter, she will be able to call the laraken."

"What of the mother?"

"I have other uses for Keturah," Kiva said in a voice that forbade discussion. "It is Tzigone we need."

The magehound fell silent, and her face became contemplative. "It may well be that Tzigone had not yet relieved herself of her so-called honor debt to Matteo. If Matteo were to come to grief, she might feel obligated to intervene.

"Yes," she said with greater certainty, "it is time to add some complications to the young jordain's life."

"And if that does not serve?"

The magehound gave her servant a small, cool smile. "Then at the very least, you will get your revenge upon him."

CHAPTER ELEVEN

In the days to come, Matteo was to spend many hours with Procopio Septus. He attended the wizard daily at the Ilysium, a vast pink marble building that housed the offices of city officials. When Procopio's duties as lord mayor were discharged, they usually took to the sky. This was Matteo's favorite time of day, and he was rapidly becoming adept at piloting a skyship. The evenings were a round of lavish public affairs: banquets, festivals, concerts. Since Matteo was only one of several jordaini in Procopio's service, he was not required to attend every event. He and his fellow counselors met each day at sunrise to compare notes and devise strategies that would best serve their patron.

Matteo hoped that these meetings would foster the sense of camaraderie he knew back at House Jordain—after all, some of these men had been students at the Jordaini College when he was a young lad. But it seemed to him that his colleagues were far too absorbed with jostling for position. Matteo was keenly aware of his newcomer status, and he never seemed able to move past it. Every morning he began the day in a circle of white-clad men who eyed him with open resentment.

Slowly he began to understand why this was so. He spent more time at Procopio's side than any jordain other than Zephyr, the wizard's high counselor. It didn't help matters when the old elf took upon himself the role of Matteo's mentor. Each morning after the jordaini meeting, Zephyr and Matteo spent an hour walking in the villa gardens and discussing the politics of the day.

As Zephyr had predicted, Procopio arranged several more tests of Matteo's skills and knowledge. The young jordain passed them all with ease. Riding an unbroken horse was little challenge after his experiences with Cyric. When a wizard "assassin" magically burst into Procopio's dining chamber, Matteo took a page from Tzigone's book and coolly deflected the sun arrows with the mirrorlike finish of a bronze plate. Procopio had howled with laughter at the sight of his hired wizard rolling on the floor in agony, and he'd sent Dranklish, the jordain who before Matteo's arrival had been second in rank to Zephyr, like an errand boy to fetch a cleric of Mystra to heal the unfortunate man. It was that event that cemented Matteo's position in the household, for it became clear to everyone that the new jordain was being groomed as Zephyr's successor. The tests ended, and so did Matteo's hope of finding friends among the household's jordaini.

His days were busy, but from time to time an image edged into his thoughts: a small, pointed face with big brown eyes and an irreverent grin. He didn't expect to see Tzigone again. Her last words to him indicated that she believed she had discharged her mysterious debt. Matteo didn't understand what exactly she thought she had done, and he wished, more than once, that he could have the opportunity to ask her.

But the days quickly settled into an orderly pattern, one suited to the life of a jordain and not disrupted by the "assistance" of roguish street waifs. Each day after the skyship flight, Matteo and Procopio would retire to the wizard's study. The wizard had a passion for games of strategy, and Matteo obliged him with seemingly endless games of chess, castles, and complex card games.

One morning he answered an unexpected summons to Procopio's study to find that the wizard had acquired a new diversion. An enormous table took up half the study, displacing the large cages of birds that Procopio kept in nearly every room of the villa.

The wizard glanced up when Matteo entered, and his face lit up in an unexpectedly boyish grin. "I ordered this a year and three moons before your arrival. I'll be a necromancer's apprentice if it wasn't worth the wait! Come see."

Matteo approached his patron's side and studied the vast table. It was no ordinary piece of furniture but a wondrous recreation of a wild land: a section of high plateau surrounded by hills and mountains.

"The Nath?" guessed Matteo, naming the wild region in the northeastern corner of Halruaa.

Procopio beamed. "Well done. Wait—you've not seen the best of it."

The wizard gestured with a long, slender wand. Several drawers hidden along the edges of the table opened, and tiny, magically animated figures poured out onto the table. Halruaan soldiers marched in formation across the wild terrain toward a mountain pass. A wizard, seated cross-legged on a flying carpet, whizzed out of the drawer and began to circle over the troops. A small horde of mounted warriors burst from the foothills and charged the Halruaan forces, and the faint pounding of their hooves reminded Matteo of the sound of distant rain. They pulled up at the far end of the mountain pass and faced the Halruaans.

All of the miniature troops were marvelous, but it was these mounted figures that drew Matteo's eye. They were rendered in shades of gray. All the horses were dappled grays, and the warriors were elflike females with dusky skin and dull silvery hair.

"Shadow amazons," Matteo marveled. For as long as he could remember, he had been fascinated by the Crinti, and he longed to pick up one of the tiny figures and examine its artistry and detail.

Some of this must have shown on his face, for Procopio chuckled. "Go ahead," he urged. "They're not alive, so you needn't be afraid to handle them."

"It is not that. The jordaini are forbidden to own, use, or even knowingly handle any magical item."

The diviner frowned. "How can you possibly refrain from doing so when you are in a wizard's service? I require you to engage me in a game of military strategy. Must I refrain from magic to accommodate you? Who is the master here, and who the servant?"

This was a reasonable question, and suddenly Matteo wasn't entirely satisfied with the traditional answer. He gave it anyway.

"Jordaini are forbidden by law and tradition from handling magic or benefiting from it. This ultimately safeguards the wizards we serve."

"What of the skyships?" Procopio said slyly. "Does this mean you intend to forego your daily flight?"

Matteo blinked, startled by this logical but unexpected application of the rule. "I never thought of skyships in that light," he said slowly. "They are so integral to Halruaan culture that the jordaini have ceased to think of them as common magical artifacts. I suppose by strict application of law, skyships are also forbidden."

"Yet no one would censor you for flying with your patron. Nor will anyone gasp with shock if they learned you were commanding toy troops," Procopio said, sweeping a hand toward the tiny figures on the table.

Matteo considered this. "Would it be possible for you to remove the enchantment? We could move the figures about by hand."

"Certainly not!" the wizard protested. "I will not suffer such a barbarian inconvenience. If I go down this path, where will it end? Would you expect me to refrain from using magic in battle for fear of offending your sensibilities?"

"Of course not. But this is a game, not a battle."

"A game I require you to play," Procopio said forcefully.

"There are exceptions to every rule, and the sooner you learn this, the greater your service to me. But calm your scruples. You need not fear the taint of magic today. You are here to advise, not to do. I will move the troops."

Matteo nodded slowly. As Procopio said, it was impossible for a jordain in a wizard's household to remain entirely beyond the touch of magic. Every jordain he knew coveted the chance to ride a skyship, and no one thought this unseemly.

He studied the placement of the tiny figures. "This looks very much like the skirmishes that preceded the battle of Mycontil's Stand," he said, referring to the archmage who died defeating a massive invasion of Crinti-led warriors.

"That depicts Mycontil himself," Procopio agreed, pointing to the figure that buzzed about like a particularly colorful fly. "He was a great wizard, but no strategist. At this battle, he lost over a hundred men because the Crinti outflanked him. Like so."

The wizard touched his wand to the foothills on either side of the warriors. Bands of shadow amazons materialized in response to his summons and began to box in the foot soldiers.

Procopio looked to Matteo. "If you were Mycontil, what would you do to minimize your losses?"

Matteo thought for a moment. "Create an illusion of sound that echoes throughout the area held by the two flanking bands, a sound that will frighten the Crinti and cause them to scatter into the hills. Then the soldiers can engage the central band."

"And what, pray tell, could frighten the Crinti?" Procopio said in scathing tones. "They lull their girl children to sleep with battle songs that would raise a pirate's gorge!"

"Have you never heard the songs of the Unseelie folk? I have, and found it an uncanny, unnerving experience. But to the Crinti, the Unseelie music holds the essence of terror," Matteo explained. "It is part of the legend of the Ilythiiri. Do you know it?"

"I know little of the Ilythiiri, other than they were dark elves who inhabited the southern lands in ancient times. They were the ancestors of the drow, who were in turn the ancestors of the Crinti. What of it?"

"Legend has it that once, many thousands of years ago, an Ilythiiri wizard stumbled through the veil that separates the world we see from the unseen world of the Unseelie Court. There she learned some of the magic of the dark fairies, most of it by unfortunate firsthand experience. After much torment, she escaped, now utterly insane but carrying a knowledge of fell magic that surpassed any wizard in the land. She began a rise to power that attracted the darkest hearts of her time to her court. Her name is lost to memory, and she is known only as the Spider Queen. It is said that the evil goddess of the drow, Lolth, assimilated the wizard into her own being, taking for herself both the wizard's name and her dark magic. It is said that something of the wizard's memory remains within the goddess, and as a result, the drow, even Lolth herself, fear the Unseelie folk. What, then, could be more frightening to the Crinti than the songs of the dark fairies?"

Procopio nodded slowly as he took this in. "Interesting notion. I had not heard that tale."

"Few men make a study of drow legends. There are perhaps three libraries on the surface of this world that contain reliable lore books. Halruaa, of course, has one of them."

"You think the Crinti are better informed than we in such matters?"

"They cherish their drow heritage. They would pass it on."

"Hmm." Procopio considered this, then shrugged. "Very well. Let's see what happens."

The wizard moved the wand in a slow, complex pattern over the table. A faint melody, dark and compelling and chilling, began to rise like mist from the hillside.

The tiny shadow amazons that came in from the flank positions halted their charge. Chaos swept over them like an evil wind. The horses reared and pitched. Some of them, riderless, milled frantically about. In moments the warriors and their horses were gone, melting off into the hills and leaving exposed the central band of Crinti, who were panicked into utter disarray, too far from the hills for retreat. The Halruaan soldiers charged and easily overtook the advance band. In short order, the table was littered with the tiny gray corpses of the shadow amazons.

Procopio smiled and nodded. He made a quick gesture with one hand, and the figures, both victors and vanquished, disappeared from the table.

"Who would have thought a song—no, a mere illusion of a song!—would have such power against those she-demons? Fascinating how so simple a ploy could turn the tide of battle! Have you more Crinti secrets to teach me?" Procopio spoke eagerly, and his animated face betrayed a more than casual interest.

A suspicion that had been growing in Matteo's mind for some time began to take solid and disturbing form. "A few," he said slowly. "I begin to see why you bid for my services. You are most avidly fond of strategy games, and as a master of games, I was first in my form."

"There is that," the wizard said in neutral tones.

Matteo pressed on. "We jordaini believe that such games train the mind and character, for a truly responsible man understands that every action prompts a reaction."

There was an edge to Procopio's smile that acknowledged the subtle layers in Matteo's comment. "I am in training, that is certainly true. He who would command must understand the art of war. It is no secret that games provide preparation. Kittens stalk imaginary prey, and small boys whack each other with sticks in anticipation of their first swords. What we do here is not so different."

Matteo shifted uneasily. "You speak plainly. I will do the same. Action prompts reaction. I know enough of history to understand that men who prepare so assiduously for battle seldom fail to find one."

"But the land is at peace, and has been for many years. Do you think that would be true if no one was prepared for battle? Why do you think our enemies stay away? The Crinti elf-breeds and their Dambraii subjects, and the Mhair savages, and the barbarians of the Shaar desert, and the wizards of Thay and Unther and Mulhorand, and Mystra only knows where else? Because we remain strong," Procopio concluded in a tone that rang with certainty.

Matteo had heard this argument many times before. It was a difficult one, for the line between a strong defense and a strong nation inclined toward offensive action was thin and nebulous. He couldn't help but wonder how this passion for military strategy fit into Procopio's personal goals. If the wizard deemed that the best way to ascend Zalathorm's throne was as a war hero, how far might he go to ensure his goal?

The wizard seemed to sense his counselor's unease, for he broke off the session and strode over to his desk. He opened a drawer and took from it a small scroll.

"I would have you take a message for me to Xavierlyn. You know of her?"

Matteo nodded. Zephyr had described in great detail all the wizards of the city's Council of Elders. Xavierlyn was a powerful diviner, a distant relative of King Zalathorm, and touted by many as his probable successor. As such, she was Procopio's most obvious rival.

"I have met Frando, her jordain counselor. It is his habit to speak in the Arbor Square before the sunsleep hours."

"No doubt many come to listen in preparation for midday slumber," Procopio said dryly. "I have heard the man. His lectures induce slumber more effectively than charms and potions."

Matteo's lips twitched, but he refrained from agreeing with his patron's assessment of a fellow jordain. He took the scroll Procopio handed him and scanned the writing upon it, then handed back the scroll and repeated the message word for word. The wizard nodded, satisfied, and Matteo went his way.

He set a brisk pace and reached Arbor Square shortly before highsun. It was a pretty place, cobbled with pink and green stone and surrounded by elaborate iron trellises and arches. The air was rich with the scent of ripening grapes, as well as the savory odors that wafted from the nearby market. Chairs and small tables had been scattered about so that passersby could take advantage of the shade.

In the center of the square was a raised platform, which was variously used for town criers, street musicians, and wizardly exhibitions. Frando, a dark, thick-bodied man some fifteen years Matteo's senior, was currently holding forth on the topic of pirate raids. With an alchemist's skill and a pompous voice, Frando transformed that exciting topic into a sleep-inducing drone. Matteo settled down under an arbor of pink grapes and tried to look politely interested.

Finally the jordain concluded his lecture and acknowledged the patter of applause with a deep bow. His self-satisfied smile broadened when his gaze fell on Matteo. Matteo rose and came to greet his colleague.

"Well, if it isn't the newest gelding in Procopio's stables," Frando said in a faintly nasty tone. "Come to listen and learn, I suppose?"

Matteo's brows lifted. For once it seemed appropriate to forego the usual polite phrases of greeting. "My patron has sent me with a message for the wizard Xavierlyn," he said curtly. "He bids me give it into your keeping."

It was a common enough task, but to his surprise, Frando hissed with exasperation. "It is clear that you don't mind playing the part of an errand boy, but I occupy my time with more important tasks. Why couldn't Procopio simply send a scroll? Or if he is as powerful a diviner as he claims to be, why not use magic?"

Matteo blinked, startled by this response. "Scrolls can be stolen, scried, or magically altered. Messengers can be waylaid, bribed, threatened, or magically influenced, or information taken from their minds. Even magically sent messages can be intercepted. There is also the possibility that a magically gifted messenger could influence the hearer, much as the minor magic of a bard lures an audience into receptivity," he explained patiently. "Any first-form jordain knows this."

Too late, Matteo realized how his words could be taken. Frando's face darkened with anger, yet he could not dispute Matteo's assessment.

"Give me the message," he said shortly.

To Matteo's surprise, the jordain did not receive the message on first hearing. Frando repeated it back with several alterations and two outright errors. Matteo patiently repeated Procopio's detailed report, once and then again, insisting that the man repeat it back precisely.

"Enough," the jordain finally said, his face crimson. "You change the words to mock me."

Matteo quickly swallowed the surge of rage that accusation brought. "I am charged with bringing a message to your patron, untainted by error or magical persuasion. Perhaps I had better repeat it to her myself." He turned away, intent upon doing just that.

Frando caught Matteo's arm and spun him around. "You would offer such insult?" he said incredulously.

"Less insult than you offered me," Matteo retorted as he jerked free of the big man's grasp. "You all but called me a liar."

"And so you are."

Impulse overtook training. Matteo's fist flashed out and connected squarely with Frando's jaw. The man staggered back and tripped over a chair. He went down heavily and came up with his hands on the hilts of his daggers.

This put Matteo in a serious quandary. It was against the law for one jordain to draw a weapon on another. If he defended himself, he and Frando would be judged equally at fault, for Matteo had struck the first blow. Yet judging from the fury in the other man's eyes, Frando intended to attack whether Matteo drew weapons or not.

Before he could respond, a small woman dressed in an eye-searing combination of scarlet, orange, and yellow breezed between him and Frando. Matteo's heart jolted with a mixture of pleasure and apprehension when he recognized Tzigone. She was clad as a street performer, wearing brilliant yellow pantaloons, an orange shirt, and a red vest encrusted with shiny bits of glass cut and polished to look like gems. Around her head was a turban fashioned of multicolored scarves. Her face was scrubbed clean and painted so that her eyes look huge and exotic. Even her fingernails were tinted in gaudy citrus shades. To his surprise, Matteo realized that this display was actually an effective disguise. Few would see past the color and the costume to take note of the small woman's features.

She hopped up onto the dais and clapped her hands. "Gather round," she called in a clear, ringing alto. She gestured for the crowd to fill in the space between Matteo and Frando, quite effectively cutting off the angry jordain's attack.

"Watch carefully and see if you can detect the skill in what I am about to do. For it is skill alone, not so much as a drop of magic!"

She called up a child, and with much flourish, she pulled a skie from behind his ear.

"A simple conjurer's trick!" scoffed someone from the audience.

Tzigone dropped her arms to her side and turned, staring incredulously at the heckler. Matteo followed the line of her gaze. The man who'd spoken was young and obviously wealthy, for he was clad in violet silk and decked with far too much gold and amethyst jewelry. There were many like him in Halruaa's cities: sons and daughters of successful merchants who had time and means to while away their hours in the shops and festhalls.

She took hold of the hems of her gaudy vest and spread

it open. "If I could conjure as many coins as I'd like, would I spend them on such elegant, subtle garments? And judging from your raiment," she added dryly, "I doubt you're of the conjurer's school either."

A ripple of laughter went through the crowd, and the fop shrugged self-consciously. Tzigone pointed at a street merchant, a plump woman with a half-full basket of oranges balanced on one generous hip. The fruit was past ripe; the sticky scent of it was strong in the air, and a few bees buzzed and circled over the basket.

"Toss me a few of those fruit, if you please."

The woman reached into her basket and took out three oranges. Tzigone deftly caught them and started tossing and catching them. With a challenging smile, the merchant threw another orange, and then several more in rapid succession. Tzigone caught them all and added them to the dancing pattern, which she constantly shifted and varied. The oranges circled and darted, crossing and leaping and changing direction in her deft hands. The crowd's murmurs of approval deepened and turned into applause.

"Illusion!" hollered a skinny youth.

Without breaking pace, Tzigone caught an orange and hurled it at her detractor. The ripe fruit splattered on his chest and splashed sticky juice into his face and hair.

"No need to wash that tunic," she told him sweetly, juggling still. "The juice is just an illusion. And so are the bees that it will likely draw."

At that moment the youth let out a howl and slapped at his neck. The orange merchant convulsed with laughter, doubling over and nearly spilling the contents of her basket.

When the crowd's mirth had died, Tzigone tossed the oranges one by one back into the merchant's bin. She then struck a haughty pose, an eerily precise imitation of Frando's stance and expression. Matteo raised a hand to his lips to suppress a smile.

"Consider the problem of pirates," she droned in obvious mockery of Frando's lecture. As she spoke, her head rolled back and her jaw fell slack into an audible snore. She pantomimed a startled awakening at the crowd's laughter, and then shook herself as if to banish the last vestiges of sleep.

"The problem with pirates," she said in a far more animated tone, "is that they occasionally come ashore. Then they become your problem and mine. I bid you good folk to hear this cautionary tale, and leave this place the wiser for it.

"A lady jordain was sent to carry a message for her patron. With her was another counselor in need of training, who for our purposes need not be named." Again she puckered her face into an approximation of Frando's prissy expression, and the crowd chuckled and looked about for the jordain.

"As night began to fall, their path took them through streets that wiser men avoid. Before long, a large, ill-favored man in a pirate's rough garb began to follow the two jordaini." Tzigone's brow beetled, and she took a couple of steps forward in deftly feigned menace.

"The lady's companion glanced behind them and took note of the danger. 'We are being followed,' he said nervously. 'What could that big fellow want?' "

The tone of Tzigone's voice was eerily like Frando's, and several people in the crowd chuckled and glanced at the crimson-faced man. Tzigone waited for silence and then continued her tale.

"The jordain woman shrugged. 'The usual, I suppose. He wishes to rob you and ravage me.' "

This was an unexpected turn, and the crowd began to shift and exchange uncertain glances. Bawdy stories were not unknown in taverns, but never were they told in this respectable forum. Tzigone's mimicry might be clever, but her words were unseemly and far beyond the bounds of polite convention.

Tzigone seemed not to notice her audience's distress. "The woman's companion wrung his hands and asked what they should do. 'Why, the only logical thing,' said the woman. 'We walk faster.'

"They quickened their pace, but their pursuer easily matched them. 'He is gaining!' wailed the jordain.

" 'Indeed,' the woman said calmly. 'By my ciphering, the pirate should be upon us before that cloud passes over the moon.'

" 'What should we do?' her companion all but wept.

" 'The only logical thing. You run one way, and I will run another. It is well known that jordaini carry little and own no valuable items. If the pirate must choose between robbery and ravishment under those circumstances, which would be the logical choice?'

"This reasoning lifted the man's spirits considerably. Without hesitation, he turned tail and scurried back toward the safety of their patron's house."

Tzigone paused again for the slightly mocking laughter directed toward Frando.

"Much later, the lady jordain arrived at the patron's house. By now Fran—that is, her companion—was nearly giddy with worry. He pounced upon her and demanded full details.

"The lady regarded him with puzzlement. 'What happened?' she repeated. 'Why, the only logical thing that could have happened. The pirate gave chase and overtook me before the shadow of the cloud cleared the moon.'

"The other jordain swallowed hard. 'What happened then, my lady?'

" 'I did the only logical thing,' she told him in a matter-of-fact tone. 'I pulled up my skirts.' "

Several people in the crowd gasped. Tzigone nodded. "Yes. The jordain responded in much the same way when he heard this. He demanded to know what happened next. 'Why, the only logical thing,' said the lady. 'The man pulled down his leggings.'

" 'And what happened next? Tell me everything!' " Tzigone spoke the words with breathless eagerness, leering as a salacious jordain might have done. Matteo noted that her expression was identical to that on Frando's face.

Before he could catch himself, he laughed aloud. Tzigone caught his eye and winked.

"The lady Jordain looked her companion in the eye. 'The only logical thing happened. A lady with her skirts up can run much faster than a man with his breeches down.'"

The unexpected ending brought a round of laughter and then applause. Frando, however, was tight-lipped with rage. He shouldered his way through the crowd with as much dignity as he could muster. As he passed Matteo, he leaned in close.

"We will finish this another time. I am certain that my patron will support my wish to challenge you to a public debate."

Zephyr's warnings flooded into Matteo's mind, and he understood the smug gleam in the other jordain's eyes. Frando's patron, Xavierlyn, was the Chief Elder of the city of Halarahh. She was one of the few wizards that Procopio Septus held in esteem, and the last person he would wish to challenge. Yet a debate between jordaini was the equivalent of a wizard's duel between their patrons—indeed, they were sometimes considered to be duels by proxy. Matteo watched as Frando sauntered off, no doubt dreaming of his coming vengeance.

Tzigone hopped off the dais and breezed through the crowd to his side. "No need to thank me," she said cheerfully.

"On that we are in accord," Matteo said, throwing up his hands in exasperation. "Have you any idea what you've done?"

She frowned. "Distracted a challenger? Stopped a fight? Made a few coins?" She jingled her bag. "Come on. I'll buy ale and sweet bread for us both."

Matteo took her arm and drew her to the far side of the market square. They stopped in the vine-covered shadows of a thick, high wall.

"Frando was not my friend. Now he is my enemy," he said tersely. "He challenged me to public debate to avenge the insult you dealt him. Win or lose, this will utterly destroy the hopes of my patron. Procopio Septus will not thank me for this day's work. My position with the lord mayor is as good as ended."

Tzigone took this in. She considered it for a moment, then shrugged. "That's easy enough to resolve. Find a new patron." She snapped her fingers. "I know just how to go about it. That ought to settle things between us for once and all!"

"Thank you for the kind thought, but, please, no more 'help,'" Matteo said earnestly.

Tzigone wasn't listening. She busily scanned the market. Her eyes lit up suddenly and a smile curved her lips. "Wait here," she said happily and dropped to the ground. She wriggled through the thick, flowering vines and disappeared from sight.

Like the crowd, Matteo was suddenly suspicious of magic surreptitiously used. He bent down and parted the bushes, but there was no sign of Tzigone or her escape route. He searched for quite some time before he found an explanation. Behind the vine, the stone wall had crumbled, leaving a hole big enough for a child or very small woman to crawl through.

"You have lost something, other than your judgment and your dignity?"

The rounded alto tones struck a chord in Matteo's memory. He scrambled to his feet. There stood a tall, regal woman clad in a simple, elegant white gown that left her arms bare and draped low over her bosom. Her glossy black hair had been elaborately dressed and coiled about her shapely head, but her only ornament was the enameled pendant that proclaimed her position. Her long, narrow face would never be considered conventionally beautiful, but the intelligence in her dark eyes made it extraordinary.

"Lady Cassia." Matteo inclined his head in a respectful bow, giving honor to the most powerful jordain in all of Halruaa. "How might I serve you?"

The words were polite, but they brought a small, hard smile to the jordain's lips. "Badly, no doubt. Who is your patron?"

Matteo told her. Her ebony brows lifted in surprise. "And does Lord Procopio know that you consort with base entertainers? That you enjoy listening to the mockery of your fellow jordaini? Is this typical of your service?"

"I would like to think it is not, my lady."

"To the contrary, I would like to think that it is," she said slyly. "It is reported that Queen Beatrix is in need of counsel. If you were to serve her, most likely you would also serve me, provided you could survive long enough. Clockwork devices are so unreliable, and Beatrix is so fond of them. Such a pity, what happened to her last counselor. They intend to bury him with full honors just as soon as they gather up enough pieces."

The smile she gave Matteo was as cold and reptilian as a crocodile's. "Prepare yourself for a promotion, boy. And while you're at it, you might want to put your affairs in order."

CHAPTER TWELVE

Matteo watched as Cassia swept through the market, as queenly and formidable as any woman who'd ever worn a crown. The short encounter left him stunned, and for the first time in his life, he felt himself at an utter loss for words.

"You're gaping like a hooked fish," intoned a rich alto voice at his elbow.

The voice was Cassia's. Matteo jumped, startled by the seeming split of sight and sound. In the next heartbeat, he realized who the speaker had to be, and he whirled to face the troublesome Tzigone. To his surprise, the young woman wore an expression of extreme self-satisfaction.

"That was easy," she said brightly. "All I had to do was mention in Cassia's hearing that you and that Frando person were planning a public debate, and she came right over. Did anything interesting come of it?"

"You might say that," he said shortly.

Tzigone frowned and handed him a small burlap sack. "You can carry this for me. That will help restore your image as a polite and proper jordain."

Matteo absently took the sack and slung it over his shoulder. "You have no idea what you've done, do you?"

"Of course. I got Cassia's attention for you. Again, there's no need to thank me."

Matteo cast his eyes toward the sky. "Again, I concur wholeheartedly."

She gave him a suspicious look. "You don't sound pleased. I must say, you're a hard man to repay. But I know just the thing—something not even you could fault or refuse."

She took off through the crowd, weaving through the throng of shoppers and buskers as she moved confidently toward her destination. Matteo followed, fearful of the trouble her next well-meaning act might cause.

They wound through the market to a small side street lined with stalls, each of which was shaded by silk awnings dyed in brilliant rainbow hues. The afternoon sun filtered down through the trees that shaded the street, providing pleasant shade for those who lingered for a midday meal. Murmured conversations and savory fragrances filled the air.

Tzigone came to a stop under a crimson canopy. She inhaled deeply as she eyed a row of braided pastries drying on a T-shaped wooden rack. Several more pastries swam in a cauldron of bubbling fat, rapidly turning plump and brown and filling the air with the scent of frying sweet bread. The baker was dredging a fresh batch in finely ground sugar mixed with rare spices: allspice and cardamom and mace. Tzigone patted her pockets and produced a few of the wedge-shaped electrum bits that passed as small currency.

"Two of the hangman's nooses," she instructed the baker, pointing to a long braided pastry with a loop at one end. "And can you swirl them around in the spice again? Make them good and sticky?"

Matteo shook his head when she offered him one of the powdery treats. He pointed to the cauldron's underside, which was red and glowing without the benefit of fire.

"The pastries are cooked by magical means," he explained. "Such things are forbidden to a jordain."

For a moment she gaped at him, then she shrugged and took a big bite of the sugary bread. "Tastes the same, either way. But there'll be no waste. I'm hungry enough to finish them both," she assured him. "What about you? Let's stroll about and find something that pleases you."

He shifted the bag from his shoulder. "There's no need and little time. I'm due back at my patron's villa by sunset, and before then I must see that Procopio's message is properly delivered."

Tzigone grinned and gave him a playful shove. "Aha! Then you're not so out of favor with him as you implied."

Matteo sighed and slumped against the broad, silvery trunk of one of the massive trees that shaded the lane. "I will be, once Lord Procopio hears of Frando's challenge."

"Why should he care? That Frando is an idiot, even by the standards of the jordaini. I've met donkeys who could best him in debate."

"That may be so, but he is counselor to the mage Xavier-lyn. A challenge between counselors reflects upon their patrons. At this point, Procopio has no desire to best Xavier-lyn, but neither would he care to lose to her."

Tzigone nodded sagely. "Ah. He has a standing bet, with large sums placed on either gamecock. He'll suffer no great loss that way, but such things can be inconvenient if he hasn't the ready coin to float."

The notion scandalized him, as did the comparison between a jordaini debate and the vulgar practice of gambling upon cock fights. "This has nothing to do with money! It is a matter of politics. Xavierlyn is the Chief Elder of Halarahh. For Procopio to challenge her would be tanta-mount to announcing his aspirations to her position. He cannot afford to appear too ambitious at this time."

She shrugged again, not seeing the sense in it. "What did Cassia have to say?"

"I think she intends to recommend me to Queen Beatrix," Matteo grumbled.

Tzigone brightened. "That's a good thing, isn't it? Becoming the queen's counselor?"

"Not if it means going to the palace in disgrace, as a means of saving my current patron trouble."

"After you've arrived at a destination, does it truly matter if you traveled by horse or mule?" she pointed out. "Once you're there, the journey is quickly forgotten."

Matteo had to admit that there was a certain practicality to this. "I am beginning to follow the paths your arguments take," he told her, and then sighed. "This worries me."

She laughed merrily and linked her arm through his, pulling him back into a slow walk. "Didn't I tell you that you'd get used to me in time?"

"That is something we must discuss," he said slowly. "I cannot deny that I enjoy your company, and I have thought of you often since last we met. Believe me when I tell you I have no wish to give offense, but I must insist that you stop interfering in my affairs."

Tzigone stopped dead and stared up at him. "Interfering!"

She looked so dumbfounded that Matteo felt compelled to provide illumination. "Meddling. Or influencing, if you prefer that term. The most recent example was your performance in the Arbor Square."

"A man was getting ready to pull two very nasty-looking knives on you. My story served as a distraction," she pointed out.

"A distraction that offended a fellow jordain and prompted him to issue a challenge."

Tzigone folded her arms. "Which in turn brought you to the attention of the king's high counselor."

"Not all attention is desirable. Cassia thinks me an inept fool, and for that reason, she intends to recommend me to her rival."

"Who happens to be the Queen of Halruaa," Tzigone concluded, exasperation edging her tones. "I thought jordaini were supposed to be ambitious! Who cares how you arrive at such a high place? Once you get there, you set about to make your mark." She struck a haughty pose. "If you cannot do so, then you're the fool that the king's counselor named you," she concluded in Cassia's voice.

The imitation was uncannily accurate, more precise than an echo. Matteo shook his head in amazement. "How do you do that?"

"The voices?" She shrugged. "I'm told that I'm a natural mimic. I used to travel with a troupe of entertainers who hawked me as 'The Human Mockingbird.' It was fun for a while," she confided, "but the feathers on the costume made me sneeze. You've heard of Old Bess?"

It took Matteo a moment to follow the abrupt shift in her conversation, but he nodded. Few people in the coastal lowlands did not know of the notorious pirate. A plump, middle-aged woman with the cheery manner of an aging milkmaid, Old Bess was nonetheless among the bloodiest and most ruthless captains to sail the Great Sea.

"I have had occasion to speak with her," Matteo admitted. "Two years past, she spent part of the summer rains at the jordaini house, insensible with fever."

"That old shark?" Tzigone said incredulously. "I'm surprised the jordaini would have anything to do with her."

"Sometimes criminals and foreigners are brought to the house for treatment so that the students might observe the course of serious disease and injury and learn of their treatments," he explained. "In all truth, no one expected her to live. When she recovered, she insisted upon paying for her keep and her care by instructing some of the students in tides and currents. It was her tales of battle, however, that provided the liveliest lessons," he confessed with a little grin.

"Then you know the voice." Tzigone cleared her throat and pursed her lips as she smiled, in a manner that made her cheeks puff up and her eyes appear to twinkle. To complete the illusion, she stepped under the crimson awning. Light filtered through it, adding reddish lights to her hair and painting her face a wind-burned pink. Without changing her form or features, she managed to portray the essence of the jovial, apple-cheeked pirate.

"Wot'll ye be havin' now, dearie?" she said with bright charm and a thick north-isle Moonshae accent. "Will it be a fish knife through yer gizzard, or will ye be having a sit-down on the business end of a pike?"

She went on, cheerfully listing increasingly gory methods of death in a tone more suited to a tavern wench's blithe recitation of the night's fare.

As he listened, Matteo felt his lips twitch and his ire begin to fade. It was difficult to remain angry with Tzigone for long. The wench was amusing, and in her own way, she truly did seem to mean well.

He also found her interesting in a manner that went far beyond her tall stories, for there was about her something of a puzzle. It did not escape him that Tzigone's speech dropped easily into Common, the widely used trade tongue that few Halruaans, who were in general both insular and proud, saw need to master.

"And now a recitation from the decadent northlands," she suggested, her voice smoothed from a Moonshae burr into an affected drawl.

> "They're far from staid after a raid,
> These men of Zhentil Keep.
> They kill off all the women,
> For they much prefer the sheep.
>
> "The men don't eat their ill-got treat.
> Not one of them's a glutton.
> So isn't it a marvel
> That they always smell of mutton?"

She declaimed the verse in ringing metered speech, much as a classically trained bard might deliver news of battle or recite an epic of long-dead heroes. The combination of her cultured tone with the bawdy verse had Matteo shaking his head in amazement.

"Wherever did you hear such a thing?"

"Great songs endure, but bad ones travel," she informed him with a grin.

He chuckled. "I'm not familiar with that proverb, but it seems to hold true."

"Proverb?" A flicker of annoyance crossed her face, but she quickly shrugged it aside. "So what shall we do now?"

Matteo knew the answer but found that he didn't relish speaking it. "I'm afraid we part ways," he said with genuine regret as he prepared to drop her burlap bag at her feet.

Her eyes widened in alarm, and she flung out a hand to stop him. "Don't put that down!"

Suspicion bloomed anew, and with it came a sharp, painful stab of self-reproach. Jordaini had a strong resistance to magic, including all means of magical inquiry. Since they could seldom be seen through scrying devices or seeking spells, they were natural couriers. Elaborate protocols ensured that they could not be used as such, even by their patrons. They carried only what they could place in the leather bags at their belt, and they memorized messages rather than carry scrolls. By accepting the bag from Tzigone, Matteo had gone against tradition and broken several core rules. And in not questioning her intent in handing him the sack, he had proven himself to be as naïve as she had named him.

"What's in here?" he demanded.

Not waiting for an answer, he jerked open the sack and thrust one hand into it. His fingers closed around a smooth, hard cylinder. He drew it out, his heart pounding as he regarded the wood and leather scroll case.

"It's a spell book," he said incredulously. "You told me that you were no wizard."

"You don't need to be a wizard to know the price of such things," Tzigone retorted. "It'll bring a good profit in the markets, provided I sell it after dark and well away from this part of the city."

Relief swept through Matteo. The reaction surprised him, as did the realization that it was easier for him to deal with Tzigone as a thief than as a wizard. Surely he did not approve of thievery, but in his world, wizards could play only two roles: patrons to be served, or enemies to be outwitted and defeated.

The thought of battle prompted him to glance at the arcane markings on the case, looking for some indication of the school and the power of the wizard who owned the scroll. This was important. Battle was to be avoided if possible, but he doubted that the cheated wizard would allow him time for explanation.

After a moment's study, he found what he sought. Lightly etched into the dark wood was the outline of a raven perched upon the point of a triangle. These were the symbols of death and the renewal that death offered, so it seemed likely that this had been the property of a necromancer.

Matteo grimaced and dropped the scroll case back into the sack. Necromancers were not considered the most honored or powerful of Halruaa's wizards, but he disliked dealing with them.

"What's wrong?" Tzigone asked quickly.

"Apart from the fact that once again you've had me carry stolen property?" he retorted.

She looked at him keenly. "No offense, but you don't seem all that bothered by theft. When I told you that I acquired this spell scroll with resale in mind, you looked positively relieved. So I take it I've stepped on one of your precious jordaini rules."

For a troubling moment, Matteo considered that perhaps he was more concerned with the rules of his order than with simple matters of right and wrong. Theft, in his opinion, was wrong, while, strictly speaking, magic was not. But although consorting with thieves was hardly the accepted thing, friendship with a wizard could get him censured or even slain. This seemed oddly out of balance.

He made a note to consider this at a later time, and he explained the matter to Tzigone as best he could.

"A jordain may not use magic or pay for it to be used on his behalf. He cannot own or use magical items. He cannot have personal dealings with wizards. Even handling magical items is suspect. The purity of the order is rigorously ensured by the magehounds and the Jordaini Council, and the penalties for violating any of these rules are stern."

Tzigone made a wry face. "As bad as all that, is it? Well, don't concern yourself. I'll be rid of this by dawn," she said as she reached for the sack.

At that moment a passerby jolted them, and the bag fell from Matteo's fingers. Tzigone lunged for it, but she couldn't get past him in time to get at it. The bag thudded onto the cobbled street.

Immediately a flash of arcane light darted from the bag. Deeper than crimson in hue, it sizzled out like the strike of a preternaturally quick snake.

The sudden burst of magic unnerved the midday diners. Chairs overturned as they moved away. Pasties and cheeses dropped unheeded to the cobblestone. Coins and merchandise lay forgotten on the counter as both merchants and customers thought of things that required their urgent attention. Spell battles were uncommon in the streets of Halruaa, but they were not so infrequent that people considered them a novelty worthy of the risk.

"Red lightning. That's never good," muttered Tzigone. She began to edge toward the yellow awning of the fishmonger's stall nearby.

Suddenly the lightning sizzled back, retracing the path of the spell of seeking. The light and power of the bolt seemed greatly increased in power; it was brighter and somehow weightier.

Matteo frowned. He hadn't expected this conclusion to the spell of seeking. Few wizards could travel along the path forged by the seeking magic. The wizard he was soon to face was more powerful than he had anticipated.

He placed his hands on the hilts of his daggers as the wizard manifested before him, not drawing them but prepared to defend himself if need be.

The victim of Tzigone's latest theft was a tall man, exceedingly long of limb and narrow through the shoulders. His lanky frame was swathed in the black-red robes of a necromancer, which swirled about him like storm clouds at sunset. A faint odor of a charnel house clung to him, whispering softly but unmistakably of death. By some coincidence of fate, the man was paler than a corpse, a true albino, with eyes the color of water and skin whiter than the underbelly of a fish. The black robes cast grayish shadows on his skin.

With almost theatrical menace, the wizard began to advance, one thin hand leveled at Matteo. His skin grew paler still, so that the flesh became as clear as crystal and the skeletal form beneath was revealed.

"Behold the fate of the hands that touched my spellbook," intoned the wizard.

"Sure, give or take sixty years," Tzigone muttered from somewhere behind Matteo.

He shared her confidence—as a jordain, he was immune to most spells. But he wondered briefly how Tzigone might explain her own resistance to magic. After all, the spell of seeking had not worked when she carried the bag, either.

The necromancer made a sharp, quick gesture with his skeletal hand and then waited expectantly. His grim hauteur quickly changed to anger when no one obliged him by withering away to bone.

He followed with a series of quick, impatient gestures. At his command, dozens of smooth, polished sticks rose from a basket in a nearby stall, all of them edged in tassels—juggler's tools sold in groups of three as toys for children. The sticks flew into the midst of the now-empty square and clattered into formation. An odd, angular skeleton, the bones of a creature that had never known life, began to advance on Matteo.

Matteo quickly adjusted his stance and his strategy. He had never faced such a foe before, but he reasoned that every creature, alive or dead or fabricated, was held together in much the same way.

He dropped and spun as the wooden skeleton advanced. As he turned, Matteo slashed out at the joints where one of the knees might have been. The silver blade cut deep into something he could not see—not flesh, but an energy that was almost as palpable. The magical bounds were strong and did not sever entirely, but the necromancer's creation seemed to be effectively hamstrung. It stopped suddenly, listing hard to one side as its "arms" flailed about in a quest for balance.

Matteo ducked under the wildly swinging limbs and wedged one dagger between two joints of the construct's wooden spine. He held the blade firmly in place as he kicked the other leg out from under the magical creature. The skeleton went down with a clatter and lay twitching, but it was no longer able to move its parts. The magical flow that held the thing together followed much the same path as the energy that coursed along a living man's spine. Sever that, and the rest was all but over.

The necromancer shrieked with rage. He advanced upon Matteo, gesturing wildly. In one hand, he held a thin strip of ripe and reeking fish. The disgusting thing flapped about as the wizard formed the gestures of his spell, gradually dissolving to an eerie, greenish light that leached into the necromancer's hands.

For a moment Matteo froze. He didn't recognize the spell or know how to counteract it.

But Tzigone took inspiration from the necromancer's attack. She snatched up handfuls of eels from the fishmonger's baskets and hurled them at the wizard. The snakelike fish tangled about his ankles, stopping his advance and distracting him from his spell. He nearly tripped, and his bobbling attempt to regain his balance would have been comical in less grim circumstances.

The necromancer ripped the entangling eels away and flung them aside. The touch of his hand turned them a glowing green and left them as rigid as sticks. One of the eels shattered against a tree trunk with a sound like breaking crockery. Shards of eel flew like a volley of arrows, bespeckling the necromancer's robes with glowing green.

"Hey, dragon snot! Over here!" hooted Tzigone, waving her arms and attempting to draw the wizard's attention from Matteo.

This affront to the wizard's dignity enraged him as much as the theft of his spellbook. Crimson light began to gather in his colorless eyes, and he kicked aside the last of the eels and lunged at her.

Matteo felt the rush of cold as the necromancer closed in, and he understood the nature of the spell. A rare few necromancers could summon a lich's touch, a dangerous spell that copied the paralysis of limb and spirit caused by the touch of an undead wizard. But Matteo stepped between the wizard and Tzigone and seized the glowing hand that reached out to seize her.

He accepted the terrible numbing chill, an attack that would have frozen most men in place as surely as the blast of an ice dragon's breath. Forcing aside the icy pain, he tightened his grip on the wizard's hand and gave it a hard, quick twist. The delicate bones gave way with a sickening crunch.

It was a cruel defense, one Matteo hated using, but he knew of no other way to stop the wizard's magical offensive short of killing him.

The necromancer howled in pain and fury, a lingering sound that rose in pitch to become an eerie wail. He fell away, backing off from the jordain and quite literally shrinking as he retreated.

He also began to change. Bones creaked and popped as they took new form. His nose bulged, then snapped outward into a long muzzle. His robes fell away, and white hair sprouted from his pallid skin. In moments the wizard's human shape was entirely gone, replaced by that of a lean and ghostly wolf.

It was a reasonable strategy, one that Matteo had anticipated. Although the wizard's spellcasting was finished for quite some time by the injury to his hand, any necromancer of power kept several spells at the ready, magic that could be activated without word or gesture. And now, as a wolf, the wizard would not need magic to attack.

Apparently he'd also had the foresight to unleash magic designed to leave Matteo vulnerable to fang and claw. As the jordain raised his daggers into guard position, he noted that the tips were beginning to glow with heat. He quickly tossed them aside, steeling himself to do what he would have to do.

The ghostly wolf's lips curled, baring preternaturally long, sharp fangs and an expanse of blackened gums. The creature snarled and crouched for the spring.

Matteo timed his defense, then leaped forward to meet the wolf-wizard. He spun on one foot and kicked out high and hard with the other as the creature rose to the apex of its leap.

His booted foot caught the creature squarely in the chest. He danced back as the wolf dropped to the ground, a look of human surprise on its pale face. But no breath stirred the great white chest, and the wolf-wizard never uttered another sound. The heart stopped on impact and would never beat again.

Numbly Matteo watched as the wolf slowly melted back into human form. If possible, the waxen, white body of the wizard seemed even more inhuman than the abandoned wolf shape.

He was aware of Tzigone edging close. The girl prodded the still figure with a tentative foot, then touched her fingers to the silence pulse on the necromancer's white neck. She rose and stared at Matteo, her eyes huge.

"You killed him," she said incredulously. "With one kick, you killed him."

"I could have stopped him without great injury had he permitted me the daggers," Matteo said shortly, mistaking her astonishment for disapproval.

In truth, he was far more stunned than Tzigone by the

ease of the man's death. Matteo had trained for battle since he was old enough to hold a wooden pole without falling on his backside, but this was the first time a man had died by his hand. It seemed to him that such a thing should not have been so easy. Something so momentous, so final, should have been harder to do, and it should have taken far longer.

Perhaps then he would have had time to reconcile himself to his actions. Perhaps then he would not be standing here staring at the dead man, marveling at the cold hollow place the unknown man's sudden absence left within his own heart. It seemed to him that a hidden room within him had been opened, one whose existence he had never suspected. He could kill. He had killed.

"He need not have died," he said softly. "I wish that he had not, even though he meant us harm."

"Poor bastard," Tzigone said in full agreement.

For some reason, her cavalier choice of words grated on nerves left strangely raw.

"The man is dead," he said coldly. "He died trying to retrieve his rightful property, which you took from him. I do not expect you to take any measure of responsibility for his death, but I will not listen as you deal him further injury. Who are you to malign his name so foully?"

Tzigone fell back a step. For a moment she stared at Matteo, her painted eyes huge in a face gone suddenly pale. She couldn't have looked more startled and betrayed if he'd dealt her an open-handed blow.

She recovered quickly, gave another of her expressive shrugs, and disappeared around the corner with a speed that Matteo, had he not seen some of her other tricks, might well have considered magical.

CHAPTER THIRTEEN

Zephyr reached into his pocket for a coin. It was a small task, one that should have been easy, yet the elf jordain was hampered by his palsied hand and the slow, tremulous movements of extreme age.

He marked the impatience on the urchin messenger's dirty face and cursed his own frailty. Of a certainty, he had lived too long.

Yet the information the street lad had brought him was worth the fee, worth the trouble it took to retrieve it, and perhaps even worth the terrible chore that living these last few years had become. According to Zephyr's informants in the markets, the girl who now called herself Tzigone had been spotted in the city wearing the garb of a street performer, and in the company of Procopio's newest and most earnest jordain.

This was an unexpected stroke of luck. Zephyr was certain Matteo would tell him what there was to know. He doubted the young man was capable of dissembling even if he wished to do so.

With a personal link to Tzigone established, Zephyr would have her in hand in no time. Then he would be able to pass the girl along to Kiva, and the terrible evil that the two elves had set in motion nearly two centuries past would finally be destroyed.

The thought cheered Zephyr considerably. It

was for this purpose that he lived, and only for this purpose. When the laraken died, Zephyr could leave his worn-out body and travel to Arvanaith, the final homeland of the elves.

An almost overwhelming flood of emotion swept him, carried by the beckoning voices of all those who had gone before so very long ago. The elf squeezed his eyes shut and fought against the ways of nature and his own deepest longings.

With difficulty, he composed himself and dismissed the urchin, then hobbled off in search of his patron. It was his job to provide Procopio Septus with information, but on occasions such as this, it was far more important to control what and how much the wizard heard. Matteo's involvement was a mixed blessing. The young man might be able to help Zephyr find Tzigone, but it wouldn't do to have Procopio inquire too closely into his counselors' affairs.

The elf found Procopio in the kitchen garden, admiring the silhouettes of the serving girls as they stretched high to pick fat crimson pods from the bean trellis.

The old jordain sighed. His patron had children enough, born on both sides of the blanket. While it was true that a future king needed heirs, a surplus of potential successors seldom boded well for a kingdom. Some other time, Zephyr would have to remind Procopio of his history lessons.

The elf saw no real need for urgency; in his opinion, Procopio was no king. Nothing about the man suggested Zalathorm's fabled judgment and foresight. Zephyr considered Procopio Septus to be reckless and impulsive and far too open with his ambitions. But then few humans had an elf's patience, and few elves possessed Zephyr's resolve. The old jordain knew only one other elf willing to work for more than two centuries to right an ancient wrong.

The old elf firmly put aside such thoughts and hobbled into the gardens. It was wise to bury one's secrets before entering the presence of a Halruaan diviner.

The real reason for Procopio's presence among the kitchen servants soon became apparent. A basket of doves stood ready for plucking, and several more of the birds flew circles about the tall, hive-shaped dovecote that dominated the south side of the kitchen gardens. Auguries were usually read from the random flights of wild birds, but Procopio had devised a way to read the future in the flight of birds lured in for table use. The diviner was quite fond of roasted dove, so the spell served two purposes at once.

"What counsel do the doves offer, my lord?"

The wizard glanced up at Zephyr's hail, and his satisfied smile broadened. "Enough to know that you have news for me."

The elf acknowledged this with a slight bow. "That is true, my lord, but bear in mind that no news is entirely unmixed. The birth of spring heralds the death of winter."

Procopio dismissed this cautionary proverb with an impatient wave. "This much I know from the birds: There was a disturbance in the market, one that can shift the course of my future. From you, I require detail."

"Your auguries tell true." Zephyr briefly related the story of Matteo's misadventure.

Procopio paled when he heard of the challenge between his new counselor and a jordain employed by his most serious rival for Zalathorm's throne. As Zephyr hoped, Procopio was too concerned for his own political future to inquire into the identity of the young woman who had played the part of alchemist in this particular brew.

"This contest would no doubt prove interesting, but there is both reason and means to avoid it. Lady Cassia took an interest in young Matteo and expressed her intent to commend him to the queen."

The diviner laughed without humor. "Did she, now? A most laudable act," he said dryly.

"Since when, dear Procopio, has any of my actions been otherwise?"

Procopio turned to face the king's counselor. He was smiling widely and looking not in the least surprised. "Welcome, Cassia. All is well with the king, I trust?"

The raven-haired woman glided forward and allowed the wizard to kiss her fingertips. "Zalathorm is well as ever, thanks be to Lady Mystra. It is the queen whose welfare concerns me."

"It is so?" the diviner said innocently. He gestured to the pile of dead birds. "Yet there were no dire signs among the auguries."

Cassia sent a quick, disparaging glance at the basket. "I see you have provided the second remove for the evening meal. Well done. It's a pity you couldn't conjure the final course instead. I am rather fond of sweets."

The wizard stiffened at the subtle layers of insult in his visitor's words. Zephyr lifted a hand to his lips and coughed slightly, not only to signal disapproval but to give an excuse to hide his smile. Conjurers held less status than diviners, and to be compared unfavorably to a wizard of that school was highly displeasing to his ambitious patron. It didn't escape Zephyr's notice that Cassia had not bothered to greet him, a fellow jordain, but he didn't take offense. To the contrary. The less attention he drew from such as Cassia, the better.

"I do not waste magic on such matters," Procopio said loftily. "As you can see, I have servants to fetch wine and honey cakes. But I hear that it is not my household servants who interest you, but my counselors. You believe that young Matteo may be of service to our queen?"

The jordain's smile was thin and cool. "Let us speak plainly. Your new counselor is a green youth, too hotheaded for delicate court matters and, by all appearances, sorely lacking in judgment. He laughed when a common street performer ridiculed a fellow jordain, which provoked the man to offer challenge. Had he any grasp of your interests and ambitions, he would have avoided this situation at almost any cost. Here is my counsel, Procopio: Be rid of him. This debate will do you no good, but Beatrix will not be harmed by it."

Procopio stroked his chin as he considered this path out

of his dilemma. "But does the queen truly require a new counselor?"

"Conveniently, yes. Of late, she has become increasingly obsessed with creating clockwork devices. One of them went amok in most spectacular fashion. Her favorite messenger was killed, and she is in need of a reliable substitute. Do you think the young jordain's talents will be too tasked by this?"

The wizard thought of the daring skyship challenge, the hours Matteo had spent schooling him in military history and tactics, and the uncanny feats of memory and logic that had been reported of the young jordain—grudgingly reported, for that matter, by the men he was likely to replace.

"I daresay his capabilities extend thus far," he said dryly. "Zephyr? Has Matteo delivered all missives faithfully and well?"

"Perfectly, my lord. Whatever his shortcomings may be, his memory is admirable," the elf replied, taking his cue from the tone of his patron's response.

"Then I am satisfied," Cassia said. "That is all Beatrix will require."

"If she wishes Matteo's services, of course I will release him," the wizard said. "And I must say, your interest in the queen's welfare is most admirable."

"And surprising?" Cassia said with the candor of the very powerful. "Not surprising at all, if you remember Keturah."

With difficulty, Zephyr managed not to gasp aloud. He had come here to steer Procopio gently away from any potential interest in Tzigone. And now it appeared that Cassia's purpose was precisely the opposite.

The diviner's brow creased, then cleared as he recognized the name that he hadn't heard spoken for years. "Yes, now that you mention her. A wizard of the evocation school, rather well regarded but a little eccentric. It has been twenty years and more since Keturah's death. What part could she possibly have in your interest in Matteo?"

"Your new counselor has apparently befriended Keturah's daughter."

Procopio's eyes widened. "I understood that the girl had been found and dealt with years ago."

"That is what they would have us believe. The child was caught, that much is true, and the official word was that she was too young and fragile to survive the rigors of magical inquiry. I know otherwise, and now you know as well. In his wisdom, Zalathorm does not admit to knowledge of certain things, but that does not mean his counselors should not be informed."

"Of course," Procopio murmured, his face thoughtful as he considered the uses of this information—and Cassia's likely purpose in sharing it with him.

Procopio knew that the mysterious "they" Cassia referred to were also known by another name. Halruaa's wizards ruled on many levels. A mysterious group known as the Cabal guided one of the most personal and important aspects of Halruaan life, the future of her wizards. This group kept detailed records of each wizard's heritage and skills, and matched them in marriage with wizards of compatible talents. This was one of the primary reasons why Halruaa could boast of so much magical talent and such highly specialized schools. Wizards in other, less civilized lands married for whim or fancy or political alliance, but in Halruaa, such things were never left to chance. The Cabal held enormous power, for they molded the future in directions they deemed desirable. A regrettable but necessary part of their duties was weeding out dangerous or wild talents, eliminating failed experiments, and dealing with wizards who became either inept or too ambitious.

But Procopio gave that grim reality no more than a passing thought. Membership in the mysterious Cabal was a sure path to power, and he coveted it nearly as much as he longed for Zalathorm's throne. And now here was Cassia, dropping hints and asking for him to release his most promising jordain! Zalathorm's high counselor was here to make an exchange, of that Procopio was certain. But on whose authority? Her own, or the king's? Either path was strewn with possibilities.

"I am honored that you would share these confidences with me," Procopio ventured. "If I might ask, how did you learn of Keturah and her daughter?"

"Not easily," she said dryly. "Amazing secrets sleep behind the queen's porcelain mask."

Procopio fell silent, stunned by the implied connection between the mysterious Cabal and Halruaa's queen.

Zephyr, though he himself was greatly troubled by the jordain's revelations, noted with approval that his patron did not question Cassia about Beatrix. To do so would be unwise and perhaps treasonous.

"Would I have met this young woman?" Procopio asked carefully.

"Not on purpose, that I assure you! Suffice it to say that, but for the circumstances of her birth, she is no one of consequence. What concerns us is that the wench seems quite taken with your young jordain. They were together in the market and looked to be on very good terms."

"Matteo," Procopio murmured thoughtfully, as if divining new possibilities in his newest counselor. He darted an accusing look at Zephyr, though there was no logical reason why his jordain should have known the identity of the street performer with Matteo.

Cassia paused for a long, slow smile. "You begin to see, dear Procopio, why it is wise for you to put distance between yourself and this youth. A man of your ambitions and talents would not willingly pit himself against the Cabal."

Zephyr noted the quick surge of disappointment on his patron's face. Was it possible that Procopio was actually hoping for an invitation to join this mysterious group?

The old elf studied his patron and their visitor and realized that this was so. Though it seemed beyond belief, these two people, the man he served and the jordain he was taught to honor above all others, could casually discuss the legacy of an evil that had destroyed Zephyr's people and ripped apart his life forever. The Cabal had ancient roots in a time the elf knew all too well. Yet here stood these two ignorant and short-lived humans, discussing the Cabal as if it were just another political consideration, another carved figure on one of Procopio's strategy game boards.

Wrath, deep and ancient and searing, rose from the old elf's heart.

"And what is your purpose in this, Cassia?" he demanded. "What do you hope to gain by sending Matteo to the service of the queen? Surely you are not driven by concern for Lord Procopio."

The woman's black eyes widened with shock at being addressed in such fashion, then she burst into genuine laughter. "All that I told your patron is true. But you are wise, elf, in suspecting that there is more. The diviner Xavierlyn is worming herself into the king's favor. I do not think Zalathorm would be pleased if Xavierlyn's jordain challenged the queen's counselor. The king might not be as besotted with Beatrix as he once was, but he will not look with favor at any woman who appears to contest for the queen's place."

"Very clever," Zephyr said coldly. "You pit your rivals against each other. But only one will lose, and how will that benefit you?"

Cassia's face turned pale with anger, except for a flush of red high on her cheeks. For a moment Zephyr thought she would strike him. She quickly gathered herself and gave him a small formal bow.

"You are quick to find the salient point, elf. I see why Procopio keeps you on, even though you are so obviously past your time. Xavierlyn is no match for Beatrix, that is true. But I know the Cabal far better than you do."

Zephyr's only response to this was a bitter smile.

"Matteo is entangled with Keturah's daughter, and hence

he is certain to fall under the Cabal's eye," the woman continued. "Therefore it stands to reason that wherever Matteo goes, trouble will follow."

The king's counselor turned to the watchful Procopio and offered him a conspirator's smile. "And if this trouble goes to the doors of Xavierlyn and Queen Beatrix, I daresay that both your cause and mine will be well served."

❂

Tzigone wandered through the city, keeping, for a change, to the well-traveled roads. Her keen senses felt the frequent touch of magic as spells of warding or scrying or seeking or divination slid over her like raindrops off a frog. She'd heard that the experience was unnerving to those who had newly come to the land. It would be, she supposed, if any of the spells could actually have some effect on her.

Magic she found rather boring. Far more interesting to her was the beauty of this place. Twilight was her favorite time, and Halarahh was one of her favorite cities. She loved the pink coral houses, the towers of white or blue or green marble, the streets cobbled in semiprecious stone, the fanciful fountains that filled the air with a pleasant splash and bubble. The bright rim of the sun was sinking below the western walls, turning the distant mountains a deep purple and gilding the snow-capped tips of the highest peaks with golden light. Starsnakes winged toward the trees, seeking refuge for the coming night. The air was soft and still, redolent with the exotic blossoms that seemed to grow everywhere. Tzigone skirted a trellis covered with jasmine. It was the one flower she disliked, for reasons that she only dimly recalled.

A frustrated sigh escaped her. There was so much that she couldn't remember. She had spent years trying to pick up the stray pieces of her life, but she couldn't put together a meaningful picture without the vital bits that still eluded her.

She had been very young when she was forced to make her own way in the world. Some of her memories of those early years were mercifully scant, and she didn't regret their loss. But the years that had come before— Why couldn't she grasp those?

If only she could hold on to her infrequent dreams. They faded so fast, leaving her with fleeing images and shadowy emotions of great poignancy, both of joy and intense loss. It seemed impossible that something so powerful could be forgotten.

Tzigone hissed through gritted teeth and swerved up toward the sweep of marble stairs that led to the promenade. Atop the city wall had been built a broad avenue. Here the fashionable people of Halarahh came to stroll, to meet, and, most importantly, to be seen.

They were out in full force on such a fine evening, clad in bright silks and brocades. Magical wands, staves, and weapons were prominently displayed; indeed, the people of Halruaa decked themselves with artifacts as freely as the wealthy folk of other lands loaded themselves with common gems.

Many of the people who came out for an evening walk were accompanied by exotic pets. Tiny gem-colored fairy dragons and winged cats flew overhead in the tight circles their leashes allowed them and enduring the promenade with ill grace. Most of the flitter-kittens were about as happy with their lot as any common cat might be, writhing and tumbling and tugging at the leashes that kept them tethered. Tzigone saw one particularly recalcitrant cat winging away toward the trees of the city green, trailing its leash like a second tail.

Lizards were among the most popular pets. Reptiles of all kinds were plentiful in Halruaa, and lizards were bred for their brilliant colors and extravagant back rills or neck ruffles. Some of the more daring folk even walked miniature behirs. The monsters' crocodilian snouts were invariably muzzled with contraptions of leather and electrum, but they were no less dangerous for it. They walked with a curious undulating motion, rolling along on their six or ten or twelve legs, their amber eyes glazed with the spells that kept them docile. But even in this enchanted state, behirs could let off lightning bolts powerful enough to reduce the finery of their wizard captors to smoke and ash.

The promenade went on for nearly a mile, and for its entire length, there was nary a side street, a nearby tree, or a building to give cover and offer a quick escape. Tzigone usually avoided such places, but tonight she didn't draw a second glance. She'd found a cast-off gown of pale green brocade airing on a rosebush and decided to spend a handful of coins for a snood of matching color. That net, tied onto her head and filled with hair carefully clipped from the tails of several chestnut horses, lent her the illusion of a noblewoman's long hair.

She strolled along, looking for someone who would provide her with an introduction to Kholstar, the city's master behir keeper. Before long, she noted a pale blue behir, glittering with scales the color of fine topaz, trudging behind a woman who minced along in a slim dress of a similar substance and hue.

This wizard was particularly arrogant. The leash that held the magical beast was braided leather, threaded with silver, which proclaimed that her control of the monster was so firm that she needn't fear its breath weapon. Chances were the wizard had warded herself against accidents, but the display was as ostentatious as any that Tzigone had seen in a fortnight.

This mixture of arrogance and style appealed to Tzigone. If she had to spend time in the company of a wizard, she might as well pick one who exhibited a certain flair.

She reached into her sleeve for a handful of tiny caltrops she'd prepared and let them fall between the wizard and her behir. The creature stepped on the first of them and let out a startled, angry whuffle. Arcane lightning sizzled up the metal threads and jolted the wizard's beringed hand.

The woman shrieked and dropped the lead, and the behir bolted in the opposite direction. Tzigone darted forward and planted her foot down hard on the leash before the creature could make good its escape.

She picked up the leather and metal strap, ignoring the indignant little sizzles that continued to pulse up the wires, and dragged the creature back over to its mistress.

"Not exactly a dutiful pet," she said sympathetically. "But he is one of the finest behirs I've seen. Such a lovely color! Do you show him?"

"He has seen it all," the woman said grimly. "You can't show him a damn thing."

Tzigone chuckled, an infectious sound that coaxed an answering grin from the wizard. "Well, the redeeming feature about behirs is that you can always treble your investment by selling them for spell components."

The woman grimaced and nodded, but she didn't seem eager to take back the lead Tzigone offered. "I would deliver it to Kholstar to be slaughtered tonight, but that thrice-bedamned behir keeper keeps the most inconvenient hours."

Tzigone lifted her eyebrows as if an idea had just occurred to her. "As it happens, I have three behirs, larger than this one but not so finely colored, that I'd just as soon sell for parts. We will bring Kholstar this one, I will promise him three more, and he will not mind the hour. What shopkeeper would turn away so much business?"

The woman considered this, eyeing Tzigone with new respect. "Three, you say?"

"They will be coming with my caravan in the morning, along with my household goods," Tzigone said smoothly.

"You are moving to Halarahh, then? From whence?"

"Achelar," she said, naming the city most remote and farthest off the commonly traveled roads. She grimaced, mimicking the woman's sudden expression of genteel distaste. "I can't tell you what a relief it is to get out of that backwater! But I am remiss in my manners. I am Margot, of the illusionist school, entirely at your service."

"And I am known as Sinestra," the woman said in a tone that was both grand and self-mocking. "I am a diviner, apprenticed and, alas, wed to Uriah Belajoon. I doubt you've heard of him."

"Who has not heard of so great a wizard?" Tzigone lied, broadly pantomiming wide-eyed awe. "You have my sincere condolences."

She had no idea what Sinestra would make of this mixed pronouncement, but apparently it fit well with the wizard's opinion. Sinestra chuckled with dark appreciation. "Welcome to Halarahh, Margot. We're destined to become great friends."

"Who am I to argue?" Tzigone said with a grin. "You're the diviner."

Sinestra's pronouncement of friendship did not keep her from taking the usual wizardly precautions. Tzigone felt the subtle touch of the woman's spells, seeking to measure the truth of everything Tzigone had said. Of course Sinestra's efforts yielded her nothing, but neither did her face reveal any surprise over this fact. Tzigone decided that if she needed a partner in a card game, she could do worse than enlist this woman's aid.

They chatted lightly as they made their way down from the promenade and through the streets to the behir keeper's shop, Sinestra providing a great deal of useful gossip to her supposed equal. Tzigone responded with completely fabricated stories of the wealthy and powerful folk of Achelar, taking pains to make them as amusing and scurrilous as possible. By the time they reached the weirs of Kholstar, Sinestra had extracted a promise from Tzigone to meet the next day for a midday meal and more gossip.

As Tzigone anticipated, the behir keeper was more than happy to unbar his door to this much business, especially when Tzigone expressed an interest in acquiring some ornamental monsters for the moat surrounding her new villa.

Sinestra left the blue behir to his fate and went on her

way. Kholstar ushered Tzigone to the back room and left her to study the behir breeding books in search of a combination of color and magic that pleased her.

Tzigone quickly decided upon a pair of rose-colored hatchlings and devised a suitably dizzy story about wanting moat guards that would match the color of the water lilies. It was just such detail, she'd learned long ago, that made her stories and her borrowed personas both plausible and entertaining.

She left the hatchling records on the table and quickly surveyed the other books on the shelf. Despite what she'd told Matteo, she hadn't come to Halarahh merely to complete her obligation to him. Word had it that the behir keeper in this city was a talented generalist wizard who specialized in the breeding of magical creatures. Moreover, his wife was the city's premier matchmaker. Their combined library was precisely the sort of treasure trove that Tzigone had been seeking, and an introduction by Sinestra, an established patron, had gained her access to it.

She quickly took down book after book, placing each one atop the behir records and running her finger down the pages as she searched for anything that might be useful.

Unfortunately the lineage records were listed by gifts, naming first the school of magic and then delving into specific talents. Tzigone's problem was that she had no idea what her gift might be. That she had magical ability was beyond doubt, but she'd picked up what she knew one spell at a time, learning whatever was available, interesting, or useful.

"Have you made a decision, my lady?"

Tzigone glanced up, tilting the big book as she did to obscure the smaller, more important one within.

"I think so," she said in vague, ladylike tones. "The rose hatchlings are a good choice, don't you think? They're just exactly the color of the first water lilies to bloom. But I also have some yellow and cream blossoms coming later in the season," she mused. "Perhaps I shall have to purchase a half score of your lovely behirs to achieve the correct effect."

The prospect of so large a sale smoothed the impatience from the man's face. He bowed and backed out the door. "Please, take all the time you need."

Tzigone smiled and bent back over the volume. When she was alone, she slammed the smaller book shut and tried another. This one was no more useful to her, but it had an entry that caught her eye.

"The jordain school," she murmured.

A thought took root and grew into new and unexpected form. She'd seem Matteo shrug off magical spells that would have knocked most men flat on their backs, if not into whatever afterlife they had right to expect. His resistance was nothing like hers, but it was impressive. Was it possible that the two might somehow be related?

She propped her elbows on the table and dropped her chin into her hands as she pondered this. This was something she had to explore, and as luck would have it, she knew a jordain who was likely to answer her questions, if for no other reason than to be rid of her.

But she hadn't intended to seek out Matteo again. His harsh words had hurt her feelings, something that hadn't happened for a very long time—not since she'd been a very small girl and Sprite had teased her mercilessly.

Tzigone abruptly sat up straight, startled by this sudden remembrance.

"Sprite," she whispered, marveling as the tiny shadow of this distant memory took shape. She hadn't thought of her old friend for many years; at least, she had not remembered him during her waking hours. It seemed to her that she had dreamed of him, but she couldn't recall the details.

Sheer frustration assailed her, and she snatched up an inkwell and hurled it at the wall. Emerald green ink splattered against the white plaster and dripped onto the carpet. The mess immediately began to disappear, just as it would on any written contract about which the behir keeper had second thoughts.

Tzigone sighed again. Memory. It both eluded her and obsessed her. She made it a point to remember everything she could, learning languages, committing names and faces and songs and maps of city streets to memory. More importantly, she searched for ways to reclaim those things she could not remember. But she had never thought to seek out the jordaini.

The jordaini made a special study of memory. It was said that they could retrieve the smallest scrap of information from the storehouses of their minds. Perhaps she could learn from Matteo.

This was reason enough to seek him out. Tzigone suspected she had another purpose, but the words to describe it were unfamiliar to her.

With a shrug, Tzigone picked up the book and began to read about the secret lineage of the jordaini.

❦

That night Matteo accompanied Procopio Septus to court for the first time. No mention was made of the events of the day, but Matteo had no illusion about the reason for his inclusion in his patron's plans. Even so, he steeled himself for the unexpected. Unforeseen events had become common since the day Tzigone had started haunting the edges of his life. Her meddling had brought him to this place, and he didn't believe that she was done with him.

The first surprise was that the king and queen held separate courts. Zalathorm held sway in a vast chamber defined by soaring rounded arches of green-veined marble. Large windows had been placed high on the walls, and beyond one of the largest windows was a docking platform for skyships. Ornate carvings lined the walls and arches, and the ceilings had been enspelled to resemble a night sky.

Matteo glanced up and saw that the rumors about the ceiling were true. The "stars" overhead truly did form constellations unknown to nature, shaping and reshaping to form the crest or sigil of each wizard who entered and was announced.

Nearly everyone in attendance was a wizard of considerable power. There were seventeen members of the Council of Elders in this city, and all but one was present when Matteo and his patron arrived. The final member was Xavierlyn, a tiny woman who liked to be called the Dawn Wizard. Matteo watched as her skyship, a gilded marvel with sails painted in soft, sunrise hues, floated gracefully to the dock. The wizard walked across the last few feet of air without aid of plank or platform, then floated down to the main floor. It was a remarkable entrance, and Matteo noted that Procopio took more than a little interest in his rival's appearance.

Matteo expected Zalathorm's court to display power and splendor, and he was not disappointed. Many of the wizards wore the old-fashioned ceremonial robes of their office and school. Others courted current fashion. The women dressed in exquisite gowns, and men donned silken plumage that was equally bright. Quite a few of the wizards were accompanied by their counselors, who were simply dressed in white linen. But that very simplicity was a statement of power, as were the pendants worn by all the jordaini but Matteo. He resolved to replace his missing emblem at first opportunity.

King Zalathorm was something of a surprise. Despite all his training in the ways of wizards, Matteo wouldn't have picked the man out of a crowd as someone of power and importance. The king was no more than average height, with thick hair and a full beard of a soft brown hue. His gaze was mild, his speech soft and almost diffident. To all appearances, he was a man in his fifth decade of life. Yet Matteo knew this was impossible, for Zalathorm had held the throne for more than sixty years. No one knew for certain how old the wizard was, but all agreed that he was one of the most powerful wizards in a nation full of magic.

"Tell me what you see," Procopio demanded in a soft voice.

Matteo tore his gaze from the king and looked about the room. "The woman in the yellow gown, the one standing by the harpist, is a priestess of Azuth. She must be quite powerful, for several wizards of high rank are laughing and drinking with her."

"True enough. Azuth's clergy is not highly esteemed, and the wizards would not bother with her unless her rank was high. What else?"

"The tall, auburn woman is Rhodea Firehair. She seldom leaves the city of Aluarim, for she is kept busy supervising the mint and commanding the soldiers that protect and transport the new coin. Her presence here indicates one of two things: Either a battle is on the horizon, or King Zalathorm has called council. She is never known to miss either. The presence of all seventeen members of the Council of Elders indicates that the king has issued a summons. The fact that the wizard Rhodea is garbed in silk rather than battle leather indicates that the council deals with matters of peace."

Procopio nodded but looked mildly impatient. So far Matteo's comments had required little special knowledge or discernment. "Continue."

The young man scanned the room. "Those three men speaking to Basel Indoulur are laden with magical devices. Do you notice how the thin one flaunts the rings on his hand, much as a man unaccustomed to wealth might display his coins? None of the three are particularly powerful wizards, but they wish to appear so. You would do well to learn why."

The diviner lifted one snowy eyebrow. "And why is that?"

"The ornaments they wear on their hands and about their necks are of Moonshae gold," Matteo explained. "Nowhere else is that particular shade of pale rose-gold mined. If these men were capable of crafting magical items themselves, they would do so. Nor are they overburdened with coin. Had they the means to buy the best, they would purchase Halruaan magic."

Procopio smiled and nodded in approval. "That goes without saying, but it's pleasant to hear nonetheless. Go on."

"The question is, how did they acquire these items, and for what purpose? It is said that the Llewyrr elves gave such gifts to the High Queen of the Moonshaes when she succeeded her father, King Kendrick, along with the prophecy that her line will continue for as long as the elven magic endures. This was no doubt meant as an elf blessing, but there are factions in that kingdom that might see opportunity in these gifts and this pronouncement."

Procopio studied his counselor with interest. "I begin to see your reasoning. Where else could such magic be studied and counteracted but in Halruaa? If the artifacts are what you think they are, their reappearance in the hands of the Moonshae queen's rivals, their magic depleted, might prove a rallying point to mount a serious challenge to the throne."

"Therein lies the problem. Halruaa can have no part in such games. Our magic is too widely feared. If the ruse were discovered, it wouldn't matter to the world if the Halruaan wizard who altered the artifacts knew nothing of their intended use. The Moonshae Islands have powerful allies. Most certainly there would be harsh reprisals."

Procopio nodded thoughtfully. He looked at Matteo with genuine regret. "You have counseled me well. I will seek a private audience with Zalathorm, and we will get to the heart of this. You, however, must present yourself to the queen's court."

He gave Matteo a small parchment card etched with sapphire ink. "Give this to the seneschal. He will endeavor to get you an introduction."

The wizard hesitated, then clapped Matteo on the shoulder. "May Mystra smile upon you."

Matteo heard the dismissal in the words and nodded his response. With a sigh, he turned toward the corridor that separated Zalathorm from his queen.

As he walked, the sound of music and conversation faded slowly away. The tap of his footsteps echoed along the marble floor, and the corridor became increasingly chill. Paradoxically, bursts of steam jetted out into the hall at intervals of increasing frequency.

He carefully came closer to investigate. A sudden, sharp hiss drew his gaze to his left, and immediate he reached for his daggers. Crouched in an alcove, looking like a giant, ice-white cat ready to spring, was a white dragon.

The beast was still a juvenile, judging from its size, but deadly just the same. The dragon's maw was wide and curved upward in a wicked smile, parted slightly to reveal rows of lethal ivory fangs. Two horns curled back off the beast's forehead, and a third, shorter one in the center jutted forward, swirled like a long, slender seashell. It looked very like a unicorn's horn, but for the barbed tip and the taint of long-dried blood. The dragon's talons were equally stained, and each was nearly as long as Matteo's hand. Its ice blue eyes regarded Matteo steadily and glittered like malevolent jewels.

A moment passed before Matteo realized his mistake. In his surprise, he looked directly into the dragon's eyes. And in looking, he felt nothing—none of the fear that turned bones to water and made strong men forget their resolve. This had nothing to do with his resistance to magic, but with the dragon itself. It was no true beast, but an elaborate clockwork device.

Matteo held back until the thing emitted two more puffs of cold steam, then leaned in closer for a look. Sure enough, the scales were bits of electrum, hammered smooth and thin and cunningly fitted together. He could glimpse the gears inside the creature's mouth and the large block of ice within its body. Periodically a small vial tipped, pouring a few drops of some unknown mixture onto the ice, which immediately sizzled and sent forth a cloud of cooling vapor. The dragon was an elaborate cooling device, nothing more. Even the apparent blood on its horn and claws was nothing more than a bit of rust.

Even so, Matteo proceeded with caution down the hall, his hands near the hilts of his daggers and his eyes keenly aware of the alcoves that lined the corridor. Such a device could easily lure a visitor into a sense of security. Three false dragons could leave one complacent and trusting, and thus easy prey for a fourth, real dragon. After all, the surest way to hide a tree was to plant a forest around it.

But Matteo got to the end of the long corridor without incident. He presented Procopio's card to the soldier at the door. The man examined it and then fixed a wry smile on the young jordain.

"I say, you're the least likely of the bunch. I could see at a glance why the rest of them got sent up here. Damned if I wouldn't have exiled them myself! What the nine hells did you do—bugger the lord mayor?"

Matteo sighed. "Figuratively speaking, I suppose you could say that. Procopio Septus, the lord mayor, is my patron. I became embroiled in dispute with the patron of Lady Xavierlyn."

The soldier raised one hand. "Say no more. We speak of those who would be king. Along with a dozen others, of course, but Procopio and Xavierlyn are the biggest roosters in the ring. Not that it's my place to talk of such things."

It certainly wasn't, but Matteo could almost understand the man's desire for conversation of any sort. He had seen no other soul since he'd left Zalathorm's court, and he didn't hear any evidence of human occupation behind the great door. A series of faint clicks and taps and whirs emanated from behind the thick wood, but no sound that could be considered remotely human.

"I have been instructed to present myself to the queen," Matteo said, determined to get on with things.

The seneschal shrugged and pulled a small silver rod from his sleeve. He touched this to the massive lock, which promptly began to fade. The door turned translucent as well, thinning and finally disappearing with a soft pop. A few paces behind it stood another door, which dissolved in much the same manner.

"Magical wards," the guard explained. "Keeps things from getting out. Can't be too careful, with the king just down the hall and all."

It seemed odd that the queen's guard should be concerned about protecting the king rather than tending his own charge. But Matteo nodded politely and waited until the third and final door swung open, this time on hinges of solid iron. He stepped inside, aware that the man was hastily barring the heavy door behind him.

The scene before him was like nothing he had ever seen or imagined. Long tables lined the room in precise rows. Here and there stood movable walls covered with large sheets of parchment. Upon them were written incomprehensible patterns of lines and runes. At second glance, Matteo recognized them as sketches for some new sort of clockwork device.

These were everywhere. A climbing vine, too vividly green to be a living thing, was studded with purple flowers that budded and bloomed and closed, over and over again. Several tiny birds darted among them, "feeding" upon the blossoms. The soft whir of their wings was faintly metallic; incredibly, these were not true hummingbirds but flying toys. A metallic tiger, its markings a lifelike pattern rendered in gold and onyx, prowled about the queen's throne, keeping guard over its mistress.

Queen Beatrix was not at her throne. She stood quietly to one side, studying one of the drawings. So still was she that for a moment, Matteo mistook her for one of her own clockwork devices. When she turned and regarded him with cold brown eyes, he wasn't entirely certain that he had been wrong.

Once she might have been a beautiful woman. Her form was small and slim, and her still features were finely molded and without blemish. But her face was utterly white, painted to resemble fine porcelain. Her mouth was a prim crimson curve and her eyes deeply framed with skillfully applied kohl. She wore a wig of mingled white and silver, elaborately curled and studded with pearls and electrum netting. Her white gown was stiff, formal, and encrusted with silver embroidery. The effect was beautiful, but cold and not quite human. Matteo wouldn't have sworn whether she was woman, goddess, machine, or some combination of all three.

"You may come forward," she said in a flat but unmistakably human voice.

Matteo dipped into a bow and gave his name and that of his patron. "Lord Procopio sends his respects."

"And has the wit not to deliver them himself," Beatrix said, without inflection of anger or humor. She turned away and gestured toward the drawing. "So, jordain. If you would be my counselor, come and tell me what you see."

He came over and studied the complex pattern of sweeping lines and curves. "In form, it looks a bit like an elephant, Your Majesty."

"Will it move? Walk? Attack?"

"I am no artificer, but I think not." He pointed to a series of connected gears. "These do not seem of sufficient size to provide much power."

"The gears provide a small amount of motive force, which is greatly enlarged by the life-force planted within," Beatrix said. "A true elephant is a rare thing and difficult to bring over the Muaraghal Wall," she said, naming the mountain range that divided Halruaa from the lands to the east. "We have tried and failed thrice."

Matteo tried not to show the horror this news evoked. Elephants were rare and wondrous creatures. Though they didn't have speech or work magic, some sages thought them to be at least as intelligent as dolphins. "You will place the life-force of an elephant within this device?"

"No. A donkey perhaps, or a Durparian merchant," the queen said in the same even, emotionless tone. "They are much the same."

From another person's lips, this might have been a dark jest. Matteo realized that Beatrix was speaking simple truth as she saw it.

"Who builds these?" he asked, with a sweep of his hand that indicated the entire collection of strange contraptions.

"I send for artisans and wizards as I require their services. There are none here now," she added unnecessarily.

The queen didn't seem bothered by her isolation, but it seemed unnatural to Matteo. "There is music and feasting in the halls of the king," he said. "Will you allow me to escort you there?"

She considered this and placed a small white hand at her waist. "I should eat," she said, as if calculating how long it had been since she had bothered to think of such things.

He nodded and walked over to tap at the massive door. The guard let them out, and together they walked down the long corridor. Each of the clockwork dragons bowed as the queen walked past, dipping its metal head until its rusty horns rasped against the floor.

Their appearance in Zalathorm's hall created quite a stir. For a moment conversation stilled altogether, which in mannered Halruaa was as obvious as a smokepowder blast might be in any other court. The king quickly excused himself from his courtiers and came forward, his hands outstretched and his ageless eyes alight with youth and hope.

"Beatrix, my dear, this is a most unexpected pleasure."

The queen responded with a single remote nod, but she put her hands into his. Matteo fell back as they spoke for a few moments, Beatrix answering in cool, measured phrases.

After a few moments she excused herself and lifted a hand to summon one of the servants who carried trays of goblets and fruit around the room. The king sighed and turned to Matteo.

"Walk with me," he said abruptly.

The young man fell into step. They left the main council hall and entered an antechamber, which in turn led to a hanging garden. The king didn't stop or speak until they reached the rail and the city was spread out before them, twinkling with magical lights.

"The queen was not always like this, you know," Zalathorm said abruptly, his eyes fixed on the city below. "When she came to the city fifteen years ago, she was a marvel. So beautiful, and so full of light!"

Matteo nodded. Over the long years, Zalathorm had had several queens. Beatrix was the latest. She had been much admired in the early years of her reign for her intelligence and courage. The daughter of reclusive wizards who lived in a remote mountain village, she was the sole survivor of an attack by Crinti raiders. She didn't speak of her early years beyond that fact, but she had been tested and shown to be a generalist mage of middling ability. But as the years passed, she took more interest in clockwork than in magic and seemed to prefer the company of mechanical creatures to that of her human subjects.

Worse yet, she had not provided Zalathorm with an heir. There were many in Halruaa who thought it past time for the king to put Beatrix aside and find a more suitable queen. Though it seemed likely that the king would outlive most of his subjects, the issue of succession was of no small importance. If Zalathorm didn't have an heir, ambitious wizards would vie for his throne. Halruaans knew their history and remembered the devastation that such a contest could cause.

"You persuaded Beatrix to come tonight," the king said. "For this I am grateful."

"It was no great matter. She is no clockwork device, and she needs food and music and company as much as any other."

Zalathorm's smile was tight and wry. "A fact that she seldom remembers. It has been some time since the queen appeared in court. You have done well. I am delighted to see that she will be well cared for."

Matteo nodded, hearing his fate in the king's words. He wasn't happy about it, but he saw no way to evade what was apparently his fate and his duty. Still, there was something he had to know.

"What happened?"

The king didn't need to ask what he meant. "Magic," he said shortly. "It is a great boon, the noblest of arts. But its effects can be as deadly to the spellcaster as the most potent poison. No one knows what spells Beatrix cast against the Crinti, or how she survived the raid. She doesn't recall anything about it; moreover, she has lost memory of all that happened to her before she came to Halarahh. No diviner could learn the queen's story. It took the most powerful of inquisitors to pull even this much memory from her. But something shattered within Beatrix, something that no magic can repair. In fact, she turns away from magic more and more with each day that passes."

Zalathorm passed one hand across his face as if to erase the pain written there. "And Halruaa being what it is, that means she shuns the land and all who live within it. Where she has gone, no one may truly follow. I will speak plainly to you and admit what many of my subjects whisper. The queen, the woman whom you must serve, is no longer sane."

Matteo listened with great sympathy, chilled by the king's obvious grief and by the enormity of damage that magic had wrought. He knew the queen's scant history, as did most of Halruaa, but for the first time, it occurred to him that perhaps more could be learned. If he was to serve Beatrix, he would need to know all he could.

"The inquisitor who learned of the queen's past . . . do you recall his name?"

"It was a woman," the king said without much interest.

"Or more strictly speaking, an elf woman. No, I do not recall her name."

A chill swept through Matteo like the passing of a vengeful ghost. There was only one elf in all Halruaa who had risen to the rank of inquisitrix: Kiva the magehound.

CHAPTER FOURTEEN

Zephyr stood at the rail of his patron's skyship, watching the small dark cloud that brooded over Lake Halruaa. The wind whipped the sparse white strands of his hair about his shoulders and sent a cruel chill through his bones. But he dared not go belowdecks until he was certain of his course. The gales that came off the lake were strong and dangerous. He wouldn't take any more risks with the skyship than he needed to.

The elf had leave to take the Starsnake up whenever he chose, and the crew were instructed to follow his bidding and speak nothing of what they heard and whom they saw. It was among Zephyr's tasks to gather information, and few Halruaans would not eagerly accept an invitation to fly on one of the wondrous ships. Once away from port, the visitors were quite literally captive audiences until whatever time Zephyr chose to put down. Over the years, he had coaxed amazing secrets from people who were too thrilled or unnerved by sky travel to guard their words. It was a fine arrangement, and one of the few occasions in which Zephyr felt truly in control.

Today, however, the elf had few illusions about who commanded whom. He had taken to the skies at Kiva's call.

It occurred to him that the beautiful magehound

had come a very long way from the bedraggled, terrified girl-child that Akhlaur's men had dragged from the trees of the Mhair. She had been nearly insensible with shock and grief, for she had escaped the first attack upon their village only to witness the slaughter of her people. Like Zephyr, she had survived years of torture and degradation at the hands of the wizard Akhlaur. But unlike him, she had escaped Halruaa and made a life for herself. Many years later, she had returned to learn the famed magic of the land, determined to use it to right this terrible wrong. For what she had endured and all she had accomplished, Zephyr admired her.

Recently, however, he had also begun to fear her. He wished he could explain why this was so. Wasn't her life's quest, grim though it was, the same as his own? Didn't she bear the same grief and guilt over the creature that haunted Akhlaur's swamp? Hadn't they both sworn not to rest until the laraken was destroyed?

The old elf squinted at the sky, cursing his fading vision as he tried to divine the nature of the small dark cloud. Yes, it was almost certainly the awaited signal. There was no lack of clouds over the lake, but most of them sailed briskly on the winds. This one sat and brooded, looking as if it wished for fingers so that it could drum them impatiently. More importantly, it lay just beyond the reach of the city's magical wards, powerful spells that informed the city guards whenever a wizard of power approached the city. Kiva would know of these wards and keep just beyond them.

Zephyr gave the order to the helmsman to change course and sail through the dark cloud. He went below to await his visitor.

He felt her presence in the sudden cool mist of the cloud that enveloped the ship. He watched as the fine droplets condensed into a solid female form, a wild elf with jade-green curls and skin of deep burnished gold, an unusually pale hue for a forest elf from this clime.

"Greetings, Kiva. You look chilled."

The magehound glared at him, then strode across the

cabin and picked up a decanter of haerlu wine from the captain's table. She poured a small measure of the pale golden liquid into a goblet and then tossed it back with a single swallow. She grimaced at the fiery taste, but Zephyr noticed that some of the coppery color crept back into the golden pallor of her face. Apparently there was cold comfort to be found in the arms of a storm cloud.

She turned to the old elf. "Do you have the girl or not?"

"I will have her," Zephyr said stoutly. "She has been most bold of late. We have spotted her several times over the last few days. So far no one has been able to lay hands on her, but it is only a matter of time."

"Has Matteo been of help?"

The elf grimaced. "Not as much as I had hoped. The lad has changed service. I haven't seen him since he went to the court of Queen Beatrix."

Kiva turned sharply to stare at him. "You cannot be serious. Whose doing was this?"

"Procopio let him go, but at Cassia's urging."

The elf woman nodded grimly. "I should have surmised. Cassia has long been suspicious of the queen. I hadn't suspected, however, that she knew so much."

"Most likely she doesn't realize the full implications of her action. Matteo can be impulsive, and Cassia claims that she hopes to see him bring trouble or at least embarrassment to Beatrix's door. Perhaps that accounts for Cassia's first impulse, but I suspect she has other, more complex desires."

"Such as?"

Zephyr told her the story of Matteo's battle with the necromancer. "He killed Azgool Njammian, in combat, which, although impressive, fixes wary eyes upon him. All jordaini are taught to fight, but few of us actually kill. Matteo will be regarded as warily as a half-feral hunting hound. What is even more significant is that Azgool located Matteo through a spell of seeking. A difficult task, for as you know, few jordaini can be observed magically. If Matteo is one of these few, then Cassia might well have gained a window into the queen's chambers."

"Cassia, that most honored of jordaini, using forbidden magic to observe a rival?" Kiva said with ironic surprise.

The elf shrugged. "There is little that Cassia would not do. But don't credit her with too much knowledge of Beatrix. I think her primary goal is to supplant the queen in Zalathorm's affections."

"More fool she. Cassia will never be queen. Jordaini cannot marry."

"As she well knows. But Cassia already has the king's ear; perhaps she aspires to his heart as well. At present, Beatrix still holds Zalathorm's affections, but with each day that passes, the clamor for him to take a new queen and get himself an heir grows louder. I suspect that Cassia would be pleased to see Zalathorm put aside Beatrix and take a new queen. He is likely to resent whatever woman supplants Beatrix, and that would place Cassia foremost in his regard."

Kiva sniffed. "Cassia might be a fool, but she is an ambitious fool. We will have to watch her closely."

The elf inclined his head. "As you say. How do the plans for battle progress?"

"Very well," she said with great pleasure. "The first great test lies ahead. If we do battle successfully in Kilmaruu Swamp, we will bring tested weapons and methods into the Swamp of Akhlaur. I am confident that before the summer rains come, the source of the laraken's power will be no more."

"This is not what we agreed!" Zephyr protested. "The laraken must be destroyed outright!"

"Of course," Kiva assured him in soothing tones. "The creature is tethered to the swamp by the spill of magic from the Elemental Plane of Water. Once that gate is closed, the laraken will be desperate to feed elsewhere. We will lure it away and see that it is appropriately dealt with."

"You swear it?" the elf persisted.

The magehound's face became deadly still. "By the graves of our people, by the trees of the Mhair, by the injustices visited upon us both, I swear that this evil will be set right."

Zephyr nodded, satisfied by the solemnity of her oath. "I regret that I have not yet been able to deliver the girl Tzigone to you, but I must admit that I am not sorry to see young Matteo move clear of the matter. The lad might become something rather special, given a chance."

"More likely one of Beatrix's machines will grind him up to oil its gears," she commented. "What a ridiculous risk to take! Warriors like Matteo should die in battle, not in some insane workshop."

"You are one to talk of risk. Do you still intend to enter the Swamp of Akhlaur, knowing that the laraken could strip the magic from you?"

"I'm working on that. There is no need to concern yourself."

The elf shook his head. "There is need. There is a bond between us. We share a history, a homeland. We have both known great loss, and our secrets are mirror images." He fell silent for a long moment, then added in a softer tone, "We share blood."

"Blood? Ichor, more likely!" she spat out. She took a moment to compose herself and then continued in more modulated tones. "We will be avenged, Zephyr. Never doubt that."

For a long moment the gaze of the two elves locked, bound by shared memories of long-ago wrongs.

Kiva shared the passion for vengeance that shone in the old elf's eyes, but she also harbored ambitions that went far beyond retribution. The laraken would be destroyed sooner or later—the wizards of Halruaa were too resourceful to let its rampage continue forever—but for many moons to come, the evil that the wizard Akhlaur had created would be visited upon his descendants. That was right and fitting. But Kiva wanted more. She wanted the dark power that Akhlaur had amassed at such unspeakable cost.

And then, once she was strong enough, she would have Akhlaur himself.

"You said that Matteo was well out of this matter," she said, schooling her voice into a mild tone. "Does the girl Tzigone seem to share this opinion? Has she finished with him?"

"They have not been seen together for several days. I've had him watched, so I'm quite sure of this."

"Perhaps she considers her debt paid," Kiva mused. "But we cannot be too certain. She might present herself on the doorstep of Beatrix's palace at any time, and that we must avoid. We need the girl and cannot risk letting the Cabal get hold of her. Not that there is much risk of that. For all anyone knows, they did away with the child years ago."

Zephyr was silent for a long moment. "Cassia has learned otherwise. She also knows that the girl is in the city and has told this news to my patron, Procopio Septus."

Kiva's amber eyes narrowed to feline slits. "And you only now see fit to mention this? What else might Cassia know?"

"That I cannot say."

The magehound poured herself another glass of wine and sipped it as she considered. "Perhaps there is a way to use this new development," she said at last. "Let Cassia seek Keturah's daughter. Nothing will lure the girl into our nets like the mystery of her past.

"Yes," Kiva said with more confidence, "we shall soon have Tzigone, and if we play the game well, Matteo as well."

"Do you really need the lad?" Zephyr said tentatively.

Kiva's smile was cold and hard, and in her eyes glittered something that went far beyond hatred. "You've seen the laraken. You know its power better than most. All your magic and centuries of your life were stolen in the making of that monster. You aged hundreds of years in a matter of hours as you watched it tear its way toward life. You know the scars that the birthing left behind, for you cared for me after I was tossed out to die."

"Kiva, no more," he begged, appalled by the memories she evoked and the rising hysteria in her voice.

But the elf woman would not be deterred. "You saw the monster that Akhlaur summoned to mingle with your magic and mine. You know what the laraken is, and you know how powerful it has become. And yet you tell me to leave Matteo out of this! He is a jordain, and I am a magehound, and his fate has been in my hands since before he was born. He is nothing."

"No soul is without worth, Kiva. Not even a human soul."

"I did not come to discuss philosophy with you. Matteo is a good fighter with nearly total resistance to magic. He is precisely the sort of weapon we seek. Knowing all you know, can you begrudge me a single blade that I could take into that swamp?"

The elf bowed his head in defeat. "Do what you must," he said softly. But at that moment he wasn't certain what he feared more: the laraken or the magehound.

❂

Cassia stood on the parapet of the palace, watching the scene below her with disbelief. Queen Beatrix walked the promenade, her pale, gem-encrusted gown glittering in the faint light of late afternoon and her elaborate white-and-silver coif anticipating the moonlight. Beside her strolled her new counselor, pointing out sights in the city below and nodding in polite deference to the wizards who passed by.

The jordain noted that every wizard the pair encountered stopped to speak with the queen, and that quite a few didn't move on after the time required by the proper greetings had elapsed. Cassia remembered all too well the charm that Beatrix could use when it suited her to do so.

Cassia spun on her heel. She strode quickly back into her chamber and began to pace. Apparently Matteo had managed to persuade Beatrix that there was a realm outside her workshop. He might even convince the queen, Mystra forbid, that she was still a human woman!

That was not a thought that Cassia relished. Granted, it was hard to find a weakness or a misdeed in a woman as cold and brilliant and solitary and mysterious as the queen. Who knew what damning secrets might flow forth if Matteo could effect a thaw?

On the other hand, Cassia's position as high counselor would be compromised by Beatrix's return to court. Cassia was at Zalathorm's side more often that anyone else, and she wouldn't readily relinquish this spot, not even to the queen.

Perhaps especially not to the queen.

Clearly she had erred when she sent the young jordain to Beatrix. She didn't doubt her assessment of Matteo. The young man was impulsive and passionate, and such people tended to attract trouble. Wasn't his apparent friendship with Keturah's daughter proof of this? What Cassia had neglected to consider was that where there was great risk, there was also great potential.

Fortunately she had other ways to bedevil the queen. Cassia glanced toward the cot, where a grotesque figure writhed and moaned as it struggled against its bonds, near death but taking its time.

Her "guest" was the Cabal's latest find, a misbegotten creature that was obviously intended to be a centaurlike warrior, half panther, half Crinti. The result was horrific: an elflike body supported by four twisted, feline limbs, and a dark, feral face that was neither elf nor panther, but a mirror into some nether world. The creature's body was covered with a mottled mixture of dusky skin, patches of gray fur, and reptilian scales. It was, beyond doubt, a wizardly experiment gone wrong.

The jordaini had a proverb about the danger of dancing to songs that gods had written. Never had Cassia seen such vivid proof as this wretched, dying cat-thing.

But the greatest crime, in her opinion, was that the

creature had been allowed to live this long. Halruaa was a land of powerful magic carefully constrained by rules and customs. This was necessary, or ambitious wizards would soon reduce the land to chaos.

But such control had its costs. Magical experiments that went wrong, and often the wizards who erred, were quickly done away with. The "crintaur" should have been slain before it drew its first breath. Yet it had been found wandering in the queen's forest. Cassia's scouts had shot and mortally wounded it. Nor was it the first such creature her scouts had found.

That led to an interesting question. Few people knew of the Cabal, a society of wizards who controlled magical use and dealt out penalties for misuse. Cassia had little doubt that Beatrix was somehow involved with this mysterious group. But did the queen work against the Cabal, or did she command it?

There were possibilities either way. Most wizards feared the secret Cabal and wouldn't take kindly to news that the queen controlled its activities. Of course, Zalathorm knew of the Cabal, but he kept himself apart from the darker realities of his realm. He was widely loved and revered. He had ruled well and led his people to victory in many battles. His people would forgive him much. But if it was proved and quietly revealed that Beatrix was connected with the Cabal, he might be forced to put her aside.

But the fact that this creature had been caught in the queen's forest was not sufficient proof of the queen's complicity. The girl Tzigone, on the other hand, might be. She had escaped the Cabal. Perhaps she could be induced to remember who had questioned her and who had aided her escape. This would yield the first steps along a path that Cassia dearly hoped would end at the door of Queen Beatrix.

There was much about Tzigone that interested Cassia. Her inquisitors hadn't been able to detect a drop of magical ability, but simple observation indicated that the child possessed a volatile combination of wild talents, as well as an almost total resistance to magic.

Magic resistance was a highly desirable trait, and the regard that Cassia and her fellow jordaini enjoyed was proof of this. But a wizard who possessed a jordain's resistance provided new and unpredictable possibilities. No one knew how talents such as Tzigone's might develop if trained, and, even more ominous, how they might pass down to future generations. Magical gifts were to be strengthened through careful selection and guided marriages, but only along prescribed lines. Tzigone would not have been the first wild talent removed by the Cabal. Society demanded it, much as it safeguarded itself through the destruction of a rabid and unpredictable hound.

Yet Tzigone lived. More interesting still, she seemed to have caught the interest of the magehound Kiva.

The same magehound, Cassia noted, who had examined Beatrix before her marriage to a smitten Zalathorm.

There was a connection there, but one that eluded Cassia.

The jordain sat down at her desk and began to write, meticulously piecing together the information from a dozen scrolls. She traced the magehound's path over the past several years and noted that Kiva's travels intersected frequently with reports of trouble caused by someone who was variously described as a street urchin, a street performer, or a young girl. Tzigone, it seemed, had had a very busy life.

A pity, thought Cassia, that she couldn't trace Tzigone back to her origin. She would have given a great deal to know the name of the girl's father. Perhaps then she might be able to find a damning connection between the girl, the magehound, and the queen.

As it was, Cassia had information sufficient to create trouble. She quickly penned a letter to Sinestra Belajoon, a diviner who had been seen in Tzigone's presence. Cassia commiserated with the wizard about her loss. Whether Tzigone had actually stolen anything from Sinestra, Cassia didn't know or care. The very suggestion would have the wizard patting her pockets and coming up with a loss of some sort. She commented that Sinestra was not the only person of wit and talent to be taken in by this clever thief. Matteo, counselor to Queen Beatrix, was a friend of the girl.

With great satisfaction, Cassia sealed the letter and sent a servant to deliver it. She turned back to the bits and pieces of Tzigone's history, tracing the determined magehound's efforts back five years, ten, nearly twenty.

"Another few days' study, and I shall have all the puzzle pieces in place," she murmured.

"Then perhaps I should return," said a sweet, bell-like voice behind her. "I do hate to leave things unfinished."

The jordain leaped from her chair and whirled, twin daggers gleaming in her manicured hands. Her fury changed to fear as she regarded the small, strange figure seated in her favorite chair. Long ringlets of jade green cascaded over a gown of green and gold and framed a face that held the color and the coldness of polished copper.

Cassia drew herself up with all the dignity she could muster. After all, she was the king's high counselor, and this creature, despite her position, was merely an elf.

"How dare you enter my chamber uninvited, and by magical means?"

The magehound's smile made the room feel suddenly chill. "I go wherever my duty takes me."

"What is that to me? You have no business here."

"Don't I?" Kiva rose in a single swift, fluid motion. "The ranks of the jordaini must be kept free of magic's taint. No one, no matter how high her rank or how powerful her patron, is immune to that rule. If I decide to call inquest against you, no one will question my right."

Cassia hadn't considered this possibility. It was a potent threat. She swallowed with great difficulty. "What do you want?"

The elf extended a peremptory hand. "To begin with, you can give me those papers."

After a moment's hesitation, Cassia handed them over. Kiva studied them and then fixed a challenging stare upon the jordain.

"As you have gone to such trouble to learn, I have sought this girl for quite some time. She is wanted for inquest. This is my duty, and I will brook no interference. This quarry is mine, jordain. Back away, and perhaps I will not need to seek another."

Cassia didn't need to ask who the second quarry might be. "I accept your terms," she said quickly.

"You are hasty," the elf said with a cool smile. "I wasn't quite finished. Have you spoken to anyone about what you have learned?"

The magehound reached into the folds of her yellow sleeve and produced a silver wand, the instrument that could find magic wherever it hid and condemn any jordain who knew Mystra's touch.

Cassia's gaze did not waver, and she spoke words that were partial truth and careful falsehood. "I did not speak to anyone, nor will I," she vowed, omitting mention of the letters she had penned. She felt safe in doing so, for by tradition, jordaini did not write and send messages.

Kiva accepted this with a nod. "Good. If I hear you have broken silence, we will meet again. And I assure you," she said softly, "on that day you will be far less happy with the bargain we make."

❂

Matteo's new quarters were in the south wing of the royal palace, far from the council chambers and several floors up from the queen's clockwork court. Although this was not the most prestigious part of the palace, it was by far the most luxurious suite he had ever occupied. There was one room for sleeping, another in which to receive company, a study lined with books, and a bath so large and luxurious that it was almost an embarrassment.

As he entered his rooms, the faint splash and murmur of water caught his ear. Carefully he eased one dagger from its sheath and crept to the door of the bath. The sight before him froze his feet to the marble floor and left him uncertain whether to smile or groan.

Tzigone had returned, and she had made herself very much at home. She was sprawled in the bath, her small bare feet propped up on one end and her head lolled over the other. Her eyes were closed, and her short brown hair had disappeared into a foamy, fragrant mass. More suds filled the tub like cream on a trifle.

He cleared his throat.

"Come on in," Tzigone said without opening her eyes. "I've been waiting for you for hours. Not that I'm complaining, mind you. I've waited in far worse places."

For a moment he wondered whether "in" referred to the room in general or the bath. Neither course of action seemed wise.

"How did you get into the palace?"

She cracked open one eye. "You always start conversations with a question. Are you aware of that?

"I started in the bilboa tree over by the harbor park," she went on, not waiting for an answer. She lifted one arm out of the water to brush aside a fleck of soap that dripped onto her face. "It's amazing how far you can travel in this city without once touching the ground."

His gaze shifted to his open window, which was at least six stories off the street, and marveled. Whatever else this girl might be, she had a powerful sense of honor if she would go to so much trouble to fulfill her perceived responsibilities.

Or was there another reason for her presence here?

"Is there still a debt between us?" he asked tentatively.

She shrugged, a movement that had Matteo averting his eyes again quickly. "That depends. How are things working out at the palace?"

"Strangely," Matteo said honestly. "I have yet to find a way to truly serve the queen."

"Hmm." Tzigone took this in. "Well, what can you do?"

This drew his attention back to her. "Excuse me?"

"What kinds of services are you trained for? Besides battle, of course. I've seen what you can do with a blade."

"Many things—history, battle strategy, etiquette, protocol, languages, customs, heraldry. It is difficult to give counsel without knowledge of such things. We must also study magic and learn its strengths and weaknesses."

She nodded, her eyes huge and bright. "How do you remember half of that? This is no idle question. I really want to know."

"I can see that," he murmured, puzzled by her intensity. "The memory is both a talent and a skill. Some have more capacity than others, just as some men are born with better singing voices than others. But there are ways to develop the memory. From a very early age, jordaini work to build a palace of the mind, one room at a time, with corridors between them. It is all very deliberate and meticulous. Each fact and idea is affixed to a particular place." He tapped his forehead and closed his eyes. "I can almost literally envision the pathways I must take to get to a needed room."

"What's in the root cellars?" she demanded. "And how about the dungeons?"

His eyes popped open. "Excuse me?"

"How far back can you go?"

He considered this. "I have some memories that go back to the age of two or so. There are also a few earlier memories, mere impressions—vague and warm but unformed by words." He paused and met her incredulous stare. "It is often so with the jordaini. My friend Andris claimed he could remember things that he must have heard while in his mother's womb, but perhaps he was jesting."

"Show me how," she demanded.

Matteo tossed her a towel. "Meet me in the sitting room and we will do what we can."

She padded in a few moments later, clad in green

leggings and tunic and looking rather fetchingly like a dew-soaked dryad.

"Tell me," she said, and plunked down cross-legged on the floor.

Matteo instructed her to close her eyes and bring to mind the earliest memory she could grasp. "Tell me what it is."

"Sprite," she said in a soft and faintly childlike voice. "That's what I called him. It was also what he was—a sprite. I suppose he had another name, but I don't remember hearing it."

"You were how old at the time?"

She shrugged. "Five, maybe six. But before Sprite, there's nothing."

"That's not so unusual. Many people retain few memories from their early years. Is it so important?"

"Yes."

She spoke the word with such finality and depth of emotion that Matteo didn't think to question her. "Then we will try another way. Envision in your mind—literally in your mind, in the physical paths that your thoughts take—where this memory of Sprite resides. Can you picture it?"

Her brow furrowed, but after a moment she nodded. "I think so."

"Move deeper and slightly to the left," he instructed softly.

She envisioned sliding back into her mind. For a moment there was nothing but blackness, and then she caught a glimmer of silver and felt a rhythmic, reassuring touch. "Someone is brushing my hair," she murmured. "My mother?"

"Stay where you are. Quiet your mind and imagine that you have just entered a dark room and are waiting for your eyes to adjust."

Tzigone nodded and sat still for a moment, her face a mask of concentration. Finally she shook her head. "Nothing," she said sadly.

"We will try again later," Matteo said, placing a consoling hand on her shoulder. "The memory is a palace constructed with patience. It cannot be built quickly, nor quickly explored."

"Not later," Tzigone said grimly. "Now." She closed her eyes and fiercely banished thought. When her mind was finally calm and still, she found the place where memories of Sprite dwelled, and then she slid farther down the dark pathways.

The gentle rhythm of the hairbrush pulled her back into the memory. But for some reason, the motion was not soothing. Tzigone felt her mother's tension as surely as if it were her own.

Her mother! Tzigone sank deeper still into memory, desperate for a glimpse of her mother's face or the sound of her voice. She saw herself as she might have then—the bare brown legs with their brave collection of childhood scrapes and bruises, the tiny hands clenched in her lap, the glossy brown hair that spilled over her shoulders.

"There, now. All finished," the woman said with forced gaiety. "With your hair so smooth and shiny, you look too fine for sleep. What if we run across the rooftops until we find a tavern still open? We could have cakes and sugared wine, and if there is a bard in the house, I will sing. And, yes, I will summon a fierce creature for you. A behir, a dragon— anything you like."

Even as a child, Tzigone hadn't been fooled by the brittle gaiety of her mother's tones. Quickly she bent down to tighten the laces on her soft leather shoes.

"I'm ready,"she announced.

Her mother eased open a shutter and lifted her onto the ledge beyond. The child leaned her small body against the wall and began to edge around the building, as confident and surefooted as a lemur.

Something on the ground caught her eye, drawing it to a disturbance several streets to the east. A tendril of magic, so powerful that her eyes perceived it as a glowing green light, twisted through the streets below. Like a jungle vine it grew, sending off seeking tendrils, moving purposefully toward whatever sun drew it.

Quicker than thought it came, and then it hesitated at the door to their inn as if it were momentarily confused by this barrier, or perhaps by another barrier that Tzigone could not see. Then the door exploded inward—silently, but with a force that stole her breath and nearly dragged her from the ledge.

Her mother was suddenly beside her, gripping her hand painfully. "This way," she urged, no longer making any attempt to hide her fear.

They scuttled sideways on the ledge like fleeing crabs, moving toward one of the elaborate drainpipes that decorated the corners of every building, providing beauty and status in addition to carrying away the heavy summer rains. This one was fashioned to resemble a pair of entwined snakes. It was easy to climb, and in moments the girl's small fingers grasped the leering stone mouth of one of the snake-headed gargoyles that capped the pipes.

Her mother placed a shoulder under the child's small rump and heaved. Tzigone lurched up, hit the roof, and rolled once. In a heartbeat, she was on her feet and racing for the roof's southern edge.

Tzigone remembered their games and the glowing threads that wove maps of the city against the night sky. For the first time, she understood their practical side. Her mother always pointed out the surrounding buildings and byways, and together they improvised a "what-if" game of pursuit and capture, one that was often whimsical and sometimes hilarious, but always, always in deadly earnest.

It felt strange to be a child again. The roof felt endless as Tzigone ran across on her short, thin legs. She reached the edge without slowing and launched herself into the night. The fall was brief, the landing hard. She rolled across the hard surface of the tiled roof of a bathhouse. Her leg burned from a brush with a jagged bit of tile. She touched it, and her hand came away wet.

"Run," her mother whispered as she dragged her to her feet. "Stop for nothing. Nothing!"

She made herself forget the pain as she and her mother raced across the bathhouse roof. Together they scrambled down the far side of the building, hands fisted in fragrant bunches of the night-blooming flowers that climbed the wall. The crushed flowers gave off a strong scent and a swirl of golden pollen. Musky sweetness surrounded them like an oppressive cloud. Never before had a fragrance seemed sinister, but to the terrified child, it seemed that the flowers were in league with her pursuers. They taunted her with their vines, so like the dangerous, seeking magic, and tried to trick her into revealing herself. Tzigone cursed them silently and struggled mightily not to sneeze.

Finally her small feet touched cobblestones. Across the street loomed a high wall of pink stone, against which was built a raised pool shaped like a half-moon and enlivened by a softly playing fountain. The wall enclosed a familiar villa, one that had entered into their games on a previous trip to this city.

Confidently they plunged into the water and wriggled through the small tunnel that circulated water back into the interior moat. Tzigone swam like an eel, but the wall was thick and the tunnel deceptively curved. She bobbed to the surface of the pool, choking and sputtering.

As she blinked water out of her eyes, she noted the pair of jeweled eyes that moved purposefully toward her, lifted above water by the crocodilian shape of a behir's head. Her mother flung out a hand to ward it off, but no magic spun out, just a splash of moat water. She changed tactics and dragged Tzigone to the edge of the moat with a haste that fairly shouted panic.

Tzigone remembered this villa. They had slipped through before during their nighttime wanderings. It was well guarded by monsters and magic. The first wave of defensive magic hit the intruders as soon as their feet touched dry ground. Her mother jolted and let out a small cry, just as the thief in the marketplace had done recently when he'd sagged upon the watchman's dirk. Tzigone felt none of the magical wards and did not expect to.

"Come," her mother gasped as she staggered toward a round freestanding tower that overlooked the garden and had no apparent connection to the villa itself.

Though the tower appeared utterly smooth from even a pace or two away, a narrow flight of stairs had been carved into the pink stone. They stumbled up the stairs, frantic now, all pretense of adventure forgotten. When they reached the top, her mother bent over, hands on her knees as she struggled for breath and speech. Tzigone could barely make out her request for light.

She had been schooled in which light to conjure during just such a "game," and she quickly cast the little cantrip. Light appeared, softer than moonlight and shaped like a giant teardrop, but visible only to her eyes. It illuminated not the natural material world, but the created magic that embellished it.

The faint light revealed a glassy, translucent path that stretched from the tower to a nearby villa, one on the very shores of the lake.

But something about it was wrong. This wasn't how Tzigone remembered the path. She sent a questioning look at her mother. The woman nodded. Without further hesitation, Tzigone stepped out into the seemingly empty air. Her mother followed closely, trusting her daughter to see what she herself could not.

No moon shone that night, but suddenly the two fugitives were silhouetted against a large, softly glowing orb. Tzigone muttered a ripe phrase she'd overheard from an impatient sea captain who'd cursed the fickleness of Selûne and her inconvenient tides. For once her mother did not reprove her for her inelegant speech.

They ran the length of the gossamer path and scrambled over the wall of the strange villa. Before them was a flight of stairs leading down toward the courtyard. In the center of the courtyard, a large oval pool brooded in the moonlight.

"Let's try it," her mother said. "It looks like a weir for lake trout."

They had encountered such things before on their "adventures." Fish weirs were common in lakeside villas, for they provided sport for the children and food for the table. A short tunnel led from lake to pool, and magic lured the fish. Swimming them was risky—there were powerful magical wards to keep anything but fish from swimming in. Swimming out was another matter. So far, Tzigone had encountered no surprises more unpleasant than the magic that tickled her skin like sparkling wine and an occasional fish that brushed past her on its way to the wizard lord's table.

They ran down the stairs, their eyes fixed on the mosaic floor below. The descent seemed to take far longer than it should have. Tzigone noticed suddenly that the floor's pattern seemed to be shifting. The color turned from its intricate inlay of deep reds and rich yellows to a uniform hue of darkest sapphire. Small lights began to twinkle in the glossy tile.

Puzzled, she came to a stop on the next landing. Her mother bumped heavily into her. Tzigone glanced back the way they'd come.

"Look," she said grimly, pointing up. Or possibly down. The pool gleamed overhead, and below them was the unmistakable void of the night sky. Inexplicably the two had changed places.

"A puzzle palace," her mother said in a faint, despairing voice. "Mystra save us."

The child's trained gaze darted around. Several flights of stairs led from the landing, some going up, some down, and some leading nowhere at all. There were four levels of balconies surrounding the courtyard, and all levels seemed to be split into several parts. Some had been fashioned with elaborately carved or tiled or painted ceilings, while others were roofed or floored by the night sky. It was as if some crazed wizard had inserted this small section of the city into a gigantic kaleidoscope, fracturing and fragmenting reality beyond logic or recognition.

"This way," she guessed and darted in the direction of a waterfall that disappeared into the air, only to resume its fall a few dozen paces to the south.

It proved to be a good choice. In moments they stood before a door—a real door, one that opened with a latch and led into the solid, staid reality of the villa beyond.

As the door swung open, her mother's amulet started to glow.

Never had this happened before, and the fearsome novelty of it froze Tzigone's feet to the floor. In the span of a heartbeat, the shining bit of electrum turned rosy with heat. Her mother let out a pained gasp and tore off the amulet, breaking the slender chain.

Instantly the courtyard was alive with verdant magic. The questing vine, fragmented into an impossible maze, writhed and twisted like a titanic snake that had been many times severed, floundering violently about in its death throes.

But apparently someone could make sense of the magical path. A shout came from beyond the villa's walls, and a door crashed open. Footsteps thundered through the building toward them.

Tzigone turned to dart back into the insane courtyard, plucking at her mother's skirt to indicate her intent rather than risk speech and discovery. But the woman gently pried the small fingers loose.

"Go," she said quietly. "My magic is nearly gone. The amulet is broken. They will find me soon whether I run or stay."

"I won't leave you," Tzigone said stubbornly.

"You must. It is you they seek."

She only nodded. Somehow she'd always known that. But knowing was not the same as doing, and she couldn't bear to leave.

The footsteps came closer, and the heavy tread seemed

to move the ground. Tzigone rocked back and forth, shaken violently by the terrifying approach. But she would not run. She had to see.

"Tzigone! Come back!"

It was not her mother's voice, but still filled with fear and concern. Instinctively she turned toward it. With difficulty, her eyes focused on Matteo's face.

He was kneeling in front of her, grasping her shoulders and shaking her, and his face was drawn and pale.

"I'm back," she said faintly. "You can stop rearranging my spine any time now."

Matteo released her but didn't move away. "What did you see?"

She averted her eyes. "Did I say anything?"

"Nothing I could make out. A word here and there. I did catch something about jasmine."

"I've always hated the bloody stuff. Now I remember why. I'm going back," she said in a stronger voice.

Matteo's lips thinned. "Tzigone, that would be most unwise. There are many layers of memory, and what you are doing goes far beyond anything most jordaini could dream of achieving. I've seen two other people fall into a memory trance. It seemed more taxing than a footrace or an afternoon's practice at arms. You should rest."

"I saw my mother!" she said. "I remembered the night we were separated. I escaped, but she didn't. You brought me back before I could see who took her away. I have to know! It's the only way I'll ever find her."

Matteo hesitated, his eyes searching her face. "This is so important?"

"I don't expect you to understand. You've never had any family but the jordaini. But I have to find her."

He nodded slowly, then rose and walked to a polished table. He took the cork from a full decanter of wine and poured a bit in a goblet. "Take a few moments to calm yourself. Then we will try again."

Tzigone took a single sip and placed the goblet aside.

Once again she stilled her mind and sank deep into the dark, hidden depths.

Suddenly an image leaped before her, more vivid than a dream.

She was in a forest, one as lush and thick as a jungle. Never had she seen such trees. They struck her as watchful and somehow wise. Next to them, the bilboa trees of Halruaa seemed as lifeless as furniture. The trees were massive, big enough to hold small kingdoms of birds and beasts in their branches. Insects and flying creatures that were not insects filled the air with a soft hum, and tiny toads dressed in bright patterns of red and blue and green and black sunned themselves on the branches, not fearing the birds that flitted and called overhead.

Suddenly the forest went still. Silence, immediate and absolute, hit her with the impact of an arrow to the heart. A piercing scream would have stunned her less. Tzigone jolted a second time as an invisible hand thrust into her mind and fisted itself around the threads that bound her to life, and to magic, and to this place.

No, not *her* mind. Tzigone was seized with the sudden conviction that she was experiencing memories that belonged not to her, but to some unknown other. And the companion that crouched at her side was certainly no creature that she had ever seen. It was a four-legged bird with a curved, rending beak and eyes bright with an intelligence more alien than an elf's. Its wings unfurled with a snap as it prepared to launch itself toward some unseen foe.

Tzigone most emphatically did not want to see the source of this danger. She dragged herself back up through the darkness more brutally than Matteo had done. Panting for air, she opened her eyes and willed the memory—*the* memory, not *her* memory—back to whatever place forgotten nightmares fled.

But the image remained, as visible to her eyes as it had been in her memory trance. The forest and the guardian beast were suspended in the center of the room like a ghostly vision. The color was almost as vivid as Tzigone had seen in her mind, but it was rapidly fading, and the image was growing more and more translucent. She could see through the memory, like looking through the arch of a low-lying rainbow, but it was no less fearsome for its seeming delicacy.

Tzigone scrambled away from the terrible vision, crab-walking frantically until she bumped into the far wall. Matteo also retreated, but he circled the vision and studied the ghostly bird thoughtfully.

Suddenly a vast clawed hand flashed in from nowhere. It slashed toward the avian guardian, a force too fast to evade and too powerful to stop. The bird exploded into a flurry of feathers and gore.

And then the image was suddenly, mercifully gone.

"What foul sorcery was that?" Matteo said softly, looking at Tzigone with the same horror that she had felt upon beholding the dream. Apparently he could bear the magic far more easily than he could stomach the magician.

"It wasn't mine," she said desperately. "Not my magic, not even my memory."

"It couldn't have been your memory. That much is true. That species of griffon has been extinct for nearly three hundred years. You couldn't remember what you have never seen.

"Or could you?" he said, his tone bleak but thoughtful. "A diviner can glimpse the future. I have never heard of a wizard who could look into the past, much less recall it in so vivid a fashion, but perhaps it could be done. But you are a wizard, Tzigone, no matter what tales you choose to tell."

For once Tzigone had no rejoinder. Too shaken to care about such fine distinctions, she bolted for the window. Before Matteo could say a word, she disappeared out into the night.

CHAPTER FIFTEEN

Dawn was nothing but a fond hope when the small band of warriors waded into the Kilmaruu Swamp. Andris went first, wading through the knee-deep water and carefully testing a path for the men who moved silently behind him. There were forty of them, some jordaini, some commoners, some of foreign blood. According to the magehound, none of them knew Mystra's touch.

Each man carried a pack on his back fashioned from sharkskin, and another, smaller bag hung on each side of his belt. These were filled with rations, for Andris did not trust any food or water they might find in Kilmaruu. The bags also carried an odd assortment of weapons. No magic could be used in the swamp, but Andris knew of natural substances that in certain combinations produced nearly magical effects. Each man carried several small bottles, each firmly stoppered with cork and sealed with a thin film of wax.

As he shifted his weight carefully to his next step, Andris tried not to think too much about the source of this relatively firm footing. Many years ago a terrible war had raged in this place. Hundreds had died fighting in a battle that lasted through the three days and nights of the full moon. It was said that entire villages had been emptied by the battles. Two villages had been all but swallowed by the swamp, and their ruins provided a haven for the undead creatures that haunted the land. Even Kilmaruu's quiet dead were very much in evidence. The bones of long-dead warriors provided a frame that held the silt and sand and kept Andris and his fighters from sinking into the muck.

Mist rose from the water, swirling through the already thick fog. Andris watched closely for patterns. Many of their foes were creatures that could hide in the mist, blending in like dryads in a grove of trees. Ahead and to his left, a particularly thick land-bound cloud brooded over a sleeping heron. The jordain noticed that it didn't touch either the bird or the water.

Andris nodded to one of the forward scouts—Quon Lee, a small, slight man with hair the color of polished ebony and almond-shaped black eyes so sharp that they could perceive shadows almost before they were cast. Quon Lee was a conscript, stolen from his homeland by pirates. Kiva had paid his slave price so that he could join this endeavor.

That was something else Andris tried not to ponder. True, the man stayed willingly enough, for he was eager to win his freedom. Kiva had promised that her magic could remove the ugly scar of the slave brand from Quon Lee's forehead once the battle was over. Andris would have preferred to lead into battle men who chose to fight, not men who fought because they had no other choice.

He watched as the scout broke away from the group and slipped down into the water, half swimming and half crawling toward the cloud, keeping his movements slow and fluid and doing his best to stay submerged.

Andris nodded in silent approval. He wouldn't have thought of this precaution, but he saw the wisdom of it at once. Quon Lee had been born and raised in haunted jungles far to the east. If a spirit guardian lurked within that cloud, it would be roused by the heat of a living body moving through the still morning air. But the water was as hot as blood, and it was full of darting creatures and unpredictable currents. The warm, restless water would mask the scout's approach.

The call of the heron, sudden and shrill, startled them all. Some of the men jumped, but all were too well trained to make any noise. The long-legged bird burst into awkward flight. It rose into the strange mist and immediately faltered, its wings locked into place as if frozen. Like a child's wooden toy, the bird traced an awkward nose dive and crashed into the water. The impact seemed to revive it somewhat, and it began to flail about in a wild panic.

Almost at once, the waters around the heron started to churn. In a heartbeat, a pool of deep red surrounded the bird. Frantic flashes of silver leaped and glittered in the bloody water.

Andris abruptly motioned his men to a stop. The swamp teemed with schools of silvery, delicate fish, not much bigger than a man's hand, that could strip the flesh from an ox more efficiently than a butcher. Andris didn't have to remind the men to keep perfectly still until the frenzy abated and the fish swam off in search of other prey.

One of the men lifted a hand to his heart to trace a sign of warding, a silent petition to some foreign god. Although Andris had been raised to believe that none but Mystra or Azuth were true deities worthy of veneration, he didn't begrudge the man his devotions. Jordain were taught to respect the gods of magic, but from a distance. Still, Andris suspected that all the men were calling upon every god whose name they knew. A trip into Kilmaruu, Andris noted wryly, might even make a devout man of Matteo.

He quickly thrust aside the thought of his friend and the pain that came from knowing he would likely never see Matteo again. In the eyes of his brothers, Andris was dead. Unless he kept his focus, that fiction might soon become truth. This was no time to think about what might come after Kilmaruu.

Quon Lee glided smoothly back toward the group. He rose from the water, caught Andris's eye, and gave him a single grim nod. The man's lips were blue, and under the brown of his face lay a sickly pallor. Even in the water, even without touching the cloud itself, he had been chilled by the ghostly presence.

Andris motioned the men away from the lurking mist. They moved cautiously through a narrow strip between two seas of reeds, into a lagoon shaded by leaning trees draped with moss and vines.

Andris studied the shore, looking for a likely route among the thick and seemingly impassable tangle of under-brush. As he watched, a shrike dived in, its flight awkward due to the heavy weight it bore in its talons. A long, limp brown form hung from the small raptor's grasp—a weasel, most likely. The shrike tossed its prey into the brush. It fell onto a wicked thorn, neatly impaled on a spike that was longer than Andris's thumb.

He studied the brush more closely and noted that the shrike had left several similar meals scattered among the bushes that lined the lagoon's edge. The result looked grimly like a miniature butcher shop, and Andris quickly decided against attempting a land passage. Jungle shrikes chose only the most secure sites for their larders, places that could not easily be penetrated or despoiled. Better to risk the water than attempt passage through those rending thorns.

Even as the thought formed, one of the scouts suddenly disappeared beneath the water. Andris stooped and plunged both hands into the dark water, groping about until he seized a handful of hair. He dragged the man up, unharmed and wearing an expression of chagrin. The scout pan-tomimed a ledge with a sudden, quick drop. They moved as close to the shore as they dared and kept to it, testing for ledges with each step.

"Ledges," Andris said softly, remembering what he had read of such formations. Ledges of submerged rock or roots offered ideal places for underwater storage. Some water monsters were known to drag their prey into the water, drown them, and leave them wedged under a rocky ledge until they had softened and aged. Ledges, he concluded grimly, were not a good omen.

The crocodiles appeared so suddenly that Andris had the uncanny feeling he'd conjured them with a thought. One moment the lagoon was limpid silver, as still as a mirror beneath the rising mist. The next, a semicircle of reptilian eyes regarded the men with a cold, incurious stare, and over a dozen snouts pointed toward the scent of living meat.

Andris nodded to Iago, his second-in-command. The thin man quickly pointed to six of the quickest fighters. Andris chose seven more. Each man took a coil of rope from his belt and tested the noose at the end. Then each man silently chose a partner. They moved in pairs, spreading out to face the approaching crocodiles.

The fighters readied their nooses while their partners cupped their hands, as if to give their comrades a leg up onto a horse. When the crocodiles were near, the men tossed the chosen fighters up and over the approaching creatures. The men twisted nimbly in the air and came down to straddle the crocodiles' backs.

Instantly the water exploded into churning foam. Some of the crocodiles reared up, jaws snapping at the air, and then splashed down hard. The men riding them lunged forward at once, struggling to get the nooses around the fanged jaws.

The crocodiles instinctively dived and went into furious spins, trying to dislodge the men or drown them. But the men had trained too well, and they knew their opponents. Once a crocodile clamped its jaws down, the strongest four men among them couldn't wrench them open. But the muscles that opened these massive jaws were not strong at all. Holding the jaws shut and tying them required not massive strength but timing, dexterity, and nerves of tempered steel.

In moments the crocodiles were muzzled and floundering about, tossing their heads and pawing at the ropes. The men struggled back to the ledge. They fell back into formation and quickly left the lagoon, fearing that the struggles of the helpless crocodiles might draw even worse creatures.

They walked throughout the morning, sometimes splashing through water, sometimes walking on narrow strips of spongy land. The mist faded as the sun rose, but the air remained thick and damp. Insects, some of them larger than birds of prey, darted across the water or skimmed its surface. Once a giant wasplike creature dipped low over the water and flew off with a large eel, snapping and writhing in its grasp.

Andris hadn't expected the Kilmaruu to be so noisy. Birds called and shrieked and laughed in the trees overhead. An occasional snarl of a hunting cat echoed through the trees. Grunts and whuffles spoke of the great wild pigs that roamed the jungles, swifter and deadlier than wolves. Insects chirped among the ferns or whined around his head. Giant frogs groaned and burped, bull crocodiles roared. Monsters whose voices Andris had never heard added to the cacophony.

Despite the noise that surrounded them, the men didn't talk. They moved along in silence, marking the swamp's every rustle and cry. Many of them kept their hands resting on their weapons. Their faces became increasingly drawn and tense, their muscles as tight and ready as a wound crossbow.

Even so, they failed to see the giant dragonfly until it dropped among them, fast as a striking hawk. Barbed, sticky talons drove deep into the shoulders of Salvidio, the smallest man among them. Two pairs of iridescent blue wings beat furiously as the creature changed direction. The reeds along shore bent under the sudden onslaught of air, and the small man was jerked from the water before he could reach for a weapon or form a startled oath. The dragonfly darted off with its struggling prey, heading for the dark, deep waters to the west.

For a moment the sheer size and speed of the creature stunned Andris into immobility. He quickly gathered himself and turned to Danthus, another jordain and the best archer among them. "Use a tethered arrow, and quickly!"

Danthus snatched his bow from his shoulder and fitted to it a stout arrow. He took aim at the dragonfly and let fly. The bolt rose, trailing a length of rope. Five men darted to the archer's side, each taking a two-handed grip on the rope's end and bracing his feet wide for the coming jolt.

The archer's aim was true, and the arrow tore through the gossamer wings and sank deep into the insect's body. The dragonfly screamed, an unexpected and chilling sound that broke off abruptly as the creature reached the end of its tether and jerked to a stop.

Down went the giant insect, but it didn't relax its hold on Salvidio. They slammed into the water. The dragonfly's wings continued to beat as furiously in the water as they had in the air.

All six men began to drag in the rope, working hand over hand as they pulled the struggling insect into the shallows. The creature's movements began to slow, and the water went still as the dragonfly and its prey sank out of sight. Andris waded in as deep as he dared, then pulled his dagger and waited.

A round, furry head suddenly exploded from the water. Andris found himself staring into the insect's eyes. Each was a bulging orb containing a thousand smaller eyes, all as green as moss and filled with malevolence. A pair of dripping antennae quirked into a posture of unmistakable menace. The creature's mouth, a strange hooked beak, opened wide as the head reared back to attack.

Andris drew the dagger overhead and stabbed straight into the open maw. The dragonfly screamed again, a horrible, strangled sound. Hot blood gushed from the beak, and the wild light began to fade from the dragonfly's multiple eyes.

The jordain wrenched his blade free, took a deep breath,

and dived under the water. Though the creature was dead, it hadn't let go its prey. Salvidio's eyes were bulging, and rifts of bubbles spilled from his lips. Andris used his knife to pry the talons from Salvidio's shoulders. He saw at once that he couldn't finish the task in time and quickly rose to the surface.

"You three! With me!" he shouted, pointing toward a nearby trio.

He dived again. With two men working on each side, they soon had the talons pried free. Andris dragged Salvidio's limp form to the surface. The man sputtered and coughed, then staggered off to retch up swamp water.

Andris took a small bottle from his bag, an ointment that would seal the wounds and keep the insects away. Even the smallest scratch could turn deadly in a swamp. He quickly applied ointment and bandages to Salvidio's shoulder, ignoring the injured man's hisses of impatience over the delay. They continued on their way as soon as Salvidio could walk. With each step, the danger increased, for they neared the site of a lost city and its undead inhabitants.

Around highsun they paused briefly, perching on half-submerged logs by the shore as they took some of the rations of the food and water they'd carried in. Wolther, a yellow-haired northerner with odd tastes in food, collected a handful of mussels from the shallows, pried them open with his knife, and ate them raw. Before Andris could chide him about the wisdom of eating anything that lived in these swampy waters, Wolther turned a plump snail shell over and probed about inside with the tip of his knife. The man's face took on an expression of puzzlement that turned quickly to horror. He dropped the shell into the water as if it burned him.

"Look at the snails," he whispered.

Andris noted that several swirled shells inched along the driftwood-smooth bark. He picked up one of the snails, noting the tug of resistance and the single, fleshy foot of the creature within. He shrugged, then picked up another of the moving shells. This time there was no grip, and there was no creature within.

For some reason, this small uncanny fact seemed more ominous than the appearance of a rotting ghoul. The swamp was filled with undead creatures; they all knew that. Animated death held absolute sway in the depths of the swamp. But Andris's mind grew dizzy as he contemplated a power so large that it would spill over into so small a creature. He could fight a zombie or a skeleton, but could they overcome a power that permeated the entire swamp?

He carefully set down the haunted shell and eased back into the shallows, motioning for the men to follow. The ruins of the lost city must be close by.

The first sign they came to was a watery field of standing stones. Draped with moss and broken into jagged shards, they thrust up out of the swamp like the graves of drowned men. Andris eased his daggers from their sheaths and heard the soft chorus of metallic hisses behind him as the men did likewise.

Several forms burst from the water, leering at them with skeletal grins and making strange, jerky gestures with their bony fingers. Weeds hung about the skulls in place of hair, sodden tatters of once-fine robes draped over bony frames, and tarnished medallions dangled over empty chests.

Andris and Iago stepped forward to meet the first attack. It was possible that these creatures, once wizards, had managed the transformation from men to liches. A lich could cast all the magic the wizard had ever learned, and it remained a deadly foe from the day of death until the day it moldered to dust. None of the men with Andris possessed magic, but only the jordaini had much resistance to it.

But no spells erupted from the jerky skeletal hands. The undead men were merely repeating gestures they had learned in life. But Andris's keen senses felt a curious sucking sensation in the air about him, an invisible and intangible vortex. He suspected that if any of the men with him had possessed magic, something in Kilmaruu would steal it away.

Not liches, then, but something different, some creation of the swamp itself.

He led the attack with a sudden rush that sent swamp water spraying and surging. The two forces, the living and the undead, slammed together. Andris chose his target, and his daggers drove for the tattered remains of sinew that connected the animated bones. His men grappled with the skeletal fighters, hacking and tearing at them and flinging anything that came loose into the deepest tangle of reeds or underbrush that they could reach.

But these creatures didn't accept death easily. Beheaded skulls rolled and spun in the water, jaws clacking furiously. An arm slithered toward them, looking eerily like a thin white crocodile.

Suddenly Wolther started shrieking in his barbarian tongue. He stamped frantically and repeatedly, then gave that up and began to stab the water with his sword.

Andris sloshed over to give aid and swore softly at the sight before him. A dismembered hand had crawled over to Wolther. Bony fingers dug through boot leather and into the flesh beneath.

"Your sword!" Andris demanded, closing his hand around the hilt.

Wolther hesitated, then he gave a quick nod and relinquished the sword. "Get it off!" he screamed, babbling with barely constrained hysteria. "Cut it off at the knee if that's what it takes."

The jordain carefully slid the sword between the boot and the bony palm, digging the blade in as deep into the swamp bed as he could. He braced one foot against Wolther's leg and began to pry the bony fingers away. The task was distressing like pulling nails from a wooden plank, but in a few moments the skeletal hand was out. Bony fingers wrapped around the sword and began to inch their way toward the hilt. Andris whipped the sword forward and sent the hand spinning toward the fern-choked banks.

He turned to Wolther and noted with relief that no blood gushed forth and that the injured leg could still support the man's weight. None of the major veins or sinews had been breached. Wolther might always walk with a limp, but if the wound didn't turn septic, he would survive.

By the time he was finished with Wolther, his men had finished dismembering the undead wizards. Andris glanced up at the sun and was surprised to note that only a short time had passed.

"Let's keep moving," he said softly. "This promises to be a very long day."

The ground underfoot grew firmer, and the terrain began to slope gently upward. Soon they were walking on dry ground. Andris knew from his studies that in times long past, this had been a rain forest set on gently rolling hills. It was said that a trio of wizards had diverted a river just to see if it could be done. As it happened, it could, and the result was the Kilmaruu Swamp. But this deed had left a city stranded, and its furious citizens determined to reclaim their drowned lands.

The land dipped suddenly, forming what appeared to be the ruins of an ancient moat. Fortunately an ancient tree had fallen over the water, providing a natural bridge. Clumps of ferns and colorful twisted fungi grew in the rotting wood, but it looked sound enough to hold their weight.

"Prepare the saltpowder," Andris said softly.

Each man quickly took two objects from his packs: a weapon that resembled a tiny catapult mounted on a crossbow and a small bottle filled with what appeared to be finely ground greenish crystals. They cranked back the mechanism on the bow and then poured the saltpowder into the tiny shot buckets on the catapults. Once the strange weapons had been readied, the men resumed walking, their weapons held level and their fingers lightly worrying the triggers.

The log was broad enough for them to cross in pairs. Andris looped Wolther's arm across his shoulder to help him across. They moved quickly, and the log held firm. The jordain nodded to Iago, holding up six fingers to indicate that they should cross in small groups rather than all at once. All went well until the last group began passage.

The assault came suddenly as scores of creatures burst from the stagnant waters. Hideous forms, as pale as beached fish and bloated to thrice their living size, reached out with swollen hands. Incredible stench rolled off the creatures in waves; several of the fighters bent over, retching. Those who could still stand took aim. The air was suddenly filled with the snaps and whumping sounds of the miniature catapults and the sparkling flight of the strange ammunition.

The saltpowder crystals pelted the drowned creatures. Fetid steam rose from the bloated forms as the minerals seared through cheesy flesh and warred with the trapped gases beneath.

"Down!" commanded Andris. He dropped flat and threw his arms over his head.

The explosion shook the ground and sent unspeakable goo splattering over the warriors. The log shuddered and shifted, creaking as it threatened to fall into the water. Andris rose and began shouting and gesturing to the men who lay flat on the log. They struggled to their feet and hurried across.

Suddenly two enormous, skeletal forepaws slammed down on the log bridge. The massive knuckles flexed and water surged as an enormous skull broke free. Nimble as a gigantic squirrel, the undead monstrosity clambered onto the bridge.

Never had Andris seen such a creature, alive or dead. A pair of long pointed horns thrust forward out of its ridged skull, and a beaklike maw was filled with teeth that resembled those of a titanic vampire. Incisors the length and sheen of daggers flashed as the creature darted at the last man on the bridge.

The man turned, alerted by his comrades' screams, just

as the massive jaws clamped down on him. As horrid as it was to see a comrade disappear into a monster's maw, it was more terrible still to see the rent pieces fall through the skeleton form to stain the log bridge and the water below.

Horror gripped the men, lending frantic speed as they ripped through the foliage and up the hill. In perhaps an hour, they stood panting at the crumbling, vine-colored gates of the city itself.

Andris stared in awe at the remains of what had once been a wondrous town, with buildings even more fanciful than those of Halruaa's cities. Remnants of leaping towers rose into the trees, some of them almost entirely obscured by vines. None of them had been constructed with stone; indeed, they had been grown, not built. Piles of multicolored crystal lay in heaps, looking like the mounds of a dragon's hoard. A small waterfall spilled over one such ruin, and the passage of water coaxed high, ghostly notes from some of the crystal shards.

To his astonishment, Andris recognized the ruined structures as elven. The history books claimed that the town was a rough outpost inhabited by rogues and bandits. He had never heard of early civilizations of elves in this part of Halruaa.

The city was eerily silent as they worked their way through the ruined streets. The only sound was the thud of their machetes as they cut through the foliage clogging the area.

Quon Lee worked his way over to Andris's side. "There should be undead here," he said softly. "Why haven't they attacked?"

"There will be undead," Andris murmured. "I don't know why they're waiting. Perhaps they're standing guard over something that seemed important in life."

"So if we leave now without despoiling this unknown treasure, they will let us withdraw in peace?"

Andris shot an ironic smile in the scout's direction. "What do you think?"

Quon Lee merely shrugged and lifted his machete again.

Suddenly they were clear and standing in an enormous courtyard. The buildings here were nearly intact, and the fountain on the huge pool in the center still bubbled. Andris noted that the scent of the swamp was heavy in the water.

He took a vial of powder and a torch from his bag, first lighting the torch and then using his teeth to pull out the vial's cork. The other fighters followed his lead.

"What now?" whispered Iago.

"We wait," Andris replied simply.

They didn't have long to wait. A sudden clatter of bone and the reek of rotting meat announced the attack. Skeletal and near-skeletal forms rattled out of the buildings that surrounded the courtyard, brandishing priceless elven weapons in their bony fists. Andris noted that none of the undead creatures appeared to be elves. All were human. The bones of some were extremely dry and brittle, while others had obviously not been dead for long. This, then, was the resting place of the adventurers who sought to despoil the city's treasure. But what of the elves?

There was no time to ponder this question. The men tossed their open vials into the pool, followed by the torches. And then they turned and ran for the exit.

They dived back into the thick foliage, rolling as far away as they could and clamping their hands to their ears.

A tremendous roar rolled through the vine-clogged streets like the scream of a dragon taking flight. A second blast followed, a cloud of terrible heat and choking black smoke.

After a few minutes, they ventured back into the courtyard. A few charred bones still twitched, but most of the undead had been utterly destroyed by the blast. Wisps of foul steam and black smoke rose from the pool. The crystal buildings still stood, but several of the doors had been blasted inward by the force of the explosion.

Andris caught sight of a faint, greenish glow through one of those doors. He cautiously eased through the opening and found himself in a ruined temple. On the altar was a small globe, perhaps half the size of a man's head, faintly pulsating with light and power. Andris could feel the pull of it, a powerful yearning that felt more like sadness than hunger.

"What the Nine bloody Hells is that thing?" demanded Wolther, raking his straw-colored hair away from his face as he stared at the glowing sphere.

"I don't know for certain," Andris replied hesitantly, "but I think this could be what empowers the undead. Notice how they gather here. This globe is hungry for magic, and the undead creatures gathered around it like bees feeding nectar to a queen."

He carefully lifted the crystal and slipped it into his pack.

The northerner's sky-colored eyes narrowed. "So you're taking that with us? It'll draw every undead thing within calling range!"

"The return trip will not lack excitement," Andris said dryly. "But it is the only way to complete our task. The Kilmaruu will never be utterly free of undead—what swamp in any land can make that boast?—but those creatures that remain need not forage for magic."

The big northerner folded his arms. "Seems to me you're moving a problem, not solving one."

"Surely Halruaa has one wizard who can negate or contain this force," Andris retorted. "We are here to remove the thing that causes the undead to feed upon magic. Only by doing so can we eliminate the danger to outlying farms and the nearby waters. Only then will you be free to return to your homeland," he added for good measure.

Wolther shrugged. "Best be going, then."

Andris noted that none of the men suggested staying to explore and pillage the elven city. All of them were far too eager to leave Kilmaruu behind.

Very late that night, the weary survivors staggered into the compound where they had trained. Kiva and her wemic captain awaited them. The magehound took Andris's report with great satisfaction, and her amber eyes lit with sudden ardent flame when he handed her the green sphere.

A suspicion stirred in Andris's mind. Somehow he doubted that the magehound's stated mission—destroying the threat offered by the undead—was her true goal.

Kiva dismissed the other men to rest, but she took Andris to her private chambers and plied him with wine and questions. Every detail of the battle fascinated her. She presented other possible situations, similar to that which they had faced, and asked how he would address them.

Andris did not mind, despite his exhaustion. Not since his days at the Jordain College and his long discussions and arguments with Matteo had he encountered anyone who shared his passion for tactics and strategy.

But doubt, once planted, grows quickly and dies hard. He studied the softly glowing globe, which Kiva kept with her, cradling in her lap like a beloved cat.

"You seem to take scant interest in this victory. What is your true purpose? What comes next?"

She smiled at him. "You are quick, Andris. I suppose I need not tell you that Kilmaruu was little more than a test."

The weary jordain let out a small, dry chuckle. "Next you'll be telling me that fighting a red dragon is nothing but battle training. I may regret asking, but for what did Kilmaruu prepare us?"

Kiva poured more wine into his cup before answering. "What do you know of the Swamp of Akhlaur?"

The jordain choked on his sip of wine. He coughed and put the goblet down with a sharp thunk. "It is an ancient swamp with a relatively new name. Known in ages past as the Swamp of Ghalagar, it was renamed for Akhlaur, an infamous necromancer who reputedly built a tower there. The swamp grows slowly, advancing some hundred feet or so each year. No one seems to know why, and the wizards who venture into the swamp to seek answers do not return."

"Wizards," she emphasized. "Your men will do better."

Andris thought this over. "We went into Kilmaruu with

a purpose. I won't risk these men's lives again without knowing that there is just cause."

The elf woman sat silent for a long moment as if in private debate. Then she rose abruptly, the glowing sphere in her hands. Raising it aloft, she began to sing.

Never had Andris heard anything like that elven song. Naming it music would be a disservice; he would sooner refer to the finest wine as spoiled grape juice! Kiva's song was magic and starlight and wind and every emotion he had ever felt or imagined. The keen of a funeral dirge was in that song, and the exhilaration of a battle yell, and the sweetness of a first kiss.

Her bell-like voice enchanted the globe as surely as it did him. The light deepened, and glowing forms began to swirl within. Finally Kiva finished the song on a clear, ringing note. Before the sound died away, she flung the globe to the floor.

There was no explosion, no tinkle of breaking crystal. But suddenly the room was crowded with softly translucent shadows, all of them elves, all of them regarding him and Kiva with profound joy and gratitude.

Motes of lights shimmered in the ghostly forms, which began to slowly dissolve. The lights drifted through the open window and rose into the night. Andris could have sworn that the stars shone brighter.

Kiva watched them go, then turned her face to Andris. It seemed to the wondering jordain that some of the light lingered on her coppery features.

"I do not think I can explain to you what happened here, but since you will surely ask, I will try."

Andris nodded, not sure that he could speak.

"Some elves join together to work magic. One elf acts as a center, drawing together the magic of the others and that of the surrounding land, focusing it and weaving it into a spell. In the city in Kilmaruu, there once were many elves, engaged in working a great magic. You can probably guess what they might have been attempting."

"A spell battle," he said. "They fought against the three wizards who diverted the river and created Kilmaruu Swamp."

"Fought, and lost," she said tersely. "The crystal was a tool to help focus their magic. Something went terribly wrong, and some of their essence was trapped when they died. But they were also linked to the magic of the land, and this link stayed open. I suspect that this is what drew and empowered the undead. I cannot say for certain. I do not know what terrible spells the three human necromancers might have used. But the elves are free now, thanks to you."

Andris considered this. "So we serve not only my people but yours as well. This is true also of the Swamp of Akhlaur?"

"Doubly so," Kiva said in a soft, dark tone. "One of those three necromancers was named Akhlaur. Like you, he learned from his experiences in Kilmaruu and went on to 'greater things.' I will not sooth you with pretty lies: What you saw in Kilmaruu is but a preparation. Knowing this, will you follow me still?"

The jordain glanced through the open window. The sky near the horizon was beginning to fade toward silver, but the stars still blazed, brighter and more joyous than he'd ever seen them.

He turned back to the magehound, and a passion that had nothing to do with Kiva's beauty burned in his hazel eyes.

"I will follow," he swore.

CHAPTER SIXTEEN

Tzigone hauled herself over the window ledge and dropped into the chamber. She crouched low to the floor and listened for sounds that spoke of the room's rightful occupant. No lights were on, but she hadn't lived this long by abandoning caution. Nor did she feel any qualm about invading Matteo's sanctum. After all, the shutters hadn't been closed and barred. If he had truly wanted to keep her out, he wouldn't have left them open.

She rummaged through the chest at the foot of his bed for one of his white tunics. The garment was far too long for her and hung almost to her knees, but it didn't look too bad once she'd belted it up. The jordain's pendant she already had, and she quickly looped it over her neck. She already wore white leggings and a loose, long-sleeved white shirt. In this weather, the jordaini usually left their arms bare, but that would give away the game. Tzigone was strong and fit, but there was no way anyone would confuse her slender arms with those of a trained fighter.

Before she ventured out into the palace, she went into the bath and practiced before the mirror until she'd produced the calm, certain expression she associated with the jordaini. Looking the part was important. A misplaced smirk might be enough to draw attention that she could ill afford.

She walked down the halls purposefully, even though she had no idea where she was going. Whenever she passed someone, she merely put on an abstracted expression, as if she were puzzling over deep secrets or committing to memory some three-scroll epic. But an hour passed in this fashion, and she began to think that she might be wandering about the palace forever. Finally she stopped a scullery maid and asked where she might find the queen's new counselor.

"If Matteo's in the palace, he'd be in the queen's workroom, like as not," she said. She shuddered as if the thought horrified her. "No, wait. No one will be there until dusk. Matteo sent word to the kitchen to pack a picnic for the queen and her guards."

Tzigone threw up her hands in feigned disgust. "Well, that's just fine! He bade me tend an errand and didn't even tell me where to go. My first day as his assistant, and he isn't here!"

"I'll point you the way," the servant offered.

Tzigone listened to the directions and took off. To her delight, the queen's workroom was utterly abandoned but for the guard seated by the vast door, nodding and snoring. A quick pressure to his neck and temples ensured that he'd sleep a bit longer and deeper than he had intended. Tzigone quickly patted him down for keys. There were none, but she found a small silver wand. It looked a great deal like the lockpicks she occasionally employed.

With a shrug, Tzigone inserted the wand into the lock and began to tinker. But there was no mechanism inside, no gears and levers to catch and trip. Not a tool, then, but an artifact.

She heaved a frustrated sigh and stepped back a pace, leveling the wand at the door and hoping that no trigger word was needed. To her relief, the door melted away, and then another. The third door actually did require picking, but she handled the matter quickly, and in moments she stood at the entrance to the queen's inner sanctum.

The rows and shelves of clockwork creatures didn't interest her. Tzigone wanted books. There was a new rumor on the streets, whispers suggesting that the records of the secret Cabal might be kept under the queen's watchful eye. If that were true, Tzigone might finally find some clue about her ancestry, a clue that might lead her to learn of her mother's fate.

She found a small room off the workshop filled with scrolls and volumes. With a small cry of delight, she settled down to read. These were not the Cabal records—the script was Halruaan, not the unique Southern Magic runes developed to protect the land's magical secrets. But they were interesting nonetheless.

The hours slipped by as she searched, but none of the names listed in the elaborate genealogies jogged her memory. Tzigone didn't remember her own name, much less her mother's. She doubted that she ever heard her father's name spoken. She found very little that would help her, but there was some very interesting information about Matteo and his fellow jordaini.

"Here now, what are you doing here?" demanded a dry and indignant voice.

Tzigone started and looked up. A wisp of a man regarded her peevishly. He was not much older than she, but his hair was the color of dust and his frame was as insubstantial as a reed. Chances were she could burst right past him. But her chances of dashing out of the palace without being stopped were considerably less likely.

"Oh, good," she said with feigned relief. "I was hoping that a scribe would happen by. You are a scribe, aren't you?"

The man frowned in puzzlement. "Yes, of course. But what need would a jordain have of my services? You do not send or carry written messages."

Tzigone realized her misstep. "I'm sure I don't know," she said sullenly. "Matteo told me to have some spells copied out, and he also wants a shopping list of the required components. I can only assume they're for the queen."

The scribe's look of suspicion deepened. "It has been quite some years since the queen requested either spells or components."

"Well, it's been a while since she went out on a picnic, hasn't it?" retorted Tzigone.

This logic silenced the scribe for a moment. "You don't look familiar," he said, eyeing her intently. "I keep the household accounts. You are not of this house."

"No," she agreed. "I'm Matteo's friend. He sort of invited me here."

"How unfortunate for him," said a resonant alto voice at the door.

The scribe spun to face the king's counselor. "Lady Cassia! It is a most unexpected honor to see you in this place!"

Something in the scribe's voice made Tzigone suspect that the female jordain was not only unexpected but unwelcome. Apparently Tzigone wasn't the only person to take advantage of the queen's absence.

But Cassia gave away nothing. "An intruder was reported in the halls. I came myself to see how diligently the queen's servants tended their mistress's affairs." She glanced at Tzigone. "In all truth, I am not impressed."

The scribe paled. "I was about to call the guard and have this boy removed."

"A good thought," Cassia said. "Do not let me hinder you. If it's all the same to you, I think I should stay until the guard arrives."

He hastened into the next room, and in moments a tinny clockwork alarm began to sound. Tzigone heard the clatter of approaching footsteps and willed herself not to panic. Her first instinct was to bolt, but there was nowhere to go. The room had no windows and only one door, and that was barred by the imposing form of the king's counselor.

Tzigone didn't dare try her hand there. She was quick on her feet and could throw a decent punch when called upon to do so, but Cassia was a trained, well-armed fighter.

The woman looked up as the first two guards hurried forward. "Take this 'boy' to the tower and then go fetch Matteo."

The two men exchanged uneasy glances. "But he attends the queen. We cannot command him away from her side, lady, not even by your word."

"You can if her safety is threatened by his presence," Cassia returned coldly. "I have reason to suspect both Matteo's veracity and his devotion to his order. This thief wears the jordaini vestment and pendant of the queen's counselor. Pretending to be a jordain is a serious matter—a deadly one, if she is found to have any magic. Any man who would consort with such street trash is suspect, but it appears that Matteo has actually brought this thief into the palace. Perhaps I am wrong about him; I hope so. But a magehound will examine them both and decide the matter. See to it!"

The guards flanked Tzigone and hauled her out of the chair. Her first response was to blind them with a quick fireball and then run like a rat. But using magic would ensure her death if she were caught. She tamely submitted to the guards, but her mind raced as she devised ways out of this mess.

Not much more than an hour or two passed before the door to her cell opened. Matteo stepped in. His gaze skimmed her attire and then clouded with resignation.

"My medallion, I suppose?"

She took it off and handed it to him. "You're welcome to it. It's caused me nothing but trouble."

Matteo sighed and put the chain around his neck, adjusting the medallion into place. "What have you done this time, Tzigone?"

"Oh, I like that," she retorted. "All the scrapes I've gotten you out of, and that's the thanks I get?"

"The story," he prompted. "Unadorned, if possible."

She took a deep breath. "I am secretly a member of the Jordaini Council. In the guise of a clever street waif, I protect the rights of any jordain targeted by treachery or jealousy. Currently I am following you to ensure that Frando does not attempt to place you in damning circumstances."

Matteo folded his arms. "Really."

"And it's a good thing I did! Are you aware that a pair of nubile Amnian twins are being smuggled into your bedchamber even as we speak? And that they are clad in the queen's gowns, and wearing wigs and face paint so that they both resemble Beatrix? Frando plans to accuse you not only of depravity, but of theft of the queen's property and treachery against the king. I suppose that would be treachery by proxy, since the twins are not actually Beatrix," she mused. "The niceties of Halruaan law escape me."

"Indeed," the jordain said dryly. "That's an ingenious plot, considering how little time Frando had to conceive it. He must have more talent than either you or I credited him with."

"Who knew?" she marveled.

Matteo sighed. "Tzigone, why do you insist upon telling such outrageous tales?"

"It keeps me in practice," she said with a shrug, then patted the wooden bench. "You might as well have a seat. We could be here for a while."

"Until the magehound is summoned," he said grimly. "Do you realize how serious this situation is?"

She met his eyes. "All my life I have been pursued by wizards and magehounds," she said quietly. "Once before I was caught. I escaped, but not before I learned exactly how serious the situation can be. Here's a tall tale you can believe: If I don't get out, I'm dead."

Matteo nodded slowly. "Then you are a wizard after all."

"Must you keep singing that dreary tune?" she snapped. "I told you, I'm no wizard. I have never been trained, I have never gone to any of the schools, I have not even been tested for gifts."

Matteo suspected that this was true, as far as it went. He

sat down beside her. "I believe that you will be slain if the law gets hold of you. But I suspect that theft is the least of your crimes."

"Compare my situation to yours," she suggested. "I've been a street entertainer, making my way by doing tricks that supposedly had nothing to do with magic. If fraud is proved, there's a price to pay. Same as with the jordaini."

He thought of Andris and of the price that had been exacted from his friend. He couldn't stand quietly by while that happened again. After a moment he looked up and let Tzigone see the resolve in his eyes.

The girl nodded and then began to plot. Matteo could almost see the gears working behind her eyes, as if she were one of the queen's clockwork creatures.

"I want you to stand over there in the far corner, where the shadows are deepest. Put your white cloak over your shoulders. Turn your back to the door, so that the first thing someone sees is a faceless jordain. You're not much taller than Cassia. It might work."

He quickly followed the line of her reasoning. But impersonating a jordain was a serious offense, even if one jordain pretended to be another. "Is this truly necessary?"

"Depends. How attached are you to the idea of living? Personally, I'm quite fond of the notion."

Matteo nodded in acceptance. He rose and took the position she had indicated, his daggers at the ready.

Tzigone rose and walked to the door.

"Guards!" she demanded in a peremptory tone. Cassia's voice rang from her throat, strong and commanding. "Open this door at once."

The guard came over to the door, glanced at the jordain in the shadows, and made the assumption Tzigone had anticipated. He dug the key from his bag and bent to unlock the door.

Tzigone seized his hair with both hands and yanked his head into the iron bars. He fell senseless. The key remained in the lock, twisted in a half turn.

Nimbly she reached around and finished the task. Motioning for Matteo to follow, she darted toward the narrow winding steps that traced the interior wall of the tower.

Matteo followed her up the steep flight, knowing full well what he was leaving behind. Saving Tzigone's life had only one possible result. He could never return to the only life he knew.

He acknowledged that this wasn't a new choice. He had merely taken another step along the path he set upon the day he stepped between Tzigone and the deadly wemic. The day that Andris had died. The day, he realized suddenly, that his unwavering faith in the jordaini order had been shaken beyond repair.

A strange desolation assailed him as he followed Tzigone out of the tower. He was a jordain, sworn to the service of truth and to Halruaa and her wizard lords. This had been his whole life; it was all he knew. He couldn't conceive of anything that could replace it.

But first, survival. They raced to the top of the tower and then squeezed out the window and climbed down the vines that somehow found purchase on the smooth marble walls. From there they moved to the curtain walls, and from there to the branches of the first of several trees. But they didn't speak until they reached the leafy sanctuary of Tzigone's bilboa tree.

Matteo watched as Tzigone took dried rations and a flask of water from a hidden cache. "Do you know every such tree in the land?"

"One or two in every city and main village," she said. "I move around a lot. I doubt I need to explain why."

"In truth, an explanation would be in order," Matteo said. "For what are you searching? What is worth the risks that you've taken?"

For once Tzigone gave a straight and simple answer. "I'm looking for my ancestry."

Matteo's brow furrowed. "This is so important?"

"I can see why you wouldn't think so. You've never known family."

"All jordaini are taken to the school shortly after birth," he agreed. "It is the traditional way."

"But haven't you ever wondered who your family were?"

He gave that careful thought. "From time to time, I have wondered who might have given me birth. But the jordaini are my brothers, and I have known no real lack. Your situation is different, I take it?"

"Yes," she said shortly. "I had a mother, and I won't rest until I find her. Don't you ever wonder what happened to yours?"

"She was a woman grown when she gave birth. I understand that jordaini births are usually predicted by the matchmakers, so she knew from the onset that she would bear a child only to give it up. This is done willingly, for the good of the land. The parents are well compensated, as they have no children to care for them in their old age, and they are greatly honored for their sacrifice."

Tzigone stared at him for a long moment. "Come with me," she said abruptly and began to slide down the tree.

Less than two hours later, they stood in the doorway of a one-room cottage, one of several such cottages, all identical and clustered around a simple garden surrounded by a tall, thick wall.

"What place is this?" Matteo asked in a whisper. There was something about the place, pleasant though it was, that inhibited the spirit.

"Go inside," Tzigone said.

Matteo paused at the doorway and spoke the traditional pledge tradition required of all Halruaans, swearing that no magic would be worked within this house.

"Do not mock me," said a small, anguished whisper.

He came fully into the room and peered into the shadows that lingered by the unlit hearth. A woman huddled there, curled up on a chair like a weeping child.

"That was not my intention, mother," he said softly, using

the polite form for unknown women of her apparent years. "My words were a greeting such as any might speak. They are also truth, for I am jordaini."

The word hit her like an arrow. She looked up, her eyes wild in her white face. "A jordain!"

Matteo couldn't comprehend her distress, but he had no wish to add to it. "Your pardon, good mother." he said, bowing. "We will go."

The mad light faded from the woman's eyes, leaving her face listless and dull. "Go or stay. It matters not."

Tzigone shoved at him from behind, prompting him farther into the room. While Matteo stood, feeling awkward and helpless, she bustled about, opening the shutters to let in the sun, plumping up cushions, building up the hearth fire, and putting water and a handful of herbs in the kettle. She brought the woman a cup of tea and curved her thin hands around it, guiding it to her lips until memory took over and the woman drank on her own. Through it all, Tzigone kept up a soft, steady stream of chatter—gently humorous tales of life in the city beyond these walls, entertaining stories that probably had no basis in reality.

Matteo listened with only partial attention as he watched the girl tend this unknown woman. And he knew, without understanding the reason, that his choice that day had been the right one.

Finally the woman drifted into sleep. Tzigone pulled a thin blanket over her and rose. Her eyes were bleak as she met Matteo's considering gaze.

"You are kind," he said softly.

She shrugged this aside impatiently. "There is little that anyone can do for her, other than the odd small kindness."

That the poor woman was insane was obvious to Matteo. "What happened, to shatter her so?"

"Magic," Tzigone said grimly, gazing at the pale, wasted face. "Once this woman was a powerful wizard, married to another wizard in a match made by still another. It was predicted that a child of their blood would likely be jordain.

The woman wanted children of her own to keep and love, but she was assured that only one jordain was ever born to a family. So she did her duty and consented to the match.

"Time passed, but there was no child. She and her husband were greatly concerned. He offered to bring potions for her that would bolster her health and promote conception. For nearly five years, this continued. What the woman never knew," Tzigone said in a tight, angry voice, "was that she was taking potions that twisted the natural course of her magic and that of the child she would bear. All of the power that might have become magic was refocused, so that her child might have great talents of mind and body."

The words seemed too fantastic for belief. "Is this one of your stories?" he asked tentatively.

Tzigone focused her eyes on his and let him judge what he saw in them.

"The magic wasn't just taken from the potential child, but from the mother. Little by little, her gift dwindled away, retreating to a place within herself that she could no longer reach.

"When the child was born, the process was complete. The birth was difficult, as such births invariably are, and the midwife pronounced that the woman would never bear another child. At one blow, the woman lost her babe, her dream of a child to keep, and all of herself that was bound up in her magic. This proves too much for most women to bear. They become as the woman you see before you."

Matteo absorbed this in silence. He didn't doubt Tzigone's words. Grim though this explanation was, it did explain why the jordaini were usually stronger in body and mind than the average man, and why their resistance to magic was so strong. But such a price to pay!

He tried to picture the woman who had paid this price for him and the man who had let her do so unwittingly. But it was too strange, too unreal, for him to grasp.

"Have you nothing to say?" Tzigone demanded. "Do you understand now why I wonder what became of my mother in this land of magic and wizards?"

She fairly spat out the last word with undisguised venom. Matteo had been raised to serve wizards, but he didn't find her reaction at all extreme.

"All my life," he said slowly, "I have been charged with developing the strength of mind and body. The passions of man were studied as important strategic considerations, but we were not encouraged to explore or experience any of them."

Tzigone gave him a strange look. "You had friends, surely."

"Yes. But even the closest of these had the careless ease of proximity—or so I thought," he said painfully. "My dearest friend, a jordain named Andris, was condemned by a magehound and slain by the wemic who pursued you the very day we met."

"Ah." Tzigone nodded, as if a long-held question had been answered.

"The grief and guilt that followed my friend's death was my undoing. I acted in a manner that denied all my training. Emotions, it seems, have great power."

He fell silent for a moment, then added, "This is new to me, and I don't know where it will lead. I should feel outrage, but I do not. I cannot mourn a woman I never knew. I cannot hate a man I never met. Perhaps that will change. If it does, I'm not sure what I will do."

"Even in this you're honest," she said softly, her eyes searching his face. "Maybe that's not always such a bad thing."

They quietly left the cottage, each deep in thought. Tzigone had come to this place intending to tell Matteo the truth: This was the woman who had given him birth. But as Matteo had pointed out, there was no telling what he might do once he got into the habit of allowing emotion into his life. Most likely he would declare vengeance upon the wizard who had sired him. That could lead nowhere good.

Matteo spoke first. "This is why jordaini have no families, is it not?"

"Magic is toxic," Tzigone said grimly. "Apparently it isn't easy to breed magic out of a human, and there is no telling what will come of the effort."

"Precaution is the grandchild of disaster," Matteo said softly, speaking an old proverb. "For such measures to be taken, things must have gone terribly wrong."

"Mistakes happen," Tzigone agreed. She took a long, steadying breath. "I suppose that's the only possible way to explain me."

CHAPTER SEVENTEEN

Tzigone braced herself for the jordain's questions. To her surprise, she realized that she was prepared to tell him everything she knew about herself and her background, secrets that she had spoken to no one. Matteo had never been less than honest with her. That honesty created a debt, and she always paid her debts.

But Matteo didn't immediately respond to her grim pronouncement. Instead, he took a small tightly rolled scroll from his bag and handed it to her.

She took it and smoothed it flat. The message was brief, and after a moment, she lifted incredulous eyes to his face. "Reads like a death warrant," she said, only partially in jest.

"That was my assessment," he agreed.

Much as she would have liked to, Tzigone couldn't argue. Cassia, the high counselor to King Zalathorm and one of the most powerful jordaini in the land, had enlisted the help of all members of the jordaini order to find information on the whereabouts and background of a thief known as Tzigone.

A strange knot formed in the girl's throat. Matteo had helped her to escape in direct defiance of the rules of his order. For a moment, even Tzigone's nimble tongue seemed weighted down by the enormity of this revelation.

"I thought the jordaini didn't write and send messages," she managed at last.

Matteo's faint smile acknowledged her unspoken words. "It appears that in this case Cassia made an exception. I daresay that the jordaini weren't the only people in this city to receive her missive. No doubt it also went to the city guard, town criers, and city Elders."

"There's a personal message on this copy," she said, pointing to the last few lines. The script was written in a different hand and in a shade of emerald ink that few professional scribes could afford.

She read aloud, using Cassia's voice. "I give you fair warning, Matteo, that this young woman is dangerous in the extreme. You have been seen in her company, but henceforth you must avoid her at all costs. She was tested as a child and found to possess great magical talent. She has abused this power and committed a number of crimes. If you wish, come see me after she has been apprehended. You will understand at once, for the secrets of her birth explain all. One jordain cannot command another, but your assistance in this matter is most urgently desired, and will be regarded as a great service to Halruaa."

"The secrets of my birth," Tzigone said in her own voice, her tone distracted. "Do you think she really knows?"

Matteo looked dubious. "A jordain's word is inviolate. That's what I was raised and trained to believe."

"But?"

He sighed and raked a hand through his hair. "I have learned that it is possible to deceive without speaking a single false word. You may have noticed that Cassia does not actually claim to possess this information. She merely says that it will answer all. It is possible—possible, mind you—that Cassia sent this note hoping that I would pass it along to you."

"Bait," Tzigone concluded.

"It is possible," he repeated in a bleak tone. He turned his gaze to her. "And now that you have this information, what will you do with it?"

Tzigone was silent for a long moment. "Some of what Cassia says is true. I seem to have some innate magic. Wild talents, they call them. But I'm no wizard," she said emphatically, glaring at Matteo in challenge.

"So you have told me," he said in a neutral tone.

"You know I'm a thief." She laughed shortly. "That's nothing to boast of, but you and I are alike in thinking it's a better thing to be than a Halruaan wizard."

"You hate them," Matteo observed. "I would like to understand why."

"You can ask that after seeing what magic did to that poor woman?"

He didn't answer at once, nor did he meet her eyes when at last he spoke. "This process—is it the same for all women who give birth to a jordain?"

Tzigone understood what must be going through his mind. He was wondering if his own mother had suffered a similar fate, and he was picturing her in a similar situation, a prisoner in her own diminished mind. For a moment Tzigone considered telling him that he need not use his imagination, for the worst was his to know.

"I don't know," she said. "Perhaps some women give birth to jordaini without aid of potions and spells."

"Perhaps." He looked up at her, frustration in his eyes. "I wish there were something I could do for that poor woman. No jordain will ever be wealthy. Our expenses are paid by our patrons, though we may receive small personal gifts from time to time. If ever I were to find my mother in such a state, how would I provide for her?"

"You saw the cottages, the gardens. Halruaa ensures that her wizards get what they need. Your mother is well cared for."

For a moment she thought she might have revealed too much. But there was no flash of epiphany in Matteo's dark eyes. He merely nodded as he took in this new information.

There seemed to be nothing more to say. That knowledge

dampened Tzigone's spirits more thoroughly than a cold rain.

"So I suppose that knowing what you know, you can't afford to be seen with me anymore," she said.

"Knowing what we know, you can't afford to be seen at all," he countered. "Promise me that you'll leave the city at once. I will learn what Cassia knows, and somehow I will get this information to you." He smiled faintly. "All you need do is acknowledge that the debt between us is paid in full. Even a jordain knows something of honor."

It was a princely offer, far better than Tzigone had right to expect. What Matteo said, he would do. It might take him a while to talk his way around the matter of her escape, but she felt he could come up with a convincing story if pressed to do so. Even so, the thought of leaving the matter in his hands distressed her, and not entirely because of her reluctance to rely upon others. Tzigone enjoyed company; she made friends quickly and parted lightly. This time, the parting was not so easily done.

But she painted a smile on her face and extended her hand to him. "Deal."

To Matteo's eyes, the girl's smile was a brave thing, not unlike a small boy dressing up in his father's armor and weapons. He took her hand in a comrade's clasp.

Tzigone muttered an expletive and dropped his hand. She leaned forward and wrapped herself around him in a quick, hard embrace. Then she was gone, scrambling down the tree as nimbly as a squirrel.

Matteo sighed. In the sudden lull her absence left behind, he noticed the throbbing in his head and the heavy thudding of his heart. He pressed against his temples with both hands to distract the pain and then again at the pressure points at the base of his neck. His fingers brushed through his thick dark hair and stopped short—not because of what they found, but because of what they did not. No silver chain, no emblem of his order.

His jordain's pendant was missing again.

The young man's lips twitched, then he chuckled. This

was not merely a theft but a message—Tzigone's way of assuring him that they were destined to meet again.

Though his jordaini masters would certainly disapprove, the thought did not displease Matteo in the slightest.

☙

It took Matteo the better part of an hour to work his way down the bilboa tree. His first action was to find a member of the city guard and place himself under the man's jurisdiction. After all, he was being held for Inquisition, and he was currently a fugitive from the king's high counselor. They took him to the palace and sent a runner for Cassia. The lady jordain herself came to the gatehouse and took custody of the prisoner, assuring the guards that she was well able to deal with Matteo and insisting that they take no further action without her command.

He walked beside her in silence as they made their way into the palace gardens. Cassia finally came to a stop under an arbor heavy with ripe yellow grapes.

"This need not come before an inquisitor. Let us be frank with each other. I don't like you and I don't wish you well, but I dislike seeing any jordain come under the jurisdiction of those accursed magehounds. Tell me what you know about that girl. Spare yourself the disgrace of Inquisition, and save your order the trouble of dealing with your latest infraction."

Matteo spread his hands. "There is little to tell. Not long ago I defended an unknown girl against attack in a tavern. Only later did I learn that she was a thief and a fugitive."

"But you knew the identity of her attacker."

"All too well," he said bitterly. "I saw the wemic kill my best friend that very morning. I will not deny that this influenced my actions."

"Imprudent, but understandable," Cassia allowed. "Yet you continued to see the girl from time to time."

"I had little choice," he said dryly. "Tzigone considered herself in my debt and acted accordingly. She appeared whenever she thought she could do me some service, only to end up increasing her debt."

"You never made an effort to alert the authorities?"

He shrugged. "Our meetings were always at her instigation, and they were both unexpected and brief. I could not alert the authorities of something I could not anticipate."

"The girl always walked away from these meetings, unscathed and undeterred. How do you explain that?"

"How do the guards of a dozen cities explain it? Or Mbatu, the wemic warrior who serves as personal guard to the magehound Kiva? Tzigone is harder to hold than starlight. I am a humble counselor," Matteo said without a trace of irony. "It would be presumptuous to claim I could do what so many have attempted and failed."

"Humble!" The king's counselor sniffed. "That is probably the first time someone's listed that quality among your many virtues."

"Yet I owe my current position to my many failings," Matteo said wryly.

Cassia lifted one hand in the gesture of a fencer acknowledging a hit. "I am seldom wrong. Would you like to hear me admit that I misjudged you? Help me in this matter, and I will consider my error to be a fortunate thing."

He studied the woman's pale, serene face for signs of duplicity. "I was imprisoned in the same chamber as Tzigone. At your command?"

"Of course. The thief claimed that you had let her into the palace."

"I did not bolt my shutters," he said dryly. "Tzigone no doubt took that as an invitation. Let me rephrase my question. Would you be gratified to hear that Tzigone stole my medallion of office?"

Her intelligent black eyes narrowed as she tried to follow his meaning. "Not particularly. Speak plainly!"

Matteo took the message from his bag and handed it to her. As Cassia skimmed it, her lips thinned and her pale face turned nearly gray.

"You thought I sent this message to you, expecting that the girl would steal it?"

"A reasonable assumption," Matteo said.

"Entirely reasonable," she agreed. "Tell me, where is she now?"

"I do not know. She told me she planned to leave the city immediately."

Cassia's smile was mocking but brittle. "And you believed her? As a jordain, you are constrained to tell the truth. But surely you are not such a fool that you think everyone follows the same code?"

He met her mocking gaze and gave away nothing of what was in his heart. "No, my lady, I am not such a fool as that."

❂

The second note from Cassia came late that night and was not such a surprise as the first. Matteo thanked the messenger and smoothed out the parchment. Written in the counselor's emerald ink was a brief message commanding that he come to her chambers at once.

Commanding. Matteo noted this turn of phrase with deep consternation. In her first message, Cassia had admitted that she could not command him. Perhaps now she felt differently. Perhaps he was now her hound to call. All she had to do was speak the word, and his life as a jordain was over. He could continue being an honored servant of truth as long as he was willing to place Cassia's demands above personal integrity. But what of his promise to Tzigone? How could he learn what secrets Cassia held if he did not play her game for at least a little while longer?

It was a complex problem, and not at all like the sciences he had devoted his life to learning. With a sigh, Matteo tucked the message into his tunic and made his way through the palace to the luxurious apartment of the king's counselor.

He tapped at the door, which swung open slightly. This

did not surprise him—after all, Cassia was expecting him. Softly calling the jordain's name, he eased into the room.

The sight before him stopped him cold. Cassia lay on the floor, her pale face a sickly bluish gray and her black eyes bulging.

Matteo knelt beside her. Her skin was cool to the touch. He guessed that she had been dead for several hours. The cause of death was immediately apparent. A silver chain had been twisted tightly around her neck so that it dug deep into the skin.

For a horrible moment, he thought the pendant was his. He gingerly reached out and turned the small silver disk. The markings on the back was the emblem of Cassia, jordain in the service of King Zalathorm.

Matteo's sigh spoke of relief and self-reproach. Why did his first thought go to Tzigone? She had said she would leave the city, did she not? She agreed to let him get the information from Cassia. And never had she given him any reason to think of her as a murderer.

But what of the crimes Cassia hinted at? Tzigone was an admitted thief. What else might she be?

The need to know raised him to his feet and prompted him to invade the counselor's study. Matteo carefully went through Cassia's writing table, and then went through the shelves, book by book. He checked for hidden drawers, wall safes, and secret compartments. The king's counselor had an amazing total of eight hiding places. They were all empty, but for a hidden drawer that held a large wilting flower, a small sack filled with skie, and a silver hairbrush. The "damning evidence" Cassia had claimed to possess was gone.

Matteo took a deep breath and had another look around. He studied the jordain's chair, which was fashioned of elegantly carved teak and deeply cushioned in the new fashion—removable cushions stuffed with down that could be removed and fluffed. The imprint that Cassia left upon the seat was there to see, but he thought he perceived a smaller, deeper imprint within it. Cassia was a tall woman, and although not heavy, she could hardly be considered small. This second imprint had been left by someone very small, someone nearly as slim-hipped as a boy. Someone like Tzigone.

Then there was the matter of the silver brush. He recalled what Tzigone had said the day they probed her memories. She remembered her mother brushing her hair. That had seemed important to her. Perhaps this brush was important as well. If so, why had she left it behind?

Matteo searched the room again, more thoroughly this time. He found a small basket under the writing table, and in it a single piece of parchment. He smoothed the sheet flat and read a message from Cassia to the wizard Sinestra Belajoon. On the parchment was the seal of King Zalathorm. Apparently Cassia, with little use for writing materials, had taken a sheet from her patron's store.

He quickly took from his bag the notes he had received from Cassia and compared the script. The writing was not from the same hand. Since Cassia, like all jordaini, didn't send written messages, no one would be expected to know her handwriting. No one, that is, except Cassia herself.

Suddenly he understood the pallor on Cassia's face as she read the note. Someone else had written these notes, someone who wished to lure first Tzigone, and then him. Someone who had left clues, like the markings that rangers carved into the trees to mark the path for those who followed.

Matteo studied the two messages. The letter to Sinestra Belajoon had been written in deep indigo. The notes he had received were enscribed in a rare green ink. But by whom?

A fresh quill lay on Cassia's blotter, its tip stained the color of liquid emeralds. Likely the quill had been used but once; otherwise, the ink at the tip would be darker from many immersions. He tested the quill and found that the ink was dry, then took a new quill and dipped it into the bottle. He would test it at intervals and see when the ink fully dried. That would give him some idea of how long ago the note had been written.

Matteo turned his attention to the flower. It was a gentiola, a rare green blossom twice the size of his hand. He had never seen one except in sketches of Halruaa's exotic plants, for it grew deep within the swamps.

He turned the flower over and regarded the stem. A bit of dried sap sealed the cut stem, keeping in moisture so that the blossom would last several days. He noted a new scar, however, where a single leaf had been torn away, and recently. A single drop of liquid seeped from it, fragrant and tear-shaped. He wiped it away and noted the tiny design that had been carved onto the stem: a circle separated by a lighting bolt, the symbol on his stolen jordaini medallion. The same symbol had been scratched into the leather of the coin pouch, which was well worn and inexpensive.

Matteo read the message with mixed feelings. Tzigone had found this place. She trusted him to figure out what had transpired.

But she had not trusted him to do as he promised. She had taken the bait after all and had come to see what information Cassia had about her past.

And in doing so, she had condemned herself. If the forged messages had been sent throughout the city, Cassia's death would turn all eyes in Tzigone's direction. Now if Matteo were to be questioned, he couldn't deny his conviction that Tzigone had been in Cassia's chambers. The coin purse was undoubtedly hers. She had left it for him, hoping that he would understand and follow.

But what had she found? And where had she gone?

He sighed in deep frustration and studied the brush. The handle and back were of finely carved silver, the dark bristles taken from a wild boar. He pulled one of his daggers and slid the tip through the bristles. The blade caught on a single long hair, a hair that caught the light and gleamed like polished jade. His heart quickened as he pulled it free. There was no doubt. The hair was green.

"Kiva," he said grimly.

CHAPTER EIGHTEEN

Matteo quietly left Cassia's chambers and made his way down to the palace stables. The night was dark, and the grooms were snoring in a mound of sweet hay. No one challenged him as he walked softly down the long row of stalls, looking for a horse that could run long and hard. He chose a black stallion that reminded him of Cyric. The horse nipped at him when he put on the bridle. Matteo took this as a good sign. He left enough of the skie to pay for the horse's hire and led Cyric the Second out of the stall.

He rode through the sleeping city and reached the docks before sunrise. Two small temples stood at the corner of the vast public square, places where sailors and travelers could come to ask the blessing of Mystra or Azuth. Matteo slipped into Azuth's temple and persuaded the acolyte on duty to find out the whereabouts of the Inquisitrix Kiva. Grumbling, the lad went into the back room and came back with a thick tome. He thumbed through it until he found the elf woman's name.

"Last assignment took her to Zalasuu," the boy said. "She's gone to Khaerbaal. That's all I have."

"Thank you." Matteo offered the lad a skie. "For the work of Azuth."

The young man's eyes brightened, and he put the coin into his bag. "Well, whose work do you think I'm doing?" he asked defensively, noting Matteo's stare.

The jordain had no wish to argue. He hurried down to the open-air market. The stalls had not yet opened for business, and many of the merchants slept on piles of their own goods. He found a dry goods stall and bought a tunic and leggings of rough brown linen from the sleepy-eyed merchant.

So garbed, he was able to get a place as a deckhand on a ship bound for Khaerbaal, claiming that he'd served as crew on Procopio's skyship. This proved sufficiently impressive to gain him passage both for him and his borrowed horse.

Once Matteo had reached Khaerbaal, he changed back into his jordaini garb, for few people would refuse information to a wizard's counselor. It didn't take him long to piece together information on Kiva's activities. She had been very busy indeed. A rather large number of visiting clerics had been branded and taken for inquisition. This was not all that unusual, but for the whispered information that a few extra coins bought Matteo. Of these people, very few were known as professed members of the clergy and some had been vehement in their denials of vocation.

Kiva had also hired additional guards in the port city, purportedly to aid her in taking the accused clergy to Azuth's temple for examination.

All of this troubled Matteo. Her actions were too bold, even for a magehound. Though the word of an inquisitrix was accepted as law, Kiva was not invulnerable. The church of Azuth dealt with any magehound who acted for personal gain or at the behest of any person or group. Obviously the elf woman deemed her pursuit to be worthy of this risk.

Matteo rode to the north gate and confirmed from gate guards that the elf woman had indeed passed through. It was no surprise to Matteo that she headed northeast, toward the Swamp of Akhlaur.

Where else? There were only two places where gentiola blossoms grew: the Kilmaruu Swamp near Zalasuu and the Swamp of Akhlaur. Kiva had no doubt left the flower as an additional lure for Tzigone. He wouldn't be surprised if the silver brush was the clue that told Tzigone which of these choices to take.

He rode until Cyric's sides were flecked with white and the great horse's breath came in deep gusts. Near sunset, a narrow side road beckoned to the village beyond, a small farming village perched on the side of a hill and visible from the trade road.

Matteo found his way to the inn and asked about Kiva and her band. No one had seen her, but his white garments did earn him some unusually suspicious scrutiny.

Finally one of the farmhands came over to his table. The man was huge, grimy with soil from the day's labors. He looked none too pleased. He picked up the saltcellar and dumped the contents on the table. With one thick, dirty finger, he drew a circle separated by a jagged bolt—the symbol of the jordain order.

"This look familiar?" he demanded.

Matteo suppressed a smile of delight and relief. Judging from the hostile expression on the man's face, Tzigone had been through this way.

"It does indeed. A young woman—or perhaps a boy, a street urchin—may have taken my pendant. I seek this person."

"Woman or boy?" The man frowned, confounded by this unexpected choice.

"A woman," Matteo guessed. "She may have been dressed as a jordain, but she is not. Her fingers tend to be a little light."

The farmer snorted. "Don't I know it."

Matteo leaned forward eagerly. "Tell me what you know of her. And tell me also what you have lost, and I will see that you receive recompense."

"Will you, now?"

The expression on the man's face puzzled Matteo. It was not relief or gratitude, not disbelief, not greed or cunning. Try as he might, Matteo had no name to give it.

"As best I can," he added with newfound caution.

After a moment the man nodded and pushed back from the table. "Follow me."

Matteo claimed Cyric the Second from the stables and followed the man out of the village and into the hills beyond. His home was a small stone dwelling that had been carved into the side of a hill, more a cave than a cottage. A separate entrance led out into a pen, suggesting that livestock shared the shelter.

The farmer nodded toward the empty pen. "Beat me at dice, she did. When I didn't put the coin on the table fast enough to suit her, she agreed to come here and take a pig."

Matteo saw where this was going. "She took more than one, I gather?"

"You might say that." The man shook his head in disgust. "Never saw anything like it. Them pigs flew off after her like a flock o' swans."

The unlikely analogy made Matteo blink, as did the image it conjured in his mind. "Your pigs flew off," he repeated. "Like swans."

"Sounds barmy, don't it? Don't suppose I could go to the magistrate with that one, or you take it to the jordain order?"

"Ah. She was tested for magic in the inn, I take it?"

"The village midwife," the man said shortly. "Near as good as a magehound, is Granny Frost. I swore the wench witched my dice, and Granny Frost mumbled over her to test the truth o' things. Said there wasn't a drop of magic in the wench, that she was a true jordain. If I complain that the girl witched my pigs, I'd be going up against Granny Frost. That ain't a thing for a man unwed to be doing. I'd sooner wed one o' my own sows than whatever Granny might pick for me."

"I see," Matteo mused. "How can I help?"

"If you have coins, I'll take payment for my pigs. If not, I'll take the girl." The farmer grinned unpleasantly. "You're bound to find her soon or late, and bein' a jordain, you got no good use for her. Might as well bring her here. Me, I don't like to leave any job unfinished."

Wrath flamed hot and bright as Matteo understood that what Tzigone had done here probably had less to do with theft than diversion, with a bit of vengeance thrown in. As he recalled, Tzigone had an aversion to familiar sayings. He would not be at all surprised if the expression "when pigs fly" had come into play. Well, pigs had flown, and Tzigone had gotten away, leaving the farmer with "unfinished business." Matteo found enormous relief in that.

"I will pay," he said shortly. "How many pigs were there in your . . . flock?"

The farmer's eyes narrowed at the gibe, but he named a number far higher than the pen could possibly contain.

Matteo glanced at the small enclosure and then back at the farmer, one eyebrow lifted. He reached into his bag and produced the rest of the coins Tzigone had left for him. By his measure, it was a generous amount.

"This ain't the price o' twenty swine," the farmer protested.

"That may be. But it is all I have, and more than you'd get at market for the number of swine that pen could truly hold."

The man's face turned a deep, angry red. His fist came toward Matteo's face in a blur. The jordain leaned to the left and did a half-pivot on his left foot. Two quick steps brought him around behind the farmer, who was still off-balance from the first punch. He hit the man on the back of the neck, hard.

The blow would have felled any of Matteo's sparring partners, but the big man shrugged it off. He ran for the pitchfork that leaned against the front wall of his dwelling, whirled, and kicked into a running charge with weapon leveled.

Matteo let him come. He dropped to the ground just short of impalement. As he fell, he twisted and reached up to seize the long wooden shaft. The weapon tipped down, and the tines plunged into the hard-trodden muck of the farmyard. Matteo released his grip and let the farmer's momentum do the rest.

With a rising howl, the man flipped into the air for a brief, flailing flight. He cleared the fence surrounding the pigpen and splashed down into the muck.

Matteo rose, arms folded, and admired the result. It was a story Tzigone would relish, and one that he doubted even her deft embellishments could much improve.

He was congratulating himself still when something hit the small of his back with a thud that resounded through his bones and sent him pitching forward onto his knees. Pain radiated through him in blinding, pulsing rays.

Heavy footsteps thumped around him. With difficulty, Matteo focused on a visage very similar to that of the farmer, minus the muck that his first opponent was scraping from his face.

"The family resemblance is striking," Matteo muttered dazedly.

"Striking!" The second man guffawed. "Oh, I like that! Hit him and he outs with a jest. Let's see what smart boy's got to say once I fetch him upside the head."

"He's not so smart," announced a thin, querulous voice from somewhere above their heads. "Only a fool don't check a hound for ticks or ask if a bastard's got brothers."

Matteo's head was starting to clear, and he anticipated both the source of the distraction and the man's probable response.

"Granny Frost?" the second man quavered, looking warily up into the trees.

But his brother sloshed out of the pen. "That's no haunt, fool! The girl's got more voices than a village meeting. She's come back."

Ignoring the numbing pain, Matteo surged to his feet and hurled himself at the second man's knees. They went down hard, rolling and pummeling at each other as best they could. It was no strategy at all and very little skill, but in his dazed state, Matteo could do no better. To his chagrin, the big man managed to pin him. He lifted his fist, prepared to drive it into Matteo's face.

Suddenly the man reared up, shrieking like a banshee. Over him stood a grim-faced Tzigone, wielding the pitchfork like a triton.

"He won't be sitting for a while," she said with satisfaction.

Matteo pointed. "Behind you!"

She whirled to face the first man. He had a small ax raised for a killing blow.

Tzigone dropped the pitchfork and gestured sharply. The ax handle burst into flame—or so it appeared. Matteo recognized the spell as a simple globe of light, although the leaping red "flames" were far more impressive than the child's toys that half of Halruaa could summon.

The farmer dropped the weapon and backed away. Tzigone stooped and picked it up. The wizard fire darted along her arm, swiftly outlining her entire form in flame. Her hair exploded into crimson flumes that writhed like the snakes of a tormented medusa.

With a sound very much like a drowning man swallowing water, the farmer turned and fled from the terrifying figure.

Tzigone's fire disappeared like a snuffed candle, leaving her unscathed but for a tiny smudge on her nose. She caught Matteo's eye and shrugged self-consciously.

"Bullies are cowards," she said, dismissing what she had done.

"True enough, but that doesn't make your display the less impressive. If I were able to move, I might not be far behind him," Matteo said dryly. He painfully rose into a sitting position.

"You're no coward," she said staunchly. "And not that much of a fool, either. You just need to remember to check for ticks, so to speak."

She moved behind him and tugged up the hem of his

tunic. A long, low whistle escaped her. "You'll be several shades of purple by morning, but there doesn't look to be lasting damage." She ran her fingers lightly over his back. "The club hit here, to the left of the spine. That's good. He got a shot to the kidney, which isn't good. Hurts like all Nine Hells."

She dropped the tunic back into place and leaned forward to peer into his face. "I always seem to be picking up after you," she said. She silenced Matteo's ready rejoinder with an upraised hand, her suddenly subdued expression letting him know that she realized that she had caused him more grief that she intended.

"Thank for you for coming after me. I owe—"

He stopped her by placing his hand over her lips. "No more talk of debts between us," he said firmly. "No distractions. We have to do everything we can to find and stop Kiva." Tzigone nodded and pushed Matteo's hand aside.

"Finding her isn't going to be the problem. Does it seem to you that Kiva seems a bit too easy to track?"

"She wants to be found," Matteo reasoned. "She is luring us. If she were simply doing her duty, I could understand why she wished to entrap you. But there is something more happening here. I have a feeling that she has a purpose for us both. Why else would she free me from the hold or send a message that would bring me to Cassia's chambers?"

"You're a good fighter. Maybe she wanted to add you to her army."

Matteo perked up. "Army? What army?"

"I'll show you." She extended a hand and helped him to his feet. They both mounted Cyric the Second and rode to the edges of the swamp. By then Matteo felt able to walk without much pain, and he followed her as they crept through the moss-hung trees.

She stopped him with a silent gesture and carefully parted a curtain of vines.

There, in utter silence, was a training field reminiscent of his days at the Jordaini College. Over a hundred men practiced with weapons of steel and wood and bone, yet there was no sound of impact, no grunts of exertion.

Matteo marveled to see jordaini routines practiced under a magical shroud of silence. He would have sooner expected snow in midsummer.

His gaze skimmed the crowd and came to rest on a tall auburn man. His disbelieving eyes widened, and he couldn't quite suppress a gasp of astonishment.

Tzigone sent him a quizzical look.

"That tall man," he said quietly, pointing. "He is very like my friend Andris." A terrible thought occurred to him. "Or an undead creature that was once Andris! I saw the wemic kill him the very day we met."

He spoke softly, just above a whisper, and then fell silent. But some magical ward captured his words and repeated them in an echo that thrummed through the forest.

The fighters stopped and turned toward their hiding place, weapons leveled.

But Andris's face broke into a joyful grin. He made a quick, impatient gesture, as if he were tearing aside an insect netting. "Trust your eyes, my friend," he said in a clear, carrying voice. "I'm alive and well and happier than I've ever been! Come into camp, and I'll tell you everything."

CHAPTER NINETEEN

"It's a trap," Tzigone said flatly.

Matteo hesitated, uncertain whether to believe what his eyes told him. "Andris was my dearest friend. I can't walk away from him without a word. I'll understand if you don't wish to follow me, but I must go."

She thought this over and shrugged. Matteo stepped out into the clearing. After a moment, he heard Tzigone's light step behind him.

Andris strode to meet him, and the friends fell into a back-thumping embrace. Finally Matteo put Andris out at arms' length and regarded him. Andris had gained color from much time in the sun, as well as a bit more muscle on his lean frame.

"You're looking remarkably well for a dead man."

Genuine regret crossed the man's face. "My 'death' was a ruse to bring me to this cause. I have often wished I could send you word, but doing so would compromise the coming battle."

"Battle?" Matteo said incredulously. "Here, in this foul swamp? Andris, what are you thinking? How many people have survived Akhlaur? Do you have any idea what you're going up against?"

"A laraken," the man said easily. "It is a creature that drains magic. But none of these men possess any magical ability or weapons. We fight as jordaini fight against wizards, with wits and weapons."

"Wits and weapons?" echoed Tzigone. She strode over to Andris and eyed the daggers strapped to his side. "Hmm. Weapons. Looks like you're half right."

Andris lifted an eyebrow and glanced inquiringly at Matteo.

"This is Tzigone," he said simply. "Lured here by Kiva. Believe me, the laraken is not your only foe."

"Kiva is no foe," Andris said quietly. "I lead these men, but I follow the elf woman."

"Andris, there are things that Kiva hasn't told you. There are things about her that you don't know."

"No doubt. Can you claim to know every secret of the wizards you have served?"

"I'm reasonably sure that neither of them murdered Cassia," Matteo said sharply.

His friend's expression turned grave. "Cassia dead, at Kiva's hand? Are you certain of this? Beyond doubt? Has Kiva been magically tested?"

"Not yet."

"Then wait until that time to make accusations. Kiva has been traveling with us for many days. We have never gone to the city of Halarahh. She could not have killed Cassia."

Tzigone rolled her eyes. "Kiva's a wizard, isn't she? Do you think her fastest means of travel is a good horse or a quick ship?"

Andris considered this, then shrugged and turned back to Matteo. "Let me tell you what we plan to do. Listen to what Kiva has done, what she wishes to accomplish, before you judge her."

"I can't think of much that would justify taking these men into Akhlaur! This is not a fight you can win."

"We won in Kilmaruu," Andris stated. "We resolved the Kilmaruu Paradox, just as I told you."

Matteo stared at him. "So that's why Kiva took you. But how could she know of your studies of Kilmaruu? Did you tell anyone other than me and the jordaini masters?"

"No one."

"Then how did she know?"

Both men fell silent as they considered this disturbing puzzle.

"I can answer that," Tzigone said with obvious reluctance. "You told the jordaini masters, right? Well, there you go. One of them passed information along to Kiva."

"That's impossible," Andris said flatly.

"A year ago, I would have agreed," Matteo said, his face thoughtful and troubled. He turned to Tzigone. "Are you suggesting a possibility, or do you know this for truth?"

Tzigone squirmed. "Let's say that maybe one of the masters has a secret he'd just as soon not hear spoken aloud. Kiva knows this secret, and she trades silence for information. She wanted a battlemaster, right? Who were her best choices?"

"Andris and I stood nearly equal in most of our studies," Matteo said.

"Well, that explains why Kiva chose Andris. I'm guessing the master gave up without a word of protest. He probably figured better Andris than you."

"What is this secret?" Matteo said quietly.

She was silent for a long moment. "Knowing what you do, how would you respond if you knew that one of your jordaini masters was your true father? How long before you ferreted out the secrets of the jordaini class, before you found your mother? And how long before your brothers started similar searches? The entire order would be in, well, disorder."

Matteo considered this. "One of my masters sired me. And the woman you showed me. She was in fact my mother?"

"Yes."

He nodded, his face set and grim. "Then the wizard had reason to keep his secret. I would have killed him for what was done to her. I may still. You know his name, don't you?"

Tzigone hesitated, then shook her head. "I've always searched for my mother. When I saw your lineage, my eye went right to your mother's name. I read everything written about her, but I paid scant attention to the father's information. He's a wizard at the Jordaini College, that's all I know for sure."

Andris listened to this exchange with an increasingly incredulous expression. "Matteo, this is absurd! Surely you don't believe this boy's tall tales! The jordaini order has come to a sad state when the lads give in to open falsehood."

"Watch who you're calling a jordain!" Tzigone fumed, jabbing her forefinger into Andris's chest. "Don't start with me, unless you want to hear a few things about yourself that you won't like knowing."

Despite himself, the tall man looked intrigued. 'A jordain's ancestry is not important."

"You look real convinced of that," she said dryly. "So let's leave it at this: You're elf-blooded. It's back a few generations, but trust me, it's there."

Andris stared at her as if she'd run a sword through his gut. Matteo sighed and turned to Tzigone, who had apparently forgotten that she was wearing the "borrowed" vestments of the jordaini order. "Was that really necessary?"

"I've been into the swamp," she said grimly. "Not far into it, but far enough. Trust me, it's necessary. No one with a drop of elf blood ought to go near that place."

"To the contrary," Andris said softly. "I have even better reason now than I did before."

Tzigone huffed and threw up her hands. "You try to do the right thing, and who listens?"

Andris draped an arm around his friend's shoulders. "We are doing a great thing here. I hope you'll choose to join us."

They turned to watch the fighters, who had resumed their training. As Matteo studied the group, he recognized a number of men from his school, students who, at a very young age, had been found unsuitable for a jordain's life and released from service. Also among them were two or three men who had been condemned by the magehound as magic-tainted. Yet they had fought with passion and pride, preparing to serve the elf woman who had destroyed their lives.

"You and I are jordaini," Andris said quietly. "Chosen for our gifts, trained to serve the wizards of Halruaa. None of the wizards can halt the spread of the Swamp of Akhlaur. We can."

Despite himself, Matteo was interested. "You know the secret of the swamp?"

"The wizard Akhlaur opened a gate to the Plane of Water. A trickle remains, and the laraken feeds upon the spill of magic from the elemental plane. It is our task to fight through to the gate and make the way clear for Kiva. While we engage the laraken, she will enter the swamp and close the gate."

"But that is worse than the Kilmaruu Paradox!" Matteo protested. "If the gate is closed, the laraken will be unleashed upon the land. Many wizards will be destroyed."

Tzigone sniffed. "Well, there's more to Kiva than I suspected! I thought I was the only one to have that particular dream."

Andris eyed her with interest. "You do not care for wizards. That's a strange sentiment for a jordaini lad."

"I'm not a boy, and I'm no jordain!" she said emphatically. "What I am is chock-full of magic. Laraken eat magic. So as far as I can figure, there's only one reason for Kiva to want me here: bait."

The jordain's face lit up. "You are the young woman of whom Kiva spoke! The one who can call the laraken!"

Tzigone's eyes narrowed. "What makes you think this laraken will come when I call it?"

"You have the gift. Kiva says that it is so—an inheritance from your mother, the wizard Keturah."

The color drained from Tzigone's face. "Keturah," she said, repeating a name that was suddenly familiar. "Of course. All creatures came to Mother's call."

"You have both magic and resistance to magic. The laraken will be enticed by your voice. You will lure it away from the magical gate, and Kiva will close the leak forever. But if Kiva is correct, the laraken will not be able to touch the magic locked inside you."

"And if Kiva is not correct?" Tzigone asked, her voice a mocking imitation of the jordain's worshipful tones.

"I would not ask this of her," Matteo said softly. "She may have this talent from her mother, but I suspect she also has a bit of the diviner's gift. Her sight doesn't go forward, but back in time. I have seen it. This gift is newly awakened in her. I do not know if the laraken will sense it or not."

Andris considered this. "If this is true, then the battle would be dangerous to her, and to us as well. Only people who are utterly without magic can avoid the laraken."

"It is too big a risk to take," Matteo said. "Tzigone, you must leave. Go now, and quickly."

His words stirred memory, memory awakened by the sound of her mother's name.

Run, child! Keturah had said, her beautiful voice shrill with fear. *Don't stop for anything.*

The words echoed through Tzigone's mind and chilled her heart, just as they had done nearly twenty years before. She responded instinctively, like the child she had been, and she turned on her heel and fled.

She ran to the nearest big tree and scrambled up into its comforting, leafy arms. She fisted her hands and dug them into her eyes, fiercely willing herself into the darkness of the memory trance.

Tzigone slipped back, back, until once again she was a small child, fleeing with her mother. They were in the puzzle palace, a magical maze that filled a vast courtyard. Footsteps thudded through the villa toward them.

Tzigone turned to dart back into the insane courtyard, plucking at her mother's skirt. But the woman gently pried the small fingers loose.

"Go," she said quietly. "My magic is nearly gone. They will find me soon whether I run or stay."

"I won't leave you," the child said stubbornly.

"You must. It is you they seek."

The child Tzigone nodded. Somehow she had always

known. But knowing wasn't the same as doing, and she could not bear to leave.

A figure appeared suddenly in the open door, though the sound of footsteps was still many paces away. The child stared with mingled awe and fear at the most beautiful creature she had ever beheld.

In the doorway stood an elf woman of rare and exotic beauty. Her skin was the coppery hue of a desert sunset, and her elaborately curled and braided hair was the deep green of jungle moss. Rich displays of gold and emeralds and malachite glittered at her throat and on her hands. Over her yellow silk dress, she wore an overtunic of dark green, much embroidered with golden thread. A little smile curved her painted lips but did not quite touch her eyes, which were as golden and merciless as a hunting cat's. She was beautiful and terrible all at once.

"Greetings, Keturah," the elf said to the child's mother. "You have led us a merry chase. And this, of course, is your accursed little bastard."

Her voice was as sweet and clear as temple bells, but Tzigone wasn't fooled. "Bastard" was the worst epitaph a Halruaan could hurl. Tzigone understood that it was not just insult but truth.

The crescendo of footsteps came to a sudden stop just beyond the door, and the elf woman glanced back over her shoulder. "Take them both," she said with cold satisfaction.

But Tekurah leaped forward and braced her hands on either side of the doorframe. She cast a desperate glance back at her daughter. "Run, child!" she pleaded. "Don't stop for anything."

Tzigone hesitated. Green light began to encircle her mother, twining about her like choking vines. Keturah tottered and went down to her knees, her hands clawing frantically at her throat.

Terror urged the child to flee, but guilt held her in place. She had begged to Mother to summon a fierce creature. Was this what had come of her wish?

The elf woman shouldered past the faltering wizard and lunged for her small quarry. But the child dropped to the ground, and the sudden shift of her weight made her slip like a fish through the slender copper hands. She rolled aside and darted out into the courtyard.

Her mother's voice followed her, urging her to flee. She ran to the fragmented waterfall and dived in, not sure whether she would crack her head on tile or soar out toward the bright shards that followed Selune through the night sky. But she fell smoothly through the waterfall and splashed down into the fish pond. Her flailing hands found a tunnel opening in the tiled wall.

She came up for air, breathing in as deeply as she could and then diving deep. Her mother's last words followed her into the water, and haunted her as she swam.

"Forget me!"

Tzigone came out of the memory trance suddenly, gasping and sobbing. It was Kiva who had taken her mother! Kiva who had chased her even then! She shrieked aloud, giving voice to the loss and fear and rage of a lifetime.

"I will not forget," she said as she fisted the tears from her eyes. "I never forgot you."

But she had forgotten. And suddenly she understood why. Her mother's last words to her had been no mere farewell but a powerful enchantment. Apparently Tzigone's magical resistance wasn't absolute. Her mother, if no one else, could pierce it.

But the spell was broken now, and memories came flooding back. For a long time Tzigone huddled in the tree, letting the images and sounds flow through her, savoring them all. There had been bad times, but they were hers. She lingered longest on her favorite memory—listening as Keturah sang into the night wind, and then waiting breathlessly too see what creatures came to the beautiful wizard's call.

After a time, Tzigone began to sing a dimly remembered tune, tentatively at first, then with growing conviction. The sound of her voice startled her. It was rich and true, full of magic but possessing its own beauty. Her mother's voice, unpolished but unmistakable, poured from her throat.

A sparkle of light appeared beside her, whirling in a tiny vortex that slowed as it gained color and substance. When it stopped, a tiny winged lad stepped out into the empty air. Wings beating, he darted closer and peered into her face with puzzlement.

"Keturah? Where did all your hair go?"

"Not Keturah," she said softly, and suddenly she realized that she had no name to give him. Hope flared bright in her heart. Surely her oldest friend would know her true name! "I'm Keturah's daughter. Do you remember me?"

The tiny face lit up in a smile. "Child? Is that you?"

A sinking suspicion crept into her mind. "Why do you call me 'Child'?"

"Why do you call me 'Sprite'?" the creature riposted. "You couldn't say my name, and I couldn't say yours."

"What was my name?" Tzigone asked eagerly. "Say it as best you can!"

The sprite shrugged. "If you don't know it, why should you expect me to? Keturah said it wasn't to be spoken, so I didn't ask.'

Disappointment surged through Tzigone, but she understood what her mother had done. Names had power, and knowledge of her true name could become a tool in the hands of those who sought her.

She shook this off and moved on. "You came when I called," she said to the sprite.

The tiny lad shrugged again. "Had to."

Tzigone nodded thoughtfully. Apparently the redheaded jordain wasn't as foolish as he seemed. This was why Kiva had been seeking her. And once her purpose was fulfilled, Kiva would no doubt cut her throat with the knife nearest at hand.

Fury assailed her at the thought of all Kiva had cost her. "No more," Tzigone whispered. "You won't win this time."

"Win?' Sprite looked at her quizzically. 'You want to

play?" He darted aside and conjured several tiny balls of light, which he began to juggle with uncanny dexterity.

Tzigone snatched up the glowing toys and squashed them in her hand. "No magic," she said firmly. "You wouldn't like what it might attract."

The sprite flittered down to rest on the branch beside her and wrapped his wings around himself like a cloak. "Don't like this place already. It's cold here."

Tzigone's eyes narrowed. The swamp was as hot as a bathhouse. She realized suddenly the danger she had put Sprite in by calling him to this place.

"Go," she urged. "Go as far from the swamp as you can. We will play soon."

The tiny lad shrugged and disappeared. Tzigone took a deep breath and stilled her mind. When she had achieved a measure of calm, she reached out with senses that had always been finely attuned to the presence of magic.

She sensed a faint shadow of magic where Sprite had been; other than that, the swamp was oddly devoid of it. There was almost nothing, other than a soft, unfocused glow that rose from the camp.

But it was not the magic of the silencing spell. This was someone's personal mark, a "feel" that was unique to one individual. Someone in that camp possessed magic, and most likely was not aware of it. But Kiva had known. A magehound knew who possessed magic and who did not. Most likely the elf had brought someone into the swamp as bait for the laraken. Perhaps Matteo. Kiva thought she could do anything without reprisal.

"I don't think so," Tzigone said softly as she scrambled down the tree, more determined than she'd ever been. The memories that flooded her had reminded her how difficult her survival had been. Survival was a rare accomplishment. But it was time to do more than just survive.

She crept deeper into the swamp, prompted by fury and by the determination that Kiva would destroy no more lives.

As she reached up to pull aside a curtain of vines that twisted between two trees, colors spilled onto her hand, a stray bit of rainbow where there should be none. She stopped and spun to her right. Not more than five paces away stood a glassy, ghostly form.

But the spirit did not move, and after a moment Tzigone realized that it wasn't a ghost—at least, not a ghost in any conventional sense.

Beside an ancient swamp oak stood a translucent statue of a beautiful female, far too lovely to be human. The slender hand disappeared into the trunk of a thick tree, and the frozen face was upturned with the hopeful expression of one who expects sanctuary. This, Tzigone realized, had been a dryad. She took a deep breath and plunged on.

As Tzigone walked, she saw other glassy forms of creatures suddenly drained of magic, and therefore of life. There were more dryads, and among the leaves, she saw the tiny fallen bodies of sprites and pixies, many of them nothing but shards. She saw a single faun frozen in midcaper and more elves than she'd seen in all her travels through Halruaa.

She'd seen one of these crystal shadows before and had thought that only elves could suffer this fate. But the lie was all around her. All magical creatures fell to the mystery of the swamp. No wonder wizards seldom emerged from Akhlaur!

A voice in her head sounded, part warning and part taunt. *This could be you.*

Tzigone blinked away the phantom image of her own glassy shadow and plunged deeper into the swamp.

CHAPTER TWENTY

Matteo and Andris walked side by side, talking softly of all they had done since they'd parted and of the task that lay before them. Try as he might, Matteo hadn't been able to convince Andris to flee the swamp. He couldn't walk away and let his friend fight alone.

But his decision to stay went deeper still. Matteo had been raised with a firm sense of his own destiny. That had been sorely shaken. Lacking a vision of his own, he accepted the one shining in his friend's eyes. He would fight the laraken for Andris, not for Kiva. And when the battle was done, he would find a way to deal with the mage-hound.

An undulating cry howled through the forest, a terrible sound that was both deep, bone-shaking growl and raptor's shriek. Distant but powerful, it reminded Matteo of the winds that blew off the Bay of Taertal before the onset of a monsoon.

Matteo and Andris unsheathed their daggers instinctively, moving in perfect unison.

"It is still some way off," Andris said softly.

Matteo nodded. As he put away the daggers, an annoying little whine sounded just above his head. Instinctively he swatted at it, then realized his mistake and dropped to the ground, shouting for the other men to do the same.

A dark, whirring cloud swept down on them, moving in deadly formation. The cloud dived sharply, and then at the last moment swerved in a rising arc to keep from crashing into the ground.

"A stirge swarm?" muttered Andris. "What next?"

Angry and cheated, the swarm of mosquitolike creatures broke formation and began to whir around in small circles as they selected their prey.

Matteo groped for the thong that bound the four-foot pike to his back. He tugged it free and surged to his feet, thrusting at the stirge that swooped toward him.

The enormous insect slid wetly down the slender blade, its slide aided by the blood it had stolen from some hapless forest dweller. The stirge stopped only when it struck the pike's cross guard. Its long mosquitolike snout still stabbed and probed, even as it twitched in its death throes.

Matteo ducked and thrust and stabbed again and again, until the skewered bodies of giant mosquitoes filled half his pike and slowed his movements. He tossed the weapon aside and pulled his daggers, slashing at any of the creatures that came near.

The men fought furiously, and soon they were joined by unlikely allies—the stirges themselves. Desperate for food, some of the giant insects fell upon their fallen kin and thrust their swordlike snouts into their rounded bellies. Macabre little tunes, the stirge song hummed by the feeding monsters, filled the air as the creatures drank the twice-stolen blood.

Their traitorous behavior disgusted Matteo. He fell upon the cannibals, slashing and stabbing until the stirge song faded into silence and the bodies lay thick upon the ground.

Andris waded over to him through the grim carpet. "Big swarm. Even so, they had to be desperate to attack an armed band."

Matteo nodded. He stooped by one of the men, a young jordain he recognized but whose name he had never known. The man had been bitten two or three times. He was as pale as a man drained by vampires. A pike lay nearby, heavy with skewered stirges. Another stirge lay dead beside him, leaking ichor from a gaping hole in its head where the snout had been. This protruded from the man's chest. He had torn it away when he ripped the giant insect from him, but not quickly enough. Blood had bubbled from the top of the tube, but the flow was stilled now.

Andris stooped and gently closed the man's eyes. He rose and motioned for the others to follow. The ground grew soft beneath their feet, and soon bog gave way to shallow water. They waded through it, moving into the deep shadows of moss-draped trees.

Matteo bumped against someone and stopped suddenly, instinctively putting out his hand to steady whomever he'd jostled. He felt a deathly chill and snatched his hand back. Squinting in the faint light, he made out the glassy shadow of an elf. Behind the crystalline form was another elf, and as his eyes adjusted, he made out several more. Matteo would have thought them to be clever statues but for the incredible cold within.

"I'm beginning to see why Tzigone warned you away from the swamp," he told Andris, shaking his head in awe. "By all the gods that ever were! This laraken is no ordinary monster."

"Since when did monsters become ordinary?" Andris said with an attempt at lightness. But his eyes were pained as he took in the ghostly shadows. "Let's keep moving."

The swamp water grew steadily deeper, the shallows unexpected giving way to sudden dangerous drops and deep pools. As they skirted one such pool, Matteo thought he saw the crenellations of a vast sunken tower, but he couldn't fathom a valley deep enough to swallow such a thing.

As he studied the towerlike shape, the water stirred. Before he could draw breath to shout a warning, a figure rose suddenly from the water, and of the water.

Shaped more like a giant bear than a human, its form

was dark and brackish, and small fierce fish schooled frantically within the watery body.

Matteo shouted an alert and pointed to the magical creature. "Water elemental!"

For a moment the fighters paused. Such creatures were fought with spells and weapons of magic, and they had none.

Andris pulled a small bottle from his bag and shouted a command. Matteo quickly lit a torch and waited until Andris and several others had tossed the contents of their bottles into the fetid water.

He dropped the torch, and the swamp gas exploded into a ring of bright flame, which quickly engulfed the water elemental. With a roar like that of an angry sea, the creature fought to beat through the flames. Its body began to dissolve with a searing hiss. Clouds of steam billowed upward. Finally the creature could take no more and disappeared back into the pool.

Matteo and Andris regarded each other somberly. "A powerful wizard could summon an elemental, but no such person could survive here for long. Yet there is much magic here," Matteo observed.

"The water elemental was a creature of the plane of water," Andris responded, seeing Matteo's reasoning. "The gate must be near."

"And likely the laraken as well. Without Tzigone to draw it away, we will have to destroy it here," Matteo reasoned. "Then Kiva can close the gate—if that is indeed her intention."

Andris gave him an odd look. "We should split the men into two ranks. If we spread out, we may be able to flank the laraken with an all-out attack. You take the second troop."

They scattered into the swamp, creeping through the shallows and slipping through openings in the vines. The water became less fetid as they went, until it was as pure and clear as a mountain stream. One of the men bent to dip up some water in his cupped hands. Mattis gave him a quick jab with the blunt end of his pick, then shook his head sternly.

It was a moment's distraction, no more. Matteo didn't see the enormous green-black hands that slid through the curtain of vines several paces before him. But his attention snapped back when a loud ripping sound shook the swamp and echoed through him like lightning and thunder combined.

And then the laraken appeared, darting through the opening in the thick jungle vegetation.

"Mother of Mystra!" whispered Matteo.

The monster was more than twice the size of a man and hideous beyond description. Eels writhed about its huge skull like snakes on a medusa's head. Ears more pointed than an elf's rose on either side of a demonic face. Long, needle-sharp fangs dripped with luminous green. The laraken's massive back was hunched, giving it a furtive appearance. But there was nothing tentative about its movements. It came on with swift, darting jolts, zigzagging like a startled lizard.

Not startled, Matteo realized. Hunting. But what the laraken needed, none of them had.

Andris gestured for the first attack. Ten of his men nocked arrows and let fly, sending them whistling about the creature's head. The laraken swatted them aside as it might dismiss a mildly annoying swarm of gnats. The archers kept the arrows coming to distract the laraken's attention. Ten more men darted in, their long pikes jabbing at the creature's body. Again and again they struck, but none of the blades could pierce the thick greenish hide.

The laraken lifted an enormous clawed foot and stamped at one of the annoying spears. The weapon shattered and the laraken's foot bore the spear wielder to the ground. The creature shifted its weight onto that foot, crushing the man with a terrible wet, popping sound. Its other foot, dexterous as a monkey's hand, darted out and snatched up another fighter. The monster kicked out, sending the man flying toward a deep pool. Immediately the water began to roil as the jungle fish swarmed and fed. Andris called the surviving pikesmen into retreat as the laraken threw back its head and sniffed the air with a loud, grating snuffle. Its head snapped toward Andris, and it let out a shriek of triumph.

It came steadily on, swatting aside the pikesmen and archers as it advanced on Andris. Its gaunt form began to fill as it moved.

Matteo motioned to the men with him flank the creature. As he ran toward the laraken, he realized that his friend was turning pale. No, not pale—translucent! He could see the outlines of the trees behind Andris taking shape through his friend's form.

Understanding jolted him. Kiva had spoken truth the day she took Andris from the Jordaini College. He did possess a certain innate magic, if only that sleeping in his elf blood. But that was dangerous enough, and Kiva knew it well. She sacrificed Andris to the laraken, using his battle skills for as long as they lasted.

Frantically Matteo nocked an arrow and let fly, shouting for his men to do likewise. The laraken ignored the tiny missiles. They threw their spears and pikes, but the weapons bounced off the tough hide.

Matteo redoubled his pace and sprinted over the crushed foliage that lay in the laraken's wake. He leaped onto the creature's prehensile tail and ran up its back, using the bumps of its spine as footholds. He hooked the fingers of his right hand over the protruding shoulder blade. With his left hand, he pulled a dagger and stabbed again and again.

He might as well have been a stirge attaching a stone tower. Not even this attack drew the laraken's attention away from his friend.

The monster was closing fast. Andris pulled out his sword and lofted it, prepared to face the monster. He jolted as his eyes fell upon his translucent fist.

Matteo hoisted himself up to peer over the laraken's

shoulder. "Flee, Andris! Kiva has betrayed you," he shouted desperately.

Andris met his eyes and shook his head, but he didn't deny the truth of Matteo's words. How could he, when he was all but transparent?

Not far away, in the tallest tree she could find, a grim-faced Tzigone watched the battle.

"Fools," muttered Tzigone, using the old term that was strangely close to the word jordain. "Damned if those idiots weren't well named."

Wrath strengthened her resolve. She began to sing, calling to the laraken in a voice that echoed through the swamp and set the crystalline ghosts around her vibrating in sympathy. An eery keening filled the swamp, as if the voices of the dead joined the song in harmony. Tzigone kept on, singing in a voice that was full and rich and sure.

The laraken turned, uncertain. It began to move toward the compelling song, paying no more attention to the human on its back and the humans that pelted it with weapons than if they'd been mildly irritating flies.

Matteo let go of his hold and slid down the creature's back. He rolled and leaped to his feet. Breaking into a run, he outpaced the laraken and spun to face it, standing directly in its path as he drew the unfamiliar long sword Andris had lent him.

The creature plunged right over him, unimpressed. Matteo fell and then leaped up, stabbing upward with all his strength.

The sword plunged into the soft hide where the leg joined the laraken's body. With a scream like that of a titanic eagle, the laraken swiveled quickly away from the attack.

It was the worst thing it could have done, and the one thing Matteo hoped it would do. He braced the sword, holding it firm as the creature's startled reaction tore the flesh within.

The force of the laraken's movement ripped the sword from Matteo's hand, but not before the damage was done.

Matteo rolled clear and came up with his daggers in hand, determined to keep the creature away from both of his friends.

Tzigone saw her own determination mirrored in Matteo's dark eyes. She pounded the tree limb with frustration, but she kept singing. If she had her way, she would summon two dark and terrible creatures this day.

❂

In a tower room in a village on the edge of the swamp, Kiva leaned over her scrying bowl and watched as the battle played out. When Matteo struck a near-fatal blow, she gasped as if her own flesh had been pierced.

She lifted anguished eyes to her wemic companion. "They might actually do it, Mbatu. They might kill the laraken."

"That might be for the best," the wemic said.

The elf shook her head. Her painted lips firmed in determination. "Give me the portal," she said, extending her hand.

Mbatu placed the folded silk in her hands, but his leonine face twisted with concern. "Is it safe for you to go so soon?"

She rose and stroked his mane. "What place is not safe if you are with me?"

The flattery was obvious, but still the wemic looked displeased. But he stayed at her side as she flung the silk into the air and let it envelop them both.

The air was suddenly thick and hot, heavy with the scent of battle and death. Impatiently Kiva flung aside the silk portal and reached for the spell she had so carefully prepared, a powerful casting that would close the portal and free the laraken to ravage the land and leave the treasures of Akhlaur for her to reclaim.

An anguished roar sent her spinning toward the battle, a scream that carried magic as the wind carried seeds. The fighters had learned from Matteo's bold move, and they focused their attacks on the soft tissue beneath the creature's arms, inside its thighs, under its tail. The laraken was weaving on its feet, bristling with arrows and spears and looking like an enormous, hideous hedgehog. But it still lived, and it slashed out wildly with its clawed hands.

Instinctively Kiva's hand went to her leg. The creature had slashed her with those claws, tiny at the time of its birth but still sharp enough to tear down to the bone. She bore the scars still, as well as other, deeper wounds to her body and her spirit.

But it wasn't a mother's instinct that lured her to the laraken's side. All Kiva knew was that the laraken was near death and that all that she had worked for was at risk.

With a terrible keening scream, the magehound summoned her magic and prepared to destroy her own army.

CHAPTER TWENTY-ONE

Tzigone heard Kiva's cry and knew with certainty that the magehound intended yet another betrayal.

Her gaze skimmed the battlefield. Over half the fighters had fallen, but the survivors were wearing the laraken down at last. It continued to press toward her tree, compelled by the magic of her song, and each pace took it farther from the source of its power.

A shimmer of silvery motes appeared over the bubbling spring, spreading and smoothing out into a large silver form. A bucket, Tzigone realized, and she had little doubt what the magehound intended to do.

Kiva snatched the bucket from the air and dipped it into the magic-rich water. She hurried forward, ready to hurl it at the weakening laraken.

Tzigone broke off her song at last, for it was impossible to sing and curse at the same time. She squared her shoulders as she muttered a few arcane words and then flung out one hand, throwing one of the few wizard spells she knew.

A huge fireball streaked toward the elf woman, arching over the laraken's head and trailing light like a comet. As Tzigone expected, much of the fireball's power was siphoned off by the magic-draining monster. It fell toward Kiva, fading and shrinking dramatically until it was no larger or brighter than an orange.

But it was large enough for Tzigone's purpose. The diminished fireball splashed into the bucket with a searing hiss. Steam rose, and water bubbled over the rim.

The elf woman shrieked and dropped the bucket, shaking her scalded hands. She whirled toward Kiva's tree, her wild eyes searching for her attacker. The wemic came to her side, standing ready for whatever command she gave.

Tzigone began to sing again, calling the swamp creatures to her aid. A score or so of stirges answered her call and dived at the elf woman, humming in their droning voices, a grim harmony to Tzigone's song.

Kiva set her feet wide and delivered a series of fireballs. Each of the glowing missiles divided again and again as it flew, and the shards took off in search of the darting stirges. Giant mosquitoes sizzled and popped as the seeking fireballs found their targets. The surviving stirges scattered in frantic flight, closely pursued by balls of killing flame.

Kiva retaliated with a swift, angry gesture. A glowing arrow sizzled toward Tzigone. But it could not strike. It was no true arrow, but magical energy shaped into a bolt. It stopped short of its target, so suddenly that it seemed to splat against an invisible wall. Now shaped more like a plate than an arrow, the missile fell to the ground and seared the earth beneath it as it cooled.

Tzigone kept singing. A pair of centaurs came to her call, their thundering hooves echoing above the sound of battle. She grimaced. These creatures had little to do with men and were more likely to side with the beleaguered elf. But the centaurs took one look at the men engaging the laraken and decided that the foes of their foes were worth supporting. Leveling wooden staffs at the elf and her wemic guard, they charged forward like jousting knights.

Mbatu reached over his shoulder for his great broadsword. He thrust Kiva aside and stepped into the line of attack. With a roar, he swept his sword up in a rising circle, catching the oncoming staff and forcing it up. He reared, raking at the centaur's chest with his forepaws.

But the centaur also reared, and his hoofs slashed and pounded at the wemic. Both combatants dropped their weapons, grappling like wrestlers with their manlike arms while pounding and lashing at each other with the weapons of lion and steed.

Mbatu leaped up, digging his hind claws deep into the centaur's belly and pulling the massive creature down with him. The snap of the centaur's leg sent a surge of triumph through him, and he ignored the heavy impact. He rolled aside and seized his discarded sword. As he rose beside the struggling centaur, he slashed the creature hard across its throat with one forepaw. Four deep lines opened and welled with blood.

A heavy thud jolted Mbatu. Dimly he recognized that this wasn't the first such blow, and he whirled to face the second centaur, his sword lifted to attack.

But there was no power to his blow. Mbatu felt strangely weak, and he struggled to draw air into his aching chest. The centaur swung his staff again and smacked Mbatu hard against his flank. The wemic spat at the centaur's hooves in defiance and noticed that his spittle was thick and red.

The wemic lifted his hand to his face. His mane was sodden with blood. The centaur's hooves had left a deep slash on the left side of his head and removed most of one ear. In his battle lust, Mbatu hadn't noticed.

But there had been other wounds, and he felt them now as he and the centaur circled each other warily. Several ribs had been cracked. One had pierced a lung. He was drowning in his own blood even as he fought.

But fight he did, as best as he could, while Kiva hurled spell after spell at the small woman in the tree.

A flicker of fear went through the wemic as he considered the probable result of the spell battle. As he feared, the laraken reared up, sniffing the air like a tired wolf who scents an easy meal. The creature turned away from the fighters and began to wade toward Kiva.

Mbatu roared in protest and leaped directly at the laraken's throat. He held on with his leonine fangs and his claws, not expecting to deal a death blow but hoping to hold the creature off long enough to allow Kiva to escape.

But the laraken plucked the wemic from its throat and gave its latest tormenter a single hard shake. Mbatu's spine snapped with an audible crunch. The laraken tossed him aside and advanced on the elf woman and her nourishing magic. As it moved closer, its many wounds started to heal and spears dropped away as knitting tissue expelled them.

Kiva's fireball spell fizzled into smoke as the creature drew near. Her hands faltered, and her copper face began to pale as the laraken drank in her magic. In a heartbeat, she was weaving on her feet, her eyes fixed on the approaching creature as a mouse might eye a swooping hawk.

Matteo saw the course of battle reversing before his eyes. If the laraken regained strength, they could not destroy it. Again he ran up the spine of the laraken. Desperate now, he flung one arm around the creature's neck. Pulling his dagger, he reached around and pulled the dagger hard toward the laraken's face. He steeled himself for the crush of those lethal fangs.

But his aim was true, and the dagger plunged deep into the laraken's eye with a sickening pop and a hot gush of fluid.

The laraken roared, twitching and pawing at its head. Claws raked Matteo's arm, slashing through sinew and grating on bone. Bright pain darted through his arm and exploded behind his eyes. He let go and fell, rolling aside and barely escaping the pounding feet of the frantic laraken.

The creature rushed instinctively toward the spring, brushing past Kiva in its desperation to feed and heal. The elf woman was tossed aside like a leaf in the wind. She came up on her hands and knees and began to chant.

Instantly the stream began to boil, and bubbles as large as men rose from the water. The laraken dived into one of the bubbles and disappeared.

Kiva, pale as death, lurched to her feet and staggered toward the spring, brandishing a square of dark silk. She tossed this over the bubbling water. The silk turned dark as water soaked it, then sank into the spring. Water and silk disappeared, leaving a bed dry and empty except for a few fish that gasped and floundered in the thin air. Kiva sank to her knees, wavered, and then fell heavily onto her face.

Tzigone slid down the tree and raced over to Matteo's side. He struggled to a sitting position and she dropped to her knees beside him. For a long moment, she regarded the deep gashes that ran from wrist to elbow.

"Well, that's pretty disgusting," she announced.

Matteo chuckled weakly. "Get Andris. He knows how to clean and stitch wounds."

She rose and looked around for the tall jordain. Andris was bent over one of the wounded men, his touch deft and sure as he bandaged a wound. He, too, had suffered from the attack. His form still retained its distinctive colors, but it was translucent. Looking at him was like looking at a rainbow in human form.

Tzigone hurried over and grasped his elbow, relieved to find that he still felt solid. "Matteo needs you."

Andris quickly finished his work and came to his friend's side. His expression was somber as he examined the wound. He took out needle and fine gut thread and began to stitch. Tzigone paced as he worked.

"Well?" she demanded.

"Deep, but clean. There is little tearing across the muscle. Fortunately the talons on that creature were sharp as knives."

"How lucky can a man get?" she muttered. "Will he be all right? I know how quickly a wound can turn bad in a swamp."

"He'll be fine," Andris assured her in a soothing voice.

Tzigone stopped and prodded the translucent jordain with her foot. "Don't lie to me," she warned him. "I can see right through you."

"Tzigone," Matteo said wearily. "Go check on Kiva."

That struck her as an excellent idea. She went over to the elf, seized one of her limp coppery hands, and jerked her over onto her back. Stooping, Tzigone placed her fingers against Kiva's throat.

"She still lives," she said in a flat voice, and then she pulled a knife from her boot and lifted it high.

Andris darted forward and seized the girl's wrist in a translucent hand. "No," he said softly. "I will not argue that she deserves to live, but consider the good of the land."

"He's right," Matteo agreed. He rose painfully and made his way carefully through the tangle of fallen men. "Kiva didn't close the gate. She merely moved it. We must find out where. Let her live, under the guard of the church of Azuth, until she recovers enough to submit to Inquisition. If it is vengeance you seek, her own kind will deal with her less kindly than you would."

Tzigone gave him a baleful look. "Is that true?"

"I swear it. Magehounds are seldom merciful, even to their own kind."

"Hmmm." She considered this and then nodded. "Maybe I could get to like magehounds after all."

But Matteo noticed that she still gripped the knife, and she eyed Kiva with a fury than went beyond hatred. He gently took her wrist and eased the blade from her fingers.

"Our task is done," Matteo said softly. "The swamp has been contained; the laraken is gone. There is a balance in that. Halruaa is well served."

"But what about us?" Tzigone said passionately. "Who among us have been well served?"

Matteo looked at his friends and at the men whom Kiva had tricked or conscripted into service. Even the brave wemic who died defending her had no doubt been stolen as a cub and trained to Kiva's service. He considered what had been taken from all of them. And try as he might, he could not hold Kiva solely guilty.

"I'm not saying that what Kiva did was right or justified,"

he said softly. "But who knows what wrongs she sought to avenge? If such grim measures were taken to mold the jordaini, what else might Halruaa's wizards have done? What evils gave birth to what we have fought today? This is something we must know."

Andris gathered up Kiva in his translucent arms. The tiny elf woman seemed almost to float. "That is no task for a jordain," he said. "It is our duty to serve Halruaa's wizards."

"It is our duty to seek truth," Matteo said with quiet determination. "From this day on, I will follow no other master."

CHAPTER TWENTY-TWO

Kiva awakened to the chant of morning prayers. Moments passed before she realized she was in the care of the Temple of Azuth. Memory returned in a rush, dimming the pain that throbbed through her every bone and sinew. And worse still was the terrible void in her mind and soul.

She had been stripped of magic. Not entirely—no elf could be entirely devoid of magic and live—but her wizardly power was gone beyond recall. She wouldn't have felt half as bereft if she'd lost sight or hearing or touch. The elf lay back on her pillows and fought against her rising despair.

There might yet be something she could do. In fact, the loss of her magic made her quest for the treasures of Akhlaur even more imperative.

But she had few defenses now, and fewer allies. Who would rally to the cause of a magic-dead magehound? Mbatu was dead—Mbatu, who would have stood beside her if she had been halt and lame and hideous. Mbatu, at least, she had not betrayed. The wemic had gone into battle honestly, knowing the risks and accepting them for love of her. Kiva took some comfort in that, especially in the face of what she had to do.

With great effort, she managed to reach the silver bell that stood on the bedside table. A cleric of Azuth answered her call, a tall man wearing a saffron tunic and a frigid expression.

"So you have awakened. Good. I will summon servants to bring broth and bread. You will need your strength to face the coming Inquisition."

Kiva propped herself up on one elbow. "What I did was done at the behest of the queen," she said, knowing that this would slow the Inquisition until her claim was investigated.

"Queen Beatrix bade you to subvert the jordaini? That is difficult to believe."

"The queen suspects the jordaini order," Kiva continued. "I slew Cassia at her command. This was my right, for Cassia was tainted by magic's touch.

"And she is not alone in treachery," the magehound continued. "Zephyr, the counselor to Procopio Septus, is another hidden wizard. He must be destroyed."

The cleric gazed at her. "Many of Halruaa's wizards might have been destroyed if you'd had your will in Akhlaur's Swamp."

She waved this aside impatiently. "The whole story hasn't yet been told. When you question Zephyr, he will tell you that he wanted the laraken to die. But ask him who sired the laraken! He cannot deny his part in this. He is a soft old fool who could not kill a thing. He will deny this, but I swear before Azuth that Zephyr told me he wanted the laraken to live. He wanted all of Halruaa to suffer at the laraken's hands."

"But if he's a wizard, then he would die as well."

"Zephyr is over six hundred years old," she said flatly, "and though that is not so old for an elf, he was greatly aged by the magic worked upon him by the wizard Akhlaur. Ask him about Akhlaur. Ask what was done to him, and then tell me that Zephyr had no part in this vengeance.

"He wishes to die," Kiva said, speaking true at last. "But not until a great evil is avenged. Test me now. I will repeat these words, and you will see that they are true."

The cleric hesitated, but Kiva gave a firm nod. He left the

room and returned with an inquisitor. When the silver rod touched her forehead, she repeated her claim. The truth of her accusation—or at least, a damning partial truth—rang through her words like temple bells.

When the men had left to send word that Zephyr was to die at once, Kiva fell, exhausted, against her pillows. She didn't regret this betrayal, for it was a necessary thing. Zephyr suspected her. She'd sensed that for some time. When he heard she had fought to release the laraken upon Halruaa's wizards, he wouldn't rest until he ferreted out the rest of her plans.

She reached for the cup of broth the servant left and forced herself to take sips of it. When some of her strength returned, she slipped out of bed and padded over to the window.

They hadn't thought to bar it, for without her wizard's magic, she was deemed helpless. But trees grew close to the windows, and Kiva had been raised in the jungles many, many years ago.

Moving carefully, struggling against the weakness in her limbs and the lightness in her head, she eased herself into the branches. Her strength returned as she moved, as if it flowed from the living tree into her body. For she was an elf, and as long as she lived, the magic of the forest was hers to call.

And so she escaped, fleeing into the trees as her ancestors had done, as she herself had done so many years ago, when the accursed wizard Akhlaur had stripped her people of their lives and their magic.

❀

Matteo and Tzigone strolled down the promenade, enjoying the fine summer twilight and watching as magical lights winked on in the city below. Much had happened since the battle in Akhlaur's swamp. After taking Kiva to the Temple of Azuth, they had gone to House Jordain and presented themselves at the Disputation Table. Dimidis had at first been reluctant to accept Matteo's story, but his tale was bolstered by the presence of the eleven surviving men, most of them jordaini. And there was no disputing that Andris, who had "died" before their very eyes, lived on, albeit in a strangely altered form. Men who had been tested and condemned by Kiva submitted to another mage-hound's tests and were found utterly free of magic's taint.

Wizards had already begun to venture into the Swamp of Akhlaur, and they returned with tales that supported Matteo's claims. The laraken was gone, and the encroachment of the swamp seemed to be halted. A great service had been done to Halruaa and her wizards.

All of the survivors had been pardoned from any offenses and heaped with honors. The jordaini immediately went into service to some of Halruaa's greatest wizards. Tzigone, however, remained strangely secretive about her plans. But Matteo noted the abstracted expression on her face and suspected that she was ready to speak at last.

"I'll be leaving Halarahh soon," she said abruptly.

Matteo sent her a quizzical look. "The road beckons? You have not yet learned of your mother's fate. I suppose you plan to seek her."

"In time." Tzigone hesitated and gave him a sheepish, sidelong glance. "Actually, I thought maybe I should learn a few things first. Get some weapons before going into battle, so to speak. I took an apprenticeship with Basel Indoulur."

Matteo burst out laughing, drawing a glare from the girl. "Repeat after me: I am no wizard. Better say it as often as possible while you still can."

"Very amusing," she grumbled. "I've got all this magic, whether I like it or not. Maybe once I find what my true gifts are, I'll be able to trace my parents. Looking now is seeking a coin in a dragon's hoard. But what about you? Will you continue in the queen's service?"

He gave his answer careful thought. "All my life, I was raised to serve a wizard patron. But I have vowed to serve truth as my own man, and will do so regardless of my circumstances. From this day, my only master is my own conscience."

"The queen might not like that."

"The queen might be part of the problem," Matteo said quietly.

Tzigone considered this. "So you're going to stay in Halarahh and seek truth amid those who shape it to their will." She gave him a wry smile. "We're changing places, you know."

"Oh?"

"Yes. I'm going legitimate, albeit reluctantly. You're becoming a rogue. Of the two of us, you seem happier with the path ahead."

"Happy?" Matteo rejected that assessment with a shake of his head. "I did not plan a life of subterfuge and secrecy. It seems a strange way to go about the service of truth. But not all truths need to be spoken aloud."

Tzigone winked. "And some of them can stand a bit of color and flash. Call me if you need lessons in truth improvement."

She swept both arms up with a cat-quick gesture. Where she had stood was a slim flame, blazing with rainbow hues. It winked out as quickly as it came, and Tzigone was gone. With color and flash, no less.

Matteo smiled wryly and shook his head. Basel Indoulur had chosen well. Tzigone had enormous talent, and she was certain to become Basel's star apprentice. In no time at all, she would be accounted a wizard.

His smile faded abruptly. Now that Tzigone was on the road to becoming a wizard, their odd friendship was at an end. The only way he would have dealings with her was as an enemy, or . . .

"A patron," he said with a groan.

Before he could ponder that disturbing thought, the palace bells began to peal, summoning the servants in before the grounds were sealed for the night.

He went directly to the queen's chambers to see if his services would be required that evening. He entered quietly, noting that the queen was alone in her workshop. An exquisite music box sat on the table beside her, and a clockwork cat purred in her lap. The box was fashioned to resemble a gilded cage, and in it a clockwork bird covered with tiny iridescent metal feathers swung on a tiny swing.

The queen idly stroked the cat, her eyes distant as she started to sing. Her voice was faint at first, as flat and toneless as her speaking voice. But then it grew in strength, becoming rich and full. The wordless tune portrayed sadness and loss more poignantly than the funeral keen of a master bard.

Matteo stopped dead. He had heard that voice before. There was no mistaking the dark alto tone and the magic that lurked behind every note. It was the voice Tzigone had used to call the laraken. For a moment the battle flooded back to him in all its exhilaration and horror and loss.

Then the memory faded, and his moment of certainty fled with it like light from a windblown candle. Should he speak to Tzigone of this? Or was this one of those truths that should remain unspoken?

For that matter, was it truth at all?

Queen Beatrix fell silent behind the blank, inhuman mask that her face had become. She put aside the cat and took up the music box, staring at the marvel of gears and gems in her hands. Tiny bells began to chime as the clockwork bird took up the heartbreaking tune.

The Cormyr Saga
Death of the Dragon
Ed Greenwood and Troy Denning

The saga of the kingdom of Cormyr comes to an epic conclusion in this new story. Besieged by evil from without and treachery from within, Cormyr's King Azoun must sacrifice everything for his beloved land.

Available August 2000

Beyond the High Road
Troy Denning

...ire prophecies come to life, and the usually stable kingdom of Cormyr is plunged into chaos.

And don't miss . . .

Cormyr: A Novel
Ed Greenwood and Jeff Grubb
The novel that started it all.

R.A. Salvatore
Servant of the Shard

The exciting climax of the story of the Crystal Shard

In 1988 R.A. Salvatore burst onto the fantasy scene with a novel about a powerful magical artifact—the Crystal Shard. Now, more than a decade later, he brings the story of the Shard to its shattering conclusion.

From the dark, twisted streets of Calimport to the lofty passes of the Snowflake Mountains, from flashing swords to sizzling spells, this is R.A. Salvatore at his best.

Available October 2000